Copyright © 2017 by M.E. Krueger

DUST AND BLOOD

www.BeyondPublishing.net/AuthorMEKrueger

All rights reserved. No part of this publication may be reproduced, distributed, or transmitted in any form or by any means, including photocopying, recording, or other electronic or mechanical methods, without the prior written permission of the publisher, except in the case of brief quotations embodied in critical reviews and certain other noncommercial uses permitted by copyright law. For permission requests, write to the publisher, addressed "Attention: Permissions Coordinator," at info@beyondpublishing.net

Quantity sales special discounts are available on quantity purchases by corporations, associations, and others. For details, contact the publisher at the address above.

Orders by U.S. trade bookstores and wholesalers.
Email info@BeyondPublishing.net

First Beyond Publishing soft cover edition April 2017 hard cover edition April 2017

Cover design by Marcin Bystrzyki

The Author can be reached directly at
BeyondPublishing.net/AuthorMEKrueger and on
Facebook.com/AuthorMEKrueger and on
Twitter.com/AuthorMEKrueger

Manufactured and printed in the United States of America distributed globally by BeyondPublishing.net

New York | Los Angeles | London | Sydney

10 9 8 7 6 5 4 3 2 1    ISBN 978-0-9987292-5-1 soft cover edition

To my family and friends who toughed
the long ride with me.

# DUST AND BLOOD

# Chapter 1

The sun had barely broken the face of the night sky; the piercing light sparking shades of fire on the red rock mesas that dotted the landscape. The newborn light had chased the moon into the opposite horizon with its ancient bravado. The chill of the night air rose to dissipate among the cloudless sky, only to be forgotten again by the landscape for a time. Shrubs of sage and other desert plant life shrunk from their master's harshness, knowing of the vicious heat to come.

As the ancient being crested the distant mountain range, the rolling hills offered little comfort from the unforgiving sun, exposing its magnificent cruelty. Dust rose from the neighboring hill, and a smaller—though not as magnificent—being crested its brow. The newcomer to this morning's scorching was just a boy, barely sixteen years of age, sitting atop his horse. His old friend was skinny from age, and her wispy mane was a testament to her years. Complementing her delicate frame was her faded, off-white coat—likely blinding white in her youth.

With a lackadaisical snort, the mare shook her mane, and the pair descended the side of the hill. The brittle landscape had been cracked by the drawn finger of the creek. The young man had always loved this spot; a perfect perch to oversee the rugged and untamed wilds that extended to the horizon. His father had picked a unique spot for the ranch, and he loved every inch of it.

With a soft series of clucks, the young man urged his old friend into a stiff trot, a shadow of a grin tugging at his dry lips. The sun glared down in the early morning, frying the desert brush and hardpan. The smell of horse sweat mingled with old leather and dying sage drifted to the boy's nostrils. He breathed nostalgically—a familiar smell in his small world of uncertainty.

The boy drew closer to the creek, the marker of the edge of his family's new property on this frontier. This was his favorite spot, but, for some unexplained reason, his father had told him several times that he was not, under any circumstances, allowed down by that creek. It didn't make any sense to the young man. It wasn't deep, nor was it fast—far from it, especially in this deep summer heat. He suspected his father was just paranoid about wildlife.

Despite what his father had said, he tried to get to the creek as often as he could. It was the one true beauty in this harsh country. As the odd pair crossed down the hillside, the creek began to unfold all its natural curves and sharp tributaries. There wasn't much water left running through it, but it was enough to satisfy a thirsty nag. His father couldn't get too angry with him for tending to the old mare.

Seeing the water so near made the mare prick her ears forward in attention and pick up her pace in anticipation. The young man didn't slow her down; his throat was just as dry as hers was, and he would be glad to get a refreshing drink. He rounded a series of familiar red rock boulders, the size of two or three horses across, and trees that reached towards the sky in vain to shield the ground below. As far as the boy could tell, the trees and shrubs were lifeless.

The mare suddenly stopped and snorted, rearing to half-height as she pranced from side to side, nickering senselessly. The young man frowned and tried to steady his spooked old friend with amateur confidence. It wasn't like her to spook. She had never reacted this strongly to anything before. The boy was grateful that she was ancient, or he would have been sprawled on the dirt, wheezing for lost air. Finally, after a minute of coaxing her gently with words and reins, she anxiously shied from the direction of the creek.

He hoped it was a dead coyote.

With shaking hands, the boy slid out of his saddle and grabbed a worn rifle from the rifle pouch and took a nervous step forward. He gripped the stock with white knuckles as he crept through the underbrush and scraggy loose rocks; the sounds of crunching sage under his boots made him cringe. The idea to be stealthy had been dismissed before he began.

The dry air cracked the boy's lips, and his breathing sounded heavy in his own ears. He hoped that whatever he was to find wouldn't hear his ragged breathing. The bugs that screeched in protest from amongst the shrubs silenced as the boy crept past. The brush finally gave way, allowing the boy see the starving creek that ran through the property. His muscles tensed with adrenaline and anticipation as he glanced back to where he had come from. The boy licked his lips in vain to remoisten them from the heat. His gaze nervously turned back to the creek bed.

A gasp broke through his lips, and he lowered his gun immediately. A man was lying face down a mere few feet from the creek's pitiful trickling. The man was clad in black, from head to toe, his hand outstretched towards the water in desperation. The boy's heart pounded against his ribs in shock and relief, all at once, as he forced his legs to move forward. He skidded to a halt next to this strange man outfitted in black.

*Black...? He's gonna fry alive out here wearin' all that leather!*

The boy didn't know if this man was dead or alive, nor how long he had been there. Frazzled, he looked around to see if the man had a horse nearby—anything that might indicate this man's origin. The shimmering heat offered no such answer. Returning his frantic gaze down at the strange man, the boy adjusted his sweating palms on the stock of his gun and called out to the man on the ground, "'Scuse me, sir?" His voice was cracked and dry-sounding, and it was trembling with nerves. He hadn't intended to sound so mild, but he couldn't shake the feeling that this man was off somehow. He knew he should've listened to his father.

The boy set his rifle down with a clattered rush onto the stony ground. Closing the short gap between him and the stranger, he dropped to one knee. He leaned down and listened for any signs of life. This stranger couldn't possibly be alive. With wide eyes, the boy looked over the blown holes that were peppered all over the stranger's backside. Bullets had gone completely through the man. Cautiously, the boy leaned over to the stranger's head and listened for breath anyway. At first, the boy heard nothing but the whisper of the brittle tree branches, but, then, he heard it; the shallow ragged sound of breath coming from the stranger's cracked, dry lips. Being this close to the man made the boy gag. He smelled like he had rolled in something that had died weeks before, with a tinge of the metallic smell of blood.

Hastily, the boy gripped the dusty backside of the stranger and heaved as hard as he could. He needed to get this man on his back. With a grunt, the boy was able to roll the wounded stranger onto his back. The man's black hat toppled off to the side, revealing his very rugged facial features. He had a chiseled jaw line, gaunt-looking cheekbones, and dried blood splattered all over his skin. This man had definitely been in a close fight with someone. The boy gulped hard as his thoughts drifted to the worst possibility: *What if this man is a wanted criminal? Or worse?* Shaking his head of that nonsense, he quickly got back to his feet and ran back to his ground-tied mare. She nickered shyly and stepped to the side, avoiding the young man's grasp.

The boy grumbled softly and grabbed the reins close to the bit, tugging her still. She snorted with irritation as she stood still for the boy. With a shaking hand, he yanked the leather water skin from the weathered saddlebag and jogged back to the stranger. He slid to a stop and went back to his knees. His fingers felt clumsy as they desperately tried to uncork the old water skin. It was half-empty already. Finally, with a hollow pop, the cork came out, and the water sloshed within its container.

The boy licked his lips nervously again as he reached down and snaked his hand under the stranger's neck. He didn't want to be the one who struck the final blow to this man's life; death by drowning. Gently, he lifted the man's head up just enough that drowning wouldn't be an option. He tilted the water skin mouth just above the slightly parted lips of the stranger's, and let a small trickle make its way into the man's parched mouth. At first, the stranger didn't react to the cool water. Then, with a shuttering gasp, the stranger coughed and sputtered before weakly reaching up and gripping the neck of the water skin, eagerly slurping up the drizzle.

# Chapter 2

The stranger's head pounded. His body felt heavy, like an obese whore. That didn't matter now. He hoped he had finally died, for once. But the seeping pain that assaulted his senses told him that he was very much alive. Even the marrow in his bones seemed to burn with fire. Every inch ached.

With a groan, the stranger shifted and felt that all-too-familiar scratchy material under him; hay. Or straw, the man couldn't tell in his state. It was hot, wherever he was, and the air smelled of horse piss and turned hay. The man's nose crinkled with disgust, and he lifted his stiff arms from his side.

Slowly, he forced his eyes to slide open, at least enough to tell him what time it might be. A sharp click of metal made the stranger stiffen, despite the burning pain flowing throughout his body. He knew that sound. *Damn it all, if I hadn't just got out of a fight*, he thought bitterly.

With a struggle, the stranger attempted to prop himself up. Instead, he was met with the bitter, cool kiss of a barrel. Whoever was on the other end of that gun was going to regret it. The barrel of the shotgun was aimed at the stranger on the hay. A voice followed, "You just sit right there, you no good son of a bitch." The voice was definitely male. Maybe in his late 30s to early 40s. By the way the gun rested in that man's hands, the stranger knew his captor had plenty of experience behind a trigger. And he sounded like he knew him.

*Shit...another one...* the stranger thought. With a sigh, the man squinted his eyes shut and slid them open completely. Just as he thought, his vision was fuddled and fogged. He loathed being near death, and it seemed to happen more often as of late.

The man with the shotgun was silhouetted, but the stranger instantly could tell that his blind analysis was correct. Now that he had a visual, he could study him closer. He was a tall man, extremely malnourished by the looks of the clothes hanging off his bony frame. Surprisingly, however, the man didn't reek of alcohol—the normal for most types the stranger dealt with. In fact, this man didn't smell much like anything.

Puzzling.

The silence was almost deafening as the thin silhouette kept a very steady aim at the stranger. He was no fool.

"...Do I know you?" The stranger's voice was deep, and scratchy from being thirsty for so long.

The silhouette man didn't move as he spoke sharply, "No. But I know you..." *Now, that is interesting,* the stranger surmised. But, then again, he should have been used to this sort of 'hospitality'. "And I'm gonna make sure that even Hell, herself, won't let you back out."

The silhouette man began to squeeze on the trigger. The stranger rose his hands up in defense. Deep in his gut, he didn't want to die. Yet here he was. A whisker away from Death's cruel embrace. *Damn, it burns like hell...still need to turn in a job, too. Wont' get paid if I'm dead...*

These thoughts tiredly scrambled through the stranger's head as the tension built around the two men in this hot place. Muffled footfalls rushed toward the back of the silhouetted man, and a large wood door swung open, pouring scathing light into the darkened space.

The silhouetted man made an audible, irritated sigh and stopped applying pressure. The stranger's eyes squinted from the light. He attempted to shield them from it, but he was so weak. A second, smaller figure, but no less thin and bony, jogged to a halt next to the tall man.

"Pa, what are you doin'?" The second voice was younger and more fit than the other. The silhouetted man turned his iron gaze to the younger and abruptly ordered, "Jed, I told you to stay in the house."

The stranger's mouth pulled into a snarl as he felt the cool grip of darkness seep into his vision and close the door to consciousness.

# Chapter 3

Jed couldn't believe what Pa had aimed to do. The stranger on the hay had lost consciousness again, and Pa's shotgun was aimed straight for his heart.

"Pa, don't!" Jed reached out and grabbed the barrel, without a second thought. Pa turned his rigid face towards his son. His jaw was set. The veins in his neck bulged, and the one on his temple even more so. He was furious, but toward whom, Jed was unsure. It was stifling hot in the barn. "H-he's unarmed! And Marietta…" His words trailed off as Pa flicked his eyes over towards the boy's sister, her thin figure in the doorway. She was hiding. The moments dragged as Pa looked at his son, then the stranger again.

"God damn it," he uttered with frustration, lowering the weapon. He turned and briskly walked toward the door. "Get him cleaned up."

"Shouldn't we get a doctor from Junction?" Jed timidly asked, knowing that this stranger was in bad shape. Without one, he would die soon.

Pa stopped briefly, glancing over his shoulder, "No. He don't need a damn doctor." Before Jed could plead with him, he was gone. Marietta stayed out of the way of their father's wrath. Jed's shoulders sagged with relief as he let his small victory savor. At least the man wasn't shot in the heat of the day in a barn.

"Marietta, can you get some water, please?" Jed asked softly. She nodded, leaving in a rush. Jed's eyes lingered on the doorway for a moment longer before he looked at the stranger again. This man had his Pa spooked. *But…why?*

Jed eased his way over to the man he had found. He licked his lips nervously. The stranger was out cold, he knew, but he couldn't help but feel like he was being watched. Jed smelled the foul stench again and choked back a gag as he crouched by the stranger. Gingerly, Jed began pulling back the black duster coat where the blood-soaked holes rested. His heart dropped in his gut.

The holes were already festering and oozing infection. This man was going to die.

Jed heard light footsteps fast approach him, and he turned in time to see Marietta stop at his side with a deep dish filled with water and a rag. Jed smiled slightly and accepted her help. "Thank you."

She nodded with a kind smile and knelt next to her brother. Jed knew that she wanted to help. He set the dish down and handed her the rag, "Hold this for me?" She nodded again and looked at the stranger with determination.

Jed blew out a puff of air as he peeled off the layers of cloth and leather with a grimace. *Oh, please don't wake up, mister...* He knew that it wasn't proper for a young girl to see a man undressed, but he needed the help. Marietta wrinkled her nose and clamped a hand over it as Jed worked in silence. The stranger's bullet-ridden chest was exposed. Gritty, sweaty, bloody, the stranger's chest was barely rising and falling in his shallow breathing. *It's a miracle the bullets didn't punch through his lungs...*

Sweat streamed down Jed's face and back as he dipped the rag into the cool water and soaked it. He adjusted his weight on his haunches and gently dabbed away the crusted blood and the oozing infection of the first bullet hole.

Hours slid by as Jed and Marietta worked on the wounds until the smell had lessened and the holes were properly cleaned. He'd cleaned the wounds of the various ranch animals, but it was never this bad. He dropped the rag into the now pink-colored water and wiped his forehead with the back of his hand. The stranger groaned softly in his sleep and fidgeted in his resting place. Jed looked at

Marietta with a worried brow, "Can you grab some bandages or scraps of cloth? I need to wrap his wounds." The slender girl stood up without hesitation and rushed back toward the farmhouse. She was back before he knew it.

Her arms carried all the bandages and scraps of cloth she could find, it seemed. Jed gently took them from her with gratitude and began wrapping the man's upper torso, midriff, all the way down to his navel; just in case. He didn't want to risk missing a wound by accident.

By the time Jed had finished, the sun was casting its deep, gold color—a signal for sundown. The stranger lay in the hay, seemingly resting easier than before, and his breathing was steadier. *He's more comfortable, at least*, Jed thought sadly. He wasn't sure if he could save this man's life or not. Only time would tell.

He stood. Marietta reached for his hand, to comfort him he knew. He gladly accepted his sister's hand. She looked up at him with sapphire eyes. "I dunno if he'll last the night, but…at least we tried…" Jed turned and headed towards the door—Marietta with him. With a lasting look, Jed stared at the stranger.

*Who are you?*

# Chapter 4

The afternoon air was arid, as was usual this time of year. She had just finished her stitching on the clothes that belonged to the stranger. He had been there for a few days now, and he seemed to be recovering well, despite his grievous wounds.

She opened the front door of the farm house and stepped out to the yard, the clothes bundled in her arm. The air was hot and stagnant.

"Marietta!" She turned her head towards her father's familiar voice and stopped mid-stride. Her Pa and her brother were busy working on the fence that surrounded the livestock. In the middle of the night, something had startled them, and they had charged the fence. "Make it quick ya hear? I don't want you around that man."

Her cheeks flushed slightly, and she nodded. *I always am, though…don't know why he's so worried about this man…he ain't done nothin' to us.*

Marietta's strides became brisk as she strode across the barnyard. *Course…somethin' feels strange about him…* She shook her head to rid her mind of her superstitious thoughts. *Awe, what am I sayin'? He's fine!* She reached the doors, and she gently opened them, letting in as little light as possible.

The stranger was laying in the hay, just as he had been for the past few days. His bandages over his midriff and his chest were cleaner-looking than the previous ones. Her father was right, however, he didn't need a doctor. She closed the barn door with a soft clack. The hammers pounded in the distance with their muffled voices. The stranger was sleeping still. He hadn't woken yet.

*The fever dream must be real hard on him...* She quietly moved towards the man and gently set the clothes down, next to the hay stack. He was so still. His breathing was stronger, and the water that she had left this morning was completely gone. *Oh, so he did get up. That's a good sign.* She leaned down setting down his clothes close to him and quietly picked up the pail and ladle.

A glint caught her eye—A gleam that winked at her from the duster. *What's this?* With a curious wrinkle in her brow, she reached inside the duster pocket and pulled out a small medallion-like object. Marietta's slender hands held it gently, not wanting to break it. She studied it carefully, turning the medallion over and back again.

The cool medallion was deep ebony and smooth on every surface. The face had the maw of a fanged skull with raised features and deep-set eyes. The three-eyed glare followed her as she turned it in her hands, as if it were watching her. Her eyes widened as she felt a chill creep up her spine and faint whispers echoed in her mind.

"Put that back…now." The gravelly voice snapped her out of her trance. She stood abruptly and clasped the medallion to her chest. Her heart raced in surprise. *When did he wake up?!*

" 'Bout a moment ago." The stranger squinted and rubbed a hand over his face.

She stopped in confusion. *How did he…?*

Silent, the stranger slowly sat up, his eyes opening and squinting shut several times to adjust to the light. "Now, sweetheart…" he extended his hand towards her.

Timidly, she went over to him and placed the cool medallion into his rough hand. The chill drained down her spine as the strange metal passed into his hands, the odd whisperings dissipating. The strange man took the medallion in his palm and clenched it and unclenched it in a stretching motion. Her eyes widened. The medallion was nowhere in sight. *The strange coin…!*

*It's gone!* Her mouth was slightly agape as the stranger turned his back on her to retrieve his duster and his other effects.

"...Yeah, and it'll stay that way..."

She watched him as the stranger stretched his neck from shoulder to shoulder, popping and cricking noises striking through the stagnant air. *He's so different, and I can't understand why...* Her eyes drifted slowly over his bare physique. His muscles were deeply toned, and his skin was slightly shiny from the afternoon heat. She felt strange toward this man as she looked at him in subtle awe. A tingling rippled through her. *He is handsome, though. Never seen other men 'sides Pa and Jed...*

The stranger stiffly pulled on his shirt first, and, then, his well-worn vest. "Thoughts like that aren't very becomin' of a young lady like you..." He grunted and adjusted his coat and pulled his hat over his head, tugging it low over his eyes. She swallowed and took a few steps backwards, struck by how he was reading her so well. Not even Jed was that good at it.

His sharp, cobalt eyes looked at her under the brim of the hat, studying her closely. She squirmed under his gaze. He turned and strode to her, stopping mere inches away from her. Something stirred deep within her. Marietta shoved the stirring back to her core.

The stranger leaned in close, looking her straight in the eyes. His eyes were steady, as though they were focused on her very soul. A puzzled look washed over his expression as his eyes darted across her face. "What *are* you...?" His voice was a rough whisper of wonder.

Her cheeks flamed at the question.

"Marietta!" Pa's voice called, shattering the spell that bound both her and the stranger in this hot place. She glanced at the door, then, back at the stranger, who had stood to his full height.

"Marietta!" Pa's voice was more urgent.

"Best you get, little girl, before your daddy finds you here." The stranger lazily motioned to the door.

Marietta turned and briskly walked to the exit. She slipped through the open door and looked over the yard. Pa waved to her from the far end for her to come to him. Marietta drew a deep breath and jogged in his direction. A heavy thought weighed on her mind as she ran, *What did he mean by 'what am I'…?*

# Chapter 5

It had been a little over a week since the boy found him in the creek bed. His body was still sore and aching, but he could manage to walk around the confines of the barn. The stranger was restless, and felt the urgent need to move on.

He settled for pacing around the barn. He knew every plank, every beam, and every smell. He had very little else to do as it was. He sighed, pausing at his duster coat that had been clumsily patched by the strange girl. She was polite, at least, and brought him stale water and meager food. He fingered a particularly bad stitch and frowned at it, as if to make it wither away.

A dull pain seared through his chest and over his shoulders. He snarled under his breath. The flesh was knitting itself slowly back together. *Fuck my life...* he thought bitterly as he moved the duster aside and proceeded to put on his shirt, vest, and coat. The warmth of the barn was welcoming as he stretched his neck; the joints cracking with the movements, relieving the stiffness that had settled in overnight.

He had to get outside. He took long strides to the barn doors and pushed them open firmly. Fresh air and the heat of the day filled his nostrils and soaked his aching body. He tugged his hat low over his eyes, to help shade them from the harsh rays. He scanned the barnyard and over the farm house. Mr. McKay, he had discovered, was busy fixing more fencing, along with his son, Jed, whom he also had discovered earlier in the week.

It struck him funny that the famous Marshall in the territory had been degraded to this low level of profession. The stranger dug around in his duster coat for his cigarette carton as he watched the two of them try to straighten the post they had placed. It amused him to see them struggle to achieve just a simple thing. He drew out the carton and pulled out a cigarette, placing it in between his lips. He put the carton back and cupped his right hand around the end as he called on himself the power of fire. They wouldn't see his trick from this far. His thumb ignited with a tiny flame, which he let kiss the end of the cigarette.

The stranger encouraged the ember end of the cigarette a couple times before he was satisfied with the smolder. He shook his hand out, extinguishing the flame before enjoying his nasty habit. He took a deep drag as Mr. McKay and his son finally got the post where it needed to be. A metallic glint caught his eye on his right side. He lazily glanced in the direction of the annoyance, blowing out a stream of smoke. He had seen all manners of creatures over the course of his life, but this girl he couldn't quite figure out was different. The solid fact that he couldn't pin down what she was drove him crazy.

She was a quiet girl and kept mostly to herself, often going about the ranch yard with her duties. She moved with a grace that was unusual for a young woman her age, and her gaze was unnatural; he could feel it. He had come across so many things during his time in the regions of the Northern Americas, but he had never seen anything quite like her before. He wanted to find out exactly what she was. Behind the wavy, auburn hair, slender frame, and vibrant, blue eyes, was something much more powerful than she realized.

What disturbed him the most was the sense that he knew her somehow.

He took another drag as he watched her lug a pail filled to the brim with feed. She was diligent, he'd give her that, but it was much too heavy for her. He sighed, dropping the half-burned cigarette to the ground and grinding it with his heel.

He could hear her thoughts as he walked toward her, *I shoulda done this yesterday. Oh well, they should be good for a couple days now.* She rested the pail on the ground, wiping the back of her hand over her forehead. She was sweating from the heat, her cheeks flushed from the exertion. She turned her blue eyes toward him as he approached her. Her expression lit up, much like fireflies in the heat of summer.

She smiled at him courteously and grabbed the pail again with both hands. She was wearing a pale blue dress, faded from the years. He ignored the fleshly appearance and focused on her soul. It was nothing like he had ever seen. The stranger had hoped that the twisting gray aura that writhed inside of her was something his mind made in his fever state. He was, regrettably, wrong.

Without a word, he reached out for the pail and took it from her firmly; its weight was nothing to him as he looked toward the small chicken house not far off. He looked back at her and nodded toward it, "Feedin' them?"

She nodded.

He grunted as he started to walk toward them, pail in hand. He heard her follow him, flustered that he was helping her, he could sense that. She jogged up to his side and looked up to him. Her thoughts were just as loud as if she were talking, *Pa is gonna kill me if he sees him doin' my chores!*

The stranger kept a grin to himself as he reached the chicken house and the run that was adjacent to it. He wanted to be outside, and it felt good to use his muscles again, despite the stiffness. He opened the latch of the gate and stepped inside, setting the pail on the parched earth. The rustle of feathers and hens clucking expectantly filled his ears as they rushed toward their food source. The stranger stepped away from the bucket and let the girl do her work.

Her shoulders relaxed as she noted that he wasn't doing the whole task. She stooped down and started hand-feeding them. She seemed to enjoy it, he noted. He needed another cigarette. He repeated his process of digging it out and lighting it up as he watched her work. The writhing gray aura was so subtle he would have missed it if he wasn't looking for it.

He didn't know what it meant, and it made him uneasy. "Marietta…" He spoke her name firmly, but in his normal, low tone. She snapped her head up, surprised to hear her name. He had heard it several times from Mr. McKay over the week. The stranger kept her under his gaze as he observed her. She was nervous around him he could sense that.

"What are you?" He asked quietly. He needed to know.

Her thoughts flooded his mind as she looked at him, confused. *I don't know what he's talkin' about…I'm just a girl.*

"You're not just a girl…" The stranger cut her off with irritability. He wanted to know exactly what was going on with this family. It felt like the answer was in front of his face, but he couldn't see it. He despised it.

She looked at him wide-eyed. He knew that she was beginning to understand that he could hear her. It was a simple task, really, for someone like him. He could do it in his sleep if he chose to.

*How can he do that?! Maybe Pa was right…I* shouldn't *be around him—*

The stranger blew out a stream of smoke and took a couple steps closer to her. She seemed to be rooted to the spot as the hens around her pecked at the feed feverishly. "He's right…but I ain't gonna harm ya…" He assured her, though he didn't know why. She amused him somehow as he took another drag and stared into her eyes. She was wary of him, and rightfully so. Most folks were. "You don't even know what I mean by that…" He contemplated as he glanced at her aura then her again.

*No…I don't…*

He grunted and blew out more smoke. The deep burn felt good in his lungs. "Well then, I suppose it don't matter."

"Marietta!" The stranger glared in the direction of Mr. McKay's voice from the fence line. Marietta startled from the sudden break of her fixation and emptied the rest of the pail. She glanced back at the stranger as she jogged from the chicken run toward the fence line. He watched her go and felt an odd sense of attachment growing in his chest.

He grumbled to himself as he dropped the cigarette on the ground, grinding it into the hardpan again. *This is why I don't stay long. Son of a bitch...*

\*\*\*

The rest of the week seemed to crawl along in tandem with the climbing summer temperatures. Jed noted that there was more heat than in past summers, and he often had to ride out to check on the cattle. They lost one to the heat, and Jed knew that it would be a heavy toll to lose more. It was time to move them again to the farther end of the property, close to where the creek widened. There was still water there, and Jed was thankful for that.

He was in the barn, saddling his mare and getting ready for the drive.

"Jed, did you grab the rope?" He heard his Pa's voice from the next stall over, saddling his own gelding. Jed adjusted the girth strap and moved around his dozing mare to the front of her stall. Jed stuck his head out and looked toward the gelding's stall. Pa was doing the same as he absentmindedly adjusted the bridle.

"Yes, Pa, they're settin' over there." Jed pointed to a table opposite of the stalls. Two coils of rope were there, waiting to be picked up. Pa nodded his approval and moved around the gelding out of sight. Jed heard the barn door creak open wider, followed by near-silent footfalls. The only sound was the rustle of a leather duster and the jangling of gear.

Jed patted his mare and grabbed her reins close to her chin. She nickered softly and perked up, almost as though she had been startled awake. He led her out to the open area of the barn and stopped for a moment as he watched the stranger walk past. Jed still felt uneasy around the man, and, yet, he was fascinated with him. Excited almost. He couldn't figure out why.

The man walked past Pa's stall. Jed could see he was watching the stranger with a frown. He still didn't get a clear answer out of his father when it came to the stranger and who he was. All he had said was he was "a man of bad sorts". The stranger cocked his head in Jed's direction, his piercing cobalt irises chilling, even in the heat. Jed couldn't look away from them. They seemed to delve into Jed's soul, looking deep within him, seeing things that Jed didn't know about himself.

Jed couldn't tear his eyes away, until the stranger finally passed. Jed swallowed, his stomach churning with anxiety. *What did he just do...?* The mare at his side gently stretched her neck, tugging at the reins in his hands; tugging him back into reality. He shook off the anxious feeling and continued to lead her out of her stall and out toward the barnyard. Jed looked at his Pa, who watched him go. *Somethin' ain't right, but I suppose I'm just not used to people being around here.*

Jed glanced back at the stranger, who had taken up his usual spot on the hay pile. His hands were interlaced with each other and rested on his chest, his hat tipped low over his eyes. He was recovering slowly, but steadily. Jed still thought it was a miracle that he had survived his near-fatal injuries. He had a feeling, however, that this stranger had probably seen worse.

# Chapter 6

A roll of thunder made the entire house shake. Jed's eyes snapped open, surprised that a storm had rolled in. It was midsummer—it was almost unheard of to have a storm this time of year. Jed groaned as light illuminated his room for a split second, before the darkness returned. Rolling over, Jed pulled his thinning blanket up to his ears, hoping it would help. He closed his eyes as thunder clapped, louder this time. As the sound rumbled to a softer tone, Jed frowned at a new sound: rain on the slatted roof.

*Oh, no...* Jed threw the blankets off him, trying to get his sluggish body to move faster. Rain was good, but not when it posed a flashflood. The cattle would be in danger of drowning in weather like this.

He heard movement down the hall, and feet walking briskly towards his end. *Pa!* Jed groggily threw his blanket off as his door squeaked open.

"Jed, get up. Rain's comin' in." Pa's voice was urgent, laden with worry.

"Alright, Pa, I'll be right down." Pa trotted down the steps. The rain began to come down heavier than before. Jed hurriedly put his boots on and straightened his clothes out. Jed hoped they could get to the herd before the storm got too bad.

*\*\*\**

Jed's father jogged across the soggy barnyard towards the barn. Puddles were already starting to pool in large quantities. *Damn it all! I can't afford to lose more cattle!* He heaved on the now-slickened handles of the barn doors, pulling on one side. The door groaned as it swung open. He stumbled in out of the rain. Lightning pulsed in the sky above, illuminating the barn. He frowned at the stranger who was already dressed and pulling his hat on. Mr. McKay caught the glimpse of his eyes in the dark—they always flashed a predatory blue.

It always sent chills up his spine. "Where do you think *you're* goin'?" Mr. McKay growled as he went to the startled horses.

The hunter grunted and responded in his low tone, "Elsewhere…"

"Not until you pull your damn weight, El Diablo…" He grabbed his saddle from the wall of the stall and rested it quickly on his horse's back and started girding. He wasn't sure if the stranger, El Diablo, would even recognize his demand for his help in this matter. He knew he didn't give a shit about his situation, but Mr. McKay felt that he owed him for sparing his life a couple weeks past. He could have ended him there. *By rights, I should have…*

Lightning streaked the sky.

He could feel a tension in the air, making the back of his neck tingle with chills. His horse screamed. He swiftly grabbed the horse's reins right under the bit, pulling the steed's head low to the ground with all his might. Mr. McKay looked over his shoulder as he watched the stranger extend his hand in the air, fingers extended and palm facing towards the emptiness of the barn. The hunter was focused solely on his hand; still as a tree. The horses thrashed and pawed at the ground and in their stalls. Mr. McKay held his horse's head down with all his strength. His eyes never left the hunter. He'd seen this before. *I hate this shit, 'specially on my land.*

The space in front of El Diablo's hand wavered, as though there were a ripple. The darkness began to draw in on itself, contorting into a circular shape. The storm outside seemed to intensify as the air tightened around them. It was hard to breathe. Thunder mixed with what seemed like thousands of whispers and distant screams, as though millions of people were shrieking in the distance. Mr. McKay's heart clenched with bitter fear as his mind screamed for him to run. He wouldn't permit himself to indulge in that extreme desire to flee.

A hoof appeared from the tightened ripple, the color as black as sin. A head followed suit, the forelock layered with bangs and a black leather bridle framing its strong face. A neck—thick and strong—came through shortly after. Then, a chest emerged, girded with a wide, black chest collar, ornamented with deep, tinted silver plating for the center decoration. The hellish steed continued forward, until it stood in all its unholy glory. The screams of what Mr. McKay could have sworn were the screams of the damned filled the space of the barn, drowning out the panic of the other two horses. Its nostrils flared, and its blood-red eyes glowed like fire in the dark. The stallion's entire skin and unearthly tack smoked and steamed faintly in the coolness of the night air.

The stranger lowered his hand, the eerie tightness disappearing, the ripple reversing and contorting rapidly into its normality. The strange whispers and faint screams disappeared with it as the stallion nickered and pawed the dirt restlessly. Without a word, the stranger grabbed the horn, placed his foot in the stirrup, and smoothly swung himself into the saddle. El Diablo reminded him of a harbinger of death, sitting atop his hellish steed from the depths of the damned.

The barn door creaked open, snapping Mr. McKay from his wary focus on the man and his stallion. Lightning streaked again as he watched his son rush over to him, soaking wet. "Pa, it's lookin' bad." He could hear his son's voice strain with rising panic. He knew that a flashflood was here. They didn't have much time. Confident his own horse was calm enough, Pa swung up into the saddle, taking control of the reins.

"We better get out there, then." Pa answered sternly. Jed stared at the stranger suspiciously as the smoking stallion glared at them.

"Where'd that horse come from...?!"

The stranger prodded his mount forward with his heels as he spoke over the rolling thunder, "Europe." Without another word, the man rode into the storm.

\*\*\*

Jed's mare was struggling through the terrain in the dark as the trio swiftly made their way towards the grazing pasture. The rain was constantly pouring its heavy drops and the ground beneath them was slop. Jed knew that his father feared a flashflood. *It looks like it might be already...* His mare whinnied with fright as lightning struck nearby, making her rear up. Startled, Jed managed to keep a hold on her. He was thankful, again, of her age. His Pa paused, looking back at him.

"You alright, Jed?" He shouted over the sound of the torrent.

"Yeah, I think so!" Jed called back. Without another word, his father kept pushing forward. The further they pushed, the worse the storm seemed to get. Despite Jed constantly wiping rain off his face and away from his eyes, he could barely make out his Pa ahead of him, leading the way. He had lost sight of the hunter. Jed's chest and gut tightened with anxiety as they crested the rocky hill. Lightning struck again, and more than once. It provided just enough light to see the pasture below them.

"Shit." Pa cursed outwardly, as he steadied his horse. Jed could see why his father would curse; the valley below was beginning to flood, and swiftly. His gut turned, hoping they could save the herd that was bawling below them; all were huddled together in a mass on top of a rise in the terrain.

"Where's the stranger at? I thought he came with us to help!" Jed spoke loudly, so his Pa could hear him.

"El Diablo don't give a shit, son," Pa's voice sounded over the downpour.

Jed's heart stopped in his chest, not from fear, but from excitement. "El Diablo?!" Jed couldn't believe it. El Diablo had been a notorious bounty hunter across the frontier. Whenever Pa went to Junction with him to get supplies, Jed would make his way to the small sheriff's station to see if there was any news on this mysterious hunter.

The reality that El Diablo had been the one Jed found struck him with awe and excitement.

His Pa shook his head and quickly answered, "Don't matter now! We have to get this herd out of here!"

Without another word, Pa urged his mount to descend the terrain with haste. Jed urged his mare to follow. He needed to stay as close as possible to his father—and put aside the shocking identity of the stranger he had found. They wound their way down the craggy hillside to the flooding plain below them. The wind whipped around them in a fury, the tall trees in the low graze land bending in the wind. The summer had not been kind to these trees. Rain pelted their skin and stung their eyes as his Pa guided his hesitant gelding across the growing water.

Jed was always shocked to see how fast a flashflood takes place. Without hesitation, Jed urged his mare to cross the water. She obeyed, her ears flicking forward, to the side, then, back to him as they made their way across.

Pa shouted at the cattle, snapping at them with his rope. A few of the cattle were startled and bolted towards the growing moat for higher ground. Lightning forked in the sky as Jed whooped and hollered, pushing on the hinder parts of the cattle.

Jed finally got one to move, and more followed. Relief filled his chest as they were beginning to move across the water. The cattle were up to their shoulders in water, struggling to walk along the bottom of the flash moat. A bout of wind felt like needles on his soaked skin as thunder roared through the sky above. The storm was getting worse. The tree at the edge of the retreating mound was creaking and groaning dangerously. Jed peered through the darkness to find that his Pa had roped a frightened old heifer. She wasn't moving.

Jed immediately went to help him. They couldn't afford to lose any more this year. Jed urgently maneuvered his mare behind the heifer and tapped his own rope on her rump, hoping that coaxing from behind would help. *C'mon! Move already!*

Lightning tore through the sky and struck the tree next to them, causing the heifer to wail in horror before charging off. Pa tried to rein in and control his horse from the sudden charge of energy as it reared, whinnying with fright. Pa shouted with surprise as he was thrown from his rearing and bucking gelding. Jed's mare spun in place, taking off, away from the exploding tree. Jed's heart pounded in his chest as he managed to rein the mare into his control.

The haunting sound of a tree groaning, cracking, and squealing filled his ears. He looked over in panic. His Pa was struggling to regain full consciousness from being thrown into the ground.

"Pa!!!" Jed shouted in fear. The tree was going to crush his father; and there was nothing he could do to stop it. Jed jumped down from the saddle in a frenzy. His mare whinnied and moved to the side, away from Jed. He had to try.

He watched helplessly as the tree gained momentum. His father tried to get up a few times, but the mud under him was too sloppy to get a solid hold.

The tree fell faster, approaching at a greater speed. It would only be seconds before a fatal crush. Jed's heart pounded, and his mind raced. *No!!!*

Light flashed above, revealing something remarkable that made Jed stop his sprint. His breath became short with shock. El Diablo was there; the mediator between his father and death. He was holding the tree up. The impact from him catching the tree had caused him to sink into the mud, up to his ankles. One hand held the trunk steady, the rest of the weight resting on his shoulders.

His Pa looked at El Diablo with disbelief before he scurried out of the way of the tree. El Diablo's black leathers were shiny and slick from all the rain. He almost looked like something out of a ghost story. After Pa got safely away, El Diablo shoved the tree up a couple of feet as he maneuvered out of the way, before letting the tree fall with a deep boom.

El Diablo and Pa eyed each other. El Diablo moved to the far side with the horses, grabbing the reins of his own dark steed and mounting quickly to the receding bank. Pa's horse was nowhere in sight.

Jed couldn't believe what he saw. He must have been dreaming. *No man could ever be strong enough to stop a falling tree, let alone set it aside like nothin'.* It sent a chill down his soaked spine. The stories seemed to have some truth about him.

"Jed let's get out of here!" His Pa's voice jabbed through his fixation on El Diablo as he started to brave the rising water. They would need to swim, and share the same horse.

Jed tore his gaze from the hunter, the whole event unsettling in his mind. *What is he…? That can't be normal…* Jed quickly raced over to where his Pa was calming the mare down. Jed handed the reins of his mare to his father. Pa quickly mounted and offered Jed a hand up. Jed gratefully accepted and swung up behind his father. It felt awkward, but Jed was ready to get to higher ground.

Pa urged the mare toward the water, talking to her in a calm tone as she began braving the water. She was struggling, but she managed to keep her head above water. The flood around them reached up to their thighs. In different circumstances, the bitter cold of the water would have been refreshing. The odd trio moved closer and closer to the other side, until she finally emerged. With a snort, she trotted away from the water's edge, breathing hard and soaked through and through.

Jed heard a panicked whinny to their right. Jed peered through the dark and over the backs of frightened cattle and saw Pa's horse tangled up in briars. The gelding must have crossed the rising water in a panic when he bolted.

"Pa! Over there!" Jed urgently patted Pa's arm and pointed. Pa looked over and quickly dismounted, handing the reins over to Jed.

"Stay here!" He shouted before running over. Jed moved himself carefully back into the seat of the saddle, still shaken up from what had been a near-fatal tree fall.

Jed watched his Pa as he managed to get the spooked gelding to calm enough to regain control. His Pa mounted again, adjusting his weight in his saddle, and heeled his horse to come back to Jed.

The bawls of the cattle were mingled with torrential rains and shrieking wind. He looked around for El Diablo, hoping he would still be here to help them get the cattle back to the corral. El Diablo was on the edge of the herd, pacing his horse to keep them in a certain area. Jed watched him as he maneuvered his horse with skill and perceptiveness.

"Jed! We need to move them!"

Pa's voice broke his concentration again, "Alright then!" Jed gripped the wet reins tightly as Pa heeled his horse over to El Diablo. El Diablo stopped his horse when Pa approached. The two men talked for mere moments before El Diablo nodded in agreement. He didn't look pleased.

El Diablo rode wide to the right, to block off the cattle's way of escape deeper into their property. His Pa took the center. Jed knew what to do. He clucked and urged his mare to sweep wide to the left.

He had driven cattle many times before. But he had never done so in the dark. With a holler, Pa began driving the cattle further to higher ground. Jed hoped all would be well when they returned and that none of their cattle would be lost.

Jed glanced back at the submerged mound, then, at El Diablo, and, finally, focused back on the drive. This man had saved his Pa's life. He would thank him in the morning.

# Chapter 7

The night had been bizarre. Jed, Pa, and El Diablo had driven the cattle back to the corral that was encircled behind the barn, safe and out of the storm's harm. Jed helped Pa stable the horses, and the hunter had done the same to his own steed. Pa voiced an uneasy thank you to the hunter who just grunted in acknowledgement as he dug in his coat for something. He drew out an ivory-colored box that had seen better days and pulled out a slender cigarette. He hid it behind his hand as he lit a match that had been tucked in the top of the carton. Three puffs later, the cigarette smoldered and began smoking, its tendrils swirling and stretching around the brim of his hat and around the rain drops.

Jed couldn't help but be fascinated with this man. El Diablo was a rare breed on the frontier. Most said he was nothing but bad luck, roaming from town to town to make a quick profit on the weak-minded. Others said he was a demon from hell. He was dangerous—of that Jed was sure—but he only saw the man who had saved his father's life. His Pa thought otherwise. He had stiffly thanked El Diablo for his help as he finished putting up the tack; men and horses were soaked to the skin. Jed remained silent as he patted his mare and put up his own tack. El Diablo was silent in the dark barn, his eyes an eerie blue in the dark, only acknowledging Pa's thanks with a grunt.

He retired to his haystack. Pa steered Jed by resting a hand on his shoulder. They both walked back out into the rain, toward the house. Jed looked back at the barn, only to be reminded by his Pa, "Mind yourself, son…he's not a man you should be takin' a likin' to…" Jed nodded and remained silent. His body was tired, as he was sure his Pa's was as well.

In the morning, Pa had been unusually courteous to El Diablo—as courteous as he could manage, Jed guessed. He had invited him to sit with them for dinner that night as a sort of thank-you for his help and for saving his life from the tree.

The dining room was as lit as possible and furnished with very basic decor. They didn't have much, but it served its purpose well.

The smells of fresh-baked bread and salted back strap made Jed's mouth water. Pa was across from Jed, at the head of the table. Marietta sat to the left of Jed, and El Diablo to his right.

The previous night had shaken Jed to his core. He would have lost his Pa to the storm if El Diablo hadn't stepped in to help. After weeks of trying to convince his Pa to let the man sit at their table and eat like a proper man, he had finally allowed him to sit with them.

El Diablo had taken his hat off for the occasion, as well as his duster coat which hung on the back wall with the weathered hutch. The coat was patched as best as it could be, with the aid of Marietta's stitching.

Jed looked at his Pa, whose weathered face looked darker in the light. The rough road he traveled in his life had finally caught up with him. He looked world weary—exhausted. Pa thought his son couldn't see through him, but Jed knew better. He had pledged to himself to help his Pa as much as he could.

Pa looked at his children and angled his gaze at the stranger. "Let's say grace…" Jed bowed his head and closed his eyes, just as Pa and Marietta did.

The stranger almost had a gleam of disgust in his eyes, but Jed couldn't tell.

"Dear Lord, thank you for this day and for the bounty you have provided us…Lord I ask that you protect us and guide us in our everyday lives…in Jesus' name, Amen."

"Amen." Jed said with enthusiasm. Marietta smiled and tucked her curled auburn hair behind her ear. Her brilliant, sapphire eyes seemed to catch the light and gleam. Jed smiled at her and, then, at the stranger.

El Diablo was not amused. His disgruntled facial expression attested to that. Jed sheepishly looked down at his place setting, his smile diminished. Marietta covered her mouth with a hand in a subtle fashion to hide her grin. She was laughing at him. Jed frowned and playfully kicked her foot under the table. She looked at Jed and shook her head.

Pa raised his eyebrow at her as he broke a piece off the bread and passed the aged basket to El Diablo. He tore off a piece and passed it on, silent and forlorn. *He sure is hard to read*, Jed thought warily as he took his own piece and gave it to Marietta.

Even though this man seemed dangerous, he couldn't help but be curious about him. Where had he come from? Where was he going? He had held his tongue from these things at his Pa's strict instruction. Neither he nor his sister were allowed to speak with this man.

"So, El Diablo…you're a long way from the West. Business not as good?" The tone of his Pa's voice was different. It had a sharp bitterness to it as Jed watched his Pa take some back strap. Pa's eyes were wary of this man.

"You could say that." El Diablo's voice was low, rumbling like distant thunder.

"And that's why you were face-down in my crick?" Pa took a bite of back strap and gulped a mouthful of water from his tin cup. The candles in the center of the table flickered as Jed and Marietta exchanged silent glances at each other, then, back at their own plates.

El Diablo pondered the question, observing Pa. A crooked grin spread across his lips as he took a drink from his tin cup. He turned his gaze to Marietta and leaned forward a bit.

"Well, Mr. McKay, the redskins always travel with the herd…"

Marietta locked her eyes with the man's, studying him with fascination. She wasn't afraid of anything, or anyone. Jed admired her. El Diablo slid a hand in front of the flame, hiding it from all view.

"When there's nothin' left to hunt…" He lifted his hand and the flame was gone. Jed stared wide-eyed at the smoking wick and the man's hand. Marietta also watched, stunned that the man had put this fire out without touching it or blowing it out. Pa tensed at the scene as he watched with disapproving eyes.

"They move on," El Diablo glanced at Pa and curved his hand back in front of the wick, out of sight, "lookin' for somethin' greater than they had." When El Diablo lifted his hand, the tiny flame was dancing again, brighter than before. Marietta and Jed watched with slack-jawed amazement as they exchanged glances.

Pa grunted irritably, "Well, El Diablo, this is not where this "herd" has migrated to." El Diablo looked at Marietta again, who adjusted her gaze back to her half-eaten meal.

"This wasn't my intended destination, Mr. McKay." The man looked at Pa again. Silence weighed heavily over the dining table. Jed felt uncomfortable as both men went back to their meals quietly. The subject was dropped.

After what felt like hours, El Diablo spoke gruffly, "What's wrong with your girl? Cat got her tongue?" Marietta's freckled cheeks flamed pink as she concentrated solely on her plate. Jed frowned and opened his mouth to defend her. Pa shot him a glare that quickly made Jed close it.

"She's a mute…born that way." Pa said with exactness, but not embarrassment. Jed's ears grew hot as he, too, concentrated on his food.

El Diablo let a knowing smirk play on his lips, "I see. Well, I'm sure she'd have a strong voice if she could talk…"

She looked up at the man, confusion etched upon her fair features. Jed wasn't sure he liked how this man looked at her as he finished off his cup of water.

Pa cleared his throat, placing his fork on the rough table top. He was finished eating. Jed quickly finished his.

"Well, *El Diablo*, care to join me for whiskey?"

The man gave a raspy chuckle and stood, "I suppose."

"Marietta, Jed, it's time y'all head to bed." His Pa rose from his seat. Though a tall man himself, Pa was much shorter than El Diablo.

Marietta's shoulders sagged with disappointment, and Jed spoke their protest, "But Pa, we ain't tired yet!"

"I *said* it's time for you to go upstairs." Pa's voice was stern and his face sterner. His look was all it took. It was final. In defeat, Jed closed his mouth and both he and his sister rose from their places and retreated to the stairs.

*Maybe tomorrow*, Jed thought hopefully, *I can ask El Diablo all my questions*. He lingered for a moment as he watched his Pa and El Diablo retreat to the parlor.

# Chapter 8

He heard raised voices drifting through the arid evening air. Jed opened his lead-heavy eyes and rolled to his side, his clothes crinkling underneath him. With a soft grunt, he lifted himself from the skinny mattress and crept to the door of his room. Jed pressed his ear to the door's rough surface and strained to hear. Blocked by the door, he could only hear muffled words. He cringed as his hand grasped the cool, metal knob and turned it cautiously. He wanted to know what was going on, and if he needed to help his Pa. The rough, wooden door swung open, to Jed's relief, with relative silence.

"What are you really here for?" Pa's voice was rough, inhospitable toward the hunter who had been reluctant to stay and heal up from his injuries.

"Nothin' you need to worry about, Mr. McKay..." The hunter's voice was indifferent, if not irritated from the inquiry. Jed edged his way to the stairwell and placed nervous hands on the railing and leaned over. The shadows of the oil lamps flickered in the doorway, shaping the vague forms of his father and the hunter sitting across from each other in the front parlor. Jed let a small frown creep onto his brow as he strained to hear the conversation clearly.

Pa huffed, and Jed heard him take a hasty drink from the crystal glass that was surely filled with whiskey. With a gentle clink, Pa set his glass down on the side table and continued his icy prodding, "I know why you're here...*he* sent you, didn't he?"

The air was stifling now, thick with tension. Jed felt his heart drop into his gut as he continued to listen. What on earth was Pa talking about? "He" who?

A gravelly chuckle resonated in the barren parlor room, a sound that Jed had never heard before. It must have been the hunter. "Who, Marks? Tch...I think you've been hiding in yer shithole for too long, Mr. *Marshall*..." The hunter grunted in distaste at the title.

*Marshall?* Jed thought with shock and utter disbelief. Pa had told him he was born and raised a rancher. He had never mentioned working for the law.

Pa responded with subtle venom, "I ain't a Marshall...not anymore."

"And I ain't part of the Marks anymore." The silence that followed the hunter's response was saturated with deadly undertones of hatred and spite. Jed squirmed, even though he wasn't in the same room.

"I see," Pa said with an unconvinced grunt, "And you suppose that they'll just...leave you alone?" Jed caught a hitch of morbid amusement lingering on his father's words. Whoever—or whatever—they were discussing didn't sound like it would rest its rage. "You realize that if they did track you here—"

"They ain't gonna." The hunter snapped in a growling tone, ending Pa's sentence as quickly as it began, "I told ya already, McKay, I killed them..." Those last three words made Jed's skin crawl with an uncanny sensation. His tone was cold-hearted, as if life had no value. It made Jed's stomach turn.

"You and I both know that it will take more than that to stop them." Pa's tone was as grave as it was low, barely audible over the lone cricket outside. Once again, silence descended upon the parlor, enveloping the vague shadows with a seed of discomfort over some piece of information Jed couldn't grasp.

"Might wanna watch what you say, Mr. McKay," the hunter mumbled into his drink as he took a loud audible swallow. "You have a wren in the rafters."

Jed silently took a sharp intake of breath. How did the hunter know he was listening? He looked swiftly behind him to make sure that the door hadn't clacked shut. To Jed's confusion, the door was still wide open. He heard Pa set his glass down and briskly push himself out of his favorite time-worn armchair. Before Jed could hastily retreat to his sanctum, Pa stepped into the foyer and searched for this metaphorical bird the hunter had pinioned. His sharp eyes darted around the darkened room and, then, up above, to the rough banister.

"Why ain't you in bed, boy?" Pa's voice was scolding. Jed tried to shrink from it, a feeling of guilt flooding his senses. He knew better than to eavesdrop on his father's private conversation. But, for some unexplained reason, he was drawn to their topic of discussion.

"Sorry, Pa…I-I couldn't sleep, and I heard voices…" Jed shriveled under his father's piercing gaze.

His father's countenance relaxed, and the tension dissipated as he sighed, running his long skinny fingers through tousled hair, "Get some sleep, Jed. There's a long day ahead of us."

Jed nodded hurriedly and lingered for one more moment to take in his father's peculiar look. He had never seen it on his father's face before. It was the shadow of branching despair. Worry crept into his heart at the thought of his Pa's expression, but he had to push it from his mind. Whatever it was, Pa would surely straighten it out in the morning. Something had begun to feel off.

He closed his door with a soft clack at that final, uneasy thought. It was just a coincidence. He yawned, putting his nerves aside as he moved to his bed and gently lowered himself onto the thin mattress, once again. The morning would be coming sooner than he liked.

As Jed lay there under his thin blankets, he heard the men talking again. He strained to hear them, but his consciousness slipped into a dreamless slumber.

# Chapter 9

Sharp rays of light penetrated the clouded glass of the window, stirring Jed from his heavy sleep. Everything from the night before seemed like a strange dream. What his father and the bounty hunter were talking about still swirled in Jed's brain as he tried to make sense out of it. Of course, none of it did. He wanted to ask so many questions: What were the Marks? *He* who? Why was Pa trying to hide his past? Why did he lie to his children?

Morning. The realization suddenly hit him with full force.

With a jolt, Jed flung the blankets aside in a panic: he had slept in. The questions that were fluttering around his mind dispersed and were forgotten. Without so much as running his fingers through his messy hair, he sprang from the thin straw mattress and snatched his well-worn boots off the floor. His Pa was going to be furious. A guilty red flush began to creep up his neck to his ears.

Jed hastily pulled his boots on, all the while hopping from one foot to the other. He threw the door open and raced around the banister, leaping two or three stairs down at a time to the foyer. His breathing was heavy, and the sweltering heat of the day was already stifling in the mid-morning air. Jed burst out onto the front porch and skidded to a halt, turning back to close the door gently. He knew he would be in trouble for this one.

His eyes squinted from the sharpness of the sun's rays as he pressed a hand on his brow. The early morning heat was already making him sweat. It was going to be a very hot day.

He glanced over the yard, quickly finding his Pa by his old nag and El Diablo a way off, firmly saddling a large, black stallion. The stallion seemed larger than the other night, and it seemed impatient as it waited for its master to finish. He jogged out to his Pa to help.

"Sorry, Pa…" he sheepishly said as he scratched the back of his head.

Pa straightened and looked his son over as he tightened the straps and stirrups. "It's alright, boy." Pa glanced at El Diablo who mounted and began walking his steed towards them. Pa wrapped an arm around Jed's shoulders and turned them from El Diablo's face.

"Jedidiah, I need you to listen closely…" Pa's voice was low and calm; something spooked him, Jed thought with concern. But what? Jed couldn't help feel that the late-night conversation had done it.

"O-okay Pa," Jed looked up at his father. Dread seeded in his chest as he looked at his face. Something was wrong.

"I need you to take El Diablo to Junction…make sure he rides out of sight when you get there. Watch him, Jed. We don't want any extra eyes up here, understand?" Pa's voice was urgent, and Jed felt it to his core.

Pa gave him a quick, fatherly embrace and looked at El Diablo, who had stopped his steed just out of earshot. "I'm sendin' my boy with ya El Diablo. He'll show ya the way to Junction."

El Diablo looked at Jed, who carefully climbed up onto the old nag's back. The mare grunted and sighed at the small weight. The man remained silent as he waited.

Pa looked up at Jed and stroked the old mare's neck, "Jed…be careful, ya hear?"

"I will, Pa." Jed half smiled and took the weathered reins into his hands.

El Diablo watched Jed as he rode past him and to the small road towards Junction. Despite his Pa's unease, he could, at least, ask many of the questions that had plagued him. The pair of them made their way down the windy path in silence. Jed turned in his saddle to see if his Pa was watching. Jed saw him standing at the top of the hill. Jed waved to Pa with a smile. Pa waved back.

# Chapter 10

El Diablo had been quiet all morning as they rode to Junction. Jed would try to provoke conversation, but it was like trying to visit with a scarecrow. Jed sighed; he had given up most of the way there. This El Diablo didn't seem so bad. Why was his Pa so afraid of him?

Jed glanced over his shoulder at the man, and he heard his Pa's words echo in his head, *Watch him, Jed. We don't want any extra eyes up here, understand?*

El Diablo stretched his shoulders in his saddle as he glanced at the landscape. He seemed to not even notice Jed's presence as he followed him. He didn't seem dangerous to Jed. Even Marietta seemed to like him in her own quiet way.

Jed's mare carefully stepped around sage brush clumps and rocks as they traversed at their meager pace. The windy trail finally gave way to the valley below, and the town of Junction studding the dry landscape. Jed smiled and pointed, "There it is, Mr. El Diablo. We're almost there."

The man grunted and rummaged through his duster pockets. Jed surmised that this was all he would get out of this man. Jed's smile faded, and he adjusted himself uncomfortably in his saddle.

His mare made her way down with ease as they finally entered the town of Junction. The heat was sharper here, and Jed felt the sweat sliding down his skin everywhere. He knew he'd have to check on the cattle later this afternoon. Jed stopped at the edge of the town as El Diablo passed him. He turned his horse to face Jed and stopped. Jed still couldn't believe this man was wearing black in this heat.

El Diablo's eyes were shaded from the brim of his hat, but Jed could feel his gaze from under it. It made him squirm inwardly, as the stallion pawed the ground with impatience.

"Well, here's Junction. There's a general store over there," Jed pointed to his right, "and a farrier over there, in case ya need one." He pointed to his left.

The man was completely silent.

"I hope, uh, ya come back soon…Pa doesn't really mean to chase ya off. This season has been rough on us, and…" Jed let his sentence trail off. The man had looked up sharply, the way they had come. He had drawn up his reins.

Jed turned in his saddle to see what he was staring at. Heaviness slammed into the pit of gut. Fear bubbled in his throat.

Smoke.

"Pa…!" was all Jed was able to mutter. In a panic, Jed turned his mare urgently back towards the trail and heeled her sides.

"Wait, boy!" El Diablo's voice barked after him.

The words passed through Jed's ears. He couldn't stop.

# Chapter 11

Abel hadn't seen them come. It was fast and sudden, with barely enough time to yell to his daughter to get in the cellar. They were everywhere, with too many to count. The dust and smoke choked him, blurring his eyes. Their yells and whoops surrounded him. He had taken cover behind a broken cart. It wasn't much, but it was something. Splinters flew everywhere as the bullets slammed into the old wood. His breathing was heavy, and his body shook with adrenaline. It had been a long time since he was in a fight. He listened.

Quickly, Abel laid his rifle across the battered top of the old wagon and fired. He hit a couple of them as they rode by, their screams mingled with gunfire. The sound fell on numb ears. He may have been old, but using a gun was second nature to him, and killing men equally so.

The fire enveloped the barn across the yard. Abel felt anger swell in his heart. More bullets and yelling screamed past him. They were everywhere. All running or riding, taking what they wanted. He saw someone slip into the barn. Mr. McKay slid from his lead-shredded cart and moved fast towards the other side. He recognized that figure.

*Lousy shots...they're toyin' with me. If they truly wanted this place, they would have killed me by now.* He slammed his back against the barn wall and reloaded. The last of his ammunition. He should have asked Jed to bring some bullets back from town. Sweat rolled off his gaunt features, and dust collected on his damp skin. He stood and entered, alert and rifle raised. This man was in here, somewhere.

The barn roared with flame, and the beams groaned with despair. His breathing sounded heavy in his own ears. The hairs on his arms and on the back of his neck prickled. Something was off. With lightning reflexes, Mr. McKay turned around, tense and filled with rushing adrenaline.

*Shit…*

There he was. A large block of a man stood between him and the exit. "Eberhart…" He hissed through clenched jowls.

"So this is where you've been hiding, *Mr. Marshall*…" The deep, ominous voice seemed to dampen the flames around them. Sweat rolled off Mr. McKay now, dripping into his unblinking eyes, down his neck and back. "You're a hard man to find." The large man took a step forward; the wicked grin on his parched lips seemed hungry.

Mr. McKay adjusted his grip, tightening his hands around the stalk and barrel. "What do you want?" He quipped. His lips were pursed into a fine line of hatred, his sharp eyes reflecting it two-fold. It was hard to see through the thick veil of smoke and lingering embers.

The man's guffaw resonated through the space. Mr. McKay's hairs stood on end. He had hoped and prayed he'd never see this bastard again after all these years. Abel felt an overwhelming sense that he would die here. *I won't give him the pleasure…*

"You already know *exactly* what I want, Marshall." The weight of his words made Mr. McKay's heart race with anxiety.

A beam groaned overhead and snapped. In a rush of fire and smoke, the heavy wooden piece came crashing down above the two men. Mr. McKay rushed out of the way, squinting his watery eyes. The smoke was getting worse, and his lungs cried for fresh air. When the haze began to settle, he couldn't see Eberhart. *Damn it! He's gone!*

Fear pitted in the bottom of his gut as sweat poured off his skin. His sharp eyes scanned the room—Eberhart had disappeared.

His heart racked against his ribs; he knew he was still here, somewhere.

Mr. McKay turned around. His heart hammered harder. The glinting dance of the flames in Eberhart's eyes froze him in place. He didn't have any time to defend himself as he felt the sharp tines of the hay fork pierce his chest. His heart quivered, his lungs winded as Eberhart viciously staked him to the ground. He gripped the handle with all his might as he felt his body smack to the floor. His shout of surprise and pain were drowned out by the raging fire around the two men.

Eberhart uttered an unearthly snarl as he pressed down harder with jerking movements. Mr. McKay stared with wide-eyed shock as he felt the tines pierce clear through him and deep into the earth. He felt his blood well into his mouth making him cough and sputter, choking on his own life essence.

Once Eberhart was pleased at Abel's plight, he kneeled to his side and looked over his handiwork. "Now, Mr. McKay..." Eberhart's words were low and sinister. He could hear it above the chaos around him. Urgent panic flooded him as he struggled to get free. He needed to protect his children. A violent cough racked his body as he continued to slowly drown.

"I'm goin' to take your daughter..." Mr. McKay gaped at Eberhart in horror. "And that will complete what you started with me..." Mr. McKay breathed heavier as his fingers fumbled around the metal base of the tines. Blood coated his fingers as he tried desperately to free himself. He had to save his daughter. *God no, Marietta!*

Eberhart chuckled maniacally as he stood and stepped over his fallen victim. Mr. McKay reached out and gripped the man's pant leg as it brushed by. His slick fingers couldn't hold on for long, as the rough cloth ripped from his grasp. He squirmed, feeling completely helpless as he felt his life being torn from him.

\*\*\*

Jed slapped the reins on the old mare's sides frantically, urging her to go faster. Her breathing was heavy and her gallop sloppy. The smoke was billowing from the ranch.

His mare just wasn't fast enough, and Jed felt his frustration peak.

Jed crested the hilltop and watched in horror as men rode on horses shouting and firing their arms. The chicken coop was wide open with hens squawking and running, desperately seeking a way out. Jed saw his Pa's horse dead just outside of the barn. Its side was wet with fresh blood from bullet wounds. Men of all sorts were ransacking the whole estate. Jed saw several men clamor out of the house in a rush of laughing and shouting in a different language. In their arms were his Pa's various whiskey bottles he had had since Jed could remember, along with armfuls of food.

Everything was going to ruin at the hand of bandits. Everything he knew, everything that made this place home, everything his Pa had worked so hard for, was being destroyed. Anger flared in his chest as Jed gritted his teeth and urged his exhausted mare towards the chaos. He would not stand idly by and let this happen. He had to stop them, somehow.

The cellar doors busted open, followed by a couple men dragging a flailing Marietta by her hair and arms. Her pale blue dress was stained with canned goods—evidence that she had fought them furiously. Fear lumped in his throat. "Hey!!" he shouted frantically, "Let her go!!" The men ignored his shouts, if they heard him at all.

He heeled his mare urgently. She neighed and pranced side to side—hesitant to continue—but obeyed. Jed was desperate to close the distance between them and him. Just as he thought he would reach them in time, he felt hands grapple the back of his shirt and violently threw him from his saddle. Jed shouted as he fell and hit the dirt underneath him.

The mare whinnied and bucked away from the tussle. Jed wheezed as he tried to get up. Marietta needed him. A dark figure blotted the sun in his eyes, looming over him. Jed struggled to overcome his winding; he couldn't let them take her. He raised his hands up in defense as he saw the butt of a rifle come rushing down on him. The splitting blow made him cry out in pain, making Jed's world go black.

*\*\*\**

El Diablo's stallion crested the hill at blazing speed. The ranch house to his right was completely engulfed in flames, and nearly collapsed. He urged his steed to a reining stop, its nostrils flared as it pulled against the bit. His ears were laid back; El Diablo ignored him.

El Diablo scanned the area quickly, his ears attuned to the roaring flames. He couldn't see the boy, which meant that he had either been taken off or was dead. "Shit…" he grunted bitterly as he kept his stallion under control.

Faint yelling and shouting was heard over the roar of the fires that engulfed the barn and decimated farm house. El Diablo immediately heeled his steed out to the main yard. The stallion brayed and danced to the side as he pulled his gun from his holster—but he was too late. *Damn it all…* The backs of the retreating marauders were too far gone for him to shoot them down. He would hunt them later. With a grunt, El Diablo turned his stallion toward the barn and trotted over. Without stopping, he dismounted from the saddle and signaled the horse with a sharp whistle, sending him galloping off.

El Diablo slipped through the door opening and into the roaring flame. The smoke clouded his eyes, but failed to mask his sense of smell. Though fire and smoke filled his nostrils, it didn't choke him in the slightest. He paused a moment. *That smell…* He drew a deep breath, processing the new smell. He knew that smell. He knew it all too well.

Blood: it was thick and fresh. El Diablo continued, intrigued, toward the source. As a smaller beam from the loft crashed to El Diablo's right side, he raised his arm to shade his eyes from the embers and sparks. He moved over the fallen support with careful precision. The iron tinge of the blood seeped into his senses, quickening his pulse as he stopped and observed the source of the smell: a squirming man brutally impaled to the ground.

El Diablo stepped around the man, noting the oozing puddle that was growing around him like a corrupted halo. His face twisted into a curious expression; he recognized this man.

"Abel McKay…" He uttered to himself as his cold eyes glanced over the handiwork. El Diablo finally looked into the old Marshall's eyes, and was surprised. He saw anger pooled in the man's eyes—not fear, as he was expecting.

Mr. McKay coughed, spewing foaming blood over his chin, lips, and cheeks. "Eb…er…h-hart…" He uttered. El Diablo frowned and squatted down on his haunches, resting his right forearm across the raised knee, his interest piqued.

"Well, Mr. Marshall…seems you're shit out of luck."

"Took…took her…" he wheezed out before another gasping spasm took hold of his body. El Diablo's countenance stiffened, a frown creasing across his face. *The girl? Why?* "Finish…" the old Marshall choked as more blood bubbled up and spilled over his lips. His eyes fluttered closed as another wave of pain washed over the man. El Diablo could see this man's life ebbing away.

He sighed and reached for the wood handle of the fork. He could, at least, let the man die in some peace with this destruction. Abel violently gripped El Diablo's outstretched hand and drew it closer to him. His strength surprised him, but this was the last of it—he could feel it. The hand, slick with blood, drew the hunter closer to him as his other hand shakily clung at the sleeve of El Diablo's duster.

El Diablo frowned at the dying man as Abel spoke as clearly as he could, "M-my son…protect him. Protect him…save," he swallowed hard, his Adam's apple bobbing painfully, "save Marietta…" A shuddered breath wreaked havoc on the man as he convulsed in a fit of choking and coughing. Blood splattered over his face, covering the dried splatters. El Diablo was drawn to this man's plea, as though hungry for his words, "I offer…all…that is in me…"

El Diablo stared deep into McKay's eyes from under the dark of his hat, tingling running through him. He nodded curtly, licking his lips as he acknowledged the dying wish. As McKay wheezed weakly, his body seized against his will. El Diablo felt a cold power enter him, burning his chest. With a final shudder, McKay's grip fell limp, his breath sighing through his parted lips. His eyes clouded over with death: the deal was complete.

The barn around El Diablo groaned urgently as hunks of wood and charred panels began to cave in. He hissed, feeling the new burden on his shoulders. He let McKay's soaked hand fall to the side. His own hand was covered in blood, his coat sleeve smeared with it. The lust had clouded his rationale. Frustration festered in his core. This man was too clever for his own good. *He knew…Damn it!!*

Angry, he jerked the hay fork from McKay and tossed it viciously to the side with a snarl. He picked up the body and wove his way towards the half-blocked entrance, fire gleaming in his hellish eyes.

# Chapter 12

Jed felt his head pounding with an agonizing ache. He felt the heat of the day on his body and he could hear simmering flames in the distance. The scents of the smoke and dust clogged his nostrils.

Everything began to come back to him as his conscious mind struggled to come back to life. He squeezed his eyes and groaned, turning his head to the side. A sharp pain shot through his skull as he reached up, tenderly touching his temple area; it was sticky and excruciating to the touch. He opened his eyes and peered at his fingers—blood.

Jed groaned again, trying to recount what had happened. *Marietta!!* He gasped as the memories suddenly flooded his mind, making him sit up fast. He quickly regretted the action as the pounding head ache threatened to drag him back to the darkness. He held his head in his hands. *They took her. They took her, and I couldn't stop them...*

He could see her flailing against them as they hauled her away... Jed forced a sob to stay hidden as he tried to calm himself. Footsteps and gear jangled toward him making him look up to see who was approaching. He hoped it wasn't a marauder that stayed behind. Jed's sight was hazy as he slowly focused on the man in black coming closer to him.

"El Diablo...?" Jed croaked in disbelief.

The man was silent as he stopped in front of him, rummaging aggressively into his duster pockets. The hunter found the ivory cardboard box and flipped open the lid irritably pulling out a cigarette.

Jed groaned and hung his head, shutting his eyes. Stars fluttered rapidly in the dark for a moment before subsiding again. When the wave passed, he looked back at the hunter and staggered to his feet from the hard ground. His eyes finally adjusted as he scanned the remnants of his home.

*Pa...!* He thought fearfully. His heart raced in his chest again as he forced his legs to move. They felt heavy, making it difficult to move as he stumbled hurriedly toward the yard. *Where is he?!* His mind raced as he searched the wreckage.

"He's dead, boy..." The hunter's words slammed into him, making him halt his stumbling. *Dead...?!*

Jed felt his legs weaken again as he looked back at El Diablo. Raw emotion began to well inside him, worsening the ache in his head. "Where is he?" His voice cracked, but he didn't care. He needed to see his Pa. He couldn't be dead...

The hunter struck a match along his gruff jaw and let the flame lick the end of his cigarette. The scowl across his face seemed to be stuck in place as he puffed on the cigarette, glaring at Jed from beneath his brim. He didn't understand why El Diablo was suddenly so hostile toward him.

Jed frowned at El Diablo.

El Diablo returned the frown.

After several long moments, the hunter tossed his chin toward the crumbled, smoldering barn. Jed worriedly glanced toward the skeleton of charred timber, his eyes quickly searching for any sign—until he finally saw what he had dreaded.

"Pa...!" Jed whispered desperately, fear lumping in his throat. He forced his legs to move, running towards the still form of his father. He recognized that tan vest and pants with the off-white shirt. As he came closer he saw the massive blood stains that coated his front and his sides; blood was all over him.

Sliding to a stop, Jed dropped heavily to his knees, the emotion finally flooding through. Tears began to wet his eyes as he looked over the fallen body of his father. "Oh God...no..." He shakily reached out to his father, barely stroking a stray strand of graying blonde hair. He saw the splattered blood over his father's grizzled chin and down his neck. He had choked on his own blood. A hot trail of tears burned Jed's dusty cheek as he saw the gaping wounds through his father's chest.

He gently scooped up his father's upper torso and cradled him to his chest. A sob ripped through him, nearly crumpling him. He closed his eyes and rocked back and forth, weeping over the loss of his family.

They took his sister. They burned his home. They murdered his father. Everything that he had ever known had been torn from him. For the first time in his life, he was utterly lost.

## Chapter 13

A breeze sidled its way across the barren site; shifting the smoke eastward. Scavengers had begun to wander through the smoldering debris of the raid, and vultures soared overhead. The flames were still vivid in Jed's mind, the shouts and howls still prominent in his memory.

*Marietta…Oh, God, Marietta,* he thought, distraught at the image of men riding off in a flurry of dust and back-fire. The dirt was dry and brittle, cracking with each strike of the spade. The monotonous movement allowed Jed think about the day, his mind wandering the void of endless possibilities. He felt as though he was suspended in a limbo state, not sure where to go or what to do.

Jed paused and rested a moment, sweat stinging his eyes. His shoulders sagged. His throat caught, emotion, again, threatening to overwhelm him. What was a boy to do? The one person whom he could ask advice of was dead: this hole was for him.

His arms were stiff as the grating of the spade on hardpan itched his numbed conscious. The strokes were steady, but it felt like he was getting nowhere as the pile of dirt grew and grew. Pa's defiled body was burning his mind, forever searing the fate that was dealt to him. Jed sniffed and wiped the back of his hand across his mouth and nose, choking on fresh emotion. The strokes were getting increasingly hard as the hole became larger and larger, just as his despair grew in tandem. The tinge of burnt wood and death drifted to Jed's nostrils—it nearly made him gag.

A new smell of smoke accompanied destruction's aftermath, though he didn't need to look for the source. He already knew who it was. He'd been a silent spectator after chasing off the straggling members of the raid. El Diablo: that's the only name that was associated with him. El Diablo had pulled out that same beat-up ivory box that held his smokes and had taken a light to one. The smell was only slightly better than the destruction.

Sweat trickled along Jed's skin as he finally finished his grim task. He brushed the back of his arm across his face, trying to wipe the sweat from his eyes, but only succeeding in making a thin film of mud. His heart weighed down in his chest; Jed knew the next step.

A shaky breath racked through his being as he looked toward the canvas-covered shape not far from the fresh grave. A heavy sigh emanated from his strange guest behind him, the smoke from the cigarette still permeating the air.

Jed looked back at El Diablo. His gaze was turned to the barren ground, his stance shifted to one side, bored or indifferent to the situation. That black-brimmed hat shaded his eyes, a trait becoming familiar to Jed.

No words were spoken. Jed's eyes pleaded with the man to at least look at him. Anything, to show that he might still be decent—not this cruel outlaw the authorities had made him out to be.

El Diablo lifted his jaw slightly and cocked his gaze at Jed. Those eyes of his were so different, their intensity surprising Jed every time. Still silence. The cigarette was half gone, it's embers burning hellish red at the tip.

A raspy sigh accompanied the billow of smoke from El Diablo's lips, his gaze hard on the dust below. He drew in on that cigarette for the last time before idly shaking it between his fingers and flicking it aside.

Jed watched him cautiously as the bounty hunter approached. His gear rustled and chinked with every step, a harbinger of death to anything in this man's path. But not today. Too much death had happened already.

Jed turned and slowly moved to the covered form of his father. He didn't understand why this had happened. Pa was a good man.

He stared down at his father, the reality that he was gone was sinking in.

A hot stream streaked his cheek, surprising him. He would not cry. El Diablo nimbly crouched down and snaked his arms under the corpse's legs. Jed crouched and gingerly scooped up his father's arms and shoulders. Grief threatened to overwhelm his reason.

*No*. He thought strongly. *Be the man.*

Trembling, Jed aided the hunter in laying his father in the hole he had dug—his grave. El Diablo surprised Jed with his apparent respect for the dead as he laid his end gently into the earth. A respect that quickly departed as El Diablo fished into his pocket for another cigarette—his cold composure returning.

Jed understood. This man meant nothing to a hunter like himself. Jed didn't expect any compassion from him. Fear crept into his mind as the spade once again began its work. Stroke after stroke, the dirt began to fill in where it once had been. The fear began in the pit of his stomach. He was alone—his father was dead, and Marietta was taken. He had to find her. He couldn't bear the thought of leaving her out there in the hands of God only knows who.

The task was done. His cheeks felt hot as he wiped the gritty sweat with the back of his hand. Here his Pa lay to rest. The spade was sturdy, serving as a lean-on for Jed. His family had been ripped apart in a day. And for what? What cause did those bandits have to take them away? Fear became squelched by a boiling fury. It welled deep inside his chest. His face darkened with a scowl.

He would avenge his father. He would get his sister back.

Without a word, Jed strode with determination to his old friend. The off-white mare was half asleep, paying no heed to her master's approach. Jed thanked God he went to town with El Diablo, or this old nag would have been killed or stolen, like the rest of the horses.

His hands gripped the pommel and the rear of the saddle, pulling his body up and into the worn seat. His nag sighed and lifted her head, tiredly perking up an ear. He reached and pulled the leather straps into his hands, and gently urged the nag to turn in the direction the raiders had gone.

"Where do you think you're goin', boy?" The hunter's gruff voice sounded. Jed turned his head to his left. El Diablo was mounted on his black stallion with the red eyes.

He hadn't noticed the man had mounted up and nudged his stallion toward him. Jed sniffed and looked the hunter in the eye as he came near, "Getting my sister back." He knew that the odds were not weighed in his favor, but he didn't care. His sister was in peril. He was the only one who would go after her and bring her home. No one would tell him otherwise.

The hunter steadied his horse as it nickered and pawed the earth, "You think you have a chance boy?" Jed frowned at the man's words, but he would be honest.

"No...but I will try." The man reined his stallion to a stop beside Jed and sighed. As though ill, the man leaned over and rested his wrists over the pommel. Black leather reins were loosely hanging from his rough fingers.

"Well..." El Diablo finally said and sat back up into position, "Then we'd best get..." His spurs jabbed at his stallion's sides, making the horse grunt and propel into a fast-paced trot in the direction of the renegades. Jed shook himself from his disbelief at El Diablo's answer. He didn't understand why the man was coming with him, but he would accept any help.

His awkward companion was gaining distance. Jed clucked and gently nudged his old nag to follow. She obeyed, first at a walk, then, a fast trot.

He would get Marietta back. The ruined ranch still smoldered behind him. *Rest in peace, Pa*, Jed thought sorrowfully. He wouldn't look back. He feared that if he did, he would lose his burning desire. The desire for vengeance—for justice.

## Chapter 14

She awoke with a startled jolt, immediately regretting her gut reaction. Her head pounded with a primal fervor. She grimaced in silence and tried to sit up, but something restricted her movement. Her arms and legs felt numb, and something was cutting into her flesh at the wrists and ankles. Forcing the skull drum to recede, she turned her stiff neck around to see what was inhibiting her. *Ropes...?* Her mind was heavily drowsy, and her ears were muffled with a low-pitched whine. She lay there, her body aching from lying face down on hard pack dirt and rocks.

Marietta let her numb and aching limbs rest for a moment as her thoughts slowly gathered together. *Where am I...?* The one question dangled in the fore front of her mind, her senses beginning to clear up.

*Pa!!* Her memory suddenly slammed back into her conscious mind as the events had unfurled. Her heart pounded as she began wriggling her wrists against her bonds. She licked her cracked, dry lips with anxiety as she craned her neck to see her progress. She withered inside as she saw that the ropes were only rubbing her skin raw. She grimaced from the burning sensation of her skin. With a silent exasperated huff, she looked around her. Her eyes widened.

She didn't recognize anything from miles around. *How long was I out?!* She swallowed hard and closed her eyes, resting her forehead on the rocky earth beneath her. *Easy now, Marietta...you can get through this. Pa is probably looking for you.* Encouragement began to build inside her, despite the lump of panic rising into her throat.

*I must get away...if I can...just...* Marietta lifted her head up, a determined frown of concentration now carved into her brow as she began a very slow wriggle. The rocks and hard dirt beneath her scraped against her skin, renegade chunks of hardened dirt trickled into her dress, making her itch. She paused, looking back at the far campfire. The shadowed figures gathered around it paid no attention to her.

Marietta swallowed hard again and took a slow breath, before making another advance. Each scrape forward made her cringe as she prayed that those brutes wouldn't hear her escape; and each scrape was one step closer to freedom.

*Just a little more...hopefully, I can find a rock sharp enough to—*

"Guess we should check on the little bitch, shouldn' we?" A gruff voice spoke over the sound of crackling underbrush and twigs of a camp fire close by.

"Suppose ya should, since you volunteered an'all." Another man snickered, sending a wave of chuckling through the rest of the group. The first man grumbled and got to his feet sluggishly.

Marietta looked back at the figure with widening eyes. *Oh, no...*

Panic began racing through her as she struggled to creep faster away. The rocks made her skin sore as she slid by.

"Ah, shit..." The man grumbled. She heard him coming, and quickly. Her breathing hastened as she gritted her teeth. She had to get away.

"Where do ya think you're goin', bitch?" The growly voice of the man resonated darkly above her. Rough hands gripped the back of her dress and the bonds that held her wrists together. Sharp pain rang through her arms and spine as the cords dug deeper into her flesh. She opened her mouth in shock to the sensation, her voice silent.

The other men had started to get up from their spots, seeing that there might be action to be had. Marietta tried with all her might to pull herself away from the rough man. She was shoved towards the camp area, where the other men were standing and reaching towards her. She dug her heels into the earth and twisted in the man's grip. *NO!!! Let me go!*

With an aggressive shove, the man pushed Marietta into the grabbing hands of the others. Men laughed, scoffed, and hollered with excitement as they groped her and felt her dress, smelling her hair. The stench of them made Marietta dizzy, nearly gagging her. They crowded around her as she struggled against them vainly. *Stop it!!* She screamed inside.

"Did I give you permission to relieve yourselves on her?" A booming voice rumbled through the camp, making the men stop abruptly. Marietta looked towards the source of the voice. She stiffened as a chill dripped down her spine; she saw faintly glowing eyes—not unlike a wolf or a coyote at night.

"Move aside…" The voice growled. Dread seeped into her bones as she tried to look around the men surrounding her. With the firm words, the men let her go, making her stumble. She lost balance, but quickly regained her equilibrium, looking towards the large figure striding calmly toward her. A lump choked her throat. *Oh, my God…* The large man entered the light. What she saw made her tremble to her core.

The man was the tallest man she had ever seen, standing around seven feet tall—or more. The glint of the fire reflected his eyes bright as gold with a haunting predatory shine, followed by a wicked, fanged grin gleaming with saliva. His shoulders were wide, and his chest broad. His girth was as thick as the trunk of the old oak on the edge of her home. *Who is that…?* Marietta's mind fluttered in panic as she stepped back, only to be stopped by the men that had made a circle around her. She glanced briefly back at the man she bumped into and moved away from him. *His eyes glow, too!*

The larger man chuckled in amusement as he locked his eyes on her. The sensation paralyzed her to the spot; her heart pounded in her ears as she watched the man in front of her. He paused, his eyes weighing her as she glared at him. Her burning anger soon slid into unease, but the man's wry smile never wavered.

*Why is he staring at me…?* Something deep within her stirred uncomfortably as the man cocked his head to the side, as if amused at her plight.

"You look just like her…" His voice almost hissed the last word, startling her. The hair on her neck chilled. The man reached out and grasped her jaw with calloused fingers, firmly, but not roughly. He turned her face to the left then to the right, analyzing her further. After a long, agonizing moment, he released her chin and leaned in closer. His breath worse than his grin. "Marietta, was it?"

She stood there, shocked. *How did he…? No one knows I exist. Not in Junction, anyway…* She felt her curiosity grow, even though her intuition screamed for it not to. This man knew something about her—though she couldn't imagine what. Marietta slowly nodded her head, answering the man's question.

"That's what I thought, darlin'…you're where you belong now. Here, with us." She flinched slightly as he reached and twirled a strand of her hair in his meaty fingers. "With me…" Those words dashed all curiosity. She needed to get away from him as fast as she was able. Without a second thought about what he had said, the wicked man looked over the men that had gathered to watch, a frown creasing his already predatory features. "Any o' ya so much as brush a finger over her, and I'll have your hide to dry. Do I make myself clear?"

Marietta saw several men in her peripheral nod their heads vigorously. She could only assume the others agreed just as fervently. The man grunted his approval and turned his back to her as the men began to disperse. The one who had grabbed her to begin with grunted and nudged her back towards the horses where another was standing guard already.

*Whatever is goin' on, I need to find out. I can only hope Jed or Pa are comin' to get me.* The man behind her stopped her and motioned for her to lie down. He was silent, but she got the idea. As she laid down in the dirt and watched the men laugh and joke around the fire, her fear creeped back into her veins. *Pa, Jed...please find me, and soon.*

# Chapter 15

He swore the man never spoke. For the past several miles, all Jed heard was the steady plodding of hooves on cracked hardpan and the creaking of well-worn leather saddles. Jed shifted his small frame in the saddle, feeling the uncomfortable ache of prolonged riding. He hated long silences, as they let his mind think on things. Things he didn't want to concentrate on.

It had been only a couple days since the strange bandits had swept through his family's ranch and burned it to the ground. Everything had been taken from him that day. His Pa had been brutally murdered, and his little sister had been abducted. The only thing he had to go by was the vague memory of the bandit who stole her and the word of this mysterious bounty hunter. He feared for her. She was barely fourteen, as well as mute. He had to find her. Pa would have wanted him to try.

El Diablo adjusted himself in his saddle and spat to his left side with a sick hock. Jed crinkled his nose in distaste of the action. He already didn't trust this man well enough, and his identity left Jed wondering if this man was a threat or a help. This 'El Diablo' had told Jed that his Pa told him to protect his son and save his daughter. Jed had a hard time believing that. Pa was the one who wanted to shoot the man until Jed convinced him that it wasn't right to kill an unarmed man, let alone a wounded one. Jed was reconsidering his gut reaction...

"You can believe anything you want boy, but I don't go back on my word...Ever." The rugged voice from the man jolted Jed out of his thoughts. His eyes widened in surprise. He hadn't spoken aloud...had he? He must have. *The heat must be tamperin' with my senses*. His ears started to flare red at the tips from embarrassment. He was raised to always be polite to strangers and the like, regardless of their color, faction, or sex. El Diablo was no exception.

"My apologies, sir..." Jed mumbled sheepishly. All he got in acknowledgement from the man was the snort of his horse and the silence that followed. The heat of the day was starting to reach its peak, but, still, they rode on.

Jed was sweating profusely, and his light brown curls were beginning to cling to his neck. He raised an arm and wiped his forehead. It had gotten unbearably hot, and his eyes continuously squinted in a vain attempt to keep the piercing sun out of his sight. He couldn't imagine how the outlaw bounty hunter felt; wearing an all-black duster, black boots, black leather chaps, and pants. *It must be ungodly hot in this weather. He should have passed out from heatstroke by now.* This was just another mystery to add to the many.

El Diablo stopped, causing Jed's old mare to jam her nose into El Diablo's ghastly stallion. The stallion—as black as his rider—pawed the ground and emitted an unearthly nicker, pulling and biting on the glinting steel bit as he pinned his ears. A wave of unease washed over Jed, and he shivered, despite the intense heat. El Diablo lifted his gaze from the head of his horse to the surrounding hills. The way he looked at their surroundings made Jed feel uneasy about something, but he didn't know what.

Quicker than Jed could follow, El Diablo pulled his pistol from his hip holster and turned his stallion sharply to the right. Jed looked up at the crest of the hill and reached for his Pa's rifle—the last memento of his Pa he was ever going to have. El Diablo cocked the hammer and took aim right at the crest as if he knew something, or someone, was going to materialize any moment. After a few pain-staking seconds, Jed licked his lips nervously and spoke quietly, "Mr. El Diablo, sir, what are—"

El Diablo looked at Jed with the sharpest gaze that could make any man shed their skin. Jed instantly snapped his jaw shut and determined it best not to speak for the time being.

"Well if it ain't good ol' El Diablo, himself…" The strange, unfamiliar voice seeped over the hills and into the small valley the duo was stopped in. El Diablo rounded his steed in multiple directions trying to triangulate the location of the mysterious voice. "I was wonderin' when you'd show. Took your sweet time, didn't ya?"

Jed tightened his grip on the reins and adjusted his hold on the weathered stock of the rifle. He looked around in a wild fashion to try and find the source as well, but seeing nothing he just moved his old mare to the side. She snorted warily and began to fidget beneath him, the uneasiness of El Diablo's stallion rubbing off on her.

"I don't have time for this shit…" El Diablo murmured and irritably rested his pistol against his shoulder with the barrel aimed at the sky. El Diablo yanked down on his reins to keep his eager stallion from throwing him as he nickered anxiously.

"Well ya should, El Diablo. Considerin' ya owe my employer a hefty sum." The voice finally sounded closer, almost as though it were above them on the hill where El Diablo had aimed before. Jed turned his mare back in that direction and startled at the new presence. The man's shaded appearance was foreboding, dousing Jed's senses with a growing fear in the pit of his gut. The eyes of the horse seemed to gleam with an ethereal light to them, matching the rider's eerie façade. How could they not have heard him ride up? It wasn't possible, was it?

El Diablo sighed and looked back down at his horse and answered in that casual gruff tone, "I figured I could avoid this whole thing, seein' as you won't be breathin' after."

The haunting laugh was bone-chilling. Jed's hairs on the back of his neck stood on end. As the laughter echoed over the arid space, countless other figures crested the hill to stand by their leader, all armed and ready for conflict. Jed nervously flicked his eyes over the gathering gunslingers and tightened his grip on the rifle.

"Funny you should say that…my employer mentioned somethin' similar." The tension rose as various clicks sounded in the silence. This man's intent was more than just conversation: he wanted blood.

El Diablo glared back up at the man, a faint glint of interest showing in his eyes, a smirk tugging at his rugged features. The moment that glint came, the guns erupted in a roar. The shaded man had drawn his own pistol and was firing in rapid succession.

Jed's mare whinnied and reared, sending him sprawling to the ground in a cloud of dust and panic. The men on the hill had started running and taking positions around the valley's lip. El Diablo had leapt from his saddle and gave a sharp, short whistle, sending the revved horse into a frenzy of speed and dexterity. The stallion and the poor mare charged back toward the direction they came from.

Jed scrambled and covered his head with his arms as several shots grazed the ground around him. After he mustered some courage, he scurried his way in the direction of where the horses had gone. With a muffled yelp, Jed was hauled to his feet and rushed to a nearby boulder; the only semblance of cover in this field of bullets and dust. Jed was tossed to safety. El Diablo slid right behind him to take cover as more bullets barraged the boulder, sending fragments of red clay over the two.

Bullets hissed overhead and plodded into the dirt close by. Crouched behind the large, red boulder, El Diablo coolly loaded his pistol. Jed was crouched as low to the ground as he could get without lying completely flat. He was flustered at the sudden eruption.

"W-what'll we do?!" He exclaimed in his breaking adolescent voice. The hunter said nothing for a moment as more bullets ricocheted off the boulder. He finished loading his gun and lifted his steely, blue gaze to meet the young man's terrified eyes.

"Kill." Without giving Jed a chance to squeak in protest, the hunter rolled out from the natural barrier and let loose three concise shots. Distant thuds let him know that his aim was accurate—and deadly. The men who received the deadly rounds shouted and gurgled in pain as they sputtered their last breaths. El Diablo's tugging smirk finally spread over his rugged lips, like the blood seeping over the dust from his victims.

Jed clutched the rifle in his hands with white-knuckled fear. The pit of his stomach was a roiling mess of anxiety and bone-shaking terror from the onslaught. He was a rancher's kid, not a gunslinger. Though his Pa had taught him the basics of marksmanship, he never learned how to actually hit something. His heart pounded in his ribcage, and his blood rushed in his veins at the realization that he was utterly useless; utterly helpless. Jed closed his eyes tightly for a split-second and prayed to God that he could live through this. He shakily peeked out around the boulder and was greeted by another wave of deadly projectiles. Jed pressed his back hard against the rock and clutched his Pa's rifle to his chest.

"You ain't gonna fight, boy?" The shaded man's voice pierced Jed's ears like a nail to a coffin lid. He meant to kill him. "You ain't as good as your Pa, kid, so you might as well just give up!" Jed went rigid at the mention of his Pa. This man knew something. Fear melted into anger as his terrified clutch became a grip of fury. This man—if he was even a man—was going to die.

Jed clenched his teeth as his muscles tensed, the shaded man laughing again. He knew what he had to do: kill. That was El Diablo's answer after all. Before Jed let the self-doubt sink into his mind, he stood sharply and laid his rifle barrel over the rock—left eye squinting in concentration. Sweat had begun to pour from him, threatening to blur his vision. He focused on the shaded man and his antsy horse. He'd pressed his upper body flat against the hot rock and flinched from another flurry of bullets. He steeled his courage against the swelling fear. Jed fumbled with the rifle and took aim again.

He pulled the trigger.

The sound erupted, and the bullet flew. The kick-back made Jed shut his eyes and grimace, quickly crouching low behind the boulder while he reloaded. His hands shook with nervousness and adrenaline. The bullet had missed. Cursing under his breath, Jed peeked over the boulder again only to see the shaded man aiming at him. His eyes widened and ducked just in time to avoid a deadly round. He could hear the shots El Diablo was firing; men's curses and screams of pain were all around him.

*How can he live like this?!* Jed thought with exasperation. Out of the corner of his eyes, he could see El Diablo moving swiftly over the scorched earth like a shade of death. Nothing seemed to touch him.

"Can't hide forever, lil' McKay!" The shaded man sneered at him. Jed frowned, the man's voice snapping his attention. He took up the sniper position again, concentrating harder. He took in a sharp breath before blowing out steadily. His shoulders relaxed slightly as he did, his finger squeezed the trigger. Jed didn't shy from the kickback the second time as he watched the bullet hit its mark and pass right through the man, as if he were smoke. Jed's small hope of triumph was utterly shattered as he watched the small bullet-hole fill itself back in. His eyes widened in fear-struck awe as the shaded man let out a deep guffaw at his feeble attempt.

"Nice try, boy!" the man dismounted his horse, which vanished into smoke as though it had never existed. He adjusted his well-worn gear, cricking his neck from side to side, as if to loosen up before this easy kill. This man was coming for him.

The man spread his arms to the side just before disappearing into gray, swirling smoke. He reappeared in front of Jed, a wicked smirk stretched over his haunting features, "Boo." Jed dropped his Pa's rifle, clattering uselessly to the dirt. His heart leap into his throat as he backed up as fast as he could manage. He wasn't sweating just because it was hot anymore—he was sweating with terror. This panic that he had tried to squelch had taken over. This was no man. He was something out of a nightmare. Jed backed as the man coolly strolled towards him. He didn't want to die. He was afraid.

The haunting man's spurs clanged, his dark brown leathers and gear rustling with each stride, and his countenance was haunting. He was a tall man, with lanky features and a slight gimp to his gait on his right side. The skin looked as if it were stretched over the skull, pale and spider-webbed with dark black veins; sharp, angular cheeks, and sunken eyes with a wicked, fanged smile.

His face locked Jed's eyes into a terrified stare as he approached. His black, soulless eyes were full of bloodlust. *He's crazy! What the hell is this man?!* Jed tripped over something and fell flat on his back, making him yelp. Pain racked his scrawny body from the impact of the hard dirt and small rocks. The man's raspy chuckle rose above the rest of the chaotic gun fight around them, the screams and shouts diminishing as fewer and fewer shots were fired. Jed snapped open his eyes, and, to his horror, the glinting black steel of the man's pistol was winking at him—mere inches from his face.

He was a tower of pale bones, his eyes calculating as he looked over Jed's trembling form. Scars riddled his cheeks, meshing with the black veins that wove underneath the skin. His muscles twitched with the cruel smile that burned apart his lips. A line of moist fangs glinted at Jed, urging him to scramble away—fast. Those black eyes seared into his mind, paralyzing Jed's heart as he felt his lungs burn—he had been holding his breath. The beast of a man seemed to take pleasure in striking terror into his victims.

The man chuckled wickedly and let a couple rounds sing, making Jed flinch and yelp from the missed shots. Jed froze, realizing that there wasn't a way out of this, and looked his killer in the eye for the last time. The man's eyes held nothing but bloodlust and greed as he cocked the hammer back once more and hissed through his fangs, "Say g'bye…oh," he cocked his head to the side, an afterthought, "An' say hello ta yer Pa fer me—in hell." His bony finger squeezed the trigger. He wasn't going to miss this time.

A shot fired, and Jed flinched with a gasp, anticipating pain. The devilish man screeched, dropping his gun into the dirt with a thud. El Diablo stepped into view as Jed squeezed open his petrified eyes. El Diablo's pistol was smoking as the man's arm bled a red river down his coat, into the dirt. Jed shielded his eyes from the sun, focusing on El Diablo in relief and disbelief all at once.

"Bit shameful to kill a boy, ain't it?" His voice carried in mocking aggravation.

The dusty battleground was silent, except for the man's shouting, "You're one to talk, El Diablo! How many boys have *you* killed for money?!" El Diablo stiffened at the remark and cocked the hammer back again. The shaded man laughed at his response, straightening from his pained posture and sneered. Jed looked at the wicked man, then, back at El Diablo. He knew the stories of this outlaw, but he had never given them much thought.

"Your good ol' pal, Diablo, here's killed people you small folk never heard of!" El Diablo gritted his teeth as he glared at the man closely. "He's burned bigger towns than your pathetic ranch and killed more than you can count."

"Shut the hell up, Lenard." El Diablo cut the man off with a hiss, his own hardened eyes narrowing. His already thin patience was dwindling.

"Tch…you used to run with me." The man took a step toward El Diablo, who greeted him with bared teeth. The man's sneer faded, replaced with a disgusted scowl. The man started to walk around El Diablo. El Diablo's blue eyes glared from under his brim as he continued to bare his teeth. "Guess that don't mean shit to you…" He stretched his wounded arm with a hiss and snatched his last pistol from the second holster. El Diablo kept his eyes trained on his supposed ex-partner in crime and commanded Jed, "Jed, get out of here…" Without a word, Jed scrambled to his feet and slid to cover behind a new boulder.

Jed peeked out from the top of the boulder to watch the two men circle. This was his life in this game of guns. If El Diablo won, Jed would live. If this other man won…he swallowed hard at the thought of what would happen to him.

"You used to terrify me, Diablo, but, now, yer soft." His words echoed over the bloody field of still corpses and against the hillside. Still, El Diablo held his tongue as he matched the swaggering pace of the other man.

"Shoulda stayed with us, Diablo. Then, ya wouldn't have ta babysit *this* kid."

El Diablo gave a disgusted grunt as they came to a stop. Jed furrowed his brow as he continued to watch. Shadows flashed overhead as the vultures and crows began circling above—waiting for one more body to add to their vast feast.

Lenard laughed and gazed up at the birds with a crazed expression, "I don't understand you, *friend*…" He focused his pitted stare back at El Diablo and flashed those sharp teeth again. Lenard lifted his pistol from his side and immediately let loose a flurry of bullets. El Diablo moved swiftly to the side. As bullets pierced the air, he released his own retaliation. His guns blazed with shots so fast it was hard for Jed to keep up with the moving gun fight.

Lenard laughed maniacally as he dodged bullets with inhuman speed and agility. Jed wouldn't have believed it if he hadn't seen it with his very eyes. El Diablo snarled irritably as he, too, moved quickly, avoiding the shots Lenard fired. Lenard shouted with a madman's glee as he disappeared into a thick swirling mass of smoke, reappearing behind El Diablo. El Diablo grunted as Lenard took the split-second advantage, sweeping his legs from under him.

Lenard shouted with a bestial vigor as he brought his foot down to where El Diablo lay, aiming straight for his chest.

With a nimbleness Jed didn't know he had, El Diablo rolled from under the coming blow and sprang back up to his feet. He turned his pistol in his hand and used the butt to pommel Lenard's face. Lenard staggered for a moment from the blow, his nose crooked from a fracture that El Diablo had given him. Blood streamed down his lips and face, making his already haunting features more ghastly. Lenard didn't waste time. With a cry of crazed bloodlust, he became smoke once more and swirled around El Diablo's feet before reappearing behind him.

El Diablo was ready this time.

With accurate sharpness, El Diablo rammed his elbow behind him, landing the blow right into Lenard's sternum. A sickening crack rebounded off the rocks and the hillside accompanied with a piercing howl of pain. Lenard stumbled backward, clutching his chest. His soulless black eyes seethed with hatred as he screeched at El Diablo, "You can't protect that runt! What's the point?!" Lenard's gimp in his right leg seemed heavier now as he staggered back. His skeletal frame was shaking from the exertion as El Diablo took aim at the center of Lenard's chest, cocking the hammer back.

El Diablo fired. The bullet tore through Lenard's flesh, bone, and vest. The blood sprayed from the impact as he screeched in pain and dropped to the ground. The blood was draining to the dirt beneath him through his vesture and skeletal fingers—just as Jed's blood was draining from his face. He had never seen a man kill another man.

Jed stood shakily from his position, the battle was ending. El Diablo held his pose for a moment before he started to coolly walk towards the dying man. "You son of a bitch. He's gonna rip your insides out, Diablo." Lenard hissed as he strained to keep himself upright, his left hand clutching his severely bleeding wound. His eyes looked at El Diablo as he kept coming, his gear rustling with his movements.

He came closer to Lenard as the man finally collapsed to his side, kneeling on one knee. El Diablo was silent as the man wheezed, his body shaking from blood loss. He didn't have much time left. "I think you're done, old friend..." El Diablo spoke calmly as he watched his handiwork take its toll. A chill ran down Jed as the realization hit him: this was the real El Diablo. The bounty hunter. "Where is he, Lenard?" He spoke in a chilling tone.

Lenard chuckled weakly, a fresh flow of blood bubbling over his lips. His body was racked by a violent shiver, but, still, he spoke, "I don't know nothin'...you should know...I'm just a nobody to him." His body involuntarily convulsed as the smirk instantly faded. He hacked and coughed, sending splatters of phlegm and blood over El Diablo's boots but it didn't seem to concern him.

"You know no one would waste their time with one boy." El Diablo shifted his weight slightly as his tone dropped to a steely resolve, "Where is he, Lenard?"

Lenard's body allowed control again, and, with it, he spat in El Diablo's face. The bounty hunter looked down at his boots, a raging tension building. With sudden tenacity, El Diablo roughly grabbed Lenard by his coat collar and yanked him up. Lenard contorted his face in a silent scream of pain that only managed to escape as a squeak.

"I ain't got time for bullshit, Lenard! Where is he?!" Lenard's body convulsed again as his mouth moved to form words, but none came. Jed watched in shock as the man slowly slipped into the embrace of death. To Jed's surprise, El Diablo laid Lenard back down gently, staring at the corpse for a moment. The apparent moment of respect was broken as he began poking around the man's coat pockets for answers.

"H-hey wait," Jed nervously voiced, "That ain't right. Can't we just leave the dead be?"

"You want yer sister back, boy?" El Diablo answered without so much as a hitch in his search. Jed bit his tongue back and nodded solemnly. "Then don't question me."

After a long moment of searching, El Diablo slid something from one of the inside pockets. Jed drew a little closer, trying to get a better look at whatever El Diablo had found.

"Marks," El Diablo growled darkly as he tossed the obsidian coin onto Lenard's bloody chest. He stood and adjusted his hat to hide his eyes from the piercing sun. El Diablo seemed to know something.

"Marks?" Jed asked exasperatedly as the bounty hunter moved past the corpse toward the bulk of carnage. Jed watched El Diablo before kneeling next to Lenard's corpse and picking up the coin. It was black as pitch, an animalistic skull with three sunken eyes and a fanged maw carved into both sides of the coin. Jed stood, quickly putting the coin in his pocket; he'd look at it later to really study it. El Diablo was preoccupied with searching the contents of his duster jacket.

Jed asked, "Who are the Marks? Do they have Marietta? Did they kill my Pa?" The hunter remained silent, as he pulled out a well-worn coin.

His brow creased with growing frustration, knowing that El Diablo was brushing aside his anxious questions. El Diablo kneeled back down next to Lenard in ritualistic fashion, pushing the corpse to its back. "What are you--?" El Diablo placed the coin directly on Lenard's skeletal forehead. The sound of searing flesh and bubbling fluid came in a rush as Lenard's body began disfiguring into unnatural shapes. The skin around his face melted away quickly, followed by the rest of him, the oozing black mass of blood, skin, and tissue spreading over the dirt, like tar. The sight sent Jed's weak stomach into dysfunction.

After all the day's events, he turned away from the body, away from the smell, and unburdened his gut. Jed wretched heavily several times before his bowels were completely empty of its contents. He was shaking and nauseated as he heard the hunter move around the corpse and past Jed, speaking in his gruff tone, "You'll learn soon enough, boy."

Jed drew deep breaths into his chest, feeling the nausea begin to recede. The hunter whistled in a low, ear-aching tone—the sound reverberated against the hill.

Jed stood and watched, straining his ear to hear what he had whistled for. At first, he heard nothing but the various birds of carrion that had begun their cacophony of eating the flesh of the fallen. Then, he heard it. The sound of thundering hooves. El Diablo stood still, patient, as his steed blazed around the bend. El Diablo's horse ran toward them sliding to a stop in front of his still master. The large animal tossed his head with a wild snort, pawing the ground in its eager habit. El Diablo grabbed the reins, swinging himself in the saddle. The horse side-stepped anxiously as the hunter adjusted his weight—his cold gaze focused on the boy. Jed couldn't take it anymore.

"I have the right to know who you were talkin' about!" Jed corrected himself and motioned helplessly over the corpses behind them. Jed had seen and heard a lot the past few weeks—this mysterious person his Pa was talking about, then, the raid, and, now, El Diablo seemed to know who and what was going on. El Diablo eyed the boy for a moment, sighing. His steed snorted and shook its mane before resuming its habit of restlessly pawing at the ground. The hunter averted his gaze to the dirt below him and, then, back at the boy.

"Look...Jed was it?" El Diablo rested his wrists over the pommel of his saddle and leaned forward a little bit, watching the boy lazily.

"*Jedidiah...*" Jed answered irritably.

"Okay, *Jedidiah*," El Diablo snidely remarked with a frown, "You ain't ready for what's comin'." He straightened his posture in the saddle and heeled his horse forward, until he was right beside Jed. Jed licked his lips, feeling uncomfortable at the stranger's analytical gaze. "You can't handle it." The hunter's beast nickered impatiently, laying his ears back. Jed turned his eyes away from the hunter, pain searing his heart. He knew he wasn't ready. He was a coward; a rancher's boy with nowhere near the skills of this hunter.

Silent, Jed went back to his Pa's rifle, laying in the dirt. He scooped it up with the care and devotion one would a child, his eyes stinging with emotion. His hands gripped the stock in determination as he squeezed his eyes shut before walking back to El Diablo. It was time to put his fears, doubts, and anxiety to rest. He was a man now.

"Teach me, then." Jed said in a serious tone, eyes locked on El Diablo. El Diablo hocked and spat, again to his left side, and weighed Jed with his eyes.

"It's a shit life, *Jed*…you think you got the balls?" Jed felt the pricks of doubt begin, but quickly brushed them off. He had no choice—sack up or die. If he ever wanted to see his sister alive again, he had to discard the child and grow into a man.

Jed firmly nodded.

El Diablo grunted, "Fine," the hunter reined his stallion to left, "But you're gonna learn how to shoot, boy. Your aim is shit."

Jed swore he saw a grin carved on the man's rugged features, but couldn't know for sure. El Diablo reined his stallion around to face the direction they were originally heading. Even though Jed didn't entirely trust this man, there was one thing he *did* understand: he'd saved his life.

# Chapter 16

The morning ride had fared better on Jed than the previous day had. He could keep up, but he could feel the exhaustion crawling over his subconscious.

In the dead of night, Jed had woken up in a feverish sweat and pounding chest. That dream—rather, that nightmare—had been so real he'd choked back his own screams. El Diablo, Jed had discovered, had already been roused from Jed's tossing and murmurings. The thought of disturbing the hunter embarrassed him greatly. He swore to himself that he'd be braver—for Marietta. But it seemed that, even in dreams, Jed just wasn't brave enough to be a man.

"'Bout another mile will put us to town." The hunter announced. Jed discarded his self-critical thoughts for the moment, perking his head up with curiosity. He'd never been to a bigger town than Junction.

"What're we gonna do there?"

El Diablo said nothing for a moment before he grumbled, "Supplies, bounties, n' move on."

"That's it? What about those Marks?" He felt sister wasn't exceptionally high on the bounty hunter's list.

Again, El Diablo said nothing. Jed sighed and quit while he was ahead. He wasn't going to get any more answers out of this man. Jed was finally learning that the grizzled man wasn't one for talk. The rocky hills they had traversed for most of the trip had given way to the plains—a sight Jed was glad to see. At least they would be able to spot an ambush, if one ever came. The flatness of the plains was beginning to incline. El Diablo's strong steed climbed the gradual change with ease, while Jed's old nag worked to haul herself up the hill with a boy on her back.

The old mare grunted and continued at her gradual pace, tenderly placing each hoof over the clumps of desert sage brush. El Diablo's stallion crested the hill and nickered with impatience as the hunter reined him to a stop to wait for the lagging mare. The stallion snorted and pulled against his bit, pawing the ground. The mare sighed and came to a stop beside the dark stallion. Jed leaned forward, patting her neck affectionately, paying no mind to the mingling of horse sweat and dust on his bare hand.

Below them, the town sprawled across the low valley. A dusty haze hung over the town, indicating that it was alive with the prosperity Junction had lacked. The sight left Jed speechless for a time until his lips moved, "Is that the town?" Jed tore his enamored gaze from the large town to his black-clad teacher, who blew out his cigarette smoke with a sigh.

"Yep." With that, the hunter pressed his spurs into the sides of his stallion, which snorted and jolted forward. El Diablo held the reins in tight, keeping the spry animal in check. Jed gently nudged his old companion to follow the hunter. His stomach felt fluttery at the thought of heading into town. He didn't know what to expect.

The road leading into the town lay before them. Their descent toward it was a short one, and one that his mare greatly appreciated with a relieved sigh. A loaded carriage filled with household possessions rumbled past. The man and woman sitting atop it had sour looks on their faces. Jed couldn't help but stare at the two, wondering what had happened to them. The couple turned their soured faces to glare at the boy. Jed felt his face grow hot, and he averted his gaze. The people of this town were already showing their surly disposition.

El Diablo kept his gaze alert, glaring from beneath his brim and occasionally at passersby. People of all sorts and types passed by them. Jed saw families and men, women in dresses that were soiled and dusty from the hard life that they led. Jed couldn't help but take it all in, never having seen such a variety of people in one place before. The racket of the town buzzed in Jed's ears, and he gripped his old reins tighter. The masses of people seemed to look right through Jed, as though he weren't even there. The two came to the main street of the town.

The streets were bustling with stagecoaches rolling in. Jed reined his mare to a stop to take it all in. There were cowboys from the outer county lines coming in for a drink, lawmen and shady men arguing, women in lavish dresses of the most recent fashion gathered in groups for gossip, children playing in the dust with their hoops and dolls, a man was being tossed out of the saloon while shouting something unintelligible, and saloon girls rolling with laughter, hanging out of top floor windows.

"C'mon, Jed, we ain't got all day…" El Diablo grunted, not even looking Jed's direction. Jed frowned at the hunter's refusal to respectfully call him by his full name.

"I've told you not to call me that!" Jed grumbled in a very frustrated tone.

El Diablo ignored Jed's complaint and continued to ride further into the town. Jed followed with an irritated sigh as the crowds of people parted around them, like a rock in a riverbed. El Diablo dismounted and lazily hitched his steed to the post, not bothering to secure the knot. Jed dismounted and watched El Diablo.

"You ain't gonna tie him up? What if someone tries to take him?" For once, El Diablo let a grin spread against his rugged features.

"They'll get a hell of a surprise if they do." El Diablo firmly patted the stallion's neck and turned to the town, the grin gone from the public eye. Jed scratched his mare's forelock and walked over to the hunter.

"Here," El Diablo pulled out a crunched piece of paper and a wad of cash, shoving it into Jed's chest. The action brought Jed to a stop with an audible exhale. Jed took the paper in bewilderment and opened it up. He was wracked with nerves as he tried to read the illegible scrawl across the note. "Make yerself useful…"

Jed licked his lips nervously, glancing up at the hunter, "What's this?"

El Diablo frowned back at him, "Shoppin' list…general store's that way." He gave a lazy gesture of direction toward the rickety boardwalk that lined both sides of the street. "I got business to settle." Without a good bye, El Diablo melded easily into the fluctuating crowd. Jed didn't think El Diablo could blend in with his odd attire, but, before he could air his concerns, the hunter was gone, leaving Jed with the eerie stallion, the old mare, and the crinkled piece of paper. The mare occupied herself with invisible tufts of grass on the ground, while the coal black stallion watched people go by, ears pricked at attention. Jed sighed and stuffed the crushed paper in his pants pocket and headed towards the general store.

The creaky planks that formed the boardwalk ground with unsafe sounds as Jed and dozens of others treaded on them, but they seemed to hold up. Shop windows reflected the passing crowd as Jed peered into several businesses; he had never seen such variety. Where Junction barely had a general store, a tack and farrier shop, and a poor excuse for a post office, this town had more than the essentials. Some had herbs and plants drying in the window, another was flowing with gowns and dresses that, surely, would make Marietta envy the seamstresses, and there was a shop lined with a wide assortment of guns and ammunition. But he needed to focus on his task: El Diablo needed supplies, and Jed didn't think it wise to keep him waiting. With reluctance, he finally tore himself from the windows of guns and ammunition, and kept weaving through the throngs of people.

A notice caught his eye fluttering in the breeze. It was tacked to a wall, one corner ripped loose from the nail at the bottom right. Jed stopped and took a couple steps back until he was face to face with a rough piece of parchment with intricate words scrawled across the top. People huffed and avoided Jed in his halted state as he studied the notice. For a moment, he couldn't believe his eyes. The sketch resembled his travelling companion, El Diablo. Jed's brow pinched together slightly as his stomach began to knot up again.

A nearby shop bell tinkled, breaking Jed's concentration. He tore his eyes from the shady picture and saw a woman leaving with wrapped packages. *That must be it*, he thought. Jed strode toward the door, forgetting about the old parchment that held resemblance of his newfound tutor. As he approached the shop, he saw an elderly lady with a large stack of grocery parcels struggling to open the door. Jed opened the door for the elderly woman, and she stumbled through the door with a sour frown.

"Good afternoon, ma'am," Jed greeted her with a polite smile and a nod.

"Watch where yer goin', boy! I coulda run into you and dumped my week's food supply all over this here walkway!" Jed's polite smile was replaced with a look of shock.

"Er, I'm sorry, ma'am, I just thought—"

"Thought what? You could be of assistance by trippin' me? Go be of assistance to someone else!" With a huff, the woman ambled off, murmuring something about a damn fool. Jed was stunned for a moment, appalled at what she had said. He thought he was being polite by opening the door for a lady. She may have had the appearance of being a lady, but she was quite the opposite.

He shook it off and tentatively entered the shop. The bell on the door clanged when it closed, hollow like an old cow bell. Jed's senses were berated with dozens of different smells, most of which he didn't recognize. His eyes soaked in all the various jars, barrels, and shelves filled with various wares. He'd never seen so many things in one place before.

"Can I help you, young man?" The storekeeper called out, his voice slowed with an aged drawl of the deep south. Jed looked over at the man behind the counter who was leaning casually against the edge of the wood. He was an average height for a man, with a slightly protruding gut, accentuated by his stained apron and rolled-up sleeves of dark, striped cloth. His weathered hands looked like they had seen many years of hard work as they rested on the countertop. His dark, beady eyes scanned Jed from head to toe, sizing him for his worth as he twitched his bushy moustache back and forth. Jed felt uncomfortable under the older man's gaze, his hands trembling with anxiety. He didn't want to get any of the list wrong.

"Uh, yes, sir." Jed timidly approached the counter and fished in his pocket for list El Diablo gave him earlier, providing the wadded paper. He swore that it was even more crumpled than when the hunter gave it to him. A flustered feeling started to burn in his chest as he felt the store handler's beady eyes analyze him. Why did everyone seem to analyze him? It made Jed feel uncomfortable in every way. With a shaky hand, Jed handed the paper to the man, who took it from him as though it were contaminated. Jed folded his hands loosely in front of him, a habit his Pa had taught him long ago when waiting for something. The man lingered his scoffing gaze on Jed before glancing over the paper. With a belabored sigh, he looked up. "You got the money for all this, boy?"

"Yes sir." Jed quickly answered, hoping to leave the stagnant heat of the store as soon as possible. Jed could feel his ears flare hot. The shopkeeper gave him a doubtful look as Jed fished again for the wad of cash El Diablo had pushed into his hands. With relief, Jed pulled out the money and laid the bills on the worn, wooden countertop. The shopkeeper placed his clammy hand over the money, sliding it to himself and started to quickly count the bills.

Jed watched the shopkeeper count closely. The shopkeeper finished and looked at Jed, who was sweltering in the stagnant general store. "Make yerself comfortable. With all your requests, this may take a bit." The man gruffly answered, as if irritated at the prospect of work. Jed nodded curtly and stood as out of the way as he could.

***

Jed gently opened the general store door and re-entered the busy boardwalk. His arms were stiff from holding the packages just right in his arms so that they wouldn't tumble. He felt proud: he'd been useful to his adoptive teacher by getting what he needed. Jed couldn't help but feel good for once through this whole ordeal

As he weaved through the busy main street back to the horses, he saw El Diablo re-cinching his saddle and adjusting some of the black leather straps that held it together. The stallion stared absentmindedly at the passersby on the boardwalk in front of him, and the mare was half-asleep at the post, leaning slightly more on her right side. Without looking up from his work, El Diablo's gruff voice sounded over the grumble of the crowd, "You get it all, boy?"

Jed stopped a few feet away, proudly displaying his packages in his thin arms, "Yep!" He said confidently. He knew El Diablo would be pleased with his ability to do things on his own. El Diablo peered up at Jed before standing, wiping his hoof pick on his leather pants. His horse snorted and sniffed the dirt as El Diablo stood up straight. A sour frown sprawled across the man's rugged features. Jed's victorious grin melted away.

El Diablo shoved the hoof pick back into the saddle bag and strode up to the boy. Jed shifted uncomfortably and let the hunter take the packages of supplies. The hunter kneeled with surprising grace and nimbleness, unwrapping the packages. El Diablo paused as he stared at the goods and started turning things over, as though in search of something. Jed could feel the hunter's agitation rise through the hot afternoon air. El Diablo slammed a block of dried meat onto the paper and stood up, startling Jed. Jed took a couple steps back from the hunter, feeling his eyes burn into his flesh.

He'd done something wrong, but didn't understand what it could possibly have been.

"That ain't all of it! Where the hell are the rest of my supplies?!" The hunter exploded. "An' where the hell is my change?!" Jed flinched at the hunter's reaction. He'd never heard or seen El Diablo so angry before. He almost expected the hunter to shoot him for doing him wrong. El Diablo seethed, "What the hell is wrong with you, boy?! Can't you read?!"

Jed let an awkward silence fill between them before opening his mouth, "N-no sir…I can't…" Jed averted his gaze down to the dust, feeling a tinge of shame creep in on him.

The hunter's animosity disbanded, and he, too, averted his gaze to the dirt, setting his hands on his hips. His hat hid the tinge of guilt as he bit the inside of his lower left lip. After a moment, the hunter looked back up at the boy and strode past him, pulling his hat lower over his eyes. "Grab 'em." He growled in a low tone. Jed snapped his gaze back up, bewildered. He thought for sure, the hunter would have just left him here in this God-awful town.

"What?" Jed asked, in wonder.

"Grab the damn packages…" El Diablo growled again.

Without question, Jed stooped to the unwrapped packages and hastily tied them together, picking them back up. As Jed hurried to stand back up, the hunter was already entering the busy street and heading straight to the general store. "I-I have the receipt, Mr. El Diablo, sir." Jed added as he caught up to the man's long strides.

With a set jaw, El Diablo pulled his ebony pistol from its holster without so much as a care to what the locals might have thought. "I don't need a damn receipt," he hissed, venomously. Jed held his ongue as he scrambled after the hunter. People moved out of destruction's way, casting a few wary glances at the pair. The hunter's gear rustled and clanged with seething fervor as he strode along the boardwalk and right up to the general store. Jed pushed his nervous feelings out of his chest as he watched the hunter rip the door open, making it slam into the store front and cracking a window, startling some ladies in fine dresses. The bell tinkled sadly, clanging as Jed stared in astonishment, mouth agape.

Still silent, El Diablo strode into the shop and raised his gun to meet a quivering shopkeeper. The man raised his hands up a little bit and stammered, "Sir, there's n-no need for such action now." Jed cautiously followed the hunter and watched the sweating man's eyes grow as wide as the full moon. El Diablo kept his burning gaze on him as he stormed right up to him. The man seemed to think he could sink behind the sanctity of his counter and avoid the hunter's wrath. He was sorely mistaken.

With a growl, El Diablo reached over that counter and gruffly hoisted the man up by his shirt collar. Jed watched from a way back at the sheer strength of the hunter as other patrons of the store quickly scattered to the outside. He had the man held up at least two feet from the ground. The hunter cocked the hammer back and shoved the mouth of the barrel under the shop keep's chin. If the man wasn't sweating from the heat of the day, he was, surely, sweating from the hunter's terrible temper.

"W-what'd you want?!" The man managed to speak out.

"I want a refund." El Diablo said with a deadly cool hiss. The hunter's answer stunned Jed. This man was much more convoluted than he thought.

The shopkeeper looked puzzled, but the fear never left his visage, "I-I'm sorry sir, I don't know what you mean—"

El Diablo shook the man a little and really pressed the cold steel against the man's sweaty neck with an unearthly snarl, "You know damn well what I mean…You enjoy takin' money from boys who can't even read?" El Diablo nodded to Jed as he spoke, the shopkeeper's eyes darting quickly between the enraged hunter and the young man.

The shop keep's eyes widened as the reality dawned on him. He had wronged the wrong man and, as far as Jed could figure, the shop owner was just starting to understand his dire mistake. His cheeks flushed cherry red from the heat and the overwhelming aggressiveness of El Diablo. Jed stood to the side, quiet and watching the exchange with a strange interest. He never thought the hunter would retaliate on his behalf.

"I-I assure you, sir, this was all a mistake—"

El Diablo bared his teeth at the shop keep as his voice became as frigid as ice, "Refund. Now." Those two words hissed as the shop keep was unceremoniously dropped back to his feet.

In a flurry of huffed breaths and shaking hands, the shop keep opened the rusty till and started counting out bills. The hunter never took his steely gaze from the shop keep, his gun unmoving— as still as a predator locked on his prey. Jed watched, mesmerized at the overwhelming power El Diablo seemed to have over this situation. Once the shop keep finished counting back the correct amount, El Diablo narrowed his eyes further. Jed could feel the searing gaze, and he wasn't even in the line of sight.

"That ain't all of it..." His voice burned with contempt as the man let out an audible squeak of fear and started frantically emptying out all the money onto the counter with frantic clattering of change.

"Here, take it! Take all of it! I-I don't want any more trouble!" The shop keep's voice trembled as his beady eyes darted from the hunter's eyes to the black hole of the deadly weapon.

"That's just part of my refund..." The hunter kept his gaze trained on the sweating shop keep. "Jed."

Hearing his name, Jed jolted forward to the hunter's side, secretly reveling in the sweaty man's defeat. *He deserves every moment of this*...Jed thought bitterly. *Didn't realize he had swindled me...I gotta learn how to read.* His eyes rested on the man for a moment, before looking at the hunter. He could feel the anticipation and gut-wrenching anxiety begin to build in him as El Diablo spoke again, "Get us three bags o' oats, two pounds o' dried beans, plenty o' canteens, couple bags of coffee..." The hunter looked at him under his hat and nodded towards the stocked back wall before adding with casualty, "Oh, don' forget the whiskey, cigarettes, chew," A malicious grin shadowed his lips as he turned his eyes back to the beady man, "An' get yerself some o' that rock candy."

Jed nodded and hurriedly scurried to it. He began gently opening bags and shoveling the contents requested into their own containers. He struggled to hurry, trying to make out where everything was. He opened barrel tops, bags, and tin jars, looking for everything El Diablo had asked for. Once he was sure he had gotten everything, Jed warily looked at the quivering man as he approached the hunter.

"I, uh, think I got everything, El Diablo." The shop keep stiffened at the name. The hunter just grunted his approval, without glancing at it. *He has that much faith in me? Lord help me.*

Without a single word, El Diablo re-holstered his pistol and nodded toward the door. Jed quickly took his gesture and walked out the door to the boardwalk with the supplies. El Diablo hocked and spat on the counter before locking eyes on the petrified shop keep. The sweaty man looked at the black glob of chew that was beginning to stain the old wood.

El Diablo stared the man down for a moment before grabbing a store pamphlet and tipping his hat. "Have a nice day now…" A wolfish grin spread on his lips. The jangling of gear left the store and its keeper alone in stunned silence.

***

Jed followed El Diablo back to the horses, carrying half of the supplies, while the hunter carried the other half. Jed's mare perked her ears in his direction and lifted her head slowly. The stallion nickered softly and shifted anxiously. El Diablo stopped at his saddle and began packing the supplies into the black leather saddlebags. El Diablo sighed, readjusting some of his supplies as he looked over the saddle at the boy.

*Can't even read…* He sighed and watched the boy.

Jed patted his mare's neck and began packing the supplies he had, taking care not to overweight the old thing. El Diablo looked back at the supplies and rapidly tied the bags shut. He gripped the worn pommel and hoisted himself into the saddle. His stallion grunted and adjusted under the hunter's weight. El Diablo nudged his horse with the tips of his spurs to the main street.

Jed sprung up into his saddle, gently taking up the reins and following him to the main stream of the town. El Diablo adjusted his weight again as the stallion shifted to a light trot. *That will have ta change...*

\*\*\*

The previous day had been eventful—too eventful—for El Diablo's taste. The peace and quiet of the new day was welcomed. The afternoon became stagnate on the rugged terrain, but it didn't bother the hunter any. Silence had been more and more frequent between himself and the boy as they rode on, seeking more leads to help him complete his pact with the Marshall. The more he thought about it, the more burdened he felt by it. Abe sighed and rolled his shoulders. The sun's warmth felt good on his aching body.

He heard the boy barely speaking above the sound of creaking leather, horse breath, and plodding hooves. "Can't hear ya, Jed." he called out behind him, turning his head to the side, so his voice could project to the boy clearly. He made sure the sun didn't touch his eyes—it ruined his keen vision and made his head ache from the disorienting view. He had been sensitive to the sun's rays ever since he had been left in this godforsaken plane. The boy was a way behind him, but he knew he had heard him. His nag's nose was as low to the ground as the reins would physically let her. *She won't last long...* El Diablo watched the boy as he tore his eyes from the crinkled pamphlet and at the hunter. The hunter could see sweat pour off his skin. *And he won't either.*

"Oh, uh, sorry, sir." Jed answered back as he hastily wiped his forehead free from sheening sweat. "I was just tryin' to pronounce this first word." The boy fumbled with the pamphlet and juggled the reins as he tried to straighten it out on the neck of his nag. She snorted in discontent as she lifted her head slightly.

"What's the first line?" The hunter grunted and looked ahead again as he casually dug through his duster. He found a cigarette and lit the tip with his usual trick, puffing on the end till tendrils of smoke wafted up and behind him. The desert spanned miles wide, with no sign of shelter. Heat simmered in the distance, creating a watery appearance among the rocks and scarce, dead vegetation. Neither he nor his beast, Dusk, were bothered by the deep heat of the season, but it would surely kill this boy.

He waited patiently as he heard the boy rustle the pages, turning them slightly in different directions as he tried to decipher the letters. Abe could almost see the knitted brow wrought with confusion as the boy pieced together the letters silently.

"We-welcome to, uh....th—e..." The boy read slowly and with uncertainty. El Diablo could feel his patience wear thin. Dusk sighed, almost airing his irritation on behalf of El Diablo. *He's learnin'...just...ignore it fer now.* He let the kid's droning slowness fade into the background as he focused on other matters ahead of them.

El Diablo frowned in thought as the heat warmed his bones. The whole situation was unsettling to him, and the same question remained in the forefront of his thoughts: why had Eberhart taken the girl? She was different enough to pique El Diablo's interest, and it had obviously done the same for him. None of the past events had made any sense so far, making it difficult to fulfill the blood pact he made with the dead Marshall. He shifted uncomfortably in his saddle, his mind drifting through the past decade of events to try and pin down a possible lead. Nothing came to mind after all the dealings he had had with Eberhart. Things had gone sour swiftly after the convenient death of the eldest brother, Dwayne. Eberhart had eagerly taken up the mantle of the leadership for the Marks gang, unleashing hell on earth to advance his own greedy gain. One that he did not want to revisit.

The memory sent a twinge of guilty pain through his chest as the memories he had so desperately tried to lock away forever clawed back to the surface. Eberhart had made him a bargain he couldn't resist, and, in doing so, he had damned himself and those he held dear. He scowled under his hat and forced the memories to go back down into the void of his subconscious. Perhaps Eberhart was simply seeking revenge on the family that had killed his twin brother. El Diablo glanced back at the boy, who was trying to read a particularly harder line in the pamphlet. *He looks just like the Marshall...what are you playin' at, McKay?*

Jed stopped in mid-sentence, lifting his gaze up to the hunter. El Diablo turned his attention back to the desert ahead. "El Diablo?" The boy's voice carried to him through the arid air. The sun was at its strongest now. He could feel it.

"Yeah?" his voice was gruff in his own ears. He didn't care in the slightest.

"These Marks fellows...how do they know you?" The boy timidly asked.

*As he should be*, El Diablo snapped in his mind.

"That was a long time ago boy...let it rest with the dead." He was harsher than he should have been, but he had hoped it would silence the boy for the rest of the afternoon. To his dismay, it didn't deter him.

"That's all fine, Mr. El Diablo...but my sister...she's still out there, right? Do you have any idea where she might be?" El Diablo sighed, rolling his shoulders and stretching his neck. It infuriated the hunter that the boy had begun to grow on him. *Like an unwanted fungus.* He was young, none too bright, and was completely naïve about the world. *Like me, when I was found here. Damn you, David...you were always right.* He knew Jed was a complete lost hope on all accounts, and, yet, he felt a drawing need to reverse the damage that he had caused this boy. He couldn't let Eberhart continue. It was time to end it. Jed could be trained to aid him in the long, arduous task ahead of them.

"I don't know, Jed." He reluctantly answered. El Diablo knew it was a lie. There was one person, a she-devil, who would know exactly where to start. Silence sprawled between them, and he could feel the boy's eyes on his back, waiting for a reply of some sort. He sighed, pulling another cigarette from his duster before answering, "But I think I know who would."

He picked up the reins again in his hands. Dusk woke from his walking slumber, pricking his ears back in attention. El Diablo spurred his horse into a fast trot. He could hear Jed follow suit. *She's nearby, and, if I'm lucky enough, I might get a lead or two.*

## Chapter 17

"El Diablo, shouldn't we check the sheriff's office?" Jed asked in a hushed voice, which nearly drowned from the start of the night life.

"Be my guest, kid." El Diablo grumbled. The man kept riding through the darkening street, towards the heart of the town. Jed kept up with El Diablo as they neared the riotous saloon. Jed should have guessed that this was the hunter's "important" business. El Diablo stopped and dismounted his horse at the over loaded hitch post. Jed squeezed his tired old friend into a slot. Jed swung his scrawny leg over the saddle and plopped to the dirt ground below, brushing his hands on his shirt, ridding them of the day's sweat. The hunter patted his steed's jaw and stepped up onto the uneven boardwalk, fishing for something in his duster pocket. Jed stepped up next to the hunter and started to take in his surroundings. His eyes roamed over the dilapidated building. *I hope we find whatever we came here for.*

His curious gaze glanced over the outside walls of the saloon, where no lantern light touched, and saw slumped dark figures were out cold, or singing incoherently. Jed wrinkled his nose at the sight: some of the saloon girls were cooing for a night's work, others were rambunctiously staggering out of the swinging doors, and the smoke from the saloon parlor drifted through the air, like a morning fog in spring. Jed shifted a little closer to the hunter feeling out of place—again.

"Here." El Diablo grunted, shoveling rolled green bills discreetly into Jed's hands. Jed stared down at the money and looked back at the vigilante in more confusion: where in the world did this man keep getting this much cash? It didn't make sense.

"Now, keep quiet and keep out of—"

"Trouble?" A sultry voice drifted on the air directly toward them.

El Diablo audibly sighed, as though unprepared for a sudden disruption. Jed looked toward the source of the sultry voice, only to feel his flushed ears and cheeks burn. He had never seen a more beautiful and strange-looking woman in his entire life. She was an average height, with porcelain skin and a perfectly shaped body that her silken dress seemed to barely withhold. Her face was beautifully shaped with slightly high cheekbones and startling ice blue eyes that held the authority of never missing a detail. Her hair is what stunned him most; cloud white hair framed her gorgeous features and cascaded over her shoulders. Her eyes locked on his, paralyzing him for a moment. She brushed her way past the saloon doors, making her way to both men. Her boots clacked loudly with her subtle swagger until she stopped a couple feet away from the hunter.

Jed swallowed nervously as her plump, rose-red lips perked into a sly grin, her eyes changing from him to El Diablo. *She...she can't be normal...can she?* Jed turned his gaze from the exotic-looking woman back to El Diablo, who had managed to, at least, half-turn in interest toward her direction. "I think you found it already, honey." She cooed to the hunter.

"It's good to see you, Jys." The hunter responded in his gruff voice.

"It's good to see you, too, darlin', but..." she leaned in, smelling his duster collar, and wrinkled her nose in a playful manner, "You haven't bathed since we last met, have you?" El Diablo stiffened, as if resisting something deep inside of him as he growled at her—something Jed was not prepared for. All he could do was watch the exchange.

"What do you want, woman?" El Diablo snapped. She had pushed his patience.

An amused giggle aired as the white-haired vixen casually walked around the hunter, her boots clacking again, her blue eyes hungrily gazing at him, "That's not how you greet your erotic lover, Abe." She dramatically placed a hand over her bosom, stopping back in front of him. "I'm hurt."

"I don't have time for your bullshit, Jystana…" He growled at her, but his growl betrayed what his eyes spoke of. A lustful hunger was there, just beneath the surface. Jed began to feel uncomfortable as he watched the sexual tension grow between the two of them.

"Oh, I know, Abe." She frowned, the tension dissipating before it rose to its peak. Jys huffed, dropping her hand heavily to her side, resting the other on her hip. Though the tension was gone for now, her eyes hid the same hunger that dwelled in El Diablo's. "You never have time for me." Jed moved his eyes from the beautifully dangerous woman, to the stern and unwavering hunter.

El Diablo stared at her hard from under his hat, contemplating his next words. "Jystana, this isn't the time. We can discuss this later." He turned from her with finality.

She sighed and looked at her nails casually, "That's fine, Absalom. 'Course, it would be awful foolish of ya to just leave without hearing what I have heard over the recent weeks…" El Diablo stopped in his steps, craning his head back in her direction.

"You have my *undivided* attention." He spoke smoothly. Her lips plumped with a smile as she let her hand drop to her side again.

"Good." Jystana turned, motioning for him to follow her. Her silken dress brushed along the boardwalk, not muffling the clacking of her polished shoes as she entered the saloon's winged doors with a flourish. Smoke from the main parlor tumbled out to the night. Her movements left Jed speechless. El Diablo grunted and walked to the doors after her, Jed following him close behind.

"So…your name is Absalom?" Jed cautiously inquired as he followed on the hunter's heels.

El Diablo snapped his head to his direction, scowling at the boy. "Keep it to yerself," he growled.

Jed kept himself from flinching as he smiled inwardly. *Well, then, if you wanna call me Jed, I'm gonna call you Abe."*

The bar was loud with riotous clientele. Every game table was crowded with men hoping for a share of the house pot. The untuned piano sang in the darker corner of the parlor room, and the prostitutes leaned over the upper balcony railings, exposing their breasts to any who looked up. Jed averted his gaze from them as they called to him in groaning voices.

Jed ignored their calls as he tried to follow the hunter through the saloon. The hunter and the mysterious woman wove through effortlessly, as though the people were not even there. Jed tried to keep up with them as best he could, but he just wasn't able to push these men aside. They became harder to see, until they completely disappeared into the saloon.

Jed stopped and tried to look over the sea of hats and raised glasses, but they were nowhere in sight. His gut was knotted with fear as he turned around, hoping he would catch a glimpse of El Diablo's hat and duster or Jystana's cloud white hair. Jed's heart sank with anxiety as he ran his fingers through his tussled brown hair. *Shit…*

"Hey! Kid!" A voice shouted at him. Jed quickly turned and saw a table with four men sitting around it. An older man was shuffling cards expertly in his hands as he watched Jed from under the brim of his worn miner's hat. His sweaty face was round from the fat that clung to his bones and it made the rest of his body look round, too. His clothes were dirty and looked like they hadn't been washed in weeks, possibly months. The grungy men stared at Jed. "You look like you need to play around." The miner leered. Jed swallowed.

Jed warily came closer to the man, clearing his throat as he rested his hands on the back of the thin, wooden chair, "What are ya playin'?" He asked timidly.

The overweight miner shuffled the cards and began dealing out to everyone at the table, as well as to the seat Jed had yet to take. "Poker, kid...you play it?" Jed shook his head nervously and took his seat at the table. The man dealt the last card and took up his own with a smirk. "It's simple."

\*\*\*

Jystana led them through the staggering crowd and to a corner table, where she took her seat in a chair facing away from the bar. She placed her high-heeled boots on the table edge, her dress falling just enough to expose her upper thighs and over-the-knee laced boots. Her lips still held that smug, knowing smile as she offered El Diablo his seat.

El Diablo—or Abe, as Jystana had called him—glared at her. He thrust his seat to the side and slouched into it, folding his hands together to rest on the worn tabletop. Her scent was strong to his nostrils. Even now, it was almost unbearable to resist. He pretended not to stare up her bare legs in hunger. *Damn this woman. I haven't seen her in months. She knows my weakness too well.* Abe thought bitterly.

"It's so good to see you, Abe." Jystana spoke to him seductively, twirling her finger through her curls. Her eyes held the same hunger he knew was in his. His groin burned for her, to smell her, to hold her, to be with this woman forever. He could feel that same tension rising inside of him, and a whisper in the back of mind murmuring with impatience. Oh, how he wanted her, but there was something more important at hand. Abe adjusted in his seat slightly, glancing around the parlor room. He never had liked crowded spaces.

"So, what do ya know, Jys?" Abe grumbled, turning his eyes back to his lover. Jystana smiled, sweeping her feet off the table and placing her elbows in their stead. His eyes could hardly keep from glancing at her exquisite breasts and exposed neck, knowing that she was teasing him. She grinned and traced a finger on a worn ring-spot on the old table they sat at.

"I know a lot of things, Abe," she chuckled. Her eyes danced with wicked lust as she stood from her seat, her hand trailing along the tabletop. Abe felt his inner self stir with want as he watched her approach him in her devilish manner. *Ah, hell...* Her scent almost overtook his sanity as she got closer, "But, you know there's a price..."

"Damn it, Jys..." He growled, powerless as she nonchalantly slipped into his lap and laying a finger gently over his lips to silence any further excuses. He knew that she could feel his burning passion radiating from his body, could smell his rising need to have her, there and now. *Fuck, I lose it every time.* He couldn't resist her as he felt her delicate frame rest on his lap and he couldn't help but feel her sides, taking a deep breath smelling her exotic oils and perfume. He could feel the growing hunger deep within. Their eyes were locked for what seemed like decades, until she leaned down and pressed her lush lips to his rough ones.

A low growl resonated in his throat as he pulled her closer to his torso, his arms and hands wrapping around her. God how he wanted to have her, to make her his once again, like old times, when matters weren't as grave. Her passion easily matched his as the kiss intensified, like the wildfires of the great plains. His inner passion roared to be released, to have the freedom to ravage her just as much as he knew her inner self screamed for the same.

He snarled and reluctantly broke their passion before it became out of hand. The grin dropped from Jys's lips as she ran her hands over his dusty shoulders, her eyes begging to be alone with him. Abe grunted and let his fingers play with a stray pullstring that helped keep her bodice together, knowing that he didn't have the time to delay. "I don't have time for play, Jys. This is more serious than you think."

A frown creased her brow. "You don't think I understand that?" She tucked her hair behind her ear and looked at him with a cocked head. Her ice blue eyes always fascinated him. He hardly ever saw eyes of that nature. He leaned forward and spoke in a low tone, "What do you know, Jys?" He needed answers, and he needed them now.

She sighed and glanced over the parlor room, ignoring some of the attention they were receiving from onlookers. "Eberhart..." She turned her head towards Abe again, as he shifted his weight. "That's who you're after, ain't it?" Her voice was a hair above a whisper, for only his ears to hear. He understood why; Eberhart was a dangerous bastard. Ever since his...incident with Eberhart, he had been keeping eyes and ears out for him everywhere he went. Another reason he didn't like crowded spaces. Unlike Jys, he couldn't hide well in plain sight.

Abe curtly nodded and let his hands continue to run over her sides, her back, and her thighs, forcing his desire for her deep into his core. He glanced through the crowd, seeing where the boy had gotten off to. He saw Jed playing cards at the far end. *Good. Maybe he can put his 'rithmatic to use...*

"Abe." Her voice snapped his attention back to her. "It's too dangerous. We talked about this—"

"Yes, I know." He allowed himself a small indulgence, kissing the nape of her soft neck. *I need a drink...*

"Why? *Why* do you have to?" She inquired urgently, gently holding his jaw with her hands to look at her.

"I made a deal..." He let the words sink in. They felt heavy, even now.

Jystana in took a sharp breath and narrowed her eyes slightly. She, too, looked to where he had, seeing the boy. She nodded to him, "The kid?"

He reached up and gripped her hand with his gloved hand. He scoffed, "Hell no…not with him." She looked at him puzzled.

"Who?"

Abe frowned bitterly, "His Pa…Marshall McKay."

Jys's eyes widened, "Who?!" She hissed furiously. "You have some explainin'—!"

He cut her off quickly. A saloon girl stopped at their table; a half-starved, bruised brunette girl, of no more than seventeen, by Abe's guess. Abe glared at the girl as she slurred, "Y'all wanna drink?"

"Bottle of whiskey. Make it quick." She rushed to the bar. Jystana looked at him, longing in her eyes. He knew the feeling was still strong, but there was nothing he could do at the moment. The girl returned with a half bottle of whiskey and two glasses, setting them in the center.

"I asked for a bottle of whiskey—not a half. What kind of shit is this?"

"Sorry, sir. It's all the barkeep had fer me." She shrugged carelessly and worked her way to the next table. Abe grumbled, shifting Jys's weight to reach the bottle and two glasses. He sloshed a full glass for himself and did the same for Jys, handing it to her. With a sigh, he downed it and refilled the glass. After a few shots, he refilled it and fingered the rim lightly. Jys hadn't touched hers.

Jys watched him expectantly, waiting for him to continue. He sighed tiredly and avoided her gaze. "Absalom, you're a son of a bitch." She sighed and knocked her glass down, letting the liquid slide down her throat. "It's gonna stay that way." Abe growled back. He knew that she wanted to know what had happened. He just didn't want to tell her. Or, at least, as little as possible. He knocked back his glass, enjoying the smooth burn in his throat. He refilled hers, then his.

He grunted and stared hard at the remnant amber liquid in his shot glass before reluctantly talking, "The ranch was destroyed when I got there. Everything was burnin'." Abe drank down the last of his glass, as mindless as his smoking habit. It wouldn't kill him after all, and it would take more than this to make him drown out the last couple weeks.

"I smelled blood. Thick n' free-flowin'...I couldn't help myself." Abe forced himself to gaze at her again. "Headed in the barn. It was half collapsed and roarin' with flames." He hated to talk this much. It always felt foreign to him. He let a loud wave of noise surge through the saloon before he spoke again.

"Went inside..." He leaned closer to smell her skin again, his voice lowered. He didn't want any possible eavesdroppers to hear him. Absalom knew she could hear him. "The Marshall was impaled to the ground so deep..." Abe indicated to his chest, pausing for a moment. "He wasn't gonna make it. And the blood, Jys..." He closed his eyes and smelled the air, taking in the stench of sweaty men and rutty whores as he relived the erotic smell of blood. Abe pulled back to consciousness, a hiss drawing through his lips and teeth. He let his words end where they lay, not needing to go on. She knew what had happened next. Every one of their kind knew what the blood did.

She leaned back in her chair, the words sinking into her. Her arms draped over his shoulders, her fingers tracing small circles on his leather duster. Though it was faint, he could feel her touch. Abe downed his whiskey again, his deep burning lust building rapidly again with all this talk of blood. With a grunt, he withdrew his face from her skin and forced himself to steady his gaze, only on her eyes.

"So...the great *El Diablo* made a deal...with a human?" She narrowed her eyes, the tinge of dumfounded disbelief written on her features. He couldn't quite believe it, himself. "And not only a human, but the same one who nearly killed you twenty years ago?"

He knew it was coming.

"Have you completely lost your mind?!" She hissed furiously. "How many times you gonna do this, Abe?!"

Abe grabbed her hand and held it tightly. She liked to test his temper, but he held it in. He was angry with himself for doing what he had done. Something about it, though, drew him right to it. He was convinced it was the smell of the blood.

"I don't know, love. All I know is the Marks have a strange interest in the boy's sister." He squeezed her hand and let go; they were drawing attention.

"That don't make any sense, Abe. What does his sister have to do with anythin'?" Jystana leaned back slightly to refill her glass. She seemed quite content to continue sitting in the hunter's lap. "I knew he had a festering grudge against the Marshall, but that was years ago." She briefly whiffed the amber liquid before downing it slowly.

Abe shook his head. He couldn't help but feel a slight burden of knowing that it was him that brought the Marks to the McKays' doorstep. *Both of us were running from something we can't ever outrun.*

"Do you know anythin', Jys? Where he is?" Abe grumbled, eager to change the subject quickly and to move on to more pressing business. Talking about himself always wore him out.

She sighed and finished her glass, setting it upside-down on the table. "I know they ain't here, that much is for sure. They cleared out from the northern parts, as well. Sold their claim out in Deadwood to a man named Mert."

Abe grimaced at the name. He'd met the man before. Mert would slit his own kin's throat, if it would get him ahead of the game—and forget about it shortly after.

"I also hear they're more on the western side now. Less government restrictions and all that." Her voice was both soothing and arousing. "Other than that, Abe, I haven't the faintest clue. You know how he is." Abe picked up the whiskey bottle and frowned at it. It was empty of all whiskey, save a skim at the bottom. With an irritated grunt, he set the bottle down.

A roar of rage erupted from the card area, keeping Abe from asking another question, "You're a fuckin' cheater!!" Abe turned in his seat, his shoulders tensing with irritability. He tugged his hat low over his eyes, gently moving Jystana from his lap. He pushed the chair back as he stood tall. A crowd was gathering around the commotion.

*Well, shit…*

\*\*\*

The grizzled miner towered over Jed, his veins bulging in his thick neck and sweat-soaked forehead. Jed looked up at him, speechless and frozen to his seat. The table felt hostile as Jed nervously swallowed and loosened his tongue, "I-I swear I didn't' mean ta win that much, sir!"

The miner growled and lunged at Jed, grabbing his shirt collar. The man's breath stank like rotting alcohol and dirt, making Jed cough subtly. *Oh, God, he's gonna kill me!* He raised his hands in surrender, his heart thrashing against his ribcage.

"You're a Goddamned lyin' cheat!!" The man's voice boomed over the hushed crowd that was gathering. Spittle splattered on Jed's face, making him cringe—a mistake Jed quickly regretted. The miner roared, slamming Jed across the table, winding him and scattering stars across his vision. Chips and cards flew out from under him—shocked gasps and encouraging shouts sounded from the audience. Ringing filled his ears as he strained to focus his eyes, just in time to see the man raise a clenched fist. Jed panicked, bracing himself for a heavy blow, moving his hands to try and shield his face.

"It's my play." The cool, steely voice washed over them. Jed felt the overwhelming sense of relief. El Diablo had spoken.

The man turned his angered gaze to the hunter, "After this fuckin' kid gets his lesson, I'll play ya…" The man's voice trailed off as his forehead met with a cold barrel of a gun.

El Diablo spoke again, more strongly, "No. We play now." With finality, El Diablo sat in a vacant chair, the empty place had been vacant for most of the games. The miner let Jed go with a shove. Jed scrambled off the table and began to retreat toward the crowd, but El Diablo glanced at him and motioned for him to sit back down.

*He has to be jokin'.* Jed looked at him warily; he frowned at Jed. The hunter won. With an internal groan of hesitation, Jed slipped back into his chair. The miner glared at him as he sat back in his chair, the wood creaking from the weight and started shuffling the cards again. Jed averted his gaze to the table.

Cards slid into his view. The sound of cards being dealt was the only sound above the ambience of the silent saloon. He could feel the eyes from the other player at the table opposite to him. A lanky man with red-rimmed eyes—a life that had been wasting away from liquor, whores, and gambling. Jed picked up his hand of cards and looked at them. He recognized the faces and shapes of the colored numbers at the corners. He carefully glanced at El Diablo, who was eyeing his cards diligently, his hat brim covering his eyes and most of his grizzled facial expression. Jed remembered the white-haired woman, Jystana, was behind him. Her hands were lightly resting on his dusty shoulders. She pretended to be interested in the game at hand. The hunter seemed to be immune to the beauty's subtle charms as he discarded one from his hand, drawing a new one, letting the game commence.

Jed glanced back at his hand, adjusting them to where he could identify what he had. The endless possibilities streamed through his mind as he licked his lips. He didn't want to win again—he feared for his life. Jed discarded two and drew two. The lanky man sighed and drew one card, fingering the edges of the ivory paper. The miner grunted, frowning as he glared over his hand. Jed peeked at him from behind his cards. The silence surrounding them burned in Jed's ears as he felt his back sweat profusely. It sure was hot in this room.

"I'll raise a dollar," the miner said gruffly, tossing a bill to the empty middle. His eyes flitted to Jed, then, to the hunter.

El Diablo tossed in two more dollars. "Raise two." Jystana rubbed the top of his shoulders slowly as she watched over his hand, suddenly more interested than when it had begun.

The lanky man grunted and threw a fifty-cent piece into the middle, the metal clanking with its other brothers and sisters. "Fifty cents." His voice was raspy, hoarse from many years of smoking.

Jed cleared his throat and pulled out a two-dollar bill the miner had placed in earlier games, as well as a fifty-cent piece. Jed would have to thank the hunter later for making him learn his numbers and letters. "Raise two dollars and…fifty cents." Jed spoke his amount clearly—but slowly—making sure he was accurate in his counting.

The round started over. The pot was growing as the bets piled one over the other. Jed swallowed hard. He recognized his cards as he double-checked himself. A red letter "A" emblazoned the dirty ivory surface of the card with shapes of hearts on its edges. The next card had a red letter "K". Jed pondered over it, as the King's printed eyes seemed to watch his every move. Jed looked at his third card. It was red, as well. His heart skipped a beat as his mind slowly pondered the possibilities. The red queen was sitting quite still on her card, the heart-centered scepter she held was blatantly obvious. He had played enough rounds to know what his hand would have for him.

*Don't give it away*, he thought, taking a slow intake of breath and calming his excited nerves. *Remain calm.* He glanced at El Diablo—or Abe, as the woman had called him earlier—was slouched in his chair, as though entirely uninterested in the game.

And, yet, he was taking sweet time. It was his turn. The miner raised another half-dollar. Abe tossed a card on the discard pile and drew a fresh one. The lanky man shifted anxiously in his chair, attempting to taste the last of the whiskey that skimmed the bottom of his glass. The woman rubbing his dusty shoulders smiled crookedly and whispered something in his ear.

Jed thought he saw a shadow resembling a grin on the hunter's mouth. "It's your turn, *boy*," the miner sharply snapped.

Abe turned his shaded gaze to the miner, "I suggest you let the boy make his mistakes in his own damn time." The miner huffed, adjusting himself in the seat. The wood creaked under his weight. Abe turned his attention back to his own hand. Jed cleared his throat quietly and focused on his cards.

They were all hearts. Ace, King, Queen, Jack, and a six. He knew he would risk everything if he tossed the six. But what if he got the ten of hearts?

He could feel the crowd push in behind him. They were all eager to see an outcome. Jed took the six out of his hand and put it with the other rejects. He wanted to take the chance, however slim the odds.

Jed drew his new card. He could feel the burning glare on him from the miner, the red-eyed stare of the lanky man, and the steely coolness of El Diablo. His stomach roiled. The ten of hearts was staring at him. He had a royal flush in his hands. Jed wet his lips and put fifty dollars into the center. A wave of gasps and floods of whispers rippled through the parlor. He could feel the tension reach its breaking point.

Abe stiffened. The woman straightened, shock spreading across her face. The lanky man eyed Jed with suspicion. The miner's face began turning darker hues of red seeing Jed's raise.

"I'm gonna call it," he snarled, tossing his cards on the table top, "You're bluffin'…"

Eyes turned to Abe. He folded his cards with a sigh and tossed them to the center, "I fold." Jed looked over both of the men's hands. Neither was very good. The lanky man tossed his hand on the table, his set of threes splayed out in an arc.

Jed laid his cards out one at a time. Ten first, then, the Ace, the King, the Queen, and the Jack. The room resounded with excitement and disbelief at the play. Money changed hands, and voices elevated above the rising flood of emotions.

Jed looked at Abe, who had tilted his hat brim up just slightly, to look at him with those unsettling eyes. This time, however, they had the look of approval about them, accompanied by a faint grin. The lanky man grumbled, shoving his chair back as he stood. Defeat weighed on his shoulders, making them sink as he melded into the crowd.

"YOU LITTLE SHIT!" The miner's roar dampened the whole room as the chair that held his weight clattered to the ground, the table jostling to the side from the sheer force. Jed looked at his oncoming attacker. He had the eyes of a wild animal, his veins popping from his neck and face. A fist was clenched tightly, ready to land a strike on Jed.

Some of the women shrieked as the room went silent, the sound of a hammer being cocked back echoing across the room. Silence followed the eerie sound. Every person was frozen in their place. Abe was standing now, his full concentration on the miner who had just lost everything.

"Take this outside." The coolness of Abe's voice seeped into every crevice of the place, bringing the heat to a low simmer. The miner glanced at Abe's gun. Jed held his hands up to his shoulders in surrender. His heart pounded against his ribcage, his body preparing for the future beating he was sure he was going to receive.

The moment was drawn thin until the old miner broke, lowering his fist in an exasperated growl. Jed felt his muscles relax from their tension. The miner released his shirt and stormed out the swinging doors to the street, Abe following him. Jed shakily stood and smoothed out the massive wrinkle the other man had left. He could feel everyone's eyes on him as he scooped up his winnings and quickly headed to the door.

"You did good, sweetheart," a soft voice chided in his ear. Jed startled at it and looked to his right side. The woman Abe had disappeared with was close beside him, her hand gently guiding him to the outside.

"I-I, uh, sorry ma'am...I just..." Jed stammered, adjusting his winnings in his arms. He didn't want to lose any of it. He won it true and fair.

"Weren't expectin' that bastard to try an' kill ya?" She laughed to herself, amused at Jed's first exposure to the den of miscreants. Jed swallowed hard and tried to hide his flaming embarrassment. How could he have been so naïve? He should have seen it coming. The signs were there, he was sure.

Jystana stopped and gently patted his shoulder, making Jed halt in his step. "Tell me, boy, how old are you?" Jed gazed up at her, stunned still by her mysterious beauty.

"I'm sixteen, ma'am." His voice sounded shy, even in his own ears. He adjusted the winnings in his arms nervously, nearly dropping an old silver-plated pocket watch that had been lost by an earlier player that night. Jystana studied him for a moment. Jed studied her back. *She knows something...*

"Well then, boy, I suppose we should get ya back to Abe." She chuckled and strode past him, her faint scent of perfume wafting to his nose as she turned the corner to the darkened alley.

# Chapter 18

Abe watched the miner ten paces away from him. He was impatient and anxious. He could smell it on him from where he stood. Abe kept his gun raised to him, to ensure that he wouldn't do anything foolish. He heard Jystana come up behind him, and the sloppy footsteps of the boy not too far behind. Neither broke his concentration.

"Now, *mister*." The miner sneered, "This kid and I have unfinished business—"

Abe pulled out a paper from his duster pocket and showed it to the man. Abe could see the miner's face drain of color as the paper showed him his end. He had picked up the bounty a couple towns back. Several, in fact. It wouldn't hurt to do some work while he fulfilled his contract with the deceased Marshall. He lowered it and spoke coolly, "You were sayin'?"

The miner began to tremble in his place as he put up his hands. *As if that would save him...* "Wait a minute, mister, we can talk this out…"

Abe cocked the hammer back. "Good. I need answers…"

"W-what?" The man stammered, a look of confusion crossing his features.

Abe pulled out the obsidian coin Jed had found earlier and showed it to him. The pale moon's light caught it, making the material glint an eerie gleam in the dark, as if it had life of its own. "This look familiar?" The miner shook his head, his fat chin wiggling from the motion. Abe narrowed his eyes.

"I wouldn't lie if I were you…" Abe heard Jystana's voice speak for him. He could count on her when it mattered most. "He's known to have…a short fuse, shall we say?" Abe glared back at her for a moment, irritation raising his hackles once more.

"Alright, alright! Yeah I've seen it before…" Abe turned his attention to the man again, tucking the coin back into his duster.

"Then you know who I'm lookin' for…where is he?" Abe was losing his patience. Damn it, he hated it when Jystana brought that out. He knew she was right.

"Perhaps I do…" The miner shifted uncomfortably, inching backwards. Abe fired a warning shot toward the ground at the man's side, making him yelp. All his confidence drained away. "Okay, okay! I do! Eberhart! Marks, th-they're all west now! Across them mountains!" The miner covered his face with his arms in a vain attempt to shield him from another possible shot.

Abe paused, mulling the words of the man. Even if they had any truth in them, it still smelled like a ploy. Then again…

"How long?"

"Not too terribly long, mister, they just up and left, without a word! I swear that's all I know! Please don' kill me!" The man whimpered.

*Pathetic…* Abe lowered his gun for a moment, weighing his words. The man's whimpers grated on his nerves. He remembered this one from those years past. He was a new blood then. He had not been in for long with the Marks.

Abe raised his pistol again and pulled the trigger. The bullet tore through the man's knee, making him howl in unimaginable pain and sending him sprawling into the dirt. Abe tossed the bounty at the man and turned to face a disturbed Jystana and a bewildered Jed.

He strode past them both as he fished into his duster for a smoke he desperately craved. "Are we just gonna leave him there?!" Jed asked, exasperated, looking from the man on the ground to the hunter.

Abe pulled out his ivory box of cigarettes and grunted, "Yup."

"But—why?" Abe lit the tip of the cigarette dangling from the part of his lips with the tip of his thumb and tucked the box back. When he was satisfied that it had a good burn, he turned his head in Jed's direction.

"You won enough money for a month's supply, boy...get the horses."

Jed hesitated for a moment before rushing off. The man's cries of agony filled the alley and spilled to the main street as Abe stopped beside the woman, averting direct eye contact. He knew that she would try to stop him.

"Abe...don't do this," she pleaded softly. Her voice was tempting, her words pleasing to his self-conscious, telling him to turn away from this path. The lustful passion that had ensued in the saloon was still there between the two. He craved her, wanted her, and wished he could stay with her and forget what he had to do. He couldn't do it. Not now.

"Jys...you know that I have to..." Abe sighed, smoke streaming from his mouth and nostrils. The timid burn soothed his throat and lungs.

"No, you don't, and you know it." Her voice was strained, but controlled. Abe looked at her. She was scared; he could see it in her eyes.

"It has to end sometime, Jys. It just happens to be now, rather than later." He resisted the urge to take her into his arms, to hold her for just a moment more. It pained him greatly to leave her on such short notice.

He heard Jed bring the horses to the alley and stop. Dusk was pawing the dirt again, impatient as always. Jys closed the gap between them and crushed her lips to his. He embraced her, holding her slender figure against him as he feverishly returned her kiss. His inner self growled within him, threatening to overtake his sense of judgement and sense of rational thought. He wanted the moment to last forever, but each second was critical. If the Marks were truly on the move this quickly, he would need to push harder to find more of them.

Abe reluctantly parted her from him, shoving his inner self back to its void. They locked their eyes together, looking on in silence. No words were needed. Heavy-hearted, Abe stepped back, adjusting his duster as he walked to the horses. He had to contain his emotions as he mounted up into his saddle and took the reins. Jystana stood there with a longing look in her eye. "I'll see you again, El Diablo. You know where to find me?"

"I always do." Abe turned Dusk to the main street and spurred him on. Jed followed closely after him on that old nag. He pushed the words she had said out of his mind. He would see her again, sooner or later. He hoped for sooner.

# Chapter 19

His mare stumbled over a dirt clod, jostling Jed awake. He startled and looked around, breathing in sharply. His eyes squinted in the piercing morning sun as he yawned from his stiff rest. He didn't remember falling asleep in the saddle, and he was thankful that he didn't fall off. Jed stretched his arms and shoulders before patting his mare's neck gently. Last night had felt like a bizarre dream. He had won several rounds of poker, and, as El Diablo had said, won enough money for a long while of supplies. None of it, however, felt like it had been real. In fact, nothing that had happened in the past few days made any sense.

Jed sighed, reachin around to the back of the saddle and grabbing the worn rifle that his Pa had left behind. The wood was warm from the body heat of the horse, and it felt worn in his hand as he brought it to his lap. He stared at the stalk and the barrel, the memories still fresh scars upon his heart. Tears stung the edges of his eyes, but he forced them to stay where they pooled. He would not cry for the dead anymore; his Pa deserved more than that. He deserved to be avenged.

"We'll rest for a while." The hunter's voice broke his mind's wandering, catching his attention. He breathed an inward sigh of relief at the thought of resting for a while. He needed to get his mind thinking in a different direction. Jed held the gun close to his lower torso, cradling it. The hunter led them down into the sloping valley that had begun to unfold before them. The insects in the surrounding sage brush screeched loudly in the stagnant air as they approached a more clustered area of deadened trees. The brittle branches provided very little shade, but it was enough to keep the sharpness off their necks.

Absalom dismounted and Jed followed suit, tying his mare to the shadiest part of the trees. Jed glanced back at the hunter who was, again, fishing inside his duster coat—most likely for another cigarette. A slow burn of anger and impatience burned in his gut. Why would they stop when Absalom clearly had a new direction? Jed sighed, pushing away his negative emotions. *He's right...I should probably rest.*

He felt the ache of travel seep into his bones, the weight of the events crushing his stomach towards the hard pan. Jed took a deep breath as he gently lowered himself onto a half-shaded boulder. He welcomed the new shape of seat underneath him. All this riding was wearing down on him. He rubbed his face with his hands, yawning.

"Here, kid." The hunter's canteen appeared, surprising Jed. He looked up at the man and took the old canteen from his rough hand. As he heard water slosh inside of it, he realized he was parched.

"Thank you, sir." Jed answered quietly, popping the cap off and taking a swig. The water was warm and stale, but it was still water. It revitalized his mouth, as well as his voice. He took another drink before passing it back, wiping his lips with the back of his hand. Absalom took the canteen and took a drink for himself before capping it. It dawned on Jed: the hunter had shown actual kindness towards him.

Jed opened his mouth to say something, then paused. *Just ask him. The worst he can do is be silent.* He cleared his throat and tried again, pushing the lump of his throat back down, "Mr. El Diablo...?" Absalom looked up after capping the canteen and stared at Jed, silently. "Why are you helpin' me? I-I thought you, uh, hated my Pa..." The question sounded unexpected, even to his own ears, and it clearly caught the hunter off guard for a moment.

"Hate him? No." He answered shortly as he went back to his saddle. "Mr. McKay was just a damn nuisance, way back when." He firmly retied the dented canteen back onto his saddle. Jed waited for him to say more, but it never came. El Diablo—Absalom—was quiet once more. Jed stood, ignoring the ache in his legs as he watched the hunter. He was desperate for an explanation. Deep down, he knew that anyone else would have let him go on his own, and he knew he would have been killed many times over, if it weren't for this man.

"I still want to know why you're helpin' me." Jed pressed.

He watched as Absalom's shoulders sagged with a sigh, as if a heavy burden was laid upon them. He turned, his hands rested on his hips. "Now's not the time for that „Jed."

Jed felt his breaking point. He had had enough secrecy, enough riddles, enough silence. His world was upside-down, and no one would tell him the straight reality of his situation. "What the hell am I supposed to do, then?! I've been ridin' with ya for days, and no one will tell me shit about what the hell happened!" He felt his face get red with his anger, frustration, and inner turmoil. He let it flow, "My sister is out there with some gang leader I had no idea even existed until a few days ago! She could be *dead*... or worse. And my Pa..." His voice cracked as his raw emotions flooded through him. He clenched his jaw, balling his fists at his sides as he collected his thoughts for a moment, "My Pa is dead, and for what? For something that happened years ago? Hell, I didn't even know he was a lawman until *you* showed up!"

Absalom stood his ground as Jed berated him with his burst of rage. The silence spanned between them as the hunter stood there, still as could be. Jed sighed and turned from him, tears finally spilling out from his eyes. *He ain't gonna tell me nothin'. I should expect no less...*

"Look, Jed—" Abe interrupted his thoughts. Jed rounded on him, glaring at the hunter.

"And don't call me Jed. Ever. *Abe*..." His own voice surprised him as he jabbed a finger threateningly towards him. His Pa had called him Jed. To him, the name had a certain sacredness to it. A name that should only be spoken by his family. This man, this hunter, would never be family.

Absalom narrowed his eyes at Jed, his mouth pursing at his harsh words, "Fine, then...*boy*..." Jed lowered his finger, having second thoughts about disrespecting a man this dangerous, "You want to know why the fuck I'm helpin' you?" The hunter approached Jed, one step at a time. Jed's countenance fell as the intimidating man drew closer. "This ain't fuckin' charity, *Jedidiah*...it was a business transaction. Your Pa made a deal with me. I swore to protect your scrawny ass from all this bullshit." The hunter's voice was low and venomous as he backed Jed up to the boulder he had sat on.

The hunter loomed over him, his visage darker than Jed had expected. He swallowed hard. His eyes were wide with shock as the hunter continued, "Your Pa started this mess, and, now, I have to clean it up. You will do as I say, and you will do it without a fuckin' question. You'd be more-than-dead if I wasn't constantly babysittin' you." The insects surrounding them had gone quiet as the words rested over the two of them. Jed felt the burden of shame rest on his chest as he turned his gaze from the hunter. He knew it was true.

"I...I'm sorry...I just..." Jed glanced at the hunter who stepped back, his fuming irritation stemmed for now. Jed sat down again, the new knowledge making his head swim. *Pa made a deal with him...? But...why?* Absalom, seemingly satisfied with Jed's reaction, went back to his horse and started unsaddling him.

"We'll camp here for now." The hunter's tone was curt. All Jed could muster was a nod of his head. He wanted to stay quiet for now. *I've said enough, I think...* He stretched out on the boulder, embarrassed at his behavior towards the man who had saved him a few times already in just recent days. *I suppose I really don't have a choice. I have to trust him.* Jed felt his eyelids slide down lower, and lower, until they closed. The insects began their screeching again, their afternoon rhythm echoing through the dead trees, heralding the start of the scorching heat.

# Chapter 20

His head swirled as he forced himself back to consciousness. The air was cooler now, and the screeching insects of the day had switched shifts with those of the dusk; night must be nearing. Groaning inwardly with exhaustion, Jed made himself sit up from his spot. He wasn't sure if his rest was harmful or helpful—his back ached from the hard rock that supported his weight. His eyes slowly adjusted in the twilight, and they focused on a small fire several feet away. At its edge squatted the hunter, staring at the small dancing flames. Jed stood to his feet and carefully walked towards the man.

Absalom never lifted his gaze to him as Jed sat on the other side of the fire. Jed knew better; he knew that the man heard him coming. He dared to presume that he knew when he woke up as well. Jed couldn't explain how this man seemed to know so much, nor did he anticipate for Absalom to talk to him after what he had said earlier. His heart felt like lead in his chest, it was so heavy with shame. His ears turned red as he recalled what he had spouted in anger.

"El Diablo— " Abe cut Jed off as he raised his hand and lifted his eyes to Jed's through the dusk light. His eyes were still cold. Jed swallowed.

"It's done…move on." Jed wrestled his strong upbringing to apologize when he had done wrong, and finally submitted to a nod of acknowledgement. Absalom stood and dug through his pockets again, pulling out folded papers. The crackling sound filled the air as he unfolded at least five pages. He knelt to one knee spreading each one out on the dirt. The sketches on them were rough, but recognizable as men.

Jed cocked his head to look at the words at a straighter angle. "Wanted" was emboldened at the top. *Wanted posters...bounties.* Jed looked at Absalom, who had squatted back to where he was, a puzzled look knitting his brow and facial features. "I thought you said we had enough money to last us months?"

Absalom touched a few with the tips of his fingers examining each of the posters. He was looking for something in those sketches. "One of these...will have what we need." His voice was low, concentration written on his visible features. Jed didn't understand the hunter at all. How could someone possibly know what to look for, just from a drawing?

Absalom went back to one towards the center of the row and picked it up, bringing it closer. He stood, tucking it inside his jacket, while he nudged the other leaflets into the small flame. The hungering dancers eagerly consumed the paper, making the fire bigger and brighter for a moment. "So...that one knows where Marietta is?" Jed let hope enter his heart. Any possibility to find her was a good one.

"We'll find out." The hunter stated with finality as he went to his horse. He must have saddled up while he was asleep.

"Shouldn't we leave right away?" Jed asked impatiently as he watched the hunter take out a leather kit.

Absalom rounded and pointed at him with it, almost in a threatening manner, "I told ya before: you ain't ready for what's comin', boy." Jed clamped his mouth shut and stayed in his seated position. He scolded himself for his tongue as Absalom sat back down by the flame and unraveled the kit. Jed peeked at it curiously, looking at the various tools and oils that were neatly organized by size and type.

"You learn how to do basic readin' and 'rithmetic, and you think you're ready..." Absalom huffed as he drew his pistols and gently laid them in front of him. Before Jed could answer for himself, Absalom cut him off again, piercing him with his blue gaze , "There's more to learn, if you want to live."

Those words rang through Jed like a hollow church bell. Jed had agreed to learn from this man, all he could so he could save her. So far, nothing of the sort had happened. He was beginning to wonder if the hunter was truly trying to help, or just to delay the inevitable. Jed found his voice in the awkward silence as Absalom began to clean his guns by the weak firelight.

"I-I know that...and I want to learn! I wanna do whatever it takes to find Marietta." Jed licked his lips, hoping his plea would finally be heard. He was tired of waiting around. He wanted to learn.

To Jed's shock, a soft raspy chuckle came from the hunter's lips. "It's a hard life, *boy*. Skills like mine come with a rep. If you get wounded or die, no one will give a shit."

Jed squirmed at the man's blunt explanation. He knew what the man was talking about. However, he had nothing to lose. Everything he had ever known was gone. Absalom had warned him before; he didn't care. "Like I said before, I want to do whatever it takes." Jed let his words sink in. Absalom went back to cleaning his pistols diligently. "Please!" Jed leaned forward and begged. *Please...* he inwardly pleaded.

Absalom narrowed his eyes and pointed at him with the tool in hand, "You listen, and you listen good." Jed nodded and focused everything on his words. "You're gonna learn how to shoot. Your aim is shit. Ya couldn't hit the side of a barn if ya wanted to." Absalom lowered his tool and grabbed another one. He never took his icy eyes off Jed's. "You will listen and do what I say." Jed nodded, replacing his shame with the hope of redemption. "And, lastly, boy...don't ever call me 'Abe' again."

Jed suppressed a small smile. He wasn't sure why, but his demand struck him as funny. He nodded, "That's all well and good, Mr. El Diablo, but if you call me Jed, I will call you Abe."

Absalom shot him a warning glance, grunting, and refocused his eyes on the task at hand. The night air was refreshing, the stars blazing against the black sky. Jed laid on his side, his body still exhausted from the strenuous travel. *I need to do this, not only for Marietta, but for Pa. He would have done the same for me.*

# Chapter 21

"Again." Absalom's voice was stern, yet guiding. Jed adjusted his shoulders and squinted his eyes. He could feel sweat drip down his neck and his back. Even the morning heat was blistering. He concentrated on the makeshift targets Absalom had set up early in the morning, while he was still asleep. He had tied various rocks, debris, and other things, to the limbs of their dead sanctuary.

He took a breath, and pulled the trigger. The kickback rammed into his shoulder, making him wince and close his eyes. He opened them, only to find disappointment and frustration. He had been trying all morning to even *hit* a mark; anything at all. He lowered his rifle and sighed in frustration, his jaw clenching with irritation.

Absalom came from his shady post and stood next to Jed. As he approached, Jed could feel his eyes on him. He didn't want to look. Jed raised his rifle again and focused, this time closing an eye. "Don't close your eye…you'll always miss," Abe corrected him promptly. Jed grunted and opened his eye. His hands were sweating against the stock. His arms were stiff from holding his position. "Now…squeeze the trigger…" Abe grunted and dug around his duster pockets again. *For a cigarette, I'm sure,* Jed thought irritably. The heat was almost unbearable.

Jed fixed the strange, dangling target into his sights, resisting the urge to squint again. It felt as though the odds were stacked against him. Between his aching muscles, the blistering heat, and the piercing sun, it was difficult to focus. *I need to do this.* Jed adjusted his stance taking a slow breath. *There is no other way.*

The shot rang through the air again, like so many before it throughout the practice. Jed had squeezed the trigger, making the kickback softer. He still felt its sting as the target exploded from the bullet. Jed let a wide grin spread on his face, relief spreading through all his limbs and being. He had done it, at last. Abe grunted, "Better, but not good enough."

Jed looked at Abe in despair as he watched the hunter pull out his small package of chewing tobacco. He held his tongue, afraid of embarrassing himself—or worse—as Abe cut off a piece from the block of chew and tucked it into his mouth, finding respite on a boulder under the shady branches of the dead wood around them. Jed could feel his eyes on him as he sighed, tired from the heat and the shooting practice.

"Again, Jed." The hunter relaxed under the shade. Jed reloaded his rifle, determination rising in his chest once more. He saw it now. He needed to learn, or he might never find his sister. This hunter was his only option. Jed focused on another dangling target, a farther one this time. *I will learn this.* He fired, the shot just grazing the side of his target. Jed reloaded, with more fervor this time. *I'm her only chance.* He took in another breath, slow and sure. On the exhale, he squeezed the trigger again, the thundering clap echoing throughout the grove.

\*\*\*

Night hadn't come fast enough for Jed. The whole day was dedicated to shooting those targets out of the branches. He had finally gotten them all down from their swaying perches—not quite what Abe had expected from this short amount of time. Sore, sweaty, and hungry, Jed sat by the small fire Abe had whipped up. Jed grabbed a portion of his rations from his saddle pack and opened the small, wrapped parcel. Dried backstrap laid neatly inside of it, the aroma permeating his senses and leaving his mouth watering in anticipation.

As Jed chewed on the meat, he watched the hunter grab a cigarette and light it up in the coals of the fire. *He sure does smoke a lot.* As if the man knew he was being stared at, he looked in Jed's direction, the red tip burning brightly for a moment as he drew on it.

"What, Jed?" Abe's voice was strong. *I think I could get used to this,* Jed thought hopefully as he shifted and stirred the coals a little bit.

"It's just…well, thank you, Abe, for teachin' me." Abe crinkled his nose at that name, but no complaint was aired, besides a grunt as he lowered his gaze back to the fire, taking another draw.

"Gotta learn sometime, boy." Abe leaned back against his saddle, pulling his hat low over his eyes. Jed cleared his throat softly and put his back strap aside. His curiosity was getting the better of him.

"Abe?" No answer came as the crickets cried from a distance. Until he answered, Jed thought he had fallen asleep.

"What, Jed?"

"That woman…from the town past…" Jed spoke cautiously, remembering how sensitive he seemed to be towards her, "do you…like her?"

Abe's sigh was loud and drawn out, like a gust of wind across the plains, "No, Jed…I don't."

"Oh, I, uh, I just thought…by the way she looked at ya—"

"How old are you, boy?" Abe cut him off sharply, catching Jed off his guard.

"Sixteen, sir."

Abe lifted the brim of his hat to look at Jed over the small flames. "Sixteen, huh?"

"Yessir," Jed answered, a bit of pride swelling his chest.

"Ever touched a woman's breast?"

The question made Jed think about his morality. *What did he just say?!* His cheeks lit up with fire as he edged in his seat uncomfortably. "N-no Abe, I can't say that I have…"

Abe grunted and rested his hands over his chest, latticing them together, "How 'bout your "Johnson"?"

"My what?!" Jed exclaimed.

"You know...make yourself feel better?"

Jed swallowed hard as he answered in a shaky voice, "No, Abe, I-I don't think I have."

Abe sat up from his comfortable position, resting his forearms over his drawn-up knees. Jed licked his lips nervously as those eyes pierced him through once more. "Huh...you *are* a strange one."

*I'm the strange one?!* Jed's ears and face were aflame with embarrassment. Not only did Abe invade his privacy to some degree, he labeled him as the strange one of the pair. Jed let his jaw drop in horror, confused and speechless.

Abe's low chuckle resonated as he shook his head and went back to his sleeping position. "Get some sleep, Jed. We ride in the morning."

No more was spoken from the hunter. Jed laid down as he was told, the awkward exchange still strong in his mind. *I will never get used to his ways.* Jed turned his back to the fire as he fell into a light sleep.

# Chapter 22

Jed was getting accustomed to the ruggedness of the land. To his relief, so was his mare. His ass was numb from the riding, but at least it wasn't sore like it had been before. Every morning, he would recite the words written in the pamphlet Abe claimed to have "borrowed." They had ridden for several days, maybe even a week. It was hard to tell. Every evening before he laid his head to rest, he took up his practice. Every day, he was getting better and better with his aim. He let his mind wander in thought as he followed Abe who always seemed to know the way.

He could feel the sweat running down his neck and back as the sun beat down on them from behind. Jed wiped his forehead with the back of his free hand and flicked the wetness from it. *I could go for a bath.* His mare sighed, Jed reached and patted her neck affectionately. He knew she was getting tired already. Jed sighed in return, wishing she were just a few years younger.

"Hey, Abe? Where are we goin'?" Jed called out to the hunter. He could see his shoulders tense at his name. *He'll get used to it.* Jed refrained from grinning.

"Town," was all he called back to Jed. Jed frowned, a crease forming on his brow. He always had the one line answers for him. Jed drew up the reins, the mare picked her head back up, and her ears pricked toward him as he nudged her gently. She stiffly trotted to where Jed directed her before softly reining her in to a walk once more.

"Which one?" Jed persisted. Abe sighed. Jed knew he couldn't ignore him for long.

"The one we're goin' to."

"Damn it, Abe, you know what I mean!" Jed blurted impatiently. He shook his head and adjusted his weight in his seat.

"...Hern."

Jed looked at Abe again, impressed that he answered with a serious response. "Hern?"

"Yes." His answer was short, but with a tone of finality to it.

Satisfied, Jed nodded and focused on the dreary landscape ahead of them both. It hadn't changed in days. *I hope we get there soon...before my horse an' I keel over.* The silence enveloped them, only broken by the sound of hooves, creaking leather, and the smallest breath of wind in the distance.

\*\*\*

The darkness of night was a relief to Jed's back and neck. He could still feel the sting of its rays on his skin as he reached up and tenderly rubbed it. He winced. *Burned...* However, the town of Hern was much alive and well-to-do. The main street was buzzing with activity. Jed was inwardly thrilled to recognize the letters and some of the words on the shop fronts.

Jed couldn't help but observe in wonder as they passed on by. The town seemed old to Jed. The buildings crowded around its inhabitants, but the townsfolk paid them no mind as they went about their nightly business. Jed kept his thoughts to himself as Abe steered to a hard left and stopped at a hitching post. Jed followed suit and dismounted, just as Abe did. Abe was firm in his landing, while Jed staggered slightly from the sudden change of position. He inwardly cursed himself as he took a moment to steady his numb legs. *Damn it, I should be used to this now.*

"C'mon Jed, we ain't got all night." Abe's voice was gruff and low. Jed nodded, biting his tongue. He stood straighter and tied off his old mare, before following Abe through the swinging doors. Jed paused for a moment to read the half-faded letters on the slanted sign; *The Painted Rose...huh. Must be another saloon.* Jed pushed through the double doors and stood next to Abe.

The parlor room was filled with loud piano music, laughter, and a smoky haze. Jed stayed close to Abe as he glanced around the room. He was not surprised to see gambling tables of all sorts. He noted the poker table, vowing to stay away from it. The last thing he wanted to do was cause more problems. Abe wove through the crowded parlor, as if the people weren't even there. Jed followed him closely, squeezing awkwardly between a couple in conversation. He muttered an apology under his breath as he passed.

Abe finally stopped at a dark wooden counter that stretched the length of the back wall, leaning with a forearm on the surface. A well-endowed woman saw the awkward pair and sauntered up to them. Jed tried to keep his gaze over the various activities of the parlor room, instead of the woman's half-exposed bust. He could feel his cheeks flush, Abe's words from days past echoing in his mind.

"Evenin', fellas. What brings ya to my Painted Rose?" The woman's voice was charming, projecting well over the boisterous raucous of the customers. Abe didn't even lift his hat brim to gaze at her as he fished out a good bit of cash.

"Couple o' rooms would do." Abe responded. The woman reached for the bills with an unblemished, fair hand. Her fingers curled around the wad and pulled it to her. She smiled and counted the bills quickly, never taking a fascinated eye off him.

She paused in her counting and cocked her head to the side, a playful look dancing in her eyes as she asked politely, "As much as you gave me sir, you can have any room ya like. How long do ya plan to stay here?"

Abe stood and adjusted his duster before speaking coolly, "One night, Madame, will be fine."

With a nod, the woman leaned down out of view, money and all. She returned and softly clacked two painted wooden chips onto the countertop and slid it towards the hunter. Jed tried to peer over Abe's shoulder to look, but the hunter made sure his hand was directly over the wooden chips. *Those aren't room keys, are they?*

"Head upstairs and pick any room you like." The woman smiled and headed down the long countertop to a new customer, "Enjoy, fellas."

Abe didn't so much as nod his acknowledgement before heading to the grand staircase, which was on the right side of the building. Jed stayed close to him as they lighted the stairs. Jed was still puzzled at the latter part of her instructions. "Abe, I thought she was supposed to give us keys to our rooms."

Abe stopped at the landing and faced Jed. "They are, Jed. New kind of invention from back east." He grabbed Jed's hand and pressed a wooden chip in his palm. "Just take this chip, and drop it into one of them boxes," Abe said, indicating to a wood box fastened to the wall next to a door. "It'll open fer ya."

Jed looked at the brightly colored chip in wonder. *First I ever heard o' somethin' like this.* "Alright, then, I will. What about you, though?"

Abe waved him off as he headed down the hallway, "See ya in the morning, boy."

Jed stood there as he watched his partner disappear around a corner, leaving him standing there. He toyed with the chip in his palm for a moment, considering his many options for rooms. A smile cracked his lips as he began to stroll down the hallway. The thought of a warm bath and a regular bed excited him. He longed for a small taste of normalcy. He passed many rooms, slowing at some prospects. Most had signs swaying from their nodes on the handles. He took the time to read "No Vacancy" and "Vacancy". He didn't know what "vacancy" meant, but he suspected it meant it was being slept in already.

After the ninth or tenth room, a worried frown creased his forehead. *For a saloon, there sure are a lot of people sleepin' already...it couldn't possibly be that late, could it?* Jed finally stopped at one towards the end of the right turn hallway, opposite of where Abe had gone. He looked at the box, which was finely decorated with paint and patterns, before dropping his token in the box. He waited. And he waited. And he waited for a while longer.

*Abe said it would unlock itself. I didn't hear nothin'.* Jed reached out for the handle, licking his lips nervously. *Maybe if I jiggle the lock...* Jed grasped the brass knob and turned it. It creaked, but it gave way just as easy. Jed shook off the oddity and swung the door open.

He quickly regretted it. A woman with the fairest skin he had ever laid eyes on was already in his room, laying on the covers, her breasts fully exposed. She was biting her lip, watching him with tousled hair and half-undone bodice. Jed turned his gaze away, his words failing him, "Oh my God! I'm so sorry, ma'am, I-I—" Jed shielded his eyes with his hand, to prevent him from temptation. The image was burned into his mind—the damage was already done. "I thought this room was empty,"

"It is, sugar," Her voice was bubbly and light-hearted, stunning him in place. He was helpless as he glanced frequently at her as she rose from her perch and sauntered to him. Her dark hair tumbled over her shoulders and half-hid her naked upper body, making it a little more bearable. Jed forced his eyes to the old, worn floor as she stopped in front of him. The scent of musk and stale perfume clung to her as she giggled. "My, my...you *are* a strange one."

Jed frowned at her comment. He made the mistake of looking up at her. Her deep green eyes seemed to swallow him whole as he stared at her. His lips moved, but nothing came out. *Say something, damn it!* "L-look, ma'am. I don't know exactly what's goin' on here, but I'm sure I shouldn't be in here. It ain't proper."

Her grin turned into one of confusion with an underlying tone of boredom. "Proper? Look, son, you paid for a room," she spoke as she sauntered over to a slit in the wall. With nimble hands, she unhinged a small metal plate from the wall, reached in, and pulled out a wooden chip. *My "key"...* She turned and showed him the red, painted chip before tossing it into a porcelain bowl on a side table. Its clatter was hollow against its other brethren. "So...let's get this over with." She closed the door as she guided him towards the grungy bed. Jed felt helpless as he kept his wide eyes locked with hers.

With a surprised grunt, Jed felt his knees unhinge as they bumped into the foot of the bed, the metal frame squeaking from the sudden fall. Before he knew it, she was over him, touching him in ways he had never dreamed of. The thought of telling her to stop screamed through his mind, but something deep inside his groin pleaded for him not to. He gave up fighting the rising sensation. He leaned his head back into the old mattress, his morality drifting into euphoria.

# Chapter 23

Abe sat at the old, worn table in the parlor. The night had died as soon as the sun crested the horizon, and, with it, the clientele from the Painted Rose. He held his hot tin cup filled with coffee as he waited for his morning meal. He still had some money left over to order a full breakfast for himself and the boy. *If he ever wakes up.*

Abe brought the cup to his lips and gulped a hot drink. The searing heat of the liquid felt refreshing to his innards as he savored the sour taste of old coffee. It wasn't much, but, compared to nothing at all in the wilderness, it was a treat. He took another drink, a content sigh resonating from his chest, while he leaned back in his chair which creaked under his shifting weight. He leaned his head back while tugging his hat low over his eyes, contemplating his next move. It could either mean his death…or the boy's. *Eberhart is playing a dangerous game.*

He heard movement from the balcony. Boots, the rustle of trousers being adjusted, a belt clasp lightly clanking. A smirk crept onto Abe's lips. *Well, well, Jed, finally out of bed?* He tilted his hat back just enough to observe the boy. He was staggering slightly, as though sore, his cheeks flushed pink as he looked back at the dark-haired harlot who swooned from afar. She cocked an eyebrow. He nodded an awkward acknowledgement before descending the flight of stairs. Abe leaned back and extended the tin cup, as he waited for the boy to come his way.

\*\*\*

Jed tried to forget what had happened to him the night before, but it wouldn't leave him. Not only did he sleep with a strange woman, he did so eagerly for the whole night. She had told him that if he ever wanted to come back, he could always stay with her. His ears flushed at the thought of another encounter with *any* woman.

He brushed those thoughts away from his conscious mind as he approached the solo man in black. Jed pulled out a chair and delicately sat down in it. He refused to give even a hint of his soreness. *Damn...I didn't know it would hurt this much.* He scooted closer to the table, avoiding contact.

"How was she?" Abe's voice cracked through the silence that spanned between them. Jed's ears flamed red and began to seep onto his cheeks.

Jed looked at Abe, a sheepish expression on his features, before clearing his throat and answering, "Er...fine sir."

Abe leaned back in his chair, satisfied with the answer. "You're a man now, boy."

Jed nodded and leaned back in his chair as well. The morning light was piercing through the smoke-stained glass. The woman from the night before—the Madame, Abe had called her—strode towards them both and placed two plates in front of them. She rested her hand on Jed's shoulder, a proud smile on her face as she spoke kindly, "Well, I trust this will fill ya up, boys. Thank you for your lovely patronage."

Before Jed could even speak, she left in a swish of expensive silk and polished, heeled shoes. Abe was already devouring his meal in a brutish manner. Jed picked up his thin slice of bacon and took a satisfying crunch out of it. The savory flavor danced in his mouth before he swallowed it. The pair ate their meals in the silence, only accompanied by the sounds of the busy street and the early risers of the Painted Rose.

After they both had finished their meal, Abe stood and headed to the door. Jed followed suit. He took the chance to grab a last glance of the place, only to see most of the harem lounging around the banister. The dark-haired beauty he had been with must have bragged to the other ladies. Jed cleared his throat and nodded to her once more, causing the whole gaggle to giggle amongst themselves.

"C'mon, Jed, we ain't got all day," Abe's gruff voice aired through the slats of the batwing doors. Jed didn't argue. *I best get, or they'll all keep me here.*

The air outside the Painted Rose was dusty and arid, just as Jed had expected. He squinted his eyes to the brightness as Abe went to the horses tied at the post. Jed stopped abruptly when he took in what he saw: his mare was gone.

Panic overtook him as he jumped the three steps to the street level. He rushed over, looking at where he had left her. She had been replaced with a bay roan, with a white stocking foot and newer-looking tack and accoutrements. Not his horse in the slightest. He looked at Abe for help, exasperated, "Abe! Where's my horse?!"

Abe had mounted Dusk and taken the reins into his hands. On his perch, the hunter looked down at Jed, "This *is* your horse, Jed…" He nodded to the steed with the new tack. Jed looked at the stallion. His ears were relaxed, and he looked half-asleep. But he looked young, and much more prepared to endure the hard travels Jed was sure were ahead. However, he couldn't' help but feel dread well up in his chest. He grabbed the reins of the new horse gently. The steed nickered softly, waking from its drowsed state.

"But…where is she?" Jed asked, his voice cracking from his growing despair.

Abe heeled his stallion forward and stopped close to Jed, nodding to the other side of the street. Jed looked in the direction. His heart ached and filled with relief at the same time. A small girl with blond curls was leading his old friend through town. Her father not too far behind, a grin on his weathered face. The mare was plodding along slowly, sniffing at the small girl who led her.

A part of Jed felt lost without his old friend beside him. "She'll be taken care of, boy…" Abe adjusted himself in the saddle as he watched Jed from his perch, his voice as calm as Jed had ever heard it. The stallion Jed held by the reins nickered and snorted, shaking its mane. Jed took his eyes away from the little girl and his old friend. He really was a man now. The last of his family had been given away to another. Jed ran his fingers over the new tack, the horse, the shiny, new leather. The oil made the leather a deep burgundy-brown, a deep shine catching the early sun.

*This saddle and tack must have cost him a fortune.* Jed felt embarrassment settle into his chest. He didn't understand why the hunter would put money into this sort of investment. He had assumed that the hunter felt that he was a burden to him. Abe grumbled, "Well? You gonna sit in it, or just stare at the details?"

An overwhelming feeling threatened to flood his eyes as he gripped the smooth horn. The leather squeaked quietly as he swung his leg up and over, resting into the seat. The support kept him upright, a complete change from the aged saddle his father had given him. The reins slid into his palms as he took them up, different from the rough and fraying edges of the old.

Jed felt a hat being gently but firmly placed over his head, shielding his eyes from the brightness. The brim was wide, providing enough shade for any sort of weather he could imagine. It, too, smelled new.

Abe snorted, urging his horse forward at a leisurely pace, "You'll grow into it."

Jed looked after the hunter in astonishment. He cleared his throat and softly prodded the stallion forward. The horse responded promptly, nickering and eager-to-move. With a small jolt, he moved after the hunter. It took all of Jed's concentration to contain the young steed. He finally maneuvered the stallion to Abe's side. "Thank you…for all this. I-I know it was probably a lot—"

Abe raised a hand, halting Jed's words as he looked at him from under the brim of his worn hat. "Let's get movin'…" The hunter clucked. Dusk snorted and broke into a gallop Jed smiled, a sense of relief and encouragement washing over him as he, too, urged his new mount faster.

# Chapter 24

Days slipped into weeks. Weeks stretched into months. Time seemed to move at a crawling pace as Jed followed Abe through the frontier wilderness. The hunter had reinforced a strict regimen of shooting practice, followed by studies of writing, reading, and arithmetic. He also learned the skills he need to survive on his own and get his sister back. Abe had been surprisingly patient with him.

Each day, Jed could feel his shy nature meld into a new creature—one that would be hardened from the rugged terrain and strict teachings of Absalom. He knew he was getting stronger with each successful shot, with each precise reading and calculation, and with each quick decision. The idea of getting his sister back and avenging his father drove him to do better. Jed felt more-than-ready to track down the Marks and this Eberhart, who had thrown him into this odd new life.

The sun was hanging high in the blue of the afternoon sky. The small outpost town was alive with horses and men talking in groups. The heat hardly bothered him as he glanced over the Marshall building. Its wall was plastered with yellow pages, each with a face and the crimes they committed. Each with a bounty to collect. Jed pushed his hat brim up a little, so he could see all the wall had to offer.

No clue yet. He always looked for a particular man—or any man for that matter—bearing the weight of the Marks. The very name left a bitter taste on his tongue.

*I will find you, Marietta.* His inward promise reminded him every moment of his oath. They ventured from town to outpost,

outpost to mining camp, searching for any sign, any indication, as to where Marietta was. The Marks were like smoke in Jed's hands. He just couldn't seem to catch them.

One of the faces stood out, blatantly catching his attention. He outstretched his hand, a concentrated frown on his brow, and snatched the half-applied paper from the siding. He studied the poster. It was an old posting, but it was still valid. The man in the black-lined box was round in the face with short, sloppy, black hair. His untamable excuse for a beard seemed it would overtake the man in a night. He was definitely a Mexican. Jed closely studied the man's face. The eyes had a certain eerie look about them, almost animalistic in nature. Jed flicked his eyes to the top of the page, reading the faded text,'WANTED: El Cabrio'. *El Cabrio, huh?* Jed glanced at the wall with all the different fugitive's faces staring back, his heart filled with conviction; this man was connected somehow. He could feel it. *I need to show Abe. I think this name means, the goat…? I ain't too sure.*

He folded the poster and placed it in his bandolier. Now that he had a lead, El Diablo would have to stop this aimless drifting. Pulling the brim of his hat down over his eyes again, Jed turned and stepped into the dusty street.

The outpost was a small, shack-style of a town with a lot of traders and people passing through. The only building that people took much note of was the saloon, which served as a saloon, hotel, and, if you had the cents, a brothel. It was always busy.

He stepped up onto the front porch and moved to the swinging door, which rested crooked in their threshold. The smoke veiled the entryway ceiling and disappeared into the outside air. Shouts of excitement could be heard from inside. *Must be a good game.*

The doors creaked and cricked, threatening to fall to the floor. Jed let the doors rest to their original spots as he entered the saloon. For midday, it was just about a full house. The smoke hung heavy around the tables. A whore was busy playing with a potential client in the corner. Jed averted his eyes. The bartender was mixing at least five separate drinks for thirsty customers. The piano player was blacked out on the keys.

Jed was unnoticed. Good. He looked over the clientele, searching for Abe. If he was anywhere, it would be where a bottle of whiskey was available. He saw him. The anticipation of a new lead made Jed anxious to get going as soon as possible. A drink could wait. Abe sat at a corner table, facing the room and its inhabitants. He was watching them, as he always did.

As Jed neared, a chair moved out from the table. Abe knew he was coming. Gratefully, Jed sat heavily into the chair and leaned forward. "Abe, I got a lead." He reached for a half-clean glass, wanting a taste of whiskey before he had discussion of business. Jed was used to talking strictly business when it came to being in the saloon. This poster—this man named El Cabrio—was most definitely business. "El Cabrio…"

Abe stiffened, lifting his eyes to stare at Jed with the piercing blue of his irises. He was silent, and Jed could feel the heaviness of the hunter's hesitation at the sound of the name. He reached and grabbed his glass, filled with golden liquid. Still, he said nothing. Jed waited a moment as a roar erupted from the card table. *What's his deal? He should be glad I found this.*

"You won again!" A man shouted.

"Lucky son of a bitch." Another groused.

The roar calmed, and silence persisted. Abe had drunk his entire glass and was going for another. Jed felt his irritation begin to build in his chest. He began to think that Abe just didn't care, or didn't notice that he had possibly found a lead at long last. He reached into his bandolier and pulled out the folded poster. "Look at it, Abe." He smoothed the paper hastily on the stained tabletop and pushed it to the hunter.

Abe glared at the page. He touched the lower corner of the page and lifted his cool gaze. "Shit bounty boy." Abruptly, the hunter pushed the page back at Jed, draining his glass completely.

Jed couldn't wait any longer, "Damn it, Abe! We finally get a lead on the Marks, and all you can say is 'shit bounty'?" He felt his ears begin to flush. He didn't care. Eyes were glancing at them. He didn't care about that, either. His sister's life was in danger. A rage began to fester in him. He was going to go after this man. Any information—anything at all—would help them. Abe was purposely hiding something, and he didn't know why. *What is he hidin'?* Jed thought suspiciously.

"Causin' a scene, kid." Abe spoke low and poured himself another glass. His eyes strayed to the poster again and slid it back to him. At least he was looking at it again. "He ain't a Marks, boy."

With finality, he pushed it back to Jed. Speechless, Jed took it back and stared at the man. Not a Marks? You can't tell by just a picture. Then again, this was El Diablo, and he's been at this game for most of his life.

Jed would prove him wrong. The man on the poster stared back at him. There was no question: Jed could get some answers from this him.

\*\*\*

The night air provided little comfort from the heat of the day. The blistered earth still wept warmth from the sun, even though it had set an hour or two ago. Jed stirred the fire pit, sending sparks to the sky. It was almost ready to make coffee. Jed and Abe had ridden out of the outpost town in the late afternoon, in the direction of Abe's choosing.

Jed rested on his heels in his crouch, watching the flames lick at the brittle wood. It reminded him of his own inner flame to chase down that lead—with, or without, Abe. But he knew that Abe wouldn't let him leave, and his acute hearing would give away his silent escape. While Abe was preoccupied, Jed had taken to the outpost in search of the orient—Chinks, as Abe had corrected him several hundred times it seemed—a strange people by Jed's standards. They usually were more toward the edge of a town or outpost, and mostly kept to themselves.

It wasn't hard to find their small settlement within the outpost limits. Jed had carefully wandered into their area, not without several wary and suspicious onlookers as he passed by. He needed to find something that would help him temporarily get Abe out of the picture. Jed couldn't wait on Abe's seemingly lax accountability to time. The Chinks moved quickly out of his way as he wandered through, ignoring the various calls in sparse English. Jed's eyes took in the sights and smells of their world. There were open-aired markets with various foods and spices, dead chickens and geese hanging from ropes that spanned across a shambled stand. There were trinkets from their home in another stand; children ran and played amongst the rundown area.

The sense of being out of place had stopped bothering Jed after a time. There had been one last 'store' at the end of the small market row that was covered in drying herbs, various objects and liquids in jars, and a burning stick that let off thick, curling ribbons of smoke into the open air. The smell was distasteful to Jed's nostrils, and the smoke burned his eyes, but he hoped that the stand would have what he needed. The elderly woman sat on a low stool, quietly working her gnarled hands on a small needlepoint frame. For a moment, Jed watched with intrigued fascination as she swiftly worked the small threads of fabric into the larger piece of silk she was working on.

The threads danced together as the woman orchestrated them, weaving them into an exquisite pattern of a creature Jed had never seen before. It was jade in color, and the scales reflected the light of the sun with brilliance. The face was wider than the body, and the eyes were perfectly round and bulbous with thick, pearl-colored whiskers on the jaw. Jed broke his brief trance and looked at the woman. She was frail-looking, with heavy lines in her face and eyes that seemed to be nearly closed. Her gray hair still had remnants of black throughout, and it was neatly bunched into a bun on her head, kept still by a brooch of some sort. It, too, was jade.

"'Scuse me, ma'am?" Jed said somewhat loudly, hoping that she could hear him. Her eyes looked up from her work, and her hands didn't miss a stroke as she watched him.

"You come for fabric? It not done. Come back latah." She spoke precisely, and shakily with age, as she turned her attention from Jed back to her project.

Jed had to strain to understand her English, but understood most of it. "No, no I'm not here for that. I need to purchase somethin' that puts people to sleep," Jed indicated to the various herbs that were hanging in front of him. He hoped that this woman could understand him and know what he would need.

She paused in her threading and narrowed her almost-nonexistent eyes at his request. "Put people to sleep…very difficult. Come." With stiff motions, she rose from her seat, setting her needlepoint frame to the side and toddling toward the tent structure behind her. Jed looked around hesitantly before ducking under the stringed herbs, not quite certain if she did, indeed, want him to follow her. The elderly woman appeared again, pinning him with black eyes, "Coming? I have little time." Jed cleared his throat and nodded his response. Satisfied, the woman disappeared into the tent again, followed by Jed. He lifted the tent flap aside and was immediately slammed with a wall of heavy smoke. Coughing from the sick tar smell, it nearly made him gag. There were a couple people lying about the tent, all dazed-looking and breathing easy. *The hell is goin' on here…?* Jed looked at the men with wariness before looking to the woman.

She was on the far side, digging in a chest that had step shelving when the lid was opened; a clever design to store things. Jed waited patiently, looping his thumb behind his belt as he looked about the tent. It was simple, really, with sparse decoration on the tent walls. The floor was littered with large floor pillows, blankets, and rugs with different colors and patterns. It was a completely different world in such a small space.

"Three dolla' for this." Jed snapped himself back to reality and toward the woman who had brought him a small bottle with thick, black liquid inside of it. Jed looked at the bottle and reached for it. The woman retreated the bottle from him and shook her head, "Pay now, then, you get sleep drug."

*Will it work on Abe, though?* Jed raised an eyebrow and questioned, "What is it?"

The elderly woman grinned, the wrinkles multiplying tenfold around her mouth and eyes as she tapped the cork stopper, "Opium. Powaful. Use for sleeping." She nodded to the men nearly unconscious around them.

Jed paused, pondering her words before pulling out three dollars. He could feel her eyes as he counted out the bills and handed it to her. Her gnarled hand gently took the bills and recounted before nodded with satisfaction. She handed Jed the bottle and bowed, "Come again. It be here when you need more."

Jed nodded, tipping his hat brim to her, "Thank you, ma'am, but this should be plenty." He left, meeting up with Abe as the sun was leaning toward the horizon. He had prepared himself mentally for this moment, and he tried to keep himself contained. As he waited for the sun to finally dip down, Jed learned that he was very impatient.

Abe was resting against the saddle he had retrieved from Dusk's sweaty backside. His hat was adjusted to cover his eyes completely, waiting patiently for the coffee Jed had promised he'd make. His calloused hands were interlaced with each other and resting on his chest.

If he knew Jed's intentions, Abe would, surely, stop him. He was determined to keep Abe asleep as long as possible—to get some distance. The elderly woman had given him the key to complete that obstacle. With a final stir of the coals, Jed stood and stretched, striding over to the bag of supplies. He rifled through dry goods and ammunition before he managed to find the coffee pot and beans. The opium bottle he had purchased was tucked neatly into one of his bandolier pouches. He needed to work quickly, but not raise suspicion.

Jed returned to the fireside and began preparing the coffee. The aroma began to permeate the air soon enough, piquing Abe's interest. He grunted and sat up, adjusting his hat back on straight.

As the coffee percolated, Jed licked his lips subtly, so that Abe wouldn't notice. He couldn't help that nervous habit of his. He poured two cups as the hunter stood and fished his inner pockets for a cigarette. Now was his chance. He slyly pulled out the opium bottle, undoing the cork and pouring the contents into the cup; all of it. He couldn't be too careful. Jed's fingers nimbly picked up a small flask of whiskey next, and opened it. The golden liquid of the whiskey mixed with the opaqueness of the opium to create a sickly honey color. The hunter finally found his cigarette and lit it up as he continued to Jed. He calmly poured the coffee into the tin cup and tried not to make a face.

The faint smell of hot tar, mingled with the sweet, bitter smell of the coffee, was almost enough to make him choke. He hoped that the hunter wouldn't notice the difference in the concocted drink. Jed closed the flask and set it casually behind him, out of sight. He made the coffee strong enough, he hoped. Jed offered up the cup with the pungent dose, hoping the hunter wouldn't pick up on his motive. To his surprise, the hunter took the cup without question.

He sauntered back to his spot and sat with a grunt; cigarette in one hand, coffee in another. Jed took his hot cup and blew on it, watching the hunter's every move. He was anxious to get going.

Abe brought the cup to his lips and sniffed the aroma of the coffee. Jed began to sweat. He looked up and watched Jed for a moment. Jed took a sip, and took a keen interest in stirring the coals again.

"Somethin's new about this..." The hunter mused. Jed looked and smiled his most innocent smile.

"It's a new kind of coffee. Bought it from a Chinaman back at the outpost." It sounded genuine, and Jed took another sip of his own.

Abe continued his analytical stare for a lingering moment before tasting. The taste must have enticed him.

"Never would have guessed." Abe drained his cup and came back for another cup. Jed refilled it. Abe drank again. Hours seemed to skip by as Jed refilled the hunter's cup several times. Each time, Abe seemed less cognizant. Each time, Jed's impatience grew.

Finally, his waiting paid off. Abe was slumped against his saddle, arms and legs askew, snoring as loud as Jed had ever heard him.

Jed stood, eager to see if it had actually worked. He circled the edge of the fire and crouched next to his blacked-out friend. He scratched his head, readjusted his hat, and waved a hand in front of Abe's face. The only reaction was a profound snore.

His lips pulled into a triumphant grin. He had outwitted El Diablo. He stood and quickly gathered up his saddle and tack. The Chinaman had been right about the "side effects". A grin crept onto his lips. He'd never forget Abe's tongue flapping so much and his red-cheeked boasts as he stumbled around the fire—almost dangerously so.

In the morning, when he returned, the hunter would wake up with little more than a pounding headache. He'd never know about Jed's midnight ride. Silently, he pulled himself into the saddle and took up the reins. His horse nickered softly, and, to Jed's flighty senses, Dusk trotted over snorting and pawing the ground aggressively. Jed swallowed hard and reined his mount, backing him several paces.

"I'll be back." He wasn't even sure why he bothered talking to a horse, but his whispered words seemed to have effect. The unnerved stallion nickered and tossed his head, before letting his ruby gaze rest on Jed's retreating figure. "I promise," he assured. Defeated, the stallion turned and trotted to his blacked-out master, in an effortless attempt to wake El Diablo.

Jed focused on the ride ahead. He would be back before sunrise. He needed answers. Time had already run too long. Jed had seen the supposed whereabouts of this El Cabrio from the wanted poster. The description was vague in its direction, but it was better than nothing at all. All it had said was 'toward the Northeast'.

Jed clucked as his steed's ears pricked in all directions. His nose flared, inhaling air in anticipation. Jed could feel the horse's excitement through the reins. The horse quivered from the urge to be let go, but he waited for Jed's command. Jed felt the building power beneath the leather, and it excited him too. Abe had picked this horse well for him—they were one and the same when they rode together. Jed had made him wait long enough and flicked the reins at the horse's sides. The horse sprang forward into a lope, his hooves tearing into the ground beneath them and leaving the small camp.

The hunt had begun.

## Chapter 25

The sky spread across the horizon in its familiar, inky hue with twinkling stars in the darkness. The raw power that held those ancient celestial bodies in place echoed through the pace of the night rider below.

The horse's hooves dug into the brittle face of the earth, leaving scars in its wake. Its breath was strong and deep with each surging stride, nose flared and body streamlined. Jed balanced himself atop the saddle, urging his powerful creature to keep its pace. The reins flicked to either side, reminded the horse that he was still in control.

The desert air felt chill against Jed's skin. The wind roared around him, accompanying the horses' breathing and stride. It had been hours since he left Abe behind. He knew the hunter would be pissed when he woke from his black-out slumber. Jed hoped that he could remain unconscious till he returned. Dawn was plenty long away.

The terrain sloped toward the heavens, and the horse grunted with effort as he slowed his pace to make up for the new difficulty. Jed pulled back on the reins with a gentle tug, urging his horse to slow with a firm, yet gentle, whoa. The horse tromped to a stop as he breached the crest of the hill. *That must be it.* He patted the steed's sweating neck as it tossed its head and stretched its neck to the earth—trying to catch its breath. The fortress lay sprawled out below the two, looking almost abandoned, save for the dim lanterns lit and the few patrol sentries along the top of the walls. The mud walls looked ancient to Jed, cracked and crumbling in some places. He heard faint sounds of horses, most likely within the main yard of the fortress. Jed watched the patrols for a moment, figuring the best way to enter the structure.

A confident thought culminated, *Looks easy enough.* Jed slid from the saddle, being careful not to stir up too much dust or make too much noise when his boots scraped on the hard pan and loose rock. He kept an eye on the sentries below, relieved that they hadn't noticed him—at least not yet. He grasped his father's rifle and checked it. He had cleaned it before this, but it never hurt to check. He was ready.

Jed looked around briefly to see what he could tether his horse to, and spotted a dead tree that was barely three feet high. He quietly led his horse to it, tying the reins around the dead trunk before patting his horse on the neck. *This shouldn't take long.* Jed began moving down the steep hill, placing his feet cautiously as he went. It was slow, but it was better than drawing unwanted attention. Jed's brow knitted with concentration as he skirted the hill, cringing at every small sound he made. He looked at the sentries often, acutely aware of their patterns and lazy patrol pace. When he finally reached the bottom of the hill, he breathed quietly to himself in relief; he had made it this far. He licked his lips nervously and scanned the wall he was headed for. The man up on the wall had passed already, and it left the wall exposed. His legs were cramping from the crouching position, his heart thundered in his chest, and sweat poured from his forehead and down his back. He took his moment, hurriedly moved to the wall, and sat against it—the coolness of the mud sinking into his skin.

No shouts. No footfalls. No signs of movement. He made it without being spotted. His lungs exhaled a breath of relief as he adjusted his grip on the rifle.

A door cracked open—a door he hadn't spotted before he made his rush to the wall. *Son of a bitch...* He stiffened and looked to his right, holding as still as he possibly could. If he was spotted now, it would be that much more difficult to get the information he needed. A man stumbled out with a belch, followed by a hiccup.

The man's feet nearly failed him as he steadied himself. Jed's shoulders relaxed slightly as he watched the disheveled man fumble with the front of his pants before relieving himself into the dirt with a groan of satisfaction. Jed didn't have time to think. He had to act before this man saw him and rose the alarm. He rose to his feet and silently walked up behind the man, making sure to place his steps carefully, like Abe had shown him months ago. The man grumbled something Jed couldn't catch as he began to fix his pants. Jed rammed the back of the man's skull with the butt of his rifle.

A muffled yelp sounded as the drunk crumpled into a sprawled heap in the dirt. Jed crouched over him, looking around quickly to make sure he had not been heard or seen. He held his breath for what seemed like hours as he listened closely for any sign of alarm. Jed's shoulders relaxed as pride began to bloom in his chest. He had been lucky so far, and it was paying off. Jed moved to the man's feet and grasped his boots firmly, dragging the man toward the dark part of the wall. He didn't want the unconscious body to found just yet. Jed straightened and gripped his rifle, alert to all the sounds and smells around him as he approached the open door. As he cautiously approached, the creaky hinges squealed in the slight breeze, making Jed cringe.

He raised the rifle slightly, to be ready, in case someone decided to come check on the drunk. He peered into the dark hallway leading into the fortress, feeling a nagging prick at the back of his mind. Something wasn't settling right. Jed frowned, shaking off the feeling from his gut as pure nonsense. He had been successful so far; there was no reason to think that the rest of this would not turn out just as well.

The cool of the dark weighed on Jed's clothes and seeped into his bones. His boots were almost silent on the rough mud floor as he crept deeper into the lair of outlaws. Jed's ears were highly alert as he picked out sounds, voices, and movements. He avoided open doorways as much as he could, and slipping past others cautiously.

It was no surprise that he was sweating as if it were the heat of the day. Jed had to find the man from the poster if he were to get any answers. He turned corner after corner, checking each time to see if there were any men on the other side.

The sounds of men burst through a door ahead of Jed as he rounded another corner, making the hairs on his neck stand on end as he quickly halted and pressed himself back around the corner. He gripped the stock of the rifle with white knuckles as he tried to calm his heartbeat. He swallowed, assured that they had not seen him. Slowly, Jed peered around the corner just enough to see three men adjusting their gear, britches, and hats. All were Mexican.

A short, squat man spoke nervously to the other two in a hushed tone, "Is the boss back?"

Another man, stocky and slightly taller than the rest of them, snorted and shook his hat out, dust floating off it with each brush. "Of course he's back. Cabrio always comes back."

Jed stiffened at the name. *He's here...somewhere in this rat hole.*

The third man grumbled and began walking down the hall away from Jed, a lanky, bony type of a man, "Keep your comments to yourself. I just wanna get paid." The other two men followed the lanky man. As the men disappeared, Jed quietly sighed with relief. He had to find this El Cabrio.

Voices drifted through the empty halls, catching his attention. He slowed his pace, concentrating on the voices and trying to pinpoint exactly where the voices were coming from. He crouched lower, to keep his boots from making any noise as he crept toward a light source. The glow from a lantern had pierced the cracked, open door, splashing the opposite wall with its orange hue. Jed stopped when he could hear the conversation begin to clear.

"Si, Cortez went outside for a piss. Who knows when he'll be back." Jed crept a few paces forward, keeping to the shadows of the dark hallway.

*I need to get to that door...see who I'm up against...*

"Well, then…" A chair creaked, and the second voice's movement echoed with oiled leather, the clacking of rested guns, and the jangling of coin. "Cortez won't mind if I look at his cards." The two men chuckled and snickered.

"Let's just play the damn game!" A third voice complained. "We can't wait on the bastard all night!"

Impatience bubbled in Jed's chest as he continued to wait. The hallway seemed to be crowding in on him as he dared to peek into the room. It was dark, save the lanterns along the walls and on a table. The table was unbalanced and surrounded by grungy, tired-looking men. They all wore hats of various sizes and shapes, and each of them had guns strapped to their hips, their chests, or in their bandoliers. The cards had been dealt and the center was littered with pesos and dollars; they were playing poker. The men played their rounds quickly, and the pot grew and shrank with the ebb and flow of the game. Jed sighed inwardly and began to move. He stopped as one of the men tossed money into the center with a yellowed grin, "Cabrio is back."

That name rooted Jed in place. He needed to hear this. A second voice, a short man with blotchy skin spoke up with a hiss, "*Si*, and what of it?"

The first man, the one who seemed to be the leader of the game, discarded a card and drew a fresh one, "He say we have important work ahead o' us."

Jed could feel the anticipation wind in the men as they continued their play. The third man in the room grunted and tossed in a small sum to the middle, "He alway does, *amigo*. Hopefully, with—eh—less…flesh involved."

A frown creased in Jed's forehead as he adjusted his grip on the rifle, keeping focus on the men talking. *Less flesh? The hell is goin' on here?*

The yellow-toothed man laughed, a phlegmy sounding wheeze, as he tossed in his raise. "There be always flesh wid Cabrio! It's de way of things."

"What kind of work, you t'ink?" The fourth man spoke up cautiously. Whoever this El Cabrio was, the men were extremely cautious of him.

A few Spanish words spewed as the game finished, the yellow-toothed man, scraped his winnings toward him. "There is dis, uh, kid he spoke of. Young, an' cunning. But he bein' helped by El Diablo, himself."

The table burst into a wave of laughter, not taking El Diablo in a serious manner. Jed could feel his muscles cramp in his crouched position; a signal that he had lingered to long. He inwardly sighed. They didn't say enough for him to need to hear the rest of their poker rounds, and he was impatient. Jed knew he was running out of time to find Marietta. He adjusted his weight and started to stand, making the tingling sensation bearable. *I need to move before I'm noticed...*

Jed had thought it too late.

Rough hands grabbled the back of his shirt and bandolier, his irritation overcome by panic. He had been found, and there was no going back. Without time to think, Jed clenched his teeth aggressively, slamming the butt of the rifle he was holding behind him. He heard a winded guff from the man who grappled him, as well as a Spanish curse word, the hands loosening their grip. Jed took the moment and turned to face his attacker, landing a blow to the man's jaw with a balled fist. The man cried out in surprise as Jed kept landing blows on him over and over. The man slumped against the wall with a final shout, unconscious from another rifle blow.

Shouts were everywhere, and more men poured out from side passages and down hallways. *Son of a bitch.* Jed growled and kept his ground in the shadowed hall, avoiding as many blows as he took. His rifle was ripped away and tossed aside as a squat Mexican head butted him, sending a splitting sear of pain across his cranium. He could feel the warmth of what he thought was blood as he tried to shake off the stars he saw in his vision.

Someone stronger than the rest grabbed him by the throat and roughly flung him into the room he was just eavesdropping into. His arms scraped on the packed dirt floor, his hat crumpling under his torso as his body slammed into the weak table legs. Shouts and cruel laughter echoed as the poker players gathered around Jed.

The yellow-toothed one adjusted his crotch before leaning down and grabbing Jed by the throat, lifting him up, as if he weighed nothing. The stars in Jed's vision began to clear, and the panic that he felt inside was turning into anger. He was angry at himself for being so careless. He was angry that he couldn't fight harder. Even more, he was angry that this Mexican had him in a chokehold.

Jed glared at the laughing Mexican as he struggled to breathe, his hands gripping the man's arm as tight as he could. "Well, look at dis. Is dat de kid Cabrio so worried 'bout?" Jed grunted, gasping for air. The hot stream of blood was streaming down his face and down his nose, clouding his sense of smell. The rest of the men surrounding them murmured and laughed amongst themselves. Jed could feel the air become thick with anticipation. "Don' see why..." the Mexican looked Jed up and down before sneering, "You jus' a fuckin' dumb kid." The man rammed a fist into Jed's side, stronger than Jed had anticipated.

A sick crack was heard and a splitting pain shot through his entire left side. He shouted in pain as the Mexican dropped him to the dirt floor. Jed tried to cradle his left side as he saw others move in, to satiate their bloodlust. He caught glimpses of their eyes, all burning with an eerie glint in the low lighting. *What have I done...?*

Jed heard the blow before it arrived. A boot with momentous force pummeled his gut, another his back. The blows kept coming from all directions as he tried to fend off the assault. It proved useless as he felt more and more of his body become battered, bruised, and broken. The pain was everywhere, and he swore he felt blood streaming in more than one place.

"Eh now, you tenderizing my meal." A deep, ominous voice washed over the crazed rabble of men, making them stop and move away from him. Jed coughed, tasting blood in his mouth as he did so. His whole body screamed in pain as he tried to push himself up to his feet, and failing to do so as he crumpled into the dirt. Jed's entirety shook with shock as the aching spots on him prevented him from getting get up. *I need to get out of here…!*

Boots were heard as the new man entered the dark parlor room. Jed spat out some blood from his mouth as he strained to look at the approaching man. His heart thundered in his chest when he saw the dim outline of the man. He was large, easily twice the size as the other men he had defeated. He was thick with muscle, towering over him like a mountain over a boulder. The smell of the man, however, was almost too much. He stank of rotten meat, blood, and sweat. Jed coughed and gagged on the air as he tried to get up again.

There was no need.

A meaty hand reached down, grabbing Jed by the neck in a tighter grip than the other Mexican. He was lifted completely off the ground until his feet dangled uselessly beneath him. Jed's voice was muffled due to the lack of air as he tried to endure his body's pain. He could feel that some of his ribs were, indeed, broken, along with his collarbone, ribs, and jaw. He had never felt that much pain before. The pain didn't matter as he locked eyes with the man. Jed was staring into the face of a madman. *El Cabrio!* Jed grabbed his arm in a vain attempt to loosen the grip. El Cabrio laughed, revealing pointed teeth, stained pink from whatever he had eaten last. His thick jaw was peppered with dark facial hair, contorted by various old scars, making his grin look more sadistic in the low lighting.

"There you are…We been lookin' for you, amigo." El Cabrio's breath was a buffet of foul air, making Jed gag and cough. It took everything in him to stay conscious as the man continued to talk, "You been a troublesome boy for some time now." El Cabrio turned Jed's head slightly to the side, as if examining a cut of meat. His tongue flicked over the sharp teeth with a hunger in his burning ember eyes. "You look jus' like your padre."

Jed couldn't take it anymore. He needed answers. "Where…is…she?!" He choked out. The gravity on his body was causing his wounds to pulse with more and more pain. He could feel the blood drip from his various cuts, scrapes, and wounds as El Cabrio laughed—a sound that was raspy, yet booming, all at once. "Your hermana is safe, amigo. For now."

*For now?! What the hell does that mean?* Jed struggled against the grip of the man, only to stop quickly as the grip tightened. He was choking, and he was too weak to fight back. Darkness began to creep into Jed's vision as El Cabrio dropped Jed back to the ground. His legs couldn't support him, letting him crumple back to the dirt in a cry of pain. He felt hands grab his arms and pull him back up to his feet. Jed looked up at El Cabrio just in time to see his meaty fist hurl his way. With more splitting pain and a thin, cracking sound, Jed's jaw was on fire, and his conscious mind couldn't handle it any longer. Jed was sent spiraling into unconsciousness.

*\*\*\**

Sounds murmured around him, his unconscious mind crawling from the void. Pain numbly crept through his veins and across his skin. The dull throb made his spine shudder as he tried to get his bearings. He was sitting; that much was apparent. Wood held his body in a stiff position with the unloving embrace of rough cord around his aching chest and pinched wrists. The cord was tightly binding his legs to the chair. His mind was awakening and, with it, the agony grew.

A groan slipped from his bloodied lips, nearly crippling him as sharp pain racked his chest and abdomen. The muffled sounds became clearer as his eyes cracked open, showing only hazy details. Jed felt his chin on his chest. It was too hard to move, so he just laid there.

Orbs of glowing light swayed ominously around him, casting shadows against the confines of the room. Men were starting to gather and their voices could clearly be heard.

"…Did you tell him?" A smoky voice murmured.

"Of course I did! Shit, you t'ink I'm stupid?" A pause ensued.

"Sometimes, I wonder."

"Why, you son of a bitch!" Scuffles were heard as the offended voice made a move to defend himself.

A door slammed open, stopping the scuffle. The room was instantly silenced. Dread filled his aching chest. Each breath he drew felt like a thousand knives were being driven through him. He squeezed his eyes shut, praying that the pain would subside.

"Well…" A smugness could be heard through the hissed word, "Lil' McKay's boy…in de flesh." Jed set his jaw and filled his lungs with air. He would meet what was to come with dignity. He would be a man. He recognized that voice as El Cabrio. A twinge of fear began to build in his gut.

He lifted his head with struggle. Jed wanted to see this bastard in better light. He saw the man's large, mud-caked boots. His pants were of some dark cloth, speckled with the mud from his boots. A thick belt pressed under the large fold that was the man's stomach. The shirt looked like it had once been ivory, but was now stained with sweat, dirt, and countless meals.

Jed's eyes widened with growing unease. The man's eyes burned with the hunger of a predator—he'd seen that look before. El Cabrio's wide jowl creased the rolls of his neck and face with a dark grin, the disfigured scars crinkling his tan skin. A damp, partially chewed cigar was clamped in between cat-like teeth. His eyes were burning like embers of hell, searing Jed's soul as he stared at him. His pupils were narrowed like a cat: thin, ominous, and unpredictable.

Jed's shallow breathing intensified his anguish. His wrists felt slick and warm, and they burned as he squirmed against the cords that held them. The shadowed men closed in like starving winter wolves, their snickers and cackles ringing in Jed's ears. The alpha of this mangy pack, El Cabrio, tugged his trousers up and stepped towards him.

"Eberhart said you would look li' him…" The earth seemed to tremble from the man's heavy stride, his ominous composure towering over Jed. His large hunting knife dangled in its sheathe at the man's side as he began to slowly circle him. Jed felt helpless as he heard the heavy man casually stride around him. "De Marshall's boy…"

*What have I done?* Jed thought in a rising panic. The large man stopped. Jed ceased to struggle against his restraints—there was no way out. He was trapped. Slowly, El Cabrio crouched to Jed's eye level. The smell of his breath was rancid, like one of Pa's cattle that had been dead for days under the sun; nearly enough for Jed's consciousness to leave him. Jed gagged and coughed, turning his head away from the beastly man.

"Why don' you look at me Amigo…" Sweaty, meaty fingers gripped his jaw and chin, forcing Jed to look at his bloodlust-filled eyes. Bone scraped against bone, a shooting pain that he hadn't expected. Jed yelled involuntarily, remembering briefly that El Cabrio had landed a blow on his jaw that must have broken the bones. The burning pain seeped through his veins, spreading like fire. His breathing was ragged and inconsistent as he tried to bear the pain. Stars clouded his vision as the pulsing agony ran rampant all over him. There was nothing Jed could do.

A yellow-toothed smirk spread across El Cabrio's face. "That's better…guess de Marshall never taught you manners." The man's voice was thick with an unnatural hunger as he licked his lips, saliva stringing onto his teeth as he did so. Jed's stomach turned inside out. He had to look El Cabrio in the eye. His father was known, even among men like this? El Cabrio's meaty grip released his chin and jaw, leaving Jed seeing stars.

"You know who I am, amigo?"

Jed tried to open his jaw to speak, but the bones and sinew ground against each other, screaming for mercy. He shut his eyes and shook his head, the motion intensifying the already excruciating pain in his head.

The man huffed as he stood disappointed in Jed's silent answer. *Be a man*, Jed's mind whimpered over and over.

"Mos' jus' call me El Cabrio." The name spread murmurs and chuckles once again from the men in the room, watching the large man circle his prey. "Marks told me all about you, *Jedidiah*." His tongue was thick with amusement as he lumbered around him. Jed's body pulsed with intensifying agony. "He say you were a threat..." El Cabrio said smoothly, pausing behind him, his large meaty hands slamming down on Jed's defeated shoulders. A sickening pop and grind resonated in the room, overlaid by Jed's blood curdling scream of agonizing submission. His collarbone was a rod of blinding pain.

El Cabrio took pleasure in Jed's agony for a moment, letting the scream soak into the walls around them. "He say you were jus' like 'im—an' I need to burn loose ends." Jed's brow felt cool with fresh sweat. "But I have a special method for you, lil' McKay..." El Cabrio's breath whispered into Jed's ear, making him gag violently. He returned to the other ear, "An' I guarantee dat you will be beggin' for death before I'm through..."

## Chapter 26

Light crested the flattened desert pan, bathing the red landscape in its embrace. Gentle warmth began to burn as the sun rose higher in the blue tapestry above. Dusk snorted at the dirt in boredom, still waiting for his master to wake from his drugged state. He'd been out cold since the night before, not stirring from his fixed position. Dusk breathed a drawn-out sigh and walked to his master—maybe he would wake this time.

He loomed over his master, whose dark hat still covered his eyes. Dusk's pitch-black nose sniffed Abe's duster, blowing at his hat. He knew Abe hated his hat being messed with. He nickered softly and lipped the brim until his velvet lips grasped the hat and tugged at it.

A tired grunt came from Abe, followed by movement from his neck and head as he attempted to move his face away. Dusk persisted.

"Mmn…Jys…not now…" Abe's lips murmured as Dusk pulled the hat completely off and tossed his head impatiently, smacking the hunter in the face with it.

With groggy reflexes, Abe reached for his hat, a frown plastered on his brow. His consciousness came flooding back, and an intense headache followed suit. With a snarl, Abe forced himself up off the ground as Dusk trotted away from him with a snort. Abe stumbled and tripped to his feet, the wave of primal pounding in his head was usually nothing to him—he liked whiskey, after all. But this…this was more than he was used to.

*Jed…* the name drifted bitterly into his throbbing conscious. *He must have done something.* He knew that damned coffee seemed off. He set his jaw and forced his legs to move. Dusk remained fixated, still holding that time-worn hat. Abe's eyes narrowed at the steed as he snatched the hat with a grumble, "Give me that." He dusted it off roughly against his already dirtied pants, adjusting the hat onto its natural resting place. His world was back in order. Able to stop squinting, Abe scanned the site for Jed.

His gut filled with icy dread. The boy was not in sight.

As Abe stalked over to his resting spot from the previous night and grabbed the saddle roughly off the ground, his dread was replaced with anger. An irritated growl peeled through his dry lips as he briskly stalked over to Dusk. Abe shot a warning glare at the beast, subtly warning him not to move a muscle. The beast sighed and remained in his spot as Abe slammed the leather seat onto Dusk's back. Dusk grunted in protest and turned his head to stare at his master with loathing red eyes.

He knew who the boy was after.

Abe paused as the reality of the situation dawned on him: Jed had left against Abe's instructions—the deal was broken. Why should he care what happened to the boy? If he was stupid enough to charge into the den of El Cabrio, he deserved to die.

The icy dread retuned, slowly at first. It grew deep in Abe's gut with each tightening of the girth and straps. Abe's hands slowed, and he caught himself staring into the distance. The den of flesh-eating was miles away. There was little, if any, chance that Jed had survived the night. He was just a kid.

*Protect my son...find my daughter...please...* The choked words echoed through his body, his steely resolve becoming shaken. Abe growled and gripped the saddle horn, planting his left foot into the stirrup. With ease, he swung up into the seat and reached for the reins. The black leather straps slipped into Abe's hands with familiarity. He adjusted his posture in the saddle as Dusk disinterestedly chewed at his bit.

Abe couldn't believe what he was about to do. Dusk fidgeted and pawed, eager to run. Abe jabbed his spurs into Dusk's sides, urging his steed to burst forward.

Knowing Dusk could handle it, Abe slammed his spurs into the beast until he was huffing with air in each stride. Abe gritted his teeth, his eyes narrowing as a burn began deep within his chest. He needed to be faster if he had any chance of reaching Jed while he was still alive. *If he's still alive, that is. Damn you, boy.* He let the sensation grow, allowing it to become a wildfire. Dusk hellishly screamed as his hooves began to bake in the embers, then flames began a slow crawl up his legs and fetlocks. He charged faster, surging with more power as Abe fueled them both with hellish energy.

He could feel the beast's body change beneath him as the fire began to spread more rapidly over the beast. Ligaments, bones, and muscles were more prominent, the dark ebony of his hair still an ominous shade; a contrast to the flames that now made up his skeletal frame, mane, tail, and hooves. His bloody eyes glowed brilliantly in his skeletal face, as though the pits of hell, itself, were dwelling in them.

Absalom felt the flames reach up toward him, which he welcomed. His gloved hands were aflame, as were his shoulders, boots, and legs. His inner being screamed with delight. He let it.

There was hell to pay. Whether it be done to Jed or to El Cabrio, it would be paid with blood and fury.

This was Absalom.

This was El Diablo.

*\*\*\**

He didn't know what day it was—or if it he would ever know at all. Hours seemed like an eternity. His body was writhing in agony after El Cabrio had tortured him through what he thought had been the entire night. He had been beaten brutally, stabbed, spat on, shouted at, and he could have sworn someone had pissed on him. It didn't matter now. Breathing felt like razor blades tearing through his chest and throat, his face ached unmercifully, and his bones felt shattered.

*Let me die...please.* He leaned his head back toward the clay ceiling, praying for his end from God. Laughter echoed abruptly in the room, as his head was shoved forward by a meaty hand until his chin smacked onto his chest with a whimper.

"You haven't said much, lil' McKay…" The man's voice was booming to Jed's ears, making him cringe. The continuous torture began to wear on Jed's will. "You better say somethin', you lil' shit, or I'll cut your tongue out."

Jed felt his anger rise again—he wouldn't give up. Not yet. Straining, Jed lifted his gaze to El Cabrio's. "Where…is…she…" It took every ounce of energy to speak through his broken jaw.

The cruel laughter shattered the air around him, mocking him, only quieting when El Cabrio answered, "She? She who?" He sneered. As he leaned in close, Jed couldn't smell the man's putridness anymore—not with the stench of his own blood in his nostrils. "If you mean dat scrawny bitch of a girl that Marks has, den yeah—I know where she is."

Jed pulled at his restraints again, his muscles and bones screaming.

Cabrio peeled his lips back, revealing the stained dark yellow fangs again, "She's gon' be keeled boy…for what she is…"

Jed felt his pent-up fury writhe inside him, but his body was too weak to unleash it. His life was draining from him, and he knew it. His brown eyes widened in horror at the man's words: killed? Why? She was just a girl.

"I hope Marks lets me have de first bite." Crazed laughter spewed from his cracked lips as he reached down to his belt and wrenched something from it.

The glinting teeth of a hunting knife smiled at Jed as his eyes focused on the blade. Cabrio showed amusement as he slowly twisted it in his hand, his predator-like eyes watching it. "I told you, boy, dat I would keel you. I've put dis off long enough, an' I missed my midnigh' meal 'cause of you."

Jed made himself look at the monster in front of him: he was going to die. His eyes stung as the hot liquid pooled in them. He had failed Marietta. He had failed his father.

He had failed Absalom.

El Cabrio cackled his crazed satisfaction as Jed felt hot tears burn down his cheeks. It seared paths through the grime and the blood and the dust that was caked onto his skin. If only he hadn't been foolish. Abe was right: he wasn't prepared for this den of wild dogs. He never was.

His neck muscles quivered with exhaustion as they slacked and let his head drop to his chest once more. Jed felt he was finally broken and felt nothing but agony and despair.

"Naw, boy, dat won' do." El Cabrio's voice was raw with subtle violence as his hand seized Jed's shattered jaw. "You are gon' look at me while I eat your flesh."

El Cabrio's knife dug into his flesh, the sound of tearing and rending filling the room. The sawing motion of the blade made each movement excruciatingly painful. On and on, Cabrio kept cutting, the only sound louder than the sound of cutting flesh was Jed's outburst of fresh agony. The heavy metallic smell of blood drenched his senses.

The bite of the blade was slow and jagged, taking its time to taste Jed's cheek. The metal scraped bone in one final motion before finally tearing the elongated chunk from his face. His neck was drenched in sweat and blood now. He felt it soak into his dirtied shirt and stick to his skin underneath. Jed's head spun with dizzying adrenaline. Fear ran rampant through his body.

"Dat color suits you, boy!" The man's laughter boomed over Jed's hoarse scream. Jed kept his eyes closed. He didn't want to see how much the crazed man had cut off. The thick meaty hand wrapped around Jed's throat in an iron grip, crushing his wind pipe. His eyes snapped open as he gasped for air, his facial pain forgotten for a moment. El Cabrio dangled the piece of raw flesh from the tip of the blade, the coagulating blood dripping to the dirt floor below. Jed's fresh wound throbbed with each pulse of his heart. His eyes widened in horror when Cabrio opened his mouth and lifted the piece of meat. Cabrio fondled the flesh with his tongue before he bit into it with a sickening squelch. His fanged teeth easily slicing into the meat.

Jed's stomach turned upside down as he watched Cabrio enjoy his sick torture. The room was in utter silence as the munching echoed throughout. Darkness swelling over Jed's conscious mind, his limbs felt numb and tingly.

*Marietta...* Jed's thoughts drifted to her memory, clinging to the last of his sanity—his strength.

The man's lips dribbled with blood— Jed's blood. The blade glinted red in the grim light as Cabrio leaned in for another cutlet, his teeth glinting red as he grinned greedily.

Short claps of faraway thunder resonated in the outside air. Cabrio paused and glanced back at the door. "Now what?" he growled irritably, straightening up and turning to face the door. Jed prayed desperately that those were the sounds of death; death approaching him quickly.

\*\*\*

The burning steed cleared the hill in a powerful surge, vaulting horse and rider towards the fortress that he knew lay before them. The sulfuric flames of hell engulfed them both. The horse's hooves left smoldering prints in the dust, scorching the rocks and sage. The hunter gritted his fanged teeth in furious determination as the hills finally revealed the fortress that he had tried to avoid. He saw Jed's horse tethered to a dead tree, its head low to the ground, asleep in the heat of the day. *Ah, hell...*

That boy was going to pay with his blood. If he hadn't already done so.

Abe pulled back on the reins, making Dusk scream and slide, the momentum continuing. The hell steed hadn't stopped completely, and Abe dismounted at a full run towards the thick, wooden gate. The flames diminished at Abe's will. Dusk spun and pranced in a screeching fury, sending heated dust clouds spiraling at his hooves. Abe could feel his inner being cry to remain his source of power. Abe ignored it. His hat was low over his eyes, and his black duster coat whipped from his sides and torso, revealing his black bandolier, leather chaps and pants covered in dust.

Abe drew both revolvers, faster than any human could follow. Men rushed along the wall in a skittered panic. They knew who was coming to their doorstep. *Good*, Abe thought bitterly.

The sentry above shouted in pain as Abe fired the first shot, dropping the man. Another dropped shortly after as Abe stormed up to the rustic wooden gates. Snarling, Abe lashed out with a strong kick. The thick gates dented and splintered with a deep boom. Bullets peppered the dust all around Abe. With an animalistic fury, he struck again.

Jed needed him. He could feel it.

The gates creaked and groaned at the second blow, and bullets screamed past him, nicking his coat, hat, and body. The internal rage burned inside him as he struck a third time. The gates blew open in a sea of swirling dust. Men yelled in Spanish, fear thick on their tongues. Abe let his guns blaze with anger, the blows striking each man he saw in vital points. The men scattered for cover, and some began to retreat to their sanctuary of blood and flesh. Abe was not finished with them. Not yet.

His long legs strode with brisk purpose toward the main door across the courtyard of dust and death. Screams of the dying shadowed the guns' roar as Abe crossed through.

The door to the main building crumpled under Abe's blow, his guns mercilessly killing his opponents. Abe heard a man wildly charging toward him in a series of shouts; battle cries, he assumed. It was a foolish mistake. Without turning to the man, he swiftly aimed at the man and pulled the trigger. The sound of the bullet piercing his skull and slicing through his brain and back out, hitting the wall, satisfied a small, twisted hunger in his gut. The man twitched, leaving a red trail on the clay. The labyrinth was dark, full of shouts of men scurrying to action. Abe's jaw clenched tight as he followed the scent of the boy. The entire complex was rife with the boy's blood.

The smell of fresh blood flooded his nostrils, raising the hackles of his neck and intensifying the apprehension in his guts. *No...* "Damn you, boy." Abe muttered worriedly to himself. The halls twisted as Abe briskly walked them, obliterating any obstacle that got in his path. He would find Jed. Dead or alive.

His stride became a sprint as he headed to the last door, a sickly smell growing stronger and stronger. With a burst, he rammed his shoulder into the door, bowing its back and bursting it open. His feet stumbled for a moment as he regained his balance, his pistols raised and ready. The room was dim. Sensing no immediate danger, he shoved his smoking pistols back into their exotic leather holsters and glared at the room's centerpiece.

The writhing anger and irritation that was dwelling in his soul dispersed. The sight he took in with his bloodshot eyes turned his stomach.

Jed sat lopsided and slouched in a short, roughhewn, wooden chair. His hands were tied behind his back, his shoulders protruding awkwardly. Dark stains drenched the front of his tan shirt and disheveled brown vest. His chest rose and fell in sporadic patterns—the boy was in agony.

He quickly strode to the boy, looking at the various wounds and abuse he must have suffered through the night. Any longer, and he might not have been alive. The whimpered breathing was shallow, almost nonexistent, as Abe drew closer. The smell of blood was so strong his inner self cried to be let out more so than ever, thrashing against the mental confines that Abe had carefully constructed over the years. Abe's heart weighed with despair, regret, and sympathy. These emotions were foreign to him, just as he felt when he first set foot onto this plane, into this life.

"Damn it, kid." He knelt, inspecting the grievous gash in the boy's cheek. His anger flared at the thought of the bastard who had done this.

"You...came...for me...?" The boy weakly gazed at Abe, his eyes hazy. Abe watched Jed under the brim of his hat, a grip of fear tightening his gut. He watched tears stream down the boy's cheeks and through the canyon in his cheek, dripping onto the dirt floor in a bloody puddle. Jed lethargically coughed and groaned.

"Of course I did, Jed..." Abe gently spoke. The boy's breathing was chopped as Abe set a gentle hand on the boy's shoulder, attempting to comfort him. The scream startled Abe as he quickly removed his hand and looked: the collarbone had broken through Jed's skin and flesh.

"I thought I heard de pig squeal..." Abe glared over his shoulder, towards the ominous voice. He knew who it belonged to. "But I didn't expect to find de hound." El Cabrio's smile revealed his pointed teeth, stained pink with a fresh meal. Abe knew where it came from. In silence, Abe rose to his feet, his inner being gathering its strength, waiting to be let out. He kept it contained—for now.

"Didn't tink you 'ad an ounce of carin' in ya, Diablo." El Cabrio stroked his glistening teeth with his tongue. His slit eyes gazed over Jed's suffering body before looking back at Abe. "De Marshall's boy...Jed, was it?"

Abe cursed himself inwardly. El Cabrio had seen his weakness. Abe's hands hung at rest at his sides, but close to his otherworldly weapons. He was ready. This devil would pay with his blood.

"His name is Jedidiah McKay." Abe's voice hissed with fury as he burned a glare into the monster in front of him.

El Cabrio tugged up his dirty trousers more snuggly under his hanging gut, stepping towards Abe. Abe drew his weapons, ready to pull the trigger at any second. The devil in front of him cackled madly. He was testing his distance; testing his patience. Abe knew this. And his patience was wearing thin.

"*Si, si*…McKay." El Cabrio pondered with his sausage-like finger pressed to his sweating chin. "The bane of Mark's existence…I can see why he would want dis piglet slaughtered." His laughter was cruel, rebounding off the crumbling surface of the walls surrounding them. "He was quite tasty, I give you that. I guess I should thank you for the morsel." Cabrio stopped and turned back to Abe, pulling out something from inside his dirty shirt. The hairs on Abe's neck began to hackle at the familiar call of the obsidian coin. Cabrio grinned avidly. His meaty fingers played over the surface of it as he turned it over and over, the ruby eyes glinting in the dim light. The sight of the cursed stone coin called to Abe's darkest corner of his being. The beast inside of him writhed to its whispers, a whisper that reminded him of a harlot's beckon. Abe hadn't moved his weapon from his target.

"You know what they say back home, Absalom?" El Cabrio took another step. Abe cocked the hammer back.

"Waste not, want not," Abe murmured, baring his teeth. His calloused fingers tugged the trigger, his inner being begging for more bloodshed. He was more than happy to appease the beast within. He pulled the trigger back, releasing a fresh wave of bullets, eager to slake his lust for death. El Cabrio roared as he moved out of the way of the bullet.

Abe moved quickly in front of Jed, setting his jaw square. A sick thought drifted through his mind, a wicked grin creeping across his features. He would take pleasure in ripping this devil apart and smearing his insides across the walls. His nature thrashed viciously within as El Cabrio narrowly escaped the rounds Abe was firing. Cabrio's clothes began to tatter and splay from the bullets. Red filtered through the already stained cloth.

Cabrio's veins bulged with rage on his neck, face, and arms. Abe smirked. This is what he was waiting for.

Abe paused his firing as a new sound tore through the stagnant dusty air. It was the tearing of flesh and sinew, skin stretching and morphing, bones cracking and splitting to form an entirely new horror. Abe remained rooted to his position. His thirst for blood grew stronger. His nature screamed to be let out, but Cabrio wouldn't be worth his effort.

With a hideous roar and screech, El Cabrio's body violently contorted to his new, disfigured form. His skull had twisted into the shape of a bestial creature, with uneven fangs protruding from his stretched darkened lips. The drool ran down the snagged fangs, his snout glistening with moisture. His forehead harbored two heavy horns, but they were not of equal size nor shape. They were contorted in awkward curves and were colored in hues of ivory, ebony, and rusted copper. His body grew into a larger, heavier beast, with bipedal legs. Matted hair grew in rough patches all over what was once slickened, sweaty skin. The eyes never changed, as Abe had expected. The slit, bloodshot eyes still held the crazed hunger of a half-breed.

"Still can't hold your form, half-blood?" Abe taunted venomously, watching the devilish, goat-like bastard spawn snarl and snort and breathe heavier than before. The devil in front of him held his crazed eyes to Abe's as his clawed hands clenched and unclenched. Abe knew he wouldn't be able to move as agilely in this form. He would be clumsy, short-tempered, and rash.

El Cabrio spoke in a deep, layered tone, seeming to shake the beams above and the walls around them, "I am *stronger* than any of your kind, Absalom!" His drooling mouth slobbered spittle around him, his arms swung as though numb. His wounds and scratches had healed completely. "Everyone in this world—and the one below—will see!"

Abe raised his gun again, the barrel still trailing hot smoke into the polluted air, "I doubt it."

El Cabrio leapt violently at Abe in a screeching frenzy of bloodthirst and claws. Abe let a smirk creep onto his lips as he let his metal companion roar in response. Bullets sprayed the half-blood's body. Abe could hear the bullets singe flesh and rip through his skin, deep into his torso and limbs. The half-blood screeched in pain. Abe visage was collected, yet fierce, as the creature rebounded and roared its fury. As the enraged beast charged him, Abe twisted out of the way, a near miss as the creature rammed into the wall, his horns piercing deep into the plaster and mud, covering the room in dust.

Abe took the moment to maneuver the fight as far away from Jed as possible. He could not lose the boy, whatever the cost may be. He backed toward the door as Cabrio clawed at the wall in desperation to get free from his self-made prison.

Finally, with a final burst of rage, Cabrio pulled his horns loose, taking a chunk of the wall with him. Dust swirled around him, billowing into the room like a fog.

Abe waited.

El Cabrio rounded his body to face the doorway head on, his glistening snout covered with plaster dust. Abe knew he could smell him over the dust and the blood. Without warning, the devil lunged again with inhuman speed. Abe remained still, waiting for the right moment to act. The charging beast focused his energy into running the hunter down. *Patience is a virtue...*

El Cabrio propelled his body through the door, through the billows of dust.

Abe made eye contact.

The rancid breath from the creature wafted to Abe's nostrils as the creature came near. Abe didn't flinch. He pulled the trigger, knowing he had been patient just enough to get the shot he needed. He heard the bullet meet its mark, and he saw the creature's pained, disbelieving eyes. Abe agilely twisted his body down and out of the way.

With a wheezing howl, El Cabrio landed and tumbled in a twisting heap along the earthen hallway floor. His blackened blood sprayed the walls and coated the floor in streaks.

El Cabrio writhed and squirmed, his claws digging at the hole that was squared in his chest. The spawn would die slowly. His oversized heart would quiver for the next hour. Abe had seen it many times. This time, though, he would enjoy not allowing this thing that mercy.

Abe rolled the panicked monster onto his back with a rough kick. He wanted the creature to see his end, and make him taste his own fear of a painful death.

Abe curled his lips into a snarl as he placed his boot over the wound and pressed down sharply. He reached down and grabbed his limbs in the process. The sound of crunching bone snapped through the air as his boot crushed his ribcage. With force, he pulled the creature's limbs out of place, rendering them useless. Abe wickedly grinned with dark pleasure as he released his grip from the limbs and kneeled over the howling creature. His eyes glinted with twisted euphoria. When the noise subsided, when nothing was left but the sound of wheezing breath and the silence from the fort. Abe spoke sinisterly, "Now, I believe we had some unfinished business, you and I."

El Cabrio stared at Abe in wide-eyed dismay. He squirmed in pain, screeching again as Abe applied more pressure. Abe could feel the bastard's heart convulsing under his boot.

"Marietta McKay…where is she?" Abe kept his tone cool as he watched the creature below him squirm with uncertainty.

"…Marks…" He wheezed.

Abe looked at his pistol. "Well, no shit." Abe removed his boot suddenly and jammed the mouth of his gun into El Cabrio's already festering chest wound. Abe's temper was rising. He wanted an answer. The creature let out a long, high-pitched screech that would have surely broken glass if there had been any present.

Abe gripped one of the mutated horns with his free hand and made the monster look him in the eye, "Where. Is. She?" He growled low in his throat. He deliberately slowed his words, to ensure, the creature had understood him completely.

The monster shuddered, letting out what sounded like a sob.

"She was with Marks, last I heard! I swear it! H-he mentioned that he had taken back what was his." Abe paused as he heard his natural tongue shouted at him through blackened teeth and lips. He contemplated what El Cabrio had just said. It didn't make sense.

"What was his?" Abe kept the gun in the wound, to remind the defeated goat who reigned supreme. El Cabrio nodded vigorously and whimpered again as the flesh surrounding the gun wriggled into a better resting position.

The creature nodded. "The girl..." His voice was almost a whisper, almost a fearful murmur of uncertainty. Abe felt the hairs on the back of his neck raise. This was more than just a revenge blow against the dead and gone Marshall.

Abe focused again, letting the new light of the reality soak in. "Where is the girl?" Abe cocked the pistol. His patience had run dry.

"...West...he was headin' west..." El Cabrio's chest was rising and falling in pained breaths, black blood continuously swelling up his throat and spilling through his teeth.

"...Bodie..." Abe muttered the name in fleeting thought. Bodie was a long way from here.

"*Si, si,* Bodie..." El Cabrio stammered. Abe focused again, his inner being gnawing at him for blood, to inflict pain. That's all his kind craved, after all. He would inflict that—and much more—on this pitiful creature.

Abe slowly removed the pistol barrel from the wound, shaking the strings of coagulating blood from the mouth. The creature uttered a sigh of relief amidst the cracking of rib bones. Abe never steered his steely gaze from the creature's fearful one. Abe holstered his pistol and let his prey relax under him.

*Good.*

Abe struck his right hand into the gaping hole. His nails and fingers wormed their way through skin and flesh, sifting through the cracked and misshapen bones. The abomination's agonized screech rang clear.

"This is for Jedidiah, you son of a bitch," Abe whispered vengefully. He could feel the blood seeping over his skin, the flesh squirming around his hand. The pulsing, quivering mass brushed against his fingers. A crazed smile spread on his lips. His inner being squealed with delight as he grabbed that rotten heart and tantalizingly pulled it free from El Cabrio's chest. The pulsing, black mass quaked and quivered still in his grip as Cabrio's agonized screeching ceased, only to be replaced with silence.

The hunter placed the heart to his lips and drove his teeth into its meaty succulence. Abe's eyes glowed as he watched El Cabrio's reaction with absolute euphoria: his eyes and face showed the pleasure. Abe savored the rancid taste for a short moment before swallowing the hunk and running his tongue over his own lips in ecstasy.

"You lost somethin'." Abe squeezed the heart into pulp and tossed the ruined organ to the side with a sickening splat. El Cabrio wheezed his last in defeat, the large mass quivering into the embrace of death.

But Absalom was not satisfied. El Diablo's hungry eyes gleamed as he drew his gaze to Jed's direction, the coin in his breast pocket burning.

Silence rang clear through the stronghold. Abe's mind clouded with the adrenaline Cabrio had supplied. Abe groused inwardly, forcing himself to focus. He looked at his stained hand, blackened and sticky from the blood. He frowned as his senses returned and wiped as much as he could onto his duster jacket. He would clean up later. There was something else that was more important than bloodlust.

He pushed all thoughts aside and focused back on the room of flesh-eating, where he hoped Jed was still breathing. Heart-wrenching worry gripped him as he rushed back to the room where the carnage had all started. The boy was right where Abe had left him, tied to the chair and barely breathing.

Abe went back to Jed's side and knelt, this time with a quickened purpose. He pulled his knife from his belt and deftly began cutting away the boy's bonds. The flesh beneath was raw, caked with blood, old and new. He was thankful that the smell of Jed's blood sickened him.

"I told you not to come here, boy..." His voice surprised himself. It was calm and quiet, almost comforting. The ropes snapped and fell limply away to the dirt-packed earth beneath the two of them. The rank smell of blood was still thick in the air as Jed's stiff body began to slide off the chair. Abe immediately caught him as gently as possible. To his dismay, Jed cried out again, weaker this time, but the pain certainly had not lessened. Abe let the boy breathe for a moment before he tenderly picked Jed up into his arms. The crackling of bone and tearing of tissue grated his senses.

The boy was dying.

Quickly, Abe adjusted the boy in his arms to a cradled position. Jed coughed, letting blood trickle over his lips and out of the corner of his mouth. Time was running out. Abe made his way back to the entrance of the compound, where Dusk was waiting for him. The hellish steed's ears pricked, and he raised his head high. Jed's breath was worsening. Abe gritted his teeth. *Damn it all, boy.*

Without hesitation, he lifted the boy up into the saddle, following close behind him. He didn't have much time left. He held the boy close to his torso with his arm, taking the reins into his other hand. With a rough heel, he urged the hellish steed to surge forward, steering him back toward the town. The boy was weak in his arms as he slapped the reins against Dusk's sides, the beast breathing heavily with each powerful stride.

He could feel the life ebbing away from Jed, but he didn't dare push Dusk to go any faster than he already was. It was too risky. The smell of fresh blood and the sound of wounds tearing back open sounded loud in Abe's ears as he adjusted his arm. The terrain was rugged on the boy's body, the galloping strides of his horse jostling him more than it should have. Abe knew that the town was too far, but he didn't have much choice. He needed to try to save Jed.

*Damn it, Jed. I told you not to go there,* he thought angrily. The realization that he had grown attached to this boy dawned on him as he raced through the rugged wilderness in search of a doctor. It had been months since the ranch had burned down, forcing him to help this boy and find his sister. He had grown from resenting the boy to being fond of him. *Just like David was to me.* A frown etched onto his forehead as he glanced at the paling Jed. *I fuckin' hate it when you're right, old man.*

With a shallow hitch, Jed's breathing slowed and stopped for a moment. The sound startled Abe back to the present, and he heard the boy's heart clearly. It was slow and sporadic in its rhythm. He was losing him. Fast. Without a second thought, Abe pulled Dusk to a sliding stop, Jed sinking dead-weight in his arms. His heartbeat was nearly gone.

"Goddammit, boy, no!" Abe snarled as he nearly leapt out of the saddle, dragging Jed off with him. He laid him in the hard pan and dried sage, seeing the pallid color in the boy's face. Blood was everywhere, and there was nothing he could do.

Except for one thing.

Abe hesitated for a moment at the idea that bloomed in his mind. It was unusual for a devil to give his blood freely, especially to a human. *I have no time.* Abe pulled his duster sleeve back from his wrist and drove his teeth through the flesh, into the veins just beneath the skin's surface. He tasted his soured blood flood his mouth, making him gag. After a few draws to get the blood flowing, Abe moved his open wound quickly over Jed's slightly parted lips. His blood dripped over Jed's clothes, mingling with the boy's, until the stream trickled into his mouth. He let the stream pulse into his mouth, hoping that it would give him the chance to survive. At first, the boy didn't move. His breath was almost completely stopped, and his heart was near-silent.

Abe felt fear grip his heart as he watched with impatience. The fear of losing the boy was more than just losing his deal with the dead Marshall. It was failing his duty as a teacher, as a guide, and as a friend. He pulled his wrist away, not sensing any change in the boy. *I'm all he has left, and I failed him.*

Abe started to stand, defeat seeping into his bones, only stopping when he heard the boy draw a giant breath, gagging. The hunter's fears of losing the boy seemed to be abated for now. Swiftly, Abe picked Jed back up, hauling him back onto Dusk. He swung into the seat seconds after. His blood in the boy's veins would help, but not for long. He snarled as he heeled Dusk more urgently. The steed snorted and bolted again, tearing into the landscape below them. The ride was long and arduous, and Abe constantly worried over the boy's wellbeing.

The town rose in the distance, a sight Abe never thought he would be so glad to see. He rode harder and faster. Each stride brought them closer and closer to the town. Soon, he saw people in the distance, moving about their daily lives. All Abe cared about was getting Jed to safety and fetching the doctor.

The hunter whipped the reins onto Dusk's flanks, causing him to pin his ears back. They charged toward the outskirts of town, nearly running over a family of several children and a ragged-looking mother. He blazed through the small main street, stopping in front of the inn. People's stares bore into the hunter's backside, a tendency he had become accustomed to over the years. Dusk screamed and reared, pawing the air. El Diablo knew that the beast was just as thirsty for blood as he was.

Men who had been conversing casually on the front porch quickly moved out of the hunter's way as Abe burst through the door with a slam. Jed was in his arms, not as pallid as before, but not looking well, either. The innkeeper stared at the pair, wide-eyed, and backed away from the counter. Abe shot the keeper a glare, demanding, "I need a room. Now."

The man's forehead broke out into a sweat, beading on his oily skin and blending into the wrinkles on his brow. Nervously wiping his hands on his pants, he answered, "Sorry sir, I don' have any—"

"NOW, DAMN IT!" Abe roared. He had very little patience for humans on the best of days. Today was not the best of days.

Jed groaned and winced in a fresh wave of pain. The innkeeper jumped into action, scrambling to grab a set of keys hanging on the back wall. He fumbled, dropping the set with a clatter to the wood floor. Withering under the hunter's gaze, the older man moved quickly around the corner of the counter, heading toward the staircase with as much haste as he could muster. Abe followed him, Jed limp in his arms, but still alive. Abe glanced down at the boy, silently willing, *Hold on boy. You ain't finished yet.*

\*\*\*

Sounds clattered in his ears, the noise confusing his mind. His arms and legs felt numb to the bone, tinged with a subtle hint of pulsating pain. Where was he now? Had he finally given in to the sweet embrace of death?

A gruff voice cut through the mist of his consciousness.

"...damn doctor, now..." He recognized that voice. But the name eluded him. His body in took a sharp breath, racking his body with agony. He felt his lips part and air escape, but the sound didn't feel like his own.

"Y-yes sir, right up the stairs..." the nervous one faded out for a moment and returned, "...fetch the doctor..."

He fought to raise his hand, to stop whomever it was from fetching the doctor. He didn't have the money for one.

"Jed. Be still." The gruff voice was back, but was not harsh with him. Jed felt his hand being pushed back to his body. His will wasn't strong enough to resist it.

*Abe*. That's who it was: Abe. His muddled mind finally grasped who was holding him. He was moving again. Each step shot pain through his entirety. He was afraid he'd fall apart from the movement. Jed coughed and wheezed, a muffled moan escaping his lips. If only he had died, he wouldn't feel this torture anymore.

No. He couldn't die. Not here. Not yet.

"Marietta..." His dry lips parted for breath. Abe adjusted his arms under Jed.

"I said be still, boy." Abe's voice was stern. Jed whimpered, closing his lips again. The weight of failure loomed over him, threatening to crush his already broken body. El Diablo—Abe—had saved him from the den of demons. He wanted to know why.

Jed felt a soft cloud form around his fractured frame. The coolness comforted his pain. The strong arms of the hunter slid out from under him, and he heard his gear rustle around the room, his spurs jangling.

# Chapter 27

Abe closed the door behind him, gruffly shoving people away from the door. His glare was all that was needed to warn these nosey townsfolk to stay away from the room. He needed to go back and fetch Jed's belongings. Now that Jed was safe, he could retrieve them. He shoved through people, glaring at those who dared look him in the eye as he passed. He was in no mood to entertain the masses.

The hunter's leather and gear jangled ominously as he approached the stairs and began his decent to the parlor room below. The staircase creaked with each step, the rug under his boots faded from years of feet treading on it. At the counter was the older innkeeper speaking hurriedly with a frazzled and graying doctor. The doctor had his black bag with him, and his coat was an off-black—sun-bleached, by the looks of it. Abe grunted to himself with satisfaction. He made his way to the door.

"W-wait sir!" The voice of the innkeeper grated on Abe's patience, which was already worn as thin as possible. He kept walking, ignoring the man as he continued, "You need to sign the guest roster—"

Abe felt a torrent of anger flood his veins as he drew his pistol, aimed at the large book that was the roster, and put a bullet right through the pages. Everyone close ducked for cover or cowered in their spots, women screamed, and others ducked out of the inn. His hellish blue eyes gleamed with rage as he bore his teeth at the innkeeper. He had signed the roster, in a manner of speaking.

Abe holstered his pistol and resumed his stride. The door slammed, slowly creaking closed. Abe went back to Dusk, who was aimlessly sniffing at the dirt in front of the inn. He nickered as

Abe approached, lifting his red eyes to meet his cobalt ones. He grabbed the horn of the saddle and swung into the seat. He slid the reins into his hands, turning Dusk back toward where they had come from.

Jed needed his effects and his horse. *I ain't buyin' more shit because o' you, Cabrio.* With a firm heel, Abe urged Dusk into a canter, heading out from the town again. The sound of the steed's stride, his breathing, and the creaking of the saddle was all that was heard as he pushed him into a gallop out of town. The afternoon air was stagnant, and the heat was stifling. Perfect weather for the hunter and his stallion.

He remained focused on his task ahead: gather the boy's belongings and head back to make sure the doctor didn't kill him in his stupor. The boy would be fragile—even unstable—for a few days, at least. *The blood I gave him should be more n' enough.* The terrain unfolded in front of him as he kept riding until he finally reached the fortress—the sun leaning more toward the horizon. He found Jed's stallion pawing at the ground with impatience. The animal was tired of being tied to a dead tree in the wilderness. Abe reined Dusk to a stop, dismounting and tying the beast to the ground.

Abe glanced at Jed's antsy stallion before walking down toward the fortress. The smell of the boy's blood was still hanging on the air—a good reason to leave Dusk where he was. He didn't need his steed from hell to get into a blood frenzy.

Silence encircled him, save the sound of his spurs echoing from the skeleton of the fortress and the buzzards circling overhead. Corpses littered the fortress as he passed through the busted-out gates, not even casting a glance at already feasting birds. Meat, sinew, and intestine strung in their beaks as they pecked at their meal. He didn't care if the bodies were eaten this way. They deserved it. The smells of the dead and old gunpowder covered the area in a blanket of foul memory as Abe walked toward the main body of the fortress. Even though the fresh battleground was empty, he exercised acute alertness to any foragers that might take their chance to take what they wanted. *Or any remaining Marks bastards.* He crossed the yard, keeping his temper at a low simmer.

The second door he had battered in was shattered into several pieces, the hinges sagging pitifully, squeaking at the subtle movement of air. He stepped through the threshold, taking an abrupt left and down the hallway. He stepped over more bodies, ignoring the gore and blood that was drying into dark stains, soaking into the old clay walls and flooring. Jed's blood was still thick in the air, making his inner being squirm. It wasn't hard to find his way back to the butchering room. Abe wrinkled his nose in disgust at the corpse of Cabrio as he passed, the stench almost masking Jed's blood.

The remains had expanded, splitting the skin and unleashing the full power of a decaying half-blood. The organs had spilled over the peak of the skin split, draping over the chest cavity and to the ground around him; his fanged face frozen in his last moment of terror and death. Abe narrowed his eyes at the corpse one last time as he passed, taking out another cigarette and lighting it. The door to the room Jed was in was directly across from the massive devil's corpse. The smoke from Abe's cigarette filled his lungs with a dull, welcoming burn as he paused in the doorway.

He hadn't had the time to take in the environment before. The lantern above the chair had gone out and was swaying side to side subtly. The stench of dirt, sweat, and blood clung to the walls, assailing his nostrils. A smell he had thought he had gotten used to. Nothing had prepared him to smell and see this.

Abe felt his stomach tighten and his jaw clench with anger. Jed's blood left dark stains all over the wooden chair. The ropes that had bound the boy were scattered to the side with dried blood coating different sections, indicating where he had tried to escape. He moved toward the rope and picked up a frayed end with a gloved hand, turning it slowly to look at it. The scene kept replaying in his mind; Jed tied to a chair, covered in his own blood, his chin resting on his chest, his breathing short and painful. He could hear the bones that were broken grinding against each other with each painful draw of air. The boy's heart was heavy in its rhythm.

Abe felt his breathing grow tense and his heart rate rising. He stood, remembering how the boy was badly beaten and marred. He had lost a lot of blood, and had endured so much. Jed's relieved whimper when Abe had come for him burned into his memory. Shock and relief were written on the boy's face. His eyes had said so much more.

Abe gritted his teeth and searched the rest of the room, hoping to spot some of Jed's possessions. They were scattered about the edges of the room, no doubt from Cabrio's men rifling through it. His inner self swelled in his chest as his anger began to flare into rage. He picked up the bandolier whose shells had been stripped from its pockets, his pistols, and, lastly, his hat. His hands trembled with fury.

*Eberhart...This is more fuckin' personal.*

Holding Jed's belongings in both hands, Abe turned and strode out with hell-bent purpose. He wanted to quench the rising tide of blood thirst that was screaming at him to unleash his true self. The sound of his boots grinding against the dirt floor echoed off the walls. He could feel his inner being clawing more sporadically now, screaming to be let out.

He intended to let it out before the afternoon was gone.

The sun was behind him when he came out of the fortress, the subtle breeze picking up for the coming evening. His senses were acutely tuned in to his surroundings. The sound of the buzzards was all around him, still feasting on the flesh of the dead. Wild dogs could be heard in the distance; a sound only someone like him could hear. Something else caught his attention on the other side of the courtyard.

"...I told you, they're all dead! El Diablo shot 'em up."

Sounds from the rifling through clothing and gear was heard with the voice of the first man.

"W-what if he comes back?" The man's voice was shaky. Abe glared in their direction, setting Jed's gear aside. The men had no idea that the hunter was in their presence. Abe could feel the inner being squirm more violently as he turned to them, a hunger burning in his gut.

"I told you, he ain't comin' back. El Diablo never comes back to a place he's been." The first man who spoke was a twig of a man with a wide hat to shade his weathered face from the sun's ray. The second man had a heavier build, with plenty to spare him through a winter season. Abe let loose the seal on his inner being, which inwardly squealed with glee, anticipating what would come next. *Easy meat...*

Abe let all his anger, fury, and despair flood through his veins as his flesh began to change. A familiar burn singed his bone and muscle as it all contorted into a more natural form. He felt his skin stretch and change, his clothing morphing into his body. Pitch black scales covered his body, and hadean blue eyes locked onto the two men, who were now shouting and trying to escape. Large, black wings stretched from his powerful shoulder blades as the men in front of him shouted in terror. His long, black tail lashed from side to side as he felt the surge of bloodthirst swell over him, launching him into the hunt with an unearthly roar.

Vengeance would be his this day.

# Chapter 28

Jed assumed that he had been placed on a bed. Wood scratched against wood as the hunter dragged a chair over and sat at the bedside. Even through closed eyelids, the light blinded Jed. If he died here, he prayed that Abe would fulfill his oath for him. Marietta was still out there, somewhere.

Jed wanted to see the hunter with his own eyes. One last time. With his last bit of strength, Jed forced his eyes open. Abe was sitting in a chair, hat low over his eyes; but he knew that those cobalt eyes were watching him closely. Monitoring him. He was leaned forward, elbows rested on his knees, hands loosely intertwined.

Grief flooded over him, tears stinging his eyes as his body convulsed in a fit of coughing and wheezing. His lungs felt so heavy.

"Abe…" His rasping voice choked out. "I'm…s-sorry." He had so much to say to Abe, so many things to ask him. "I…I…"

Abe leaned forward and rested a hand on his forearm, "Jed, rest now. Don't talk, yer just makin' things worse." The tears that stung Jed's eyes dribbled down his cheeks, into the gouge in his face. The salt stung, but he felt he deserved that. He had endangered both his and El Diablo's lives.

The door behind Abe creaked open, letting a frazzled doctor sweep into the room. Jed saw faces crowding the door. The doctor shooed them off with a wave of his briefcase and muffled words. Blackness threatened to take Jed away as he closed his eyes. Abe rose from his chair.

"He dies…and I will find you." Those words hung heavy in the room. The threat as red hot as the fires at night.

The door opened again. The jangling of spurs echoed.
Jed let the darkness slip him away.

\*\*\*

The sun spread over him, letting the fingers of warmth flood his senses. His body ached, but didn't agonize as it had before. His mind was clear of the mist. Jed opened his eyes slowly, letting them adjust to the early morning. His limbs felt like stones, heavy and slow.

*How long have I been gone?* This single thought floated across his waking mind. His last waking memory was of the doctor and Abe.

*Abe.* Jed sat up fast, and quickly regretted it. With a muffled groan, he felt his aches and strains more than he had before. He touched his shoulder and his collarbone tenderly, fingering the wrappings that were taught around it.

Jed observed the simplicity of the room; wood-slatted floors, a washstand in the far corner, a chair in the other. The nightstand next to him had a nearly empty yellow-stained bottle. He winced, reaching for the bottle. He clumsily grabbed it and turned it to see the intricate label.

Opiate, the bottle read. *Why, Abe? This is expensive.* Jed grunted and set the bottle down. He needed to find Abe. He took a breath and tossed the sheets and blanket off him and slowly swung his legs over the side. He was completely bare, and Jed's ears began to flush a deep red. He looked around and caught a glimpse of freshly pressed clothes sitting on the stool of the washbasin.

Jed pushed off the bed with weak arms and stumbled towards it. His steps felt foreign to him as he steadied himself along the way. He hastily dressed himself as best as he could manage and headed to the door.

The door creaked open before Jed could reach it. He let his hand drop to his side in defeat as a girl entered. Her rosy blond hair was curled around her bare shoulders and grungy ivory and powder blue dress. It seemed timeworn, as though it was all that she owned. Her eyes widened in shock as she stepped over to him, flustered.

"Oh, sir, you can't be up yet." Her instructions grated on Jed's nerves as he felt a frown chisel on his features. "The doctor said you ain't ready to be up and about yet."

"Like hell I can't." Jed had better things to be doing than lay in bed. He had done that enough as it was. He put a step forward with determination, only to stumble and be caught by the girl. His frustration grew.

"Looky here, mister…" He could almost hear the amusement in her voice as she attempted to steer him back to his bed, "You ain't well enough yet. You were half-dead when Diablo brought you here."

Jed paused and looked at her, remembering the strong arms and comforting voice of the hunter. Why would Abe save him like that? After he had drugged him to follow his own foolishness. "El Diablo brought me here? Where is he?" How long had been laying here? He judged it must have been at least one week.

He allowed the small-breasted girl to sit him back down as she walked around the bed and grabbed the bottle. "They say he's on the outskirts of town. Heaven knows why he don't just stay here." She drifted back to him, lustfully eyeing the bottle. Jed wondered if he had been the one to take all those doses, or if this girl had helped with that.

She snapped out of her trance and quickly handed him the bottle as she sat next to him. Her eyes were wide with wonder, excitement, and fear all at once as she continued in a hushed voice, "I hear that you can make deals with him…at the cost of yer soul! Can you imagine? Someone doin' a silly thing like that."

Jed focused on the bottle, ignoring the girl's bizarre intrigue. El Diablo certainly was different, but not that different. Jed added that to a long mental list of questions. He set the bottle aside and looked at her as sternly as his tired body could allow.

"Look, miss, I ain't got long...I need to find El Diablo. Now, if you'll 'scuse me..." Jed stood up again and pushed past the flustered blond.

"Sir, you can't! He'll kill us if he knows you left before you were better!" She pleaded in desperation as he batted her off his arm.

"He won't." Jed answered gruffly. His patience was wearing thin. He needed to find Abe. He needed to catch up to him before he got too far ahead. If he knew Abe at all, he knew that the man would be long gone from here by now.

Jed gripped the stair railing with white-knuckled strength as he eased himself down. The numbness was seeping from him, being replaced with aches and strains. He ignored it.

After a wordy battle between innkeeper, whore, and Jed, he finally made it to open air. There was a horse hitched at the rail. Jed sighed his relief at the familiar stud. At least Abe hadn't completely left him stranded.

The stud was still saddled and bridled. Jed was thankful for that as he stepped off the boardwalk to his horse. His hands gripped the pommel and back of the saddle. He steeled himself for the hardest part as he took a breath and heaved himself up onto the horse. Pain seared through him as he adjusted himself in the seat of the saddle and took up the reins.

The horse adjusted his weight under Jed and moved with ease at Jed's direction. Jed tapped his heels against the horse, urging him forward. The swaying motion of the horse burned his sore wounds. He didn't care. He ignored it.

Jed rode to the edge of town, feeling eyes on him the whole way. He held himself with dignity as he rode past. The boy he was before was long dead. A man had replaced him.

\*\*\*

Abe stoked the coals of the fire aimlessly. The embers drifted lazily into the sky, the wood snapping and popping with relief. El Cabrio had given him what he wanted. But it just didn't seem...right. His gut instinct was screaming inside him that it was a lie. That it was a trap set up.

*So had that fortress*, he thought, bitterly. With a growl, he stabbed the stick into the heart of the fire and laid back. This whole hunt had been a wild chase, with no predictability. He disliked the taste it kept leaving in his mouth.

He tugged his hat over his eyes as he let his mind stew over the incident. Cabrio specifically answered Bodie, though he knew that the Marks gang hadn't organized there in years. Too much attention from the law. Why would Marks be there again?

*Unless it was another trap...* Abe sighed, adjusting his position. *Almost lost the kid back there. He ain't strong enough...unless...* The thought blazed in his mind, surprising him.

He heard faint hooves in the distance. He tipped the brim of his hat to watch as a horse and rider approached. He remained in his spot, waiting to see who it was. He couldn't catch the scent from downwind. Abe would have to lay in wait.

Dusk turned his head in the direction of the rider and snorted. Abe waited in stillness with the company of the dying fire.

## Chapter 29

The sun was bearing down on Jed's back. The swaying motion of the horse's movements made Jed grimace. The once-firm bandages were damp and sliding over his wounds. He hoped it was sweat and not something else.

His cheek ached a deep, throbbing ache with each heartbeat. It was a solemn reminder of what had happened. Jed's life was testament to one man's commitment to a contract. He sought to find him. Abe was out there, somewhere around this little town. His mind still swam with the haze of the opium, but his pain had started to rise again.

*Should've taken the damn bottle,* was all that Jed could think of. The horse snorted and stumbled over a stub of brush in its lazy gait. The motion jarred Jed's tender fractures, making him growl under his breath. He frowned and leaned forward a bit, seeing stars in his eyes. When the stars subsided, Jed resumed his posture.

A fire was lit in the distance. *That must be him.* Jed thought with hope. Jed clucked and heeled his mount to pick up the pace. The horse pricked its ears and responded to Jed's direction. The small campfire drew closer as the sun in the sky began its descent behind him. He saw the ominous black steed standing off to the side, with a smaller figure laying on the ground. He was clad in black. Relief spread through Jed as he recognized the pair.

*I thought for sure he would have left me here.* The pain over his body was soon forgotten. The fire was dwindling as the ember core of the fire barely spat. Jed felt a foolish grin play on his lips; Abe certainly couldn't keep a fire going. Abe's steed nickered softly and looked at him with those foreign, crimson eyes. Jed shifted in his seat uncomfortably and reined to a stop.

The man on the ground was unmoving, even though Jed knew that he could sense his presence. "Go back, boy."

Jed looked at Abe and cleared his throat. "How long was I out?"

"Not long enough…you ain't ready to ride." The irritation in Abe's voice was apparent.

"Like hell I ain't," Jed answered softly. Marietta was still in danger—out here, somewhere.

Jed shifted his weight and slowly swung his leg over, hanging on with white knuckles to the horn and cantle. His wounds sang with burning soreness. Holding his breath, Jed slid off the saddle, feeling his knees buckle from the impact with a suppressed yell. The blackness crowded his eyesight as his healing ribs, collarbone, and other afflicted parts of his body cried out.

Strong hands caught him before his body completely collapsed.

"Damn it, boy. You'll shatter, like one of them porcelain dolls." Abe's voice was softer than Jed had anticipated. Though his current state told him otherwise, everything that had happened in the fortress felt like a distant bizarre dream. Though his current state told him otherwise. Jed welcomed Abe's strength for the time being. He knew he was still weak, but he could waste no more time.

Jed's feet tried to steady under him, as Abe helped him over to the dying fire.

"How'd you catch me so fast, Abe?" Jed looked up at him in confusion. "You was laying just there…" He indicated to the saddle.

Abe was silent for the moment as he gently set Jed down.

"I ain't like your kind, boy…"

Jed watched Abe move around the fire and back to his saddle. There he squatted down on his haunches and rummage through the saddle bags. *He's running low on things again,* Jed thought sheepishly. *Because of me.*

The guilt flooded his body as he trained his eyes to the ground. The girl back at the hotel had told him, in brief, what El Diablo had done. He had the keep give up his best room, so Jed could rest, paid in full and up front. El Diablo never did favors. Not unless there was something in it to his benefit.

*Why did he come back for me?* Jed pulled his knee up to the rest his forearm on.

A beat-up tin whiskey flask slipped into view, and Jed gladly took it. The contents sloshed as he unscrewed the cap and took a swig, only to choke halfway through.

Jed lowered his head, so that Abe wouldn't see his embarrassing moment. The hunter stood there, patient, until the coughing stopped. Jed screwed the cap back on and handed it back to him.

The hunter took it back and strolled over to his saddle again, taking a swig himself.

The silence was unbearable. Jed had to speak, "Abe…"The hunter paused, listening. "I'm sorry for what I did…I thought— "

"That you could handle things on your own?" Abe scoffed. "I told ya, kid. You ain't ready."

Jed shifted uncomfortably. He knew that he had no right to retaliate with a heated remark. Not after what he had just pulled.

The sun began to set, and the embers of Abe's fire burned low, providing just enough light to see.

"I'll get us some more firewood." Jed slowly tried getting up, but the strain on his body was enormous. He felt a hand gently, but firmly, push him back to the ground. Jed looked up at Abe.

"Stay—" before Jed could speak, he was gone. He turned his head in all directions, looking for El Diablo, but there was nothing. He had completely disappeared.

His hairs hackled and a chill seeped into his skin and flesh. *El Diablo really is…* Weariness bared down on Jed's shoulders, his mind becoming fuzzy with exhaustion. Maybe his eyes were playing with him again. Jed inched and squirmed his body to lay on the ground. The warm dirt and rocks poked his back. The feeling was more of a comfort than a discomfort now. That room felt too perfect, anyhow.

Jed hoped that El Diablo—Abe—would return.

\*\*\*

Light danced over his eyelids, the flickering movements disrupting his rest. The air was cool against his damp skin.

He was still sweating, damn it all. Jed lifted his hand groggily to wipe his forehead clear of moisture and took in a deep, shaky breath. His chest was still sore.

Jed slowly opened his eyes, only to be greeted by the hearty dancing flames of the fire, which seemed to have found a new will to live.

*Abe.*

Jed sat up sharply. The hunter had returned. Jed winced and coddled his side, winded from the sudden movement.

"Bout damn time, boy."

Jed snapped his head back up and looked across the fire. There he was. Sitting with his knees drawn up and forearms resting on them, hands dangling loosely.

A subtle smile slid onto Jed's lips. Abe had returned. "Sorry, sir, didn't know you was expectin' me." Jed let the remark linger, feeling relieved the hunter was still here. Abe was silent. Jed's smile faded.

"What am I, boy?"

"What…? I don't…"

Abe lifted his gaze from the fire and stared him down. The deep blue reflected the dancing flames.

Jed swallowed hard before his attempted answer, "Uh…you're El Diablo, bounty hunter."

"That's *who* I am boy, not *what* I am." Abe turned his gaze to his duster pocket and rummaged. He drew out a cigarette and placed it in between his lips.

"*What* am I Jed?" His eyes were stern. He wasn't playing games tonight.

Jed looked at his hands in thought, "Well…I don't know." Jed looked at him again, "Most say you're a spirit…a sort of ghost plaguing towns. Others say you're just a vigilante, roaming from territory to territory." Jed leaned in closer, "But all say that you're the devil, himself."

Abe erupted into a fit of laughter. The outburst startled him. Jed had never heard Abe laugh before. It was gravelly and rough, like an old dog.

Abe shook his head and calmed his laughter, "Well, boy, they're all wrong."

He rummaged again for his matchbook, unsuccessful. "I'm not the devil…" his voice quieted and his eyes locked with Jed's, "But I am *a* devil." Abe snapped his forefinger and thumb together, and a tiny flame remained on his thumb.

Jed stared wide eyed at it in wonder and fear.

"Jesus Christ…" Jed murmured.

"He ain't got nothin' to do with it, boy," Abe growled as the tiny flame licked the end of his cigarette. After a few satisfactory puffs, Abe shook his hand loosely, extinguishing the flame.

"He don't exist here." The smoke trailed aimlessly upward into the sky. Everything was eerily quiet. The silence was killing him.

"So, you're really a demon?" Jed was bewildered. He thought the rumors were just talk, like everything else on the frontier.

Abe jabbed his cigarette towards him with a glare, "I'm not a damn demon. I'm a devil, there's a difference."

"Sorry …" the strong reaction astonished Jed. Abe was all-business. "Didn't mean to offend…"

Abe grunted and took a long draw. "Yes. I'm a devil."

"Then, why do you do bounty huntin'? I mean, if you are what you say you are..." Jed quieted, as if doom might strike him dead if he said devil loud enough. "Can't you do whatever you want?"

Abe grinned and blew out the smoke from his mouth and nostrils. "Ain't that simple boy. We got rules, same as you. I hunt those who break 'em."

Jed knitted his brows and thought, *But his own kind?* He remembered El Cabrio. Those men were different. He could see it in their eyes. It was as though they weren't men. He was beginning to believe his delusion of Cabrio morphing into a horrific monstrosity. Silence spanned between the two again as Abe let the cigarette smoke before taking another large drag, the red tip flaring up as he did. "So...El Cabrio...he was a demon, right?"

Abe sighed and drew again, collecting his thoughts. "Jed...there's more to this world that what you've seen already. When I said you ain't ready, I damn well meant it."

Jed held his tongue expecting more. Abe paused and looked hard at Jed.

"But, given the circumstances, I oughta at least offer you the choice. Jed shifted his position, giving his hurt side a rest, interested in what Abe had to say. "Ever heard of the phrase, 'made a deal with the devil'?"

Jed nodded. *What's he on about?*

"Well, the phrase has truth in it." Abe tossed his old cigarette into the flames, its contents absorbed. "Us devils, we take pleasure in making deals with your kind to better our situations. That said, our deals require a sufficient sacrifice."

Jed didn't like what he heard or where this was going. "What kind of sacrifice are we talking about?"

"Blood. In rare cases, souls, in addition to the blood." Abe casually pulled the cigarette from the pack once again, lighting it and taking a drag. The tip glowed red as the off-white skin changed into ash. He pulled it away from his mouth and tapped the end of it, the gray ash falling to the ground.

Jed swallowed hard. His heart pounded with anxiety. He wasn't sure he wanted to hear what this choice of Abe was.

"Now, being as you're human, Jed, you won't survive much longer. 'Specially, since Marks is involved." Abe frowned at the name. Jed waited patiently with dread. But he knew he was right. He wasn't ready. His cheek was a constant reminder of that. He could still feel the biting steel of the blade.

"I'm offering you a deal, boy." His tone was deep, sinister. His eyes changed temperature. They were soul-piercing. His icy stare frightened Jed, but he couldn't turn back now.

"You need an edge in order to survive, if you want it..."

The words hit Jed like a freight train. *A deal? With El Diablo?* Jed braced himself and stood, turning his back to the fire and inspecting the vulture-like eyes of El Diablo. He was right. He knew he was right. Jed was completely helpless when he charged into the flesh-eating hands of El Cabrio. There was nothing he could have done to fight against those demons. He was powerless. Weak.

*That won't help Marietta.*

Jed rubbed his face and glanced at the sky above. The stars were dimly lit, almost as if they, too, knew the dark task that had to be done.

Jed looked at Abe again, gravity in his gaze.

"I'll do it."

Abe stood and pulled his duster coat back. He seemed taller than normal. His form seemed to meld with the darkness of the night. He truly was something unnatural. Jed didn't fear him. He'd seen things far worse.

Abe walked over to Jed and held out his right hand and motioned. Jed glanced at Abe's hand then his own hand and cautiously held out his. Abe firmly grabbed it turned it, so the palm faced skyward. Jed licked his chapped lips. Abe had mentioned blood as the price, and, sometimes, souls.

No price was too much to save his family—what was left of it, anyway. He'd sell his soul a thousand times over to see that Marietta was safe again. He steeled himself as he heard a blade being drawn from an oiled sheathe. The sound rang ominously in Jed's memory. He closed his eyes. A hot pain etched in his palm, the red oozing out of the gash that sprawled from the base of his index finger to the outer edge of his hand. The blood dripped, streaming heavily onto the ground. Jed held his tongue, his jaw clenched with determination. He opened his eyes and looked. His skin was flayed open, and it pulsed heavy with his heart rhythm. He looked at Abe, who watched the wound for a breath's spell. He released Jed's hand and took the knife to his own hand. Without any sign of feeling, Abe sliced his hand open. Jed swore he heard him hiss at the self-inflicted wound.

Abe grabbed Jed's hand and clenched their hands together, as if to arm wrestle. Jed winced, grimacing as their blood mingled. The burn coated Jed's new wound and coursed through his veins, scalding his nerves. It was almost debilitating. He couldn't help whimpering. The pain level was growing, and rapidly. His heart raced, he body sweated, and his head reeled.

Abe forced their joined hands over the flames, letting the thick drips hiss and pop. The pressure was suddenly released, and his hand was his again. The burning sensation began to simmer. Jed's breathing was heavy as he held his hand at the wrist. He didn't dare look at the gash.

Abe stretched his hand, as if to release a cramp, wiping the smooth blade over his pants to clean the blood off. He strode over to his saddle and laid down in his routine way—as though nothing had ever transpired.

Jed stared at him in disbelief as he waited for a sign that it had worked. "Was that it? That was the deal?"

"The blood pact has been sealed, Jed…the fire, a witness." Abe sighed as he relaxed on the ground with his hands clasped over his chest.

"But uh…wasn't somethin' supposed to happen?"

"If you mean somethin' like an explosion, then, nah." Abe tilted his hat low over his eyes to hide a spreading snicker, "Not yet."

Jed went rigid. *Explode?!* "What?!"

"Sometimes those that make the deal, their bodies can't handle the blood pact. Their blood rejects it and they die—vomiting for weeks until their entrails spew all over the dirt." Jed stared at Abe in jaw-drop horror. "Seen it many a time." Abe shifted a little more until he finally found his resting spot. "Get some sleep. Long ride ahead of us."

*This deal could kill me? Jesus…what was I thinkin'?!* Jed felt panic rise in his chest.

Shakily, Jed found his saddle and tack on the ground and laid down. With death smiling at him from the shadows, how could he sleep?

# Chapter 30

Jed woke with a start. The sun had just barely begun to creep out of its slumber, and its light pierced through his eyelids. He slowly sat up, rubbing his face with a hand, holding his hat with the other. *Wait...* Jed patted his midriff, his heart skipping a beat as he felt for any sign of pain. Nothing. Jed bolted to his feet, checking where all his injuries should have been. "What the hell?" Jed whispered as he felt his face. The cuts, pains, and fever were gone. With a shaking hand, Jed reached up and gingerly touched the heavy bandage that hid the worst of all his wounds. Through the bandaging, he could feel that the skin and flesh had not been completely restored. The gash was still underneath.

*Well, at least it don't hurt no more.* He looked at his hands, turning them over in fascination. He had never considered how complex hands were. Veins crisscrossed everywhere, and individual hairs were plainly visible. Even the skin lines looked like canyons sprawled across them.

"Oh good. It didn't kill ya." Abe's voice startled him. Jed nearly gasped at what he saw: his shadow was writhing around him, twisting around his feet and lower legs; black as the night. He had never seen that before.

Jed stared at it, wide-eyed. Abe looked up at him under his brim, "What do you see, boy?"

"Your shadow! It ain't right!" Jed pointed to the hunter's feet.

Abe chuckled placing his hands on his hips. Jed frowned as Abe's grin grew. "What's so funny?" Jed snapped, his eyes still trained upon the odd movements of the shadow, not trusting it.

"You, Jed. That's what's funny. Abe walked towards him and clapped his hand on Jed's shoulder, "It worked. Now, you come with me."

Jed looked at Abe, his frown melting away, "You mean...?" Abe nodded, a shadow of a proud grin seeping into his features. "Well what are we waitin' for? Let's go get her!" Jed felt the surge of excitement rush though him. Now, he could face Eberhart and get his sister back. Jed grabbed his saddle and his tack and rushed to his horse. *This is my chance! Now that I can do whatever it is Abe can do, I can get her back!* Jed's fingers rushed as they fastened the bridle on, tightened the cinch, and adjusted the belts, only slowing when Jed noticed that Abe had not moved from his spot. "Abe...?" Jed called to him, "Ain't you comin'?"

Abe was silent for a moment. His proud grin was gone, replaced by a stony expression. "Jed...it ain't that simple."

Jed fumed. He strained to control his tongue as he turned, placing his hands on his hips, "Why the hell not?"

Abe was silent, pondering. "We can't take Marks with the two of us..."

Jed could feel his anger burn inside of him. *I've done crazy shit these past several months, sellin' my own soul, even, and it's still not enough?!* He held his tongue still. He turned from his friend and mentor. He reached and placed his hands on the saddle horn and the back of the saddle. Lowering his head, he drew a deep breath. *But...it ain't proper to scream at the man that just saved my life.* He straightened again, rubbing a hand over his face as he looked at Abe. He hadn't moved a single step. "Then...what're we supposed to do?"

Jed inwardly scolded himself—he hadn't meant for the words to sound harsh. Abe didn't seem to notice, or, if he did, he didn't pay it any mind.

Abe pulled a cigarette out from the depths of his duster, placing it in between his lips, "First, Jed, I need to train you." Abe snapped his fingers, a flame emanating from the tip of his thumb. The end of the cigarette began to smolder from the flame. Jed waited patiently as the hunter drew a long drag. "You may have the abilities necessary to hunt us boy, but skill, skill is what will destroy us." Abe walked to Jed, his gear clanking softly in the morning air.

*What the hell is he talkin' about? He's taught me everything!* Jed shifted his weight uncomfortably under Abe's scrutinous gaze. "So…" he continued, "you got five days to find me."

*What?!* "But Abe! I-I don't know how! I can't find just one man in the fuckin' desert!" Jed's temper showed itself, his face reddening and his voice growing louder. Abe expected the impossible from him.

Abe tapped the end of his smoke, clearing the ashes that had steadily grown, "Sure ya can." Abe flicked his cigarette to the ground, grinding the smoldering end into the dirt with his heel. He walked back to Dusk with a lazy stride. Jed opened his mouth in protest, but stopped himself. Abe's footsteps left distinct shadowed imprints as he mounted up, taking the reins into his hands. No words were needed.

Jed nodded, finally understanding what Abe had meant. He followed suit, mounting up on his own horse. Abe sat atop Dusk, across from Jed, who remained silent. Jed glanced at the faint footprints. *The shadow…it lingers for a little while.*

"Five days, boy." Abe grunted and turned his steed towards the west before cantering off. Jed sighed and looked down at his stallion, who had his full attention towards where Abe had gone.

"Guess it's just you an' me." Jed spoke softly, patting the horse's neck.

\*\*\*

Jed had spotted the small town miles away. The dust hung over it in a haze. He was still entranced by his enhanced senses. He could hear things he never noticed before, smell things that no normal man could smell, and see things so far away it would rival a hawk's sight.

Jed reined in his horse from a lope to a stop. He'd ridden far already. A couple days, in fact. Each day still provided the same outcome; a cold camp fire and the residual footprints of El Diablo. He had to find him, and quickly. The time spent with the hunter had taught him so much already. *What I need to focus on now is the wanted board.*

Jed pulled his hat low over his eyes as he clucked and heeled his horse forward. It sighed, taking off at a lope once more. When he was close enough, Jed pulled the horse into a trot. Under the brim of the hat, he could watch the townsfolk and keep an eye out for the marshal building. Some folks stopped to watch him, others passed by. Riders, wagons, cattle drivers; all seemed to pass him by like a ghost. *Good.*

He stopped at an ancient-looking building that was clearly marked 'Marshal.' He tied off his horse quickly and stepped up to the front side. His own gear lightly clinked and clanged until he stopped at the wall plastered with posters. This time, however, he was only hunting one face out of many. His eyes carefully swept over them all, knowing that Abe's face would be easy to spot.

"You lost, son?" An older man called to him from the doorway. Jed tore his eyes from the plastered wall of papers to a stout, barrel-chested man. Jed felt his smile crease his still patched over cheek, a phantom pain stretching his skin and flesh. He ignored it.

"No, sir, just uh..." Jed casually waved an arm towards the wall of wanted faces. "Lookin' for a particular man." Jed stepped up to the man, scanning over his attire. His eyes lingered over the badge. "Sheriff" was engraved on its surface.

The sheriff looped his thumbs through belt loops, his suspicious eyes were trained on Jed. "Well, son I might be of assistance to ya."

Jed kept his hands away from his holstered weapons. He had a slight sense that this man might have an edge about him. He tipped his hat brim up a bit, so the sheriff could see his eyes. "Well, sheriff, I'm lookin' for El Diablo. He been through here recently?"

He watched the sheriff's countenance change at the name. The stout man grunted, turning his gaze to the ground before looking Jed in the eye again. "Look, son, whate'er is in yer head, you'd best get rid of it. Ain't nothin' good comes to those who chase him."

Jed expected to feel the same pull of doubt in his chest as he always had. This time, though, he felt nothing but determination. He would not fail Abe again, even if Abe's methods were a little odd. Jed sighed and leaned in a little closer, hoping to reducing his odds of being overheard. "Sir, I do appreciate your concern, I really do, but I need to find him." The sheriff and Jed looked long and hard at each other as the town bustled around them. The silence was beginning to grate on Jed's nerves. *It must be this heat.* "Sheriff, please. It's important." Jed took a chance and lightly rested a hand on the man's shoulder. The old sheriff sighed, his shoulders sagging as he wiped his forehead with the back of his hand.

"Alright, son…don't say I didn't warn ya." The sheriff glanced around him, observing the ebbing flow of this dirt town. "He rode in 'bout a day ago. Wasn't looking for anyone, far as I could tell." The sheriff motioned for Jed to follow him as he climbed the two steps into the Marshall building.

The inside was sweltering with the heat already, and it was smaller than Jed had expected. He took in the small space as the sheriff went to the desk and pulled something out of the top drawer. The tiny space was bare and simple. There was one jail cell, with lopsided bars and semi-rusted door. It clearly wasn't used much, save for the occasional local drunkard.

"He left this on the counter in the saloon," Jed returned his attention to the beat-up old canteen, his hand reaching out to meet the container. He grabbed it gently from the older man and turned it over. The contents that were left barely sloshed inside as Jed turned it. "Never thought he'd forget somethin' like this. He'll die o' thirst out there."

Jed hid his smile behind as expression of concentration. "You'd be surprised." Jed muttered.

"What was that, son?"

Jed cleared his throat and held the canteen at his side, "Just odd he'd leave this here." *His canteen? That is suicide, but, knowing Abe, he knows I'm close.*

As Jed reached the door, the sheriff added, "One more thing son." Jed looked over his shoulder, towards the old man. The sheriff sighed, scratched his chin and waved him off, "Jus' be careful, ya hear? You're too young to get wrapped up with the likes of El Diablo."

Jed paused, the words weighing heavy on his chest. For the first time, it finally broke through; He was too young. The boy he was before, however, would never have made it this far. That boy had died in the den of El Cabrio.

"You're right, sheriff," Jed replied in a somber tone, "but I'm afraid it's too late for that." Jed turned with finality, tipping his hat low over his eyes. *The sins of the father shall pass unto the son.*

Leaving the stifling heat of the sheriff's, Jed strode over to his horse, lashing the canteen to the side of the saddle. He could feel the eyes of the old sheriff on his back as he mounted up, taking the reins into his hands again. He didn't look at the old man as he turned his horse towards the other end of town.

Jed's horse snorted, eager for a ride. He heeled the horse's sides. The animal underneath him jolted forward, evening his strides to a lope. His journey, he had realized, had only just begun.

*\*\*\**

Jed stooped to his haunches, resting his weight in the balls of his feet. The fire pit before him was smoking its last breath as he examined the embers. *It's still fresh. He must be close.* Jed stood and looked over the brittle landscape. It was the fifth day. The day El Diablo had designated as the last day of the hunt. He had ridden for miles, searching for clues and remnants of his "target's" movements. If Jed hadn't known better, he would have said Abe was being sloppy on purpose.

"Not bad, boy." Jed's muscles froze in place. He knew that voice. Abe had arrived. He turned, restraining a grin. He had passed Abe's test.

"Well, Abe, you were pretty easy to find." The sun was climbing its steady pace into the cloudless, blue space above the two of them. The heat was a steady bake to the world below. It used to bother Jed, making his body sweat from morning till night, but not now. Withstanding high temperatures was another of Jed's new abilities.

Abe was standing about fifty paces from Jed, hands at his sides. He remained silent for a moment before gruffly prompting, "Well? What're you waitin' for, boy?"

Jed's grin dissipated with a fresh wave of heat. "What are you talkin' about, Abe?"

"You ain't done. The job ain't finished." Abe pulled back his duster coat, exposing his bandolier and loaded belt.

Jed planted his left foot back, keeping his body turned to the side—his instinct to shoot was ingrained in him. *He can't be serious!*

"Shoot me."

Abe's order made Jed pause with confusion. He could feel that it was written all over his face, "What…? Hell no! I ain't gonna shoot ya!" Jed shouted over the distance. His words evaporated in the dry air around them. Abe drew one of his twin pistols and aimed it towards Jed, the click of the hammer locking into place. The deadly sound echoed. Jed drew his and took aim as well. *This is insanity! I...I can't...* He drew the hammer back, never taking his eyes from Abe.

"I said shoot me, boy, now do it!" Abe snarled menacingly. In a split-second, Jed adjusted his aim from Abe's chest to his shoulder and squeezed the trigger. He had a feeling that if Jed didn't pull, Abe would.

The bullet hissed through the air, hitting its mark. Abe shouted and dropped his gun, clutching his wounded shoulder. Jed's heart dropped to his stomach, worry and guilt pouring through him. He inwardly scolded himself for going through with it. What was he expecting? Some sort of trick that Abe could pull to dodge a bullet? He ran over to his friend, hoping that he didn't wound him too much.

Abe's shouts of pain turned into laughter as Jed came closer, standing up straight from the blow. As Abe stood, he placed a cigarette into his mouth. Jed came to a stop, his worry quickly turning to irritation. He hadn't hurt him at all. "Nice try, boy," Abe managed between laughs, "but your aim is still shit." Abe lit the tip with a flame from his thumb.

Jed stood there, hands placed on his hips as his jaw set, "Damn it Abe! I thought—!"

"You what? Hurt me?" Abe stooped down picking up his pistol and holstering it. "No, Jed. There are only three spots that count on us. Here," Abe pointed to the upper left side of his chest, just under the collar bone, "here," Abe drew his hand over to his right side of his chest, but slightly lower, "and here," Abe drew a final line down to his middle, where the sternum ends and the stomach begins.

Jed's brow knitted. "But why? That don't make sense. The only one that makes sense is the mid-point." Jed gestured to the last point Abe had drawn. Abe dropped his hand it his side and stared long and hard at Jed.

"Because, Jed, we ain't like you." Abe began to pace slowly around Jed as he continued, "You humans only got one heart. We got three." The explanation sounded like something made up.

"Three fuckin' hearts?"

"You hit any of those, we won't survive for long. You shoot us anywhere else, then, we… have a tendency to heal faster than the bullet can kill."

Jed remembered Lenard, the leathered skeleton of a man who had tried to ambush them. "Like Lenard?"

Abe stopped in front of Jed again, nodding as he took a drag from his cigarette. "That's why my bullet went right through him. He didn't even slow." The epiphany cracked his blurry thoughts, giving him a better understanding of the kind of 'people' he was dealing with.

"Now you get it boy, now you get it." Jed saw Abe grin as he pulled out his whiskey flask and offered it to him. Jed grinned back. He unscrewed the dented flask and took a swig, wiping the back of his hand against his mouth and passed it back to Abe, who took a swig. With Abe's guidance, Jed felt he could do whatever it took in order to get Marietta back.

## Chapter 31

The town was growing sleepy when she directed her mare to the nearest hotel. The saloon was just coming to life as she slowed to a stop, tossed the reins over the post, and dismounted. She could instantly feel eyes picking at her skin; the looks of want and bed lust clouding their judgements. *Easier for me*, she thought with a sly curl of the lip. Her white mare nickered. She craned her neck to see a group of men walk up the steps to the saloon, each tipping their hats to her as they passed. Jystana moved her hair from both her shoulders to one, making sure her bare skin was exposed. She had a job to do, and, for Absalom, she would go to the ends of the earth.

She picked up her skirts as she ascended the steps to the porch of the hotel-saloon, making subtle eye contact with a couple men as she walked. She reached out and swung the wing doors outward as she brushed past. She was instantly bathed in the loudness of the parlor. Wherever there was a saloon, there was gossip—and, sometimes, the bits of truth that her lover desperately needed.

Jystana's senses flourished as she made her way to the bar. Her nostrils filled with the stench of old musk, sweat, and dank liquor, dousing the smells of humans and devil-kind, alike. She relied on her sense of hearing as she slipped into a space between men. Her icy blue eyes locked onto the bartender, who was immediately captivated. She smiled slyly and ordered, "Gin and tonic, darlin'. No rocks." Jystana finalized her request with a wink, making the man flush a beat red.

As the man quickly went about making her order, she turned her watchful eyes to the throng of people in front of her. The splendor of sensory overload excited her being. There were so many opportunities to exploit this night and so many opportunities to earn good money. There were also so many opportunities to make a dire mistake. The clink of glass on the hardwood counter at her elbow diverted her attention to the tender, his face a deeper blush than before. Jystana put on her sweetest smile, took a satisfying sip, and turned her attention back to the crowd. The scene tugged at her heart as she scanned the various conversations. It all felt so familiar, reminding her of her first encounter with Absalom.

From his beaten down demeanor, dull eyes, and dusty gear, she could tell he had traveled for miles. He was quiet for his age, observant as he scanned the bar with wary, tired eyes. Only after he made sure it was secure did he approach the bar counter, keeping his gaze hidden under the brim of his hat. Jystana had been watching him from the other side of the parlor, her curiosity nagging at her mind as she ignored the group clients she had been charged with 'entertaining' for the evening. She had ignored their rough hands that caressed her skin, her hair, her curves—she hadn't cared in that moment. Something about that devil intrigued her.

Jystana's ears picked up a strange conversation that didn't flow with the rest of the evening rabble, pulling her abruptly from her precious memories. She frowned subtly as her eyes rested on two men sitting at a corner table, away from the main rabble. The two men, to her, were obviously two devils, but, to the humans around them, they merely looked like weary travelers. They were dressed in grungy clothes, ranging from dark brown to shades of off-white. *Seems these boys have had a rough go of it.*

"You checked the back, right?" One of them asked the other. Jystana could hear every word. She sipped her gin and tonic, looking over the crowd as she listened. The devil who spoke was constantly checking his surroundings, his hands fidgety as they tried to clasp together. He was middle-aged and seemed to be suffering from one of the many diseases their kind can contract. His skin was blotched with scabs and sores that ruined an otherwise decent complexion. His shoulders were drooped, as if he were to be struck at any moment from unseen force.

"Keep yer damn voice down. Of course I did." The second grumbled back as he sat stiffly into the opposite chair, whiskey glasses and bottle in hand. Jystana noted that he was more collected than his partner. She placed her empty glass down and motioned to the bartender for another round. The leader of the two studied the parlor as he spoke, slowly pouring himself a shot. Jystana gently pulled a man in front of her, playfully, as the observant devil swept his eyes over where she sat. She knew she had barely escaped being discovered, as the drunken man she pulled aside stumbled off. *He knows he might be followed. What are you transporting, Eberhart?*

The scabbed devil reached for the bottle, disgruntled that his partner didn't pour him a glass. Jystana didn't need much to understand that this pair was strenuous, at best. *I could use this to my advantage...* "Shit, I ain't loud. Whole damn place is loud, anyway." The collected devil frowned at his partner and downed his shot. He leaned in close, "Regardless, keep yer damn mouth shut...almost got us killed last time."

The scabbed devil snarled and flashed his pointed teeth as he leaned in close and hissed, "I ain't the one who begged fer this job, neither..." Jystana couldn't help but smirk as she listened to the tension between them tighten. The collected devil narrowed his eyes with a burning hatred. *Perfect targets...divided amongst themselves.* She drank the last of her gin and tonic, tipping the glass upside down. She didn't need another drink.

Jystana picked up her skirts and calmly made her way toward their corner, as the collected devil snarled and stood up, "You do it yerself, then. This ain't worth the trouble."

"Go on, then, you som' bitch! I can take care of this shit myself!" The scabbed devil shouted at him. His partner didn't so much as take a glance back as he made his way toward the doors. He was of no danger to her now. As they passed each other, the two looked at each other. Jystana smirked. His eyes sparked with recognition .

He and his partner were through. He was consumed with apathy; she could see it. It was all she needed to reassure herself that the rest of this job should be easy.

She wove in and out of drunk patrons, never letting the disgruntled, scabbed devil out of her sight. Now that the second devil had removed himself, she had a better chance of getting what she needed; information. Finally, she reached his table and slid into the empty seat in front of him, making sure her bust was in his full view. The devil looked up from his glass, startled. His eyes were red-rimmed and dilated in different sizes; a sure sign that he was in fact diseased. *He must have the sickness of the devil's blood,* Jystana thought, trying her best not to gag or make any repulsive facial expressions. *I can smell it now.*

"Looks like you could use some company…" Jystana spoke smoothly as she twirled a strand of hair between her fingers.

He frowned and grabbed the bottle, taking a long swig before setting it back down with a hard clank. "I don' need yer smooth mouth. Get." He gestured away from him.

"Don' be that way…" Jystana calmly reached over and brushed her fingertips over the back of his scabbed hand. The sores, open and scabbed over, appeared infected and felt rough to the touch. It made her stomach turn. *You owe me somethin' expensive after this one, Absalom.*

Her touch caught his attention as he stared at her. His greedy eyes kept glancing at her bosom and back to her face. "What do you want, woman?" He asked, his tone calmer.

Jystana retracted her hand and leaned back in her chair, a sultry grin spreading over her lips, "I jus' wantin' to have some fun. That's all." She could feel his blood flow more rapidly through his diseased veins, and his pathetic heart beginning to race with anticipation. *There we go...men are far too easy.* "Let's say we head upstairs, *hm*?" Without another word, he rose from his chair, a gleam of lust glinting in his eyes as she too rose from her seat. *This part becomes harder and harder to go through with.* She followed him through the crowd and up the staircase that led to the many rooms throughout the establishment.

They passed door after door, until they found an unoccupied room. It was dingy, but Jystana was no stranger to shady places. She could sense the devil's presence as he shut the door behind him. In the enclosed space, his stench grew more powerful. His scabbed hand touched her shoulder, making her skin crawl. *I hate this. I hate all of this.* She could feel his rancid breath taint the back of her neck as his hands began to wander over the laces of her dress, searching for a way to undo them.

*That's far enough.* With a swift motion, she drove a fist backwards into his groin, making direct contact with a solid *thud*. The devil cried in excruciating pain as he stumbled backwards. She didn't pause in her actions as she turned and heel kicked him in the jaw. Jystana heard her heel connect with his jaw with a sick crack as he tumbled to the floor in agony. His moans fell on deaf ears as she loomed over him, pressing her boot heel over his neck and drawing her ivory pistol from her thigh holster. She took delight in this sort of 'escorting'. Easier on her nerves. "Now...I have some questions fer ya."

The devil's eyes burned with hatred as he squirmed. His hands tenderly covering his groin—he didn't want her to strike him again. "The hell is wrong with ya? Ya crazy bitch!" Jystana cocked the hammer back, aiming for his main heart, just like Absalom had taught her all those years ago. "A lot of things sweetheart, but not as much as you. Where's that cargo o' yers goin' to?" Her voice sounded cold and fluid, like the runoff from a mountain in spring.

His eyes widened, realizing his loud mouth had gotten him into a bind. Shock was soon replaced with anger as he gripped her boot to throw her off. She snarled, her piercing blue eyes flaring into a hadean glow as she squeezed the trigger. The bullet tore through flesh, bone, and ligament, his hand and fingers useless and limp. "Another wrong move, and I'll blow the rest o' yer goddamned fingers off. Where is the cargo goin'?" The devil whimpered as he stared at his hand, the blood pulsing in thick streams down his arm.

"Eberhart wanted some sort o' drug taken to the Pacific Coast," the devil pleaded with her, glancing from her fierce eyes to his crippled hand. She could see that it pained him greatly, but she couldn't have cared less. His answer was not enough.

"You still didn't answer my question." She cocked the hammer back again, sending the devil into a panic.

"No wait! We was headin' to Bodie! Silas wanted it!" He quickly spat his words out.

*Bodie? That is far from his usual territory, and I haven't heard of Silas before.* "That's better. And Eberhart? Where is he holdin' his sorry ass up?" She pressed her boot heel harder into the devil's neck, causing him to choke and sputter.

"He's just...out o' Bodie...! In...in the hills!" He wheezed. She pressed harder as she felt her inner self begin to come alive again, the blood and the agony she inflicted making it squirm deep inside of her. She didn't let it show very often. Jystana dampened it as she regained her self-control, letting off the pressure. She walked around him and toward the door, satisfied with his answer, but deeply troubled. It sounded liked Bodie was a set-up to her. Something didn't feel right.

"Oh. Before I forget, darlin'..." She adjusted her aim toward one of his minor hearts and squeezed the trigger once more. This time, the bullet tore through thick muscle, embedding itself deep into its flesh. The devil howled as she holstered her pistol and calmly opened the door, leaving as though nothing had happened. The devil's howls and shouts attracted unwanted attention as she continued her way down the hall and toward the stairs. Men rushed, and the piano downstairs stopped playing as panic began to flood the saloon. She kept her composure through the chaos as she repeated the information in her mind. She needed to get word to Absalom, and she needed to do it now, before Eberhart decided to move on.

She flew down the stairs, where her mare was standing idly by the hitch. Jystana moved to her and mounted quickly. *Abe, get your ass to Bodie, and do it fast. Time's wastin'.* If this was what Abe was looking for, she hoped, for his sake, he would heed her call.

# Chapter 32

The two men in front of Jed had sour looks on their faces as they leafed out green bills. Jed waited patiently as he counted the bills out in his head. *10...20...30...* The man sitting wore a dirt-stained bowler hat, and the other standing by wore a stained vest and bandana to match. When Jed had walked in just minutes ago with a bounty paper, these men had laughed and said he was too young, to go home. Remaining silent, Jed had pulled out a small satchel, stained dark, and tossed it onto the desk. The laughter stopped. The sneers were wiped from their expressions. Bowler Hat had hastily opened the satchel and grunted. The proof of the target's heart was in there.

They had reluctantly gotten out their lockbox from the dark, wood desk and had started to count. The count was close now; *420, 430...* It was a small bounty, Abe had said, but it would be his final test before the real hunt would begin. Jed looped his thumb through his belt loops as he watched the two flighty men.

"There, 450 dollars, kid," Bowler Hat grunted. Jed reached and grabbed the leafed stack, doing a quick recount. He'd have to thank Abe later for teaching him how to count. Jed frowned and glared at the rat of a man from under his hat. "It's short."

"It ain't short!" Bowler Hat exclaimed, looking shocked.

"You're 10 dollars short, or I could make sure your heart will join his." Jed indicated to the pouch.

The silence in that small, decrepit building was almost painful to the ears as the two men swapped glances before Stained Vest dug into his pockets. He pulled a crumpled ten-dollar bill out of his breast pocket and extended it to Jed. Jed snatched it and tucked it in with its brothers, putting the money in his own pocket.

"Nice doin' business with ya." He curtly tipped his hat, turned on his heel, and strode out into the open air street. The midmorning rush was in its thriving pulse as Jed took a moment to allow his eyes to adjust.

"'Bout damn time." Jed couldn't help but smile at the sounds of that voice. Abe moved from the shade of the rickety porch, stepping up next to Jed as he dug for something in his duster. Jed pulled out the money he had just received and subtly handed it to Abe. The hunter grunted, storing the cash in the recesses of his pockets. A full grin spread across Jed's his grizzled features. He felt the crease of his scar on his cheek. It still felt foreign to him, even after the weeks that had passed since it had occurred. Jed looked up to the street. The saloon across the way was quiet, apart from some girls on the second floor. Jed called it whoring. Abe called it advertising.

He could see one of them had a darker aura, like Abe's but not as strong. She was smiling at him and flirtatiously waving at him.

"Jed, are you even hearin' me?" Abe's voice cut through him like the wind through a gorge. Jed's ears began to flame as he looked at Abe, who now had a smoke in hand.

"Sorry, Abe…I'm still ain't used to this…aura thing just yet."

Abe grunted and looked at the woman Jed had caught eyes with, "You don't want her anyways."

"Why not?" Jed asked, looking at Abe from under his hat.

"She ain't clean. Her aura is weak." Abe tapped the end of the cigarette over the edge, letting the white ash dissipate to the dirt ground below. "Don't want any o' her infections…" Jed turned his attention back to the whore, who had moved on to her next potential client for the night to come. "We got a job to do, boy." Abe took one last drag as he stepped down to the street, tossing the used cigarette to the side. The sun's rays didn't seem to illuminate him at all, as his attire absorbed the light. Jed walked down the steps, following him.

Abe and Jed walked in tandem, the crowds molding around them like a river going around a rock. Jed was ready. Abe had been able to teach Jed within a couple weeks what normally would have taken months, had he not had his deal with this devil. *It's worth every drop of blood I gave.*

The horses were left at a hitching post, towards the edge of the town. He could see his stallion standing asleep, head low to the ground, a back leg resting while the other three supported the beast's weight. Dusk, on the other hand, was watching people stride along the boardwalk in their raucous way. Abe reached his horse and took up the reins in his left hand, his right hand holding the horn. He had never tied Dusk off.

Jed untied his horse, who nickered softly, pricking his head up in anticipation. Jed took up the leather straps in his left hand, holding the horn in his other.

Both men mounted, taking steady control over their mounts.

In silence, the two of them rode off into the grassy plains, still damp from the morning dew. Without looking back, they heeled their horses into a gallop. They had a job to do.

\*\*\*

The sun was at their backs as they raced through the rolling hills. Jed was relieved that the weather was finally giving way to fall. It meant an easier time for the horses, as well as for the two men out on the frontier. Rain meant life and food for both them and their horses. The sod under the horses' hooves was sturdy and provided them with traction, without the risk of sliding in the loose dirt of the arid summer climate.

The heavy breath of Jed's horse and the thundering of the two horses' hooves on the earth filled Jed's ears. He loved the sound of it. The rush of the wind, the smell of the fresh plains, the thrill of a fresh hunt. Jed rode next to Abe and slightly behind him, following his direction as they charged forward to a new bounty.

Jed had asked his partner about the nature of their ride, but Abe had stated that it would pay, and it would pay big. Jed had learned not to question him. You wouldn't get a straight-forward answer anyway. The rolling hills they were riding suddenly topped off at a point, indicating a valley just up ahead. Jed eased on the reins as both men came to a stop. Jed overlooked the valley below them, the mountains ahead bare rock and naked from snow. Jed wasn't interested in the mountains this time; he was looking at the snaking track that was laid in the bosom of the valley, herself. There was a small plume of white smoke that trailed behind a sleek black figure on the train that was snaking its way west.

Jed looked over at Abe, his brows furrowed with slight hesitation, "A train?"

Abe adjusted himself in the saddle as Dusk pulled and strained at the bit. As always, the otherworldly horse was ready to ride. Abe looked down the valley and at the train that was making its way slowly down below. "Eberhart is expectin' a delivery…" Abe looked over at Jed, his lips curled into a sly grin, "I aim ta interrupt it."

Jed looked back at the train, a burning anger in the pit of his stomach beginning to grow. "What's on it?" Jed growled, his grip tightening on the reins. If Eberhart was expecting a shipment, Jed would damn well try to intercept it. *He ain't gonna get shit, if I can help it.*

"Money, Jed, and lots of it." Abe heeled Dusk into a brisk descent down the slope. Jed followed suit, his jaw set and ready to destroy at least a little bit of the bastard's income. As soon as Dusk reached flat ground, he screamed and bolted off at a blazing speed.

Jed bared his teeth and urged his stallion to charge after him, "Ha! Ha!!" He shouted over the thunderous sound. Jed flicked his reins from side to side, making the stallion huff and surge forward. Jed leaned low over the horse's neck, his feet balancing his weight in the stirrups. Jed's stallion could barely keep pace with Dusk as the train slowly grew larger and larger in size. The loud *clickity clackity* sound of the train became more apparent and soon drowned out all other noise. Abe drew near the giant metal car, carrying Eberhart's precious cargo.

Abe stood in his saddle for a second as his hands grabbed the side ladder. With a smooth motion, Abe peeled off his saddle and clung to the side of the cargo car. Jed was next. His stallion snorted and huffed as he urged his mount to get closer. They were keeping pace with the train's speed as Jed drew near the side ladder. The train's hollow horn echoed throughout the valley. Jed reached for the metal rungs. His horse wavered from side to side, making it difficult to grasp the rung. His fingers brushed its metal surface a couple times before Jed finally could grasp it.

Jed's heart beat heavily in his chest, almost matching the sound of the train clacking across its tracks. His horse whinnied in anxiety, and feeling that Jed was sliding off immediately, it peeled away from him. Panic filled his chest as his body slammed into the side of the train, his arm twisting unnaturally. His hand gripped the rung tighter. He could feel his grip weaken. *Shit!!* Panicking, he could feel his fingers start to slip, and he shouted. He was going to fall to his death under the moving train.

He felt a rough grip on the back of his shirt and vest, a tight hold that caught him as his fingers lost their grip. Suddenly, Jed was in the air and on top of the train's car. With a thud, Jed landed on his back, out of breath. In disbelief, he coughed and looked over towards the edge. Abe followed shortly after, moving lithely, as though nothing had happened. Abe extended a hand out to him, his weight shifting with the swaying motion of the train. Jed gratefully took it, hoisting himself up to his feet. Abe held him steady for a moment as they locked eyes, brother to brother. Jed nodded in appreciation. Abe nodded back.

Abe had saved his life. Again. *I have to get out of that habit,* Jed thought sheepishly as Abe made his way past him and towards the front of the moving train. His duster coat blew with the wind, making Abe look like a crow in flight. It seemed that he knew exactly where Eberhart's money was hidden. Jed followed him, unsteady for a moment, as the train's swaying made his footing unsure. The wind bit at Jed's face as he held his hat in place with one hand and used the other to balance.

Abe stopped, drawing his pistol. Jed did the same, watching as a hatch in front of the hunter slammed open and a man attempted to crawl through. Without a second thought, Abe popped him. Jed watched as the man's arm went completely limp and disappear to the interior of the car below them.

Jed heard something click behind him, snapping his attention to another man who must have climbed up from the back of the car. Jed frowned as he swiftly moved aside. He elbowed him in the face, making him shout in surprise. The man staggered, giving Jed the opening he needed. Jed moved behind the man and dropped him with one shot. The corpse dropped with a sick thud and slid off the side and to the terrain that was speeding by below. *It's so damn loud up here I didn't hear him comin'.* A bullet whistled past him, making Jed duck low, searching for the marksman. Abe returned fire behind Jed as he ducked. Another man fell in between the cars. Jed looked at Abe, thankful that he had his back.

More shots whistled past them as Abe moved quickly to the open hatch and dropped down. Jed cursed under his breath, but he knew he had to follow. He was too exposed on top of the metal car. Jed ran to the open hatch, dropped his legs through the hole, and used the lip of the hatch grate to swing himself to the floor with a rough landing. His legs quivered from the impact, his muscles and tendons aching from the sudden change of stability.

Abe was finishing off some of the men that had been taken by surprise from the drop-in. Abe had disabled one man's firing arm, moving the man swiftly in front of him, his comrade shooting the man, instead of the hunter. The man in Abe's grip shouted in pain until the other's six shots were up. Abe discarded the crude living shield and shot the other man in the head. With river of blood running down his forehead, he wordlessly dropped to the ground.

Jed straightened and strode over the first man. He lightly tapped his boot against the dead man's. "These Eberhart's boys?"

Abe looked back at Jed and nodded, "Yep."

A seething hatred coiled in Jed's gut, and he leaned over, spitting on the man's corpse before moving around Abe and to the car's back door. "What you gave him was more than he deserved." Abe remained silent. Jed could feel his piercing gaze on his back as he reached the door. His own words shocked him. *What is wrong with me?*

"What, exactly, is this delivery you mentioned, Abe?" Jed wanted to forget what he had done. He wanted to get this job done and continue searching for his sister. He could feel that they were, somehow, closer to finding her.

Abe moved around the corpses to the door, looking at the latch intently, "Money. I'm sure it's a shit ton." Jed couldn't help but noticed the hint of greedy anticipation. Jed nodded, hoping that they could get it and get out quickly. If robbing this train meant hurting Eberhart's operations, so be it. The bastard deserved it and more. Jed froze in place.

They heard something. Something big.

Abe slowly backed from the door, taking out his pistols just as slowly, as if whatever the noise was could hear them. Jed's neck hair stood on end as he, too, drew his pistols in silence. He heard the sound again. It sounded like a deep growl from the other car, and thrashing like rolling thunder. Jed took a step back and grimaced as he slid in pooling blood. He frowned at the growing pool and back at Abe. He was staring at it.

*Oh, shit,* Jed inwardly cursed as the sound of ripping metal whined and screeched followed by a hollow boom. The door and the face of its wall bowed in from the impact. Abe moved back quickly, motioning Jed to do the same as the wall bowed more with another blow. The howl from whatever creature was in that other car was more deafening than the train, itself. Abe roughly twisted Jed around, shouting, "Move your ass, boy!"

Before Jed could ask why, the door split open, the metal contorting into an odd shape. A gnarled, bloodied claw and arm emerged as they heard a loud screech. The skin of the creature was slick, as if wet. It was a dark color that seemed to meld and shift in the light, as though to camouflage itself into its surroundings.

They both jumped over crates and moved towards the front of the car. The door and wall around it finally slammed open. Jed could hear the creature's long claws skid and scratch along the floor. Abe's gun roared in the dim light, flashing as the sound mingled with the shrieks of the creature. Jed reached the furthest door and heaved on the turn lock. With a slam, the metal latch lifted and creaked letting the door swing open in a rush of air. Jed was nearly blinded by the brightness of the sun.

Jed could hear Abe fire more shots as he ran. Jed quickly moved outside, Abe right behind him. Jed could hear his heart pound wildly in his chest as Abe slammed the door behind him. He aimed his pistol at the door, as it, too, bent outward toward them. The howls and screeches echoed eerily in the metal car. "What the hell was that thing, Abe?!" Jed shouted over the sound of the train.

Abe reloaded his pistol with a certain calmness that Jed prayed he would get with time. "Eberhart was transporting a damn Cucal." Jed looked at the door again as the creature slammed its whole body against the door a couple times. "A mindless demon. They eat my kind, and those that are tainted with our blood." Jed's heart dropped to his gut as the creature continued its rampage against its metal confines.

Without another word, Abe walked across the tongue and hitch to the other car and scaled the wall. The wind from the train's speed whipped his duster around him. Jed didn't hesitate to follow him swiftly, not wanting to get left behind. Not after he had come this far. This, 'Cucal'—as Abe had determined—was frantically clawing its way out of the car below them. And, by the sound of it, it was making good headway on the door.

Abe was running along the top of the car. Jed followed suit, keeping up with his friend as they raced across the top. The sound of exploding metal crashed behind them, slamming into the car they were on, making Jed lose his footing.

"Shit!" Jed cursed as he slammed onto the rooftop, winding him. He felt his hands grasp at the metal, but nothing seemed to give him a firm hold to keep him from slipping. The Cucal below screeched as it tore open the next door. None of that would matter if Jed couldn't stop himself from a fatal fall.

Jed's heart pounded in his ears as he glanced back over his shoulder. The terrain flew past. Jed would be crushed under the several tons of metal that hauled over the tracks. "Abe!" Jed cried out, more out of a need for help than of fear. He hoped Abe heard him over the low horn of the train. Jed felt his lower half drop off the edge. Gritting his teeth, he clung at anything he could, straining his core muscles to keep him from falling. He could feel sweat dripping off his forehead and down his entire body.

Gunshots were fired, piercing the metal roof to the car below. Screeches echoed in the metal confines of the car, making it rock violently as Jed felt a strong hand grab his forearm. Jed looked up to see Abe's shaded face. Relief washed over him as Abe hauled him back up to his feet. Sweating and breathing hard, Jed nodded a silent thank you. Abe grunted, turning back towards the front of the train again, "Watch your feet, boy." Jed nodded again, trying to calm his heartbeat. "What's the plan, Abe?!" Jed shouted.

"Move!" They dashed to the other car, narrowly missing the roof of the car had burst through, the sound of twisting metal screamed over the clack of the tracks below. The demon below was getting desperate now, wildly clawing. It wanted their blood and in a bad way. The hole was slowly growing.

Abe had successfully jumped to the next car, waiting for Jed with obvious impatience. Jed didn't waste any time. *Damn it all to hell*, he cursed inwardly, making a break for it. The hole in the center rang with the calamitous screeches of the Cucal. Feeling the

Cucal's fury, Jed's legs pumped as fast as they could, his feet vaulting off the surface in a giant leap. He prayed he wouldn't get caught. The Cucal must have sensed him, and its darkened claws lashed out of the darkness, hoping to catch a fresh meal.

With teeth bared, Jed felt the claws brush just past his legs. The demon had failed to snare its victim. In a rage, it tried to pull itself out of the hole. Jed didn't look back. He kept his momentum going as he vaulted to the other car. This time, he didn't lose his balance. Abe started to run with Jed, seeing he made it mostly unscathed. Jed followed Abe, fully trusting his friend's unspoken plan. The pair of them ran and ran, the metal cars passing under their feet as swiftly as they could.

Jed could hear the demon charging down the train. *Damn! I hoped it would have been stuck longer!* The sound of the train and wind, the pounding of his heart and his blood rushing, the sweat running down his whole body. He felt he could run like this forever, if need be. Each passing car brought them closer to the head of the train.

Abe stopped at the car just before the coal car, turning to face the charging Cucal. Jed slid to a stop, balancing himself. In between heavy breaths, he shouted, "Abe! What do you need me to do?"

Abe drew his pistols, cocking the hammers back. "Get to the engine! Full throttle! Then, break the handle!"

Jed nodded, hoping he could do what he asked. He'd never been on a train, and he hoped this throttle would be obvious. Jed scaled over the lip of the next car, into the bed of unburnt coals. The light material was loose and hard to keep traction on. He kept his balance by spreading his arms slightly, a precarious balancing act. He reached the edge and quickly dropped to the connecting platforms. The roar of the engine almost overwhelmed Jed's ears as he quickly moved to the main engine.

In the main engine car, the heat was blasting in steady impulses each time the hatch to the flames opened. A big, broad-shouldered man in overalls with no undershirt was shoveling the coal, and a smaller man was handling the numerous cranks and levers that were scattered across the front. Jed took a moment to admire the complexity of the metal monster.

The bigger man seemed to sense him. His thick muscles tensed, and both his meaty hands gripped the rough wood of his shovel.

Jed could see an aura, much like the others that he had encountered, flare up briefly. Jed prepared himself for a fistfight. *Don't think my gun will do me any good up here.*

The man roared, turning his body around to face Jed, swinging his shovel at him. Jed moved to the side, letting the blade of the coal shovel clank and spark on the floor from the impact. A concentrated frown creased Jed's brow as the man swung wildly to the right, making him duck under the blade. The motion whistled over his head, barely missing his skull.

*Don't get overwhelmed...it's just like your training,* Jed reminded himself, anticipating the overhead blow that came next. The man roared an unnatural tone. Instinctively, Jed shouted back, meeting the shovel handle with his hand, gripping it tightly. The impact did little to Jed, where it surely would have cracked his carpals before. The demon before him, in his human form, cocked his head, surprised that a human had stopped his blow.

Jed took the opening.

He quickly head-butted the demon right in the cranium with a sickening thwack, followed by a swift, upward jerk of the knee. The demon screeched as he doubled over, but Jed gave him no reprieve as he elbowed him hard in the back of the neck. With a shout, he fell to the metal floor, unconscious. Jed's blood pumped swiftly through his veins, and he could feel the adrenaline throughout his body. Senses heightened, he turned his attention to the only man left; the engineer. Jed adjusted his hat as he stalked over to the man, who backed up as far as he could.

*I don't think so.* With a growl, Jed grabbed the man roughly by the collar and hoisted him up to eye level. The man was quaking in his spot, his hands trembling as he raised them in surrender, "N-no please! I just run the train!"

Jed stared deep into the man's eyes, trying to see if there was any trace of evil in him. The engineer's face was plastered with fear, soot, and sweat. "Where's the throttle to this thing?" Jed shouted over the noise of the engine. He didn't have time to play games.

The engineer frantically pointed to a larger lever on the floor, with a squeeze handle on the back of the tip. Jed glance at it and back at the man, dropping him to the ground. He walked over to it, gripping the handle tightly. As he stood there, he felt the pumping and workings of the pistons and gears beneath their feet; a sensation that he could only compare to a beating heart.

With a strong motion, Jed pushed the lever forward as far as he could push it. When it clacked into place, Jed stood back and kicked at it with brute force. Jed knew what Abe's plan was: derailment. He wouldn't let him down. With a series of grunts, he struck at the lever over and over again, each time with more force. He could feel the engine beneath him hum with more vigor as he felt the speed picking up. With a final shout, the lever bent over and to the side. Satisfied, Jed turned back to the coal car and looked at the frightened engineer.

"Follow me if you want to live!" Jed ran for the car ahead. The engineer started, and quickly followed, stepping around the fallen coal shoveler.

Jed scaled the mountain of coal again, quicker this time. He heard gunshots firing, mingled with the screeches of the Cucal's rage. Jed climbed up to the car Abe was battling on and paused. His breath was tight in his chest as he looked at the thing in the daylight.

It was snakelike, with long, lanky limbs and a long torso. Its skin was thin, the veins clearly defined over large sections of its slimy body that multiple gunshot wounds had ripped through. With an elongated bottom jaw and jagged teeth, the head was the most terrifying. It had eyes, but it couldn't see through the murky clouds that covered the pupils and iris. The claws on its hands and feet were uneven, as though they were not fully developed.

*This thing isn't full grown?!* Jed thought. It's thick, black blood was smeared all over the metal roof, making it hard for Abe to balance. The demon was obviously wearing down, but it was far from giving up on the fight. Abe had managed to put several rounds into the beast's flesh, and it was profusely bleeding. The demon lunged, taking Abe by surprise as they both landed onto the car with a thud. Abe staved off its slavering mouth by using his forearm against its slimy neck. Droplets of saliva mingled with blood, oozing onto his chest, face, and hat.

Allowing instinct to take over, Jed drew both of his guns, pulling the hammer back and firing several shots to its face, hoping that it would at least knock it back. It did more than he had anticipated.

The Cucal writhed and recoiled from Abe, clutching its face with its clawed hands. It scratched at itself as though a parasite was suddenly lodged into his body. Its screeching hit a new, higher pitch, piercing Jed's ears. The pain was almost unbearable.

Abe got up quickly with lithe agility, dashing to Jed and the cowering engineer. Without a word, Abe grabbed them both by the shoulders, running to the edge at full speed.

Jed shouted with surprise as all three of them were vaulted off the edge of the train and to the fast-running river below. It felt surreal as the three of them fell yards and yards below. Something swift moved in the corner of Jed's eye. He looked over his shoulder to find the Cucal had jumped after them. Its arms were spread wide, its talons extended, and its fanged maw open wide with rage and hunger. He felt Abe's grip loosen and vanish altogether as the hunter reacted. The motion left Jed in a freefall toward the water and hidden rocks below.

Abe turned his body completely around in his fall, facing the demon that had leaped after them. Jed saw something in Abe he hadn't seen in the many months he had been with his unusual companion: Abe's body was being enveloped with writhing, shadowy tendrils from his core, wrapping around his limbs. His eyes burned a crimson red, like the fires of hell, itself.

The Cucal drew closer, its maw opened wide, anticipating a mouth full of flesh and bone. Jed was plunged into a the torrent of the river, which churned over him until he couldn't tell where the surface was. He fumbled to holster his gun, and searched desperately for something he could hold onto. His fingers brushed against a river rock. He had hit bottom. His lungs burned for air as he began to follow the rocks on the bottom. He prayed it would lead him to the surface.

The pressure of the water and the roaring of the river around him were tightening, when he finally broke the skin of the water. He gasped for air. His lungs felt relieved as the air filled his aching lungs. He was soaked to the bone, but he had survived the fall that surely should have killed him. He looked around for Abe and the engineer. He couldn't see either of them.

He heard the Cucal's roar echo in the deep river's ravine, and the rocks ricocheted its anger. As he staggered to his feet, Jed's body felt heavy with river water. He turned to his left to see Abe in close combat with the demon. Abe was soaked, and fighting with only his hands. He didn't see his guns. Jed pulled his pistol out and took aim. He cocked the hammer back again and pulled the trigger. The gun clacked in silence, spattering water droplets everywhere.

"Shit." He murmured to himself. He frantically searched for spare bullets, anything to help. He cursed again under his breath, finding nothing in his pockets or belt. Jed watched his friend, helpless.

Abe bared his teeth as he firmly grabbed the Cucal's arm, landing a heavy punch into the demon's jaw. The wet thud echoed off the rocks around them as the Cucal staggered on its feet. The heavy blow seemed to daze it enough for Abe to make his move. Without hesitation, he grabbed its arm more firmly and flung it into a giant boulder just off the river's bank. With a howl, the demon's back cracked against it. It fell to the ground, writhing and squirming. It had finally been worn down, and Abe knew it.

Stalking to it, Abe's anger seemed palpable. He picked up a large rock and raised it over his head. Jed cringed as the sound of cracked skull echoed through the ravine. Abe shouted with rage as he pounded the rock over and over on the demon's now-crushed skull. Each blow made the body twitch. Finally, it stopped.

All was quiet again, save the sound of the rushing river behind them. Jed walked over to Abe, his feet slipping on rocks along the way. Abe took his hat off with a grumble, shaking it out. Jed was just relieved that they had survived the encounter.

"You alright, Abe?" Jed called out to him. He knew Abe would be in no mood to entertain.

He grunted, rummaging in his duster. He drew out his ivory box that contained his beloved cigarettes. It was warped and soaked with the river's water; all of them ruined. He sighed, tossing the whole carton to the side.

"I need a damn cigarette." Abe walked past Jed, to the bank.

Jed couldn't help but smile at his friend's petty plight. *Well, he's obviously fine.* Jed looked behind him, remembering the engineer that had been thrown off with them. His heart sank to his gullet as his eyes caught sight of the man's mangled arm amidst the rocks downstream. His now-pale hand stuck up awkwardly, with bone and blood showing.

*Nothing left of him.* Jed swallowed hard and turned his attention forward. *May God have mercy on ya.*

In silence, they both walked the side of the river.

## Chapter 33

The wreckage had been on near-catastrophic. Abe and Jed had walked for a couple miles through the deep ravine until they found their way back to the plains. Abe had called for his horse with a low whistle that made Jed's ears ache. Dusk had come from the place they last left their horses. Jed felt the weight of the matter sink in: he was horseless again. Abe told him to wait, that, perhaps, it had been for the best. Jed took the time while he was waiting to dry out some of his soaked clothes in the high afternoon sun.

Abe returned a couple hours later, Jed's stallion in hand. As they entered town, the people stared. Jed was starting to get used to it—people often stared when the two of them came to town. Jed could feel every muscle in his weary body spasm with exertion, and he was relieved to see the local saloon. It meant beds, a warm meal, and a shot of whiskey or two.

Jed reached around to his saddlebags and tightened the strained straps firmly. When the two of them scoured the wreckage of the train, it had proven difficult. The train had, indeed, derailed. Its sleek, long body of seemingly endless cars was now twisted and contorted in unimaginable ways. The smoke was heavy and thick, the engine looked like it had exploded from the crash. Abe and Jed had managed to find a car full of valuables, no doubt some sort of payment or tribute to Eberheart. Jed was only too happy to carry off as much as his saddlebags could hold.

With a snort, Dusk stopped at the hitching post. Abe dismounted, undoing the latches of his saddlebags. Jed reined his stallion to a stop, accompanying it with a soft 'whoa'. He swung his right leg over the back of the saddle and landed on the ground. It felt good to be on solid earth. Jed loosened the straps to his own saddlebags and slung them over his shoulder. He was looking forward to all the relaxing pleasures he was sure were to come. He followed Abe up the steps, his spurs and gear clinking and rustling, still damp from their plunge. Abe pushed the winged doors aside, Jed followed.

The saloon was another smoke-filled parlor, there was another piano player on another un-tuned piano, and, predictably, there were whores weaving in and out of the tables. Abe ignored them all as he shoved himself into a spot at the bartop. The bartender nervously approached Abe. His years-old clothes were as neatly pressed as possible. Jed stood by, observing the local throng. He saw no other demons or devils in the crowd. Jed relaxed a little.

Abe leaned in close to the barkeep and spoke in a low tone, "Clear this saloon. Me an' the boy are buying it for the night."

The bartender scoffed, all nervousness was gone from his countenance. The older man looked down at the bartop, wiping at a spot complacently, "Mister, I got a whole buildin' of paying people. You'd have ta have more n' a night's worth of revenue ta—"

Abe lifted his heavy saddlebags, setting them firmly on the worn countertop. The tender pulled the black leather bags closer. He opened one bag and stopped. Jed knew what was in there. They had found unharmed stacks of freshly printed money from the East Coast. Jed had hoped it was Eberheart's. The bartender was, at least, smart enough to not pull any of it out. He cleared his throat, the thick mustache on his lip wiggling twice, as if in deep thought. Abe waited for an answer. Finally, the man nodded and called over someone Jed thought to be the bartender's son.

They talked with each other in hushed voices as the rabble of the parlor carried on. The son stood up tall and projected his voice so all could hear, "Alright! Shut yer mouths, y'all!" The whole room became silent, and the piano's out-of-tune song cut off mid-chorus. The drunks kept singing, until someone finally told them to be quiet. "This saloon is closed for the evenin'!" A wave of groans, protests, and shouts erupted from the crowd as some started to pick up their things and leave. "Y'all heard me! Saloon's closed! Now get!"

The crowd murmured and groaned amongst themselves as they filed out of the winged doors. Jed couldn't help but smile to himself, *Abe knows how to clear a room.* Once the last patron filed out, the whores who took residence there began cleaning up the very small messes here and there. The silence was refreshing to Jed's ears. Quiet was exactly what his mind and body craved.

Abe turned his attention to the half-empty bottle in front of them. The amber liquid sloshed inside the clear bottle, its label had worn off long ago. He took it by the neck and poured himself a shot into one of the many glasses that were left dry. The bartender hefted the bags over his shoulder and looked at Abe, "If'n you don't mind me askin', who are you fellas, anyways?"

Abe grunted, clearly not in the mood to talk about anything anytime soon. Jed answered for both of them, "He's my uncle, sir. Just passing through. He wanted to travel across the territories."

The bartender shook his head with a grunt, "It's dangerous out here, son. Ain't nothin' out here but outlaws, bandits, and Injuns."

Jed grinned, "I appreciate the warnin', sir, but I think we'll be just fine."

The man grunted and walked past the bar, to the back room, where Jed was certain all the finances were stored. The son grumbled under his breath and moved to the main parlor to help the girls clean up.

"Uncle?" Abe looked at Jed. Jed could hear the amusement in his friend's voice as he downed his shot of whiskey. He poured himself another drink and pulled a dry glass to him. He filled it and slid it over to Jed, who gladly took it.

Together, they knocked back their drinks. At last, in silence and relative peace, Jed's shoulders felt heavy as he set the glass down. He could feel the toll of the train incident wearing on his body. He poured another glass as his mind wandered back to his sister. He had to ask.

Somberly, Jed looked at the liquid in the shot glass, and asked in low tone, "Abe...do you think Marietta is still alive?" That question had been haunting him for several weeks now. He wanted desperately to believe that she was, in fact, alive and unharmed. But his mind had to think in the reality of the situation; the chances she was even alive were slim, and he didn't want to face the fact that she could be dead.

Abe drained his glass, pausing before filling it again, "Honestly, kid...I don't know." The words were hard to hear, even though his mind had come to that same conclusion. Neither had any idea if she was alive. Jed hung his head, trying to keep his emotions out of control. He had come so far, and had done and seen so much.

"But I intend to finish what I swore to do, Jedidiah." Jed could hear the hunter knock back his round. He felt a strong hand reassuringly clasp his shoulder. Jed looked up at the hunter, shocked that Abe had comforted him. His expression was that of one caring for someone else. He hadn't seen a similar look for many months. Not since his Pa.

Jed swallowed hard, his heart pricking with the memory of his Pa from what seemed like ages ago. He missed him so much and so many things to talk to him about. *Can't fix that now...none of this.* Jed nodded at Abe's strangely comforting words, feeling that Abe had meant what he said. *I trust him. He's been a man of his word since the beginning.* Jed took a breath, and filled his glass again.

"Why me?" Jed asked quietly as he toyed with the empty glass in his hand. The bartender had returned, seeing that the two of them had already drained the bottle of whiskey. Abe shirked his duster off his shoulders, laying it across the back of his barstool. His black vest and dark gray undershirt were wrinkled and still appeared to be damp. Abe straightened his vest and shifted his bandolier slightly. The bartender placed a new bottle on the countertop. Abe popped the cork and poured himself another.

"Why my family?" Jed's words hung in the air, as though on a thin string, as he looked at Abe, hoping he would have an answer. Abe cleared his throat, again clearly uncomfortable with the questions.

"Eberheart…he doesn't take kindly to those who…disrupt his 'business operations'." He continued his drinking as he talked, "And your Pa, Jed, he did just that."

Jed set his glass down on the counter, listening close to what Abe had to say. He wanted the truth.

"He never did tell ya about his Marshalling, did he?" Abe turned his cobalt blue gaze to Jed as he paused mid-drink.

Jed shook his head, "No, he didn't. He always told us that he had been a rancher all his life."

Abe grunted, "Best that he did after what happened."

Jed turned in his seat, the silence of the building weighing down on them both.

Abe drank again before continuing, "Your father was a territory Marshall. Roamed from town to town, bringing wanted men in from all sorts of directions. Abel McKay…" Abe half smiled to himself as he poured another glass, "Abel McKay was the most respected and well-known Marshall in the southern territory. Bane to outlaws and scourge of the desert." Abe chuckled. "To me, he was just some fresh blood bootlicker."

"If I didn't know better, Abe, I'd say you respected my Pa."

Abe sighed and leaned back, "In a way, I suppose you could say that. I stayed out of his way, and he stayed out of mine." His small smile faded. "That is, until I had gotten word about a new uprising bandit ring called the Marks…" Abe dug into his vest pocket and drew out the obsidian coin that Jed had been seeing recently. He turned it over in his fingers before setting it on the counter. The ruby eyes of the beast imprinted on the coin stared maliciously at the two of them, glinting with a burning hunger. Jed reached over and touched the edge.

"Your Pa went after them after they had ransacked a town or two, devastatin' the land in the process."

Jed looked up at Abe. *I can see that...Pa was always so willin' to help those in need, even if it meant he couldn't eat.*

"He spent months trackin' down the gang, learnin' their patterns, their tactics...he narrowed the leaders down to one person." Abe indicated the number with his forefinger before gripping the neck of the whiskey bottle in front of them. "That's where he made the mistake."

"Eberheart," Jed murmured hatefully.

"Not Eberheart," Abe corrected him quickly.

"I thought it was just Eberheart that led the Marks?" Jed asked, puzzled.

"And he does, but he had a brother. Two, in fact." The realization struck Jed to the core. *Two brother's? Christ...* His eyes widened as Abe's words filled in the puzzle to this whole mess. "Your Pa had killed the younger twin brother, Donald, in fatal combat. Abel had managed to head off a raid with several men, deputies, and sheriffs of the towns 'round about. Abel didn't realize the spark of retribution he had created." Jed retracted his hand from the odd medallion and poured himself another glass. "When Eberheart learned of his twin's death, and who had done it, you can imagine his rage."

Abe's voice grew lower in tone, and he was silent for a moment, thinking about how to word the next part of the tale. "He swore to tear apart Abel McKay's legacy, from the source to the seed." Abe looked at Jed before he took the obsidian medallion back, letting it disappear from sight once more.

Jed looked forward at the glass he had filled, "So...Eberheart is doin' this for a lifelong grudge." The truth of his father's murder and his sister's abduction made sense now. And it made Jed feel angrier at this devil than ever before. He gripped the glass as the truth mulled in his thoughts.

"Easy, Jed, I ain't gonna bandage your hand for ya," Abe grumbled.

Jed glanced at his friend, then, at the glass. The clear material was beginning to spider crack. *How…? How did I not notice that?* Jed cleared his throat and pushed his glass away. *What is happening to me?*

"You need to control yourself there, kid. You ain't used to what I gave ya."

Jed nodded and looked at Abe again, "Thank you, Abe, for tellin' me the truth."

Abe just grunted and nodded. The sun had finally set, and the many candles and oil lamps glowed throughout the parlor room. Abe had called over the barkeep and demanded a warm meal, which Jed hadn't had in a while. He didn't disagree with Abe's request.

When the food arrived, they ate in silence as Jed contemplated the discussion about his father's past and the true nature of what he did. Jed couldn't help but feel not only betrayed, but also proud of what his Pa had tried to accomplish. He tried to get rid of an evil, so others could live in peace. He always had a feeling that his Pa was not a rancher all his life. There was just something about him that Jed had never been able to put his finger on.

The meal was full of cured meat heated up over a hot stove, with week old biscuits, semi-fresh gravy, and corn. Abe picked around the corn agitatedly. "You really should eat your corn." Jed took a daring jab at Abe, a slight grin on his lips, "It's good for ya."

Abe scoffed and flicked a piece of corn from his fork, "Like hell it is. Damn rabbit food is what it is."

Jed laughed, a good long laugh, at Abe's reaction. The noise startled Abe for a moment, and he, too, started to chuckle. He knew he had been had. The rest of the evening unwound from there. Both men had opened up more to each other—thanks, in part to the drink, Jed thought—and they talked and argued about different things. Abe's bounty hunter façade crumbled, and Jed's closed demeanor dissipated into the liquor and card-playing for the rest of the night.

*** 

Jed woke in the morning with a throbbing head and a groggy body. He groaned, rubbing his face with an open palm. He could feel the heat of the day filtering through the aged linen curtains. *I can't remember what I did last night…or maybe it was this mornin'…I ain't sure.* With a sigh, he sat up slowly, holding his head in one hand. He tensed when he felt a soft hand on his lower back and heard a woman's content, sleepy groan. He turned his head to the side and looked at the half-covered woman beside him. His ears flushed red at the sight of the whore in his bed. *Oh, shit…now I remember…*

He gently placed her hand on the sheets and got up. He found his pants and boots next to the bed and began pulling those on, as she scratched her head and rolled over. Jed couldn't help but grin as he stared at her slender bare back. The memories from the previous night slowly began to trickle back into his mind, even though it was a bit hazy. Abe and Jed had a meager meal, which was more than what they usually had out on the plains, and they played cards late into the night, while the whores of the saloon watched eagerly. For hours, the two played cards, and Abe was winning almost every game, until Jed caught Abe cheating. In a playful uproar, the two had said good night, each accompanied with a woman on their arms.

Jed smiled to himself. It was a good night. He found his shirt and gun belt. He tried to remain as quiet as possible. He didn't want to wake his lovely, soiled dove. He looked at her one last time before silently tipping his hat to her in a farewell.

*I need coffee,* Jed sighed, rubbing his pounding temple and hoping that there would be at least one cup available.

"You're always late boy." Jed looked up and saw Abe sitting at a table by himself in the corner, eating what looked to be breakfast. Jed grinned and walked over to him, taking the empty chair across from him. A second plate was already there. His stomach rolled with hunger and he picked up a piece of cured ham. "Didn't want ta wake up the nice lady."

A mischievous grin that spread over Abe's rugged face, just visible under his hat's shadow. They again ate in silence, not speaking once about the night prior. When both were done with their meals, they rose. As they were leaving, the bartender called after them, "Have a good ride now! And feel free to stop by again!"

Wordlessly, Abe left. Jed paused and looked at the man, tipping his hat to him politely, "Much obliged." Jed followed his friend to the golden morning, leaving their temporary sanctuary behind.

The town was quite busy, with men and women bustling about. Abe went straight to his horse, who looked as bored as it had ever been. Jed went to his stallion and patted his neck gently and stroked his shoulder, before securing his saddle bags again and mounting up. He adjusted himself in the seat and took the reins in his hands. It felt good to be in the saddle. Abe mounted as well, turning Dusk to the edge of town.

"Where to now, Abe?"

"Deadwood." Abe gently prodded Dusk's sides with his spurs, making the black horse move. Jed followed suit. *And now the hunt truly begins.*

# Chapter 34

The rains had come with a fury from the heavens, making the roads and trails more treacherous than Jed was accustomed to. The rolling hills had made a sudden change to giant mountains and tall, pine-dominated forests. The weather was cooler here. Much cooler. Jed had stopped teasing Abe for buying heavier clothing and padded gloves after their first fall night. It had rained seemingly non-stop for weeks.

The horses snorted and chose their footing carefully as the rain continued to drip through the canopy. Jed could barely see the darkening sky overhead. He shivered, pulling his thick coat around him. Abe had been quiet, as usual. Both riders and horses were soaked to the bone, and Abe's grumpy countenance was clearly visible, even from Jed's point of view.

The trail they had set to was thick with mud and decaying vegetation. It clearly wasn't used very often, and it was said the roads to this northern territory were rife with natives thirsty for white-man's blood. Jed grunted and adjusted himself in the saddle. *They're all probably just as miserable as we are out here. Doubt we'll see any.* The rain that trickled through the forest made it hard for Jed to hear. He glanced over his shoulder, wary of possible danger here in this new frontier.

"They ain't comin' boy, so just calm yerself." Abe's grumbled voice carried over the quiet sounds of the terrain around them.

Jed snapped his attention back to his friend leading the way and called over to him, "Ya might be right, Abe, but this rain might make it hard to hear 'em comin'."

Abe raised a hand, waving his remark off as his horse stepped over a dip in the road. Jed sighed and leaned forward. After several months with his strange mentor—and, now, friend—Jed had learned that Abe was quite literally fearless of any situation. He hoped that, in time, he, too, could be that fearless.

After hours of weaving through the dense forest, Jed began to wonder if the outpost town was actually this far north. They climbed a steep hill, the ground underneath the horses' hooves slick with mud, humus, and rainfall. Abe's horse scaled skillfully and carefully; Jed's was slow and stumbling. Jed reined his steed close, making him take his time up the hill. He couldn't afford losing his horse to a broken leg, or worse. The stallion snorted, as if frustrated from the difficulty of the climb, as he carefully placed his feet. Abe reined to a stop at the top of the rise, digging around his pocket for a cigarette. Jed's stallion finally crested and stopped, blowing and snorting in satisfaction of overcoming the challenge.

Jed stared down the winding valley to the small lanter- lit town below, in the valley's gut. "Deadwood?" Jed asked. Abe drew out his long-sought-for cigarette and lit up under the cover of his hat. He cupped the tiny flame that emanated from his thumb tip as he puffed, sending fresh smoke into the drenched air. Abe breathed out, sending another stream into the air before nodding, "Yep. Lowest place you can find…far as greed and corruption goes."

Far off thunder rumbled through the black hills with a raw, ominous power. Abe clucked his horse forward again. Jed followed suit, watching the seedy town so far below with a curious eye. *Abe really **has** been all over this country.*

The sun had set long before they had hit level ground. The trail was difficult to navigate in the dark, but Jed trusted Abe and he knew that the hunter remembered the way very well. The transition from the thick forest to the main road and edge of the town was abrupt. Jed could hear the life beat of the town before they broke cover.

From what Jed had heard, he guessed there was one main street filled with late night shops and, of course, late-night entertainment. He had pinpointed three saloons, just on the basis of the badly out of tune the pianos being played were. Jed was still trying to get over the fact that his hearing was this good, even over the downpour.

Abe steered his horse to the side of the main street, to avoid the knee-deep mud pits. Not only had Jed's hearing been enhanced, but the smell was almost enough to make him gag. The stench of urine, feces, and rot drowned his senses. The faint smell of Abe's cigarette was a reprieve from the barrage.

Finally, Abe reined to a stop at one of the largest buildings on the street and dismounted, loosely tying the horse to the rotten post. Jed reined his horse to the left of Abe. He could feel the muck sink up to his ankles as he, too, tied off his horse. The ruckus coming from inside was a match to the storm outside. Loud shouts and hollers and the off-key notes of an un-tuned piano echoed through the batwing doors, accompanied by a cloud of smoke.

Abe walked around the horses after patting Dusk's neck, looking up at the darkened sign creaking in the breeze. He grunted and moved to the mud-covered steps. Jed glanced up as well, his eyes keen in the dark. Its faded letters read *The Gem*.

Jed rubbed his horse's forehead gently before following Abe up the slickened steps. The bottom step was so caked with mud that a man might slip and fall to the sodden street below it. Jed took his steps carefully. When they reached the top, Abe tossed his used cigarette to the side before walking through the door.

Jed took off his hat, shaking the water off it and, then, he put it back on his head snugly. He followed Abe, bracing for the overwhelming sensory overload that was sure to follow. As the doors swung inward with a tired groan, the sound of the parlor hit him like a waterfall on rock. Everything was so loud. His eyes swept the room, scanning over the people crowded around tables, games, and the main bar. Men and women drifted around each other in a cacophony of laughter and shouting.

The colors of the clientele are what struck him most. The miasma of colors that swirled and danced like smoke—though they were faint—were almost mesmerizing. Jed swallowed, keeping himself calm and collected. He was surrounded by demons, devils, and the lowest of humanity. None had noticed his entry. He wanted to keep it that way.

Jed slid through the crowd toward the bar and took a place by Abe's side. He nodded to the bartender and loudly asked for a shot of whiskey. The gruff, weary-looking man nodded and poured one, sliding it into Jed's hand.

Jed pulled off his gloves and tucked them away inside his heavy coat. "What do you see, boy?" Jed heard Abe's voice clearly through the commotion. No matter where they were, Jed always seemed to hear him clearly and in his usual tone. Jed knocked back his shot and cleared his throat. The burn of the alcohol soothed the ache of the cold that seemed to have taken harbor. "What *don't* I see is the better question."

Conversations were flowing around them, and Jed was sifting through to see if he could find something useful:

"—I told you not to use a belt..."

"Just one night? I'll pay double!"

"Shit! You won again!"

"...soon as we get enough money, we can get out of this shit hole..."

Jed inwardly grumbled. Always the same, routine talk with these people. And always the same result: nothing of use to him in the slightest. Jed turned his back to the saloon, resting against it. He avoided eye contact with Abe. *Don't make it obvious that you're workin' with me, boy. It makes the prey nervous and less likely to expose himself in his natural environment.* Abe's teaching had stuck with him clear as a bell. He made damned sure he would adhere to it to the best of his ability. The last thing he wanted was to get them both killed, or worse.

"Don't worry, Jed, he's here..." Abe grumbled into his shot glass before knocking it back and motioning for another. Jed nodded slightly and kept a closer eye on the mob of people.

Something caught his eye at the craps table in the far back corner. His shoulders stiffened, and his gut roiled with nervousness. He started to think that no matter how many times he would do this, the nerves would never go away. He began to feel suspicious eyes on him. He was running out of time. "Good, boy, good. Go get 'im."

Abe's encouraging words dowsed the roiling fire in his gut, giving him a boost of confidence he needed to play this out perfectly. He pushed himself off the bar. As he coursed his way through the people, he gently moved aside drunks, horny, half-dressed women with their ruined makeup and hairstyles askew, and the occasional quiet man trying desperately to fit into this low lifestyle.

The craps table was surrounded by miners and men seeking to earn their fortune of ill-begotten gold, only to spend it on women, drinking and gambling. He heard the dice roll and tumble across the green felt, and the ensuing roars of triumph and anger. One weary miner, who smelled like he was fresh from the wilds, stumbled past, defeat written all over his countenance.

Jed moved aside to let the downtrodden man past, before slipping into his spot. He could feel everyone's eyes on him as he thumbed out a few dollar bills. He didn't want to draw more attention than he already had. The dealer, who seemed to have a permanent frown on his face, took the bills and slid over some multicolored chips, all faded from use.

The men gathered around the table relaxed as the dealer began taking bets again. Jed looked straight ahead to the target across the table. He stared at him for a moment, watching his subtle, deep burgundy aura writhe behind him. The rounds flew by as he watched the target win again and again. Jed didn't mind losing a few dollars if it meant he could bring this animal out in his natural state.

The dealer rolled again, and the dice bounced along the faded felt table top and over barely visible numbers and boxes. He noticed that the dice had a pattern. A consistent set of numbers that he wondered if anyone else had noticed. *Unlikely, considering the drunken stupor most of these men are in.* The cheer of victory came from his mark over the loud groan and shouts of the men who had lost again. Jed saw his opening as the man drew in his winnings with a greasy, yellow grin.

Jed spoke calmly over the noise of the table, "Well played, for a cheatin' man."

The shouts, cheers, and groans were abruptly stopped. Every eye turned on Jed as he dug around his pockets for a dollar bill. He made himself contain a smirk of success as the target growled, "What did you call me, boy?"

"I said, you're cheatin'." Jed could feel the eyes from the crowd around them switch between him and the man. Jed knew none would intervene.

"You wanna settle this outside, boy?"

Jed looked up at the man from under the brim of his hat, "Yeah, I do." Jed knew he had him right where he wanted him. The hotter a mark was, the better off he'd be in a fight. The man stalked past Jed, making a point to look him straight in the eyes. Jed didn't look away. He wanted to see this man for what he was.

All Jed saw was corruption and greed. This wouldn't take long.

Jed followed the man through the now-silent parlor. All that could be heard were clients upstairs enjoying their dollar and the rain beating on the roof. The people parted like a wave before the two of them. The only law, Jed had gathered from the various conversations and the aura of the town, was that of dueling, or self-righteous judgement. The batwing doors creaked and swayed as the target passed through. Jed passed shortly after, leaving the smoke-heavy building.

The night air was refreshing. The weight of the stares, the noise, and the rank smells were not as bad out on the porch. The man was already trotting down the steps to the swamped street level. Jed followed, the mud under his feet squishing and squashing. He watched his target closely from under his hat. This man knew something. He could sense it. Jed looked down at his waist, peeling his duster back to grab his gun—he stopped. He felt something sharp in the back of his mind, like someone had jabbed at his skull. *Threat?*

He heard him before he saw him. The target was charging him from behind at full speed. Without thinking, Jed moved to the side slightly, planting his feet hard into the ankle-deep mud as he gripped the man's arm and flipped him over. The man made a winded sound as he fell hard into the slop and splattered mud all over Jed's boots and up his pants. He'd clean it off later. The man growled, his aura now a deep red, writhing as he agilely flipped over. His eyes were glowing red, like coals on a fire. He was on all fours. His composure was not of a human, that was for sure. His muscles were tensed, like a wild animal ready to pounce. Jed drew his pistol and pulled the hammer back. Behind him, he heard Abe do the same.

The human-looking demon paused in his growling, seeing that Abe was behind Jed. He almost seemed to tremble in fear as he watched him.

*He's notorious, even among his own kind*, thought Jed.

Abe kept his gun trained on the demon in front of them, calm as always. "Where is Eberhart Marks?"

"Ah, you seek the Betrayer!" The demon hissed, coming out of its crouch and sitting on his haunches. The demon's odd movements and way of speech unnerved Jed to the core. He was the strangest one he had encountered yet. Abe snarled at him, "Where is he?"

The demon cowered at Abe's growled reproach. He whimpered and crawled forward, as if begging for its life, "He is not here! We swear it!"

"Then, where is he?" Abe was losing his patience; Jed could hear it in his voice.

The demon fidgeted, nervously looked around, and turned its gaze back to Abe, "I-I-I can't! He will kill us!"

Jed frowned, firing a warning shot next to the demon's leg, "Better us than him…"

"Oh please! Don't kill us! We, we haven't caused any harm to anyone!" The demon swiftly changed from nervous to devious, "At least not fatally…"

"You're not of use to me, then." Jed could hear the trigger Abe was squeezing. He could only imagine that the demon heard the same.

"Wait! Wait! We'll tell you!" He wormed the rest of the way to Abe, looking to Jed nervously as he passed, "Eberheart! The Betrayer! He went further than here!"

"Well, no shit," Jed murmured.

"To the golden hills of the territory known as California! He has been busy, oh yes, very busy, indeed."

The words did not sit well with either of the men's ears. Jed looked to Abe for a second, who did not seem outwardly surprised, but Jed could sense the slight uneasiness in him. Jed worried about what might be ahead.

"Where's the girl?" Jed asked sternly. He needed to know, and the question bubbled out of his mouth.

The demon hissed under its breath and cranked its body and head in Jed's direction, "Oh, yes! The McKay girl!" He inched closer. He stopped when Jed held the pistol a foot away from him, "She is still alive, yes, still alive."

Those words nearly brought Jed to his knees with relief. All this time, Jed had no idea if she was alive or dead. This confirmation was what he needed. *She's still alive!*

"Last chance, son of a bitch," Abe barked.

The demon quickly returned to the boots of Abe's mercy, as he spurted, "Eberheart! He is in Bodie! Bodie, California! That is what he told us!"

Jed swallowed. Something didn't feel right at all. *Why would he tell this lowlife? This don't make no sense at all…it's almost like he's layin' a trap."*

A moment of fleeting silence filled the area, only to be shattered by Abe pulling the trigger to his pistol. The demon didn't have time to squeal or shout or beg as the bullet tore through his vulnerable spot; the third heart. The demon slumped with finality into the mud, the thick slop almost totally enveloping his corpse. Without a word, Abe holstered his pistol and turned back towards the main street. Jed holstered his and came up next to him, pulling his coat collar up a little higher.

"Abe, this don't seem right."

"'Cause it ain't." Abe rummaged through his duster for a cigarette.

"Why would he tell this lowlife demon his location?"

A roar from the saloon erupted with shouts and curses, mixed with laughter. Abe watched as a man was tossed, face-first, into the middle of the street. He began to walk towards the spectacle, "He's layin' a trap, Jed."

Jed followed, Abe's conclusion with the wormy demon was starting to sink deep into his mind. *He's using my sister as bait…* The thought tasted bitter on his tongue as Abe turned the corner, towards the man cursing and spitting mud out of his mouth. Abe used his foot to turn the man over onto his back forcefully.

The man shouted, "Get off me, goddammit!"

The man's defensiveness quickly melted into surrender. He held his hands up, "El Diablo! I already paid that debt!"

"You owe me a life debt, John." Abe coolly spoke as he resumed his cigarette search. The man, John, squirmed uncomfortably.

John attempted to wipe mud from his face, but, instead, just smeared it more. The rain was not helping his situation as he scrambled for a rebuttal, "W-well, lemme shoot ya in the chest—I'll miss yer heart!" Jed raised an eyebrow, surprised at how desperate this man was to leave Abe's presence. Abe, having found a cigarette, lit the tip of it with his thumb. The tiny flame illuminated the underside of Abe's hat, and most of his front, giving him ominous look about him, before the flame was quickly extinguished. John continued hurriedly as he stumbled to his feet, "Then I can rush ya to the Doc! I'll even pay for it!" The sky rolled with thunder in the distance, as the tip of Abe's cigarette burned a brilliant red.

"You got two choices, John." Abe blew out his inhalation of tobacco smoke. "Either, you do as I say, or you don't." He drew in another long drag of the cigarette, the tip burning brilliantly again. John spit out another mouth full of mud and spit to the side, weighing his chances against El Diablo.

"Fine, fine. I need a drink first, before I hear ya out." John trudged down the street, his gait a little sore. No doubt from his toss and fall. Abe grinned as he followed, with Jed not far behind.

# Chapter 35

The rain was starting to slow as the three men entered a smaller saloon. It was quieter, and was much older than the other buildings in town. The old miners mostly kept to themselves. The establishment reeked of rot and decay, making Jed crinkle his nose slightly at the sour onslaught. Jed held his whiskey to his nose, hoping the aroma of the amber liquid would help. To Jed's disappointment, it did very little, but the warmth in his gut made up for most of it.

John had found a trough overflowing with rain water in front of the saloon. He tried to clean the mud off his body, making him gasp and sputter from the chilly water. By the time he was finished, Jed thought he looked like a drowned rat. He was relatively lean, dark-haired, and of average height. His beard peppered his jaw and some of his neck, but it seemed as though he was trying to hide his almost boyish features.

The three of them sat in silence as John dripped dry in the saloon, whiskey in their hands. John didn't seem to care too much as he gratefully downed his whiskey.

"So, about this life debt I owe ya…" John spoke quietly as he poured himself another shot from the bottle Abe grabbed on the way in. "How can poor ol' John Carson help the infamous El Diablo?" John smugly sipped his second glass.

Jed was still trying to figure this man out. He was different, that was for sure, but his coloring—his aura—was something he had not seen before. He was human, Jed was convinced of that. Most humans that he had seen so far had a faint glow to them—but not John. His was faded, almost as if it were gone entirely. *There's more to him than he's lettin' on to...maybe Abe does know John can be useful to us.*

Abe was silent as he poured another into his shot glass, downing it before answering, "Need your talent, John." His cigarette smoldered away in his free hand as he downed the drink.

John's smug expression turned quickly into one of discomfort. "I don't do that no more, remember?" John grumbled, knocking back his shot.

"You will." Abe stared at John long and hard. As John squirmed in his chair, Jed couldn't help but think that he knew the feeling well. Abe's gaze was piercing, right down to the soul, and unwavering. Jed knew that he would get what he wanted; one way or another.

John muttered under his breath, "God damn, I hate that look." He frowned and looked him in eye. "Alright, fine. Point, and I'll shoot."

"Gotta find him first." Abe flicked his dead cigarette to the floor, crushing the last of it with his boot, promptly seeking a replacement.

John choked on his drink, "You ain't on his trail?! What the hell am I supposed to shoot, if you ain't got a mark?!"

Glancing around the room, Jed growled, "Keep your voice down..." The last thing they needed was unwanted attention. Thankfully, the room was full of old men, passed-out drunks, and gamblers that paid them no mind.

John frowned at Jed for a moment before settling down in his seat again. Abe not only found his replacement cigarette, but a box of half-empty matches. Abe struck a match, lit his cigarette, and tucked the matchbox back into his coat. Abe remained silent as he dug into his vest pocket. John watched in impatient silence as Abe found what he was looking for and placed the item on the tabletop. He slid the item over to John, the sound of metal grinding on wood. Jed knew what it was.

Abe lifted his hand off the dark, obsidian coin, revealing the beast with ruby eyes. John's eyes widened with fear, darting from the coin to Abe, then back again. "Is that?"

"A mark of Marks." Abe took a long drag from his cigarette.

"Now wait just a minute, El Diablo," John put his hands up defensively. Jed could feel the urge of panic rising in John's being. Something about this had spooked him. *What have you done, John?* "You know I ain't the type of man who would back down from an oath," Abe raised his eyebrow, "But this...this is Marks we're talkin' about. They're not people to trifle with."

"They ain't people." Abe corrected John sternly, grunting as he took another drag.

John nervously licked his lips as he glanced around the room. He leaned in closer, "El Diablo, this is suicide. You kill one, five more spring up in their place."

Abe said nothing.

John sighed and leaned back in his chair, "Who is it you're after that's so important?"

"Eberheart's got someone he shouldn't."

John's jaw opened in shock at the name. "Eberheart? Shit..." Jed fingered his half-empty glass, "Who the hell does he have that you wanna get back?"

"A girl. Marietta."

"Marietta, huh?" John drank the last of his whiskey. Jed glanced at Abe, noticing that he had left out the part about her being Jed's sister. *I can't help but think he doesn't quite trust this John Carson, or he is tryin' to protect me still, since my Pa was.* "She must be important," John poured again. "Alright, I'll do it. Then, our debt is settled, right?"

"Yep." Abe blew out smoke. Jed felt relief spread through him. They had gotten the help that Abe had come to Deadwood for. They finalized the agreement with a toast.

***

Abe walked out of the saloon. He needed fresh air and to get away from the confined space of that shack. He still couldn't stomach being in an enclosed space for too long. He had finished his cigarette and searched for a new one. With John's help, it would be much easier for them to strike at Eberheart.

He sighed quietly as he found what he searched for and lit it up with his thumb. *This damned blood pact is gonna be the death of me.* Dusk snorted at the sight of him, disgruntled by the weather. Abe walked over to him and rubbed his soaking neck. The rain had stopped for now.

"Ah, it ain't that bad…You've had worse." Dusk nickered and looked at Abe as he stroked him.

"You El Diablo?" Abe stiffened at his title. He hadn't been aware enough of his surroundings to hear the man approach him. With a sigh, Abe turned and looked at the man from under his hat. He was short, and his clothing had seen better days. Abe was grateful to be upwind from this man. He didn't look like he knew the meaning of bathing.

"What the hell do you want?"

"Mr. Mert wants to see ya." The man flashed a greasy grin, one that caught the lantern light.

Abe cursed to himself as he looked down to the ground, taking one final drag before tossing it into the mud. *Shit. I'm gettin' sloppy.* He glanced back at the shack and frowned. *Boys can handle bein' without me for a moment.* Without a word, Abe walked past the man and back up the main street. He knew where to go. Abe had no intention of talking with Mert while he was here, especially since the last time had been years ago when Dwayne Marks had run the business.

He approached the Gem as another patron exited the winged doors with shouts and curses. The man shouted angrily as he tried to get up, but failed in his drunken stupor. Abe ignored him as he walked up the steps and through the doors. No one looked at him, and he didn't pay anyone else mind. He preferred it this way. Less of a mess.

He weaved in the crowd. He knew Mert was here.

"Absalom! There you are, you old dog!" The familiar voice boomed over the raucous crowd of nightly pleasures. People around him spread away, leaving him exposed. Abe looked up to the banister of the large flight of stairs. He saw Mert. He was a tall man, with dark hair and dark circles under his soulless eyes to match. His dark suit was stained with booze and age. Abe remained silent as Mert motioned Abe to come up the stairs, "Come on up here!" His voice was deceptively friendly. Abe knew what he was really like.

Abe moved through the parting crowd to the stairs. Dwayne had placed Mert here to hold his northernmost 'assets'—the numerous gold claims that had proven themselves more than prosperous. Abe reached him at the top of the stairs, his grin hiding his wicked intentions. He struck out his hand as a gesture of feigned friendship. Abe stared him in the eye, ignoring the hand entirely. He took a drag, intentionally blowing the smoke into Mert's face before dropping the cigarette onto the ancient rug that adorned the space, grinding the cigarette into it, creating a charred hole.

Mert's fake smile morphed into an irritated frown as he dropped his hand to his side, tucking it into the pocket. "Fine, have it your way, Absalom." He turned and started toward his quarters, "Step into my office. We have much to talk about."

*Of course, you do,* Abe thought bitterly as he followed him down the hallway. Abe ignored the sounds from within the rooms they passed. Whores doing their work, men arguing about how much gold one took from the other; all were unimportant to him. Mert opened a door, leading into his quarters, which also served as his place of business most days. He stood aside as Abe entered before him. The door closed with a soft clack. The calamity of the saloon was quieted somewhat as Mert walked around to his desk and pulled out a pair of shot glasses. "You seem tense, Absalom. Have a drink, sit." He motioned to the chair in front of his desk as he turned to the ancient cellarette behind his desk. The top of it was strewn with all assortments of liquors, brandies, and other spirits that Abe was sure were both expensive and exotic.

He remained silent as Mert paused, glancing at him. Abe was not here for a social call. "Always the stubborn one, Absalom." Mert shook his head as he picked out his choice of brandy. The dark brown liquid sloshed inside of its exotic-looking crystal carafe. He took the crystal stopper out as he turned back to his desk and poured it into the glasses he had brought out before. Abe watched him carefully for anything suspicious. Mert's grin had a subtle maliciousness to it, as it always had, Abe recalled. Abe slowly downed his glass, exaggerating a sigh of contentment after.

Abe moved forward, taking the drink into his hand. He brought the glass to his nose, smelling the aroma before following suit. If Mert drank it, there would be no possibility of it being poisoned. He didn't care much for brandy, but Abe finished the glass and set it down as Mert took his seat. The old, padded wooden chair creaked under his lean weight as he leaned back, glass still in hand. There was just a skim left at the bottom.

"What brings you to this illegal settlement, Absalom?" Abe didn't care for Mert's tone, and he most certainly didn't care for his prodding either. *Stop usin' my damn name for starters.*

"Business," Abe curtly answered. He just wanted to grab Jed and John and be on their way.

Mert chuckled as he emptied his glass and refilled it. "And you expect me to not notice the boy you brought with you?"

The back of Abe's neck began to prick as his hairs rose. *That son of a bitch...*

"Don't worry, dear Absalom, I don't work with Mr. Marks anymore."

Abe leaned over, placing his palms on the surface of the desk. Staring him straight in the eye, he said, "Like hell you don't. No one just walks away."

"You mean like you did?"

Abe snarled at the jab and aggressively slammed his glass onto the table. He stood to his full height, his voice seething, "You're on my list, Mert. Too bad you're at the bottom of the shit pile."

Mert perked an eyebrow and leaned forward. Abe's threat seemed to have no effect on the devil. "Are you seriously threatening me, Absalom? In my own territory?"

Abe remained silent. He didn't dare push this man any further. Even though Abe had plenty of field experience, he would never be able to overthrow him. He was much, much older than he. Content with Abe's silent answer, Mert adjusted his jacket abruptly and stared at Abe long and hard, "I have a problem with a man here in town, Absalom, and you're gonna take care of it for me."

Abe snorted, backing away from the desk. He had no intention of working for him. "Take care of it yourself." Abe turned on his boot, pulling his hat lower over his eyes. *I don't have time for this bullshit.*

"Oh no, I think you might wanna listen to this…unless you don't mind what happens to John Carson, that is."

Abe stopped mid-step, turning his gaze over his shoulder. "What the hell did he do?" Abe growled.

Mert flashed a confident grin, steepling his fingers, "Well, Absalom, Mr. John Carson has been quite the busy man around here… His prospectin' career has gotten him up shit creek." Mert stood from his chair and strolled to the large bay window overlooking the street below. He clasped his hands behind his back as Abe turned back around to face him. "A lot of the people in this town want to see him fed to the Chink's hogs." Mert looked back at Abe, his soulless black eyes catching the lantern light in the room. "Unless, of course, you pay the price for his…disappearance."

*Damn it all John, you stupid shit.*

"How much?"

Mert placed a thoughtful curled knuckle to his lips. Abe knew it was for show. "I'd settle for…twelve hundred dollars. That covers payin' off the pissed miners and other locals he's managed to swindle."

The price made Abe's muscles tense with irritation. He had no other choice. If he didn't pay Mert, not only would Abe have to somehow sneak Jed and John both out of Deadwood, but he would run the risk of Mert squealing back to Eberheart. In silence, Abe reached into his duster, his hand slipping into one of the many pockets attached to the inside, and pulled out a thick roll of cash. Abe tossed the roll onto the desk and walked to the door, wrenching it open gruffly. He heard Mert's voice call after him as he ducked into the hall, "It was nice to see you again, Absalom."

\*\*\*

"And that's how I got this here pistol." John finished his long-winded tale as he tightened up his saddle straps.

Jed kept his thoughts to himself as he too prepared to ride again, *I can already tell John talks too much.* John didn't seem to be bothered by the only recognition Jed offered in response to his long tale: a grunt. His wide grin seemed to tell him that he was just glad to get out of here.

The two of them rounded up their horses, John's included, and they began preparations to leave. Jed was tired, but he was used to the rough travel he had endured so far. He heard John mount up on his horse, a dark brown quarter horse, by the look of it. "You don't talk much, do ya, Jed?"

Jed sighed, trying to calm his irritation. He had told him multiple times to call him either Jedidiah or Mr. McKay. He wouldn't say it again. Jed turned to scold John for running his mouth, but stopped as he heard the familiar sounds of Abe's gear rustling and jangling in the street. He looked towards the street as his friend rounded the corner. Jed's anticipation was met with a tingling feeling in the back of his mind. *Now what's Abe pissed about?*

He cautiously watched his friend as he made straight toward John, who looked more and more nervous as Abe approached. John's skittish horse nickered and danced to the side as John called out to Abe, "'Bout time you came back, El Diablo." His grin was devoid of all his confidence he had a moment ago.

Jed remained quiet and watched with surprise as Abe reached John, suddenly grabbing him by his shirt and roughly pulling him out of his saddle and back into the mud. The skittish horse whinnied and trotted out of the way of the commotion as Abe grabbed John's collar with a snarl and jabbed a balled fist into John's jaw and mouth. The sharp cracking sound reverberated against the wood-slatted walls of the buildings they were between.

John shouted, retaliating in a loud voice, "What the hell, El Diablo?! I ain't done nothin'!!"

Abe growled, looming over John with sinister intent, "You're a dumb son of a bitch, John. You crossed Mert?!" John rubbed his jaw, nursing the tenderness as he stood again. Jed watched the exchange in silence. According to what John had told him in the past half hour, Mert was the biggest miser in this town. He controlled everything up and down the main street. Nothing got past his desk without his approval.

"Well...not deliberately...but I guess I did, yeah."

Abe jabbed at his jaw again, with enough force to knock John back into the mud onto his back. Abe leaned down and grabbed John's collar and threatened him in a low growl. "I just paid twelve hundred dollars for your sorry ass." He roughly dropped John back into the mud, moving around him. He reached Dusk, who had remained still for the entire encounter, and Abe pulled himself angrily into his saddle, taking the reins into his hands. He turned Dusk to face John, nudging him to move next to him, who was still dazed from the two heavy blows to his jaw and mouth. Abe glared down at him and hissed, "I *own* you, John Carson. If I tell you to cut your leg off, you damn well do as your told."

John stared at Abe, wide-eyed. Realizing the grave mistake that Abe had just saved him from, he nodded in silent appreciation. He stumbled to his feet, smearing blood onto the back of his hand and spitting some out onto the street. Jed pulled himself into his own saddle, keeping his mouth shut. He didn't dare cross Abe when he was fuming. He had seen him get angry once, and he almost felt sorry for John. Jed, too, had been the subject of Abe's wrath before, but he had never done anything as serious as crossing a serious criminal mastermind.

The three riders began to leave as the first two had come. Mert watched the odd trio from his bay window with curiosity. His grin was still on his lips as they disappeared into the dark, wooded trail that lead deeper into the black hills.

*The great Absalom rides to meet his death...what does he possibly hope to achieve?*

# Chapter 36

The weather had swiftly shifted from fall to winter in the northern territory since the three of them had left Deadwood. They constantly raced ahead of the coming blizzards and storms from the far north, heading south for their next destination that Jed and Abe had obtained: Bodie. A mining community revolving around the gold strike that seemed to be in a constant flourish there.

Jed shivered against the cold as he adjusted his coat collar closer around his jaw and neck. They were pushing into a new territory known as the Dakotas, named after the prominent tribe that roamed these lands hundreds of years before the white man came. It was early morning, and a light dusting of snow covered everything as far as they could see. Abe led them ever onward. He was determined to get to Bodie as soon as possible, without killing the horses and their riders.

John rode behind Jed, rubbing his hands together vigorously to warm them. Puffs of steam streamed behind Abe and his horse, as well as Jed and his stallion. "El Diablo, when are we gonna stop for a rest?" John called ahead. Jed learned quickly that John not only talked to much, he was not well-suited for cold.

"Quit your bitchin', John," was all Abe could call out behind him as they continued their pace. Jed reached back into his saddlebags and pulled out a couple strips of cured back strap. He turned in his saddle and tossed John a piece. Even though Jed didn't much care for John, he couldn't let him starve to death, either. Jed was just as hungry. John caught the piece of meat, a smile spreading on his features, "Thanks, I owe ya one." Jed nodded to him before turning back to the front and to the view ahead.

He had to admit, it was quite beautiful. The rolling hills were glimmering with the new, fallen snow dusting them. The frigid morning air was sharp in his lungs, and it made his nose burn. The sun was paler than he was used to; a new sight he never thought he would see. *I bet Marietta would like to see this. Maybe when I get her back, we can ride up here again.*

Abe reined his horse to a stop, Dusk lowered his head and snorted hard. His ears were relaxed, half-asleep from another night's ride. Jed's body was heavy with travel as he, too, reined to a stop next to him. John came up beside Jed, leaning forward and resting his arms on the pommel of the saddle, while he gratefully chewed the tough meat. Jed felt relief spread through him as they watched a town not too far in the distance.

"There's your rest, John," Jed said with a half-smile. He looked forward to some normalcies that most take for granted. Most of all, he wanted a bed and a blanket that wasn't soaked all the way through. Abe heeled Dusk into a trot.

*Looks like Abe is hoping for the same thing,* Jed mused as he, too, clucked and nudged his stallion to follow. The three of them trotted the rest of the short distance into the small town tucked into the folds of the plains. It was quiet and still in the early morning. Abe pulled Dusk to a stop at the inn, leaving the reins laid over the hitch post. Jed dismounted and stretched. His body was stiff from the same position for days. He would be grateful to get a warm bed a hot meal. He tied off his horse and patted his neck as he followed Abe inside.

The lobby was welcoming, with bright-colored carpets and pictures. A tall, older man was behind the counter, organizing something on the desk, as the three men walked inside. Jed took his gloves off and looked around as Abe approached the counter. The older man mustered a polite smile as Abe looked at the registry book with a frown. "How may we assist you, good sir?"

"We need a room…" Abe spoke gruffly.

The older man looked at Abe with regret, politely answering, "I'm sorry sir, but we don't have enough for the three of you."

Abe looked at the man with a disgruntled look. Jed knew he was giving the old inn keep a stare that would surely make him crumple. *He has that ability with people.* Jed couldn't help but smile to himself as the man shuffled nervously under Abe's gaze, "Give us a damn room…or I'll toss out one of your patrons and make room…"

Abe's threat was quiet, but sincere. The innkeeper frowned and swallowed hard as he turned the registry towards him and flipped through the pages. He scribbled something down and turned behind him to his cabinet of hooks with keys dangling from them. He took one off a hook and handed it to Abe, "Enjoy the honeymoon suite."

John looked at Abe and stifled a chuckle as he turned towards the stairs and began to climb. Abe shot John a glare that put an abrupt end to his laughter. Jed looked at Abe and nodded his silent thank you. He could tell that they were all exhausted from their hard ride. They were so close and, yet, so far.

They couldn't press on without some serious repercussions on their bodies. Even Abe was showing signs of exhaustion. Jed climbed the stairs after John, and Abe began to follow them.

"Absalom, it's been a long time," a man calmly called out to them from the dining area as they passed. Abe stopped on the third step up, almost cringing from the sound. Their hope of a nice, quiet day's rest was, almost certainly, dashed. Jed watched the priest in the doorway with suspicion. He was tall, with faded blond hair. His black pants, shoes, and jacket starkly contrasted the white collar, drawing one's eyes to it. His eyes were piercing, but not with malice, anger, nor ill intent. All Jed could see in the man's eyes was weariness and observation.

Something was not quite right, Jed had felt. The aura that illuminated the priest was a pale, goldish glow; another aura he had not yet encountered. It made him feel uneasy. For comfort, Jed's hand drifted to his gun, resting his palm on the handle. Abe grunted back, "Too damn short, if you ask me."

The priest smiled with kindness, looking from Abe to Jed, "There won't be a need for your weapons, child." His voice was so calming, yet commanding. Jed couldn't help but retract his hand from his pistol. *What the hell is he?* The priest looked back to Abe, gesturing to the dining area, "Care to join me for a spot of breakfast?"

Abe growled and descended the steps, as if in defeat, "No, I don't fuckin' care to, but I don't have a choice, do I?" Abe tossed the key to Jed. He worried for his friend as Abe looked back to the priest. "Both of ya…get upstairs."

John didn't argue as he finished climbing the stairs. Jed hesitated, but followed John, watching as the two of them disappeared into the dining room.

*Careful, Abe…*

\*\*\*

Abe made sure to choose what table they sat at. He picked a rather dreary corner that was close to the exit, enabling him to see every inch of the room. Abe never liked to have his back to a room. The fallen angel in front of him had placed both of their orders to the old cook. He had smiled at the old man with caring, thanking him graciously for his courtesy. It made Abe's stomach turn from the sight. When the two were finally alone in the barren dining room, Abe grumbled at the fallen, disguised as a travelling Catholic priest, "What the hell do you want, Ezekiel?"

Ezekiel calmly took the napkin that held old, mismatched silverware and placed it in his lap. He promptly responded, "Other than an answer to why you are crossing our agreed territorial boundaries, nothing."

The parlor was devoid of any other patrons this early in the morning. Abe would have preferred to be sleeping off a hangover at this time of the day, rather than having breakfast with his tenuous ally. The light of the coming day was beginning to filter into the glass windows, illuminating the rickety tables and their shoddy settings. Abe grumbled at the response, digging for a cigarette. He hadn't had the time, nor the luxury, of having a smoke, and he badly craved one. Finally finding his pack, he pulled one out and lit up. He knew this would bother the fallen angel, but he didn't give a damn.

He heard the shuffling footfalls of the old cook's steps, no doubt bringing the two men their breakfast. Abe realized how hungry he was as his stomach began twisting with hunger. Cigarettes only stemmed the tide of starvation for so long. He took a long drag and blew out a stream of smoke into the air, sighing as he did so. *It ain't workin' as well as it used to.* Abe looked at the smoking cigarette in his hand for a moment, until the plate of food slid into view.

Ezekiel smiled warmly at the old cook, "Thank you, you are very kind." The old cook couldn't help but smile back, nodding as he shuffled back to the kitchen. Abe grabbed his fork from the place setting and eagerly stabbed the half-cooked rasher on his plate. He ravenously put the entire slice of cooked meat into his mouth, relishing in the flavor of it. He was almost euphoric as he began to chew, the taste of meat and curing salts permeating his tastebuds.

Out of the corner of Abe's eye, he watched as Ezekiel bowed his head and folded his hands together, his eyes closing in silent prayer. Abe reached over to the coffee pot the old cook had brought over, pouring himself some and taking a drink. He loved it piping hot. "He can't hear you," Abe scoffed as he stabbed another piece of rasher.

"He listens to those who are faithful, Absalom," Ezekiel answered calmly as he finished his short prayer. Before Abe could reply with a quip, Ezekiel spoke again as he cut up his own rasher, "You have a promising prodigy, Absalom. What is his name?"

The sport for a fight had disappeared from Abe's forefront thinking as the topic of the boy came up. "Jedidiah McKay."

Ezekiel swallowed a bite and looks at Abe with a perked interest in the name, "I see…well, he has a strong spirit. Like his father before him, it would seem."

Abe held his tongue as he drank another gulp of rancid coffee. He avoided eye contact with Ezekiel. He knew that the fallen knew. Angels were annoyingly good at being observant; it wouldn't surprise Abe that Ezekiel could see the blood pact between him and the boy.

"He's dangerous, Absalom," Ezekiel prodded quietly as he looked at Abe, "He is full of anger."

Abe looked at him with irritation. "He'll be fine…he's trained."

Ezekiel paused before he took a sip of his own coffee, "And that is what's worrisome."

"It's none of your fuckin' business, fallen." Abe defensively growled at Ezekiel. The prick of guilt in his heart brought regret. He knew he had given Jed too much blood back at the lair of El Cabrio. But he also knew if he hadn't given him that much, Jed would have been dead.

"You're right, Absalom, it is none of my business at this point in time." Ezekiel set his tin cup down gently, taking the ratted napkin and wiping his mouth clean. "However, it will become my business when he becomes a full-fledged Nephilim." The silence that spanned between them was stifling. Abe knew that was a risk, but he was too selfish. He had grown attached to the boy. He viewed him like a son.

Abe didn't like the subtle warning he took as a threat against the boy. He leaned forward, his hackles bristling in defense as he hissed at Ezekiel, "Are you threatenin' me?"

Ezekiel chuckled, "No, I'm not threatening you or the boy. I am simply reminding you of who—and what—I hunt."

Not entirely content with the fallen's answer, Abe relaxed back into his seat. He was too tired to continue a quarrel. "You still haven't answered my question…What the hell do you want?"

"You are going to need assistance to bring Mr. Marks down."

Abe stiffened at the thought of yet another tagalong. He didn't need any more help. Especially from one of *his* kind. But he knew that Eberheart had strengthened over the past decade. He doubted his ability to be able to bring this bastard down by himself. Abe was going to try, knowing he would, most likely, die from it. He did not want his own lack of skill to get Jed killed—or worse.

Ezekiel finished the last of his meal and calmly continued, "I will forgive you of this violation of our territorial agreement, and I will help you with Mr. Marks." The fallen leaned back in his chair, seemingly content with his breakfast. "And, in exchange, I will ask you for a favor in the future"

Abe cursed under his breath as he dropped his now burned-out cigarette onto the floor. Favors were never good, and they always made him uneasy. Favors meant things he wouldn't normally do. *But…I don't really have a choice.* Abe fished out a new cigarette and lit it, considering the offer at hand. He looked at the finished plate before him, then, to the patiently waiting fallen angel. "Fine. We have a deal."

Ezekiel smiled with pleasure as he stuck his hand out for a handshake, "We have a deal."

Abe reached over and grasped the fallen's hand.

The deal was struck.

## Chapter 37

Jed was thankful to have a quiet room and, for once, quiet company. John's constant chatter had worn Jed's patience thin on their ride from Deadwood. After the two of them left Abe and the priest to their morning meal, Jed and John had gone up two flights of stairs to the wedding suite. Jed didn't mind the overly decorated walls, the odd paintings of naked harems of women, or the gaudy flowery curtains that laced each window heavily like a veil. He just wanted to sleep.

John had thoroughly inspected each painting with a childlike sort of glee on his face before finally claiming the bed. Jed had taken to the window seat that was plenty big for him and was covered with dozens of overstuffed pillows. *This sort of room must normally cost a fortune.* He tossed some pillows off the window seat to the floor. Jed paused as John flopped onto the bed with a sigh of relief.

The bedframe squeaked under the strain of someone on it. Jed couldn't help but grin to himself, "You're gonna break that, Mr. Carson." Jed pulled his hat down low over his eyes to block out the rising sun that pierced through the curtained windows.

He heard John adjust some pillows as he responded with a grin in his tone, "Nah, I think it'll be just fine. I'm sure it's held up more'n just me."

Both men chuckled at the small joke. Even though John did get on his nerves sometimes, Jed was beginning to get used to John Carson and his ways. It was almost nice to have someone else of his kind to talk to, even if he didn't know when to be quiet. John fell asleep rather quickly, snoring mildly in the silence. Not even the town seemed to be awake yet. Jed adjusted in his position again, resting his upper back against the wall portion of the alcove.

It didn't feel right to sleep without Abe being able to rest as well, but he was exhausted from the past few weeks. His eyes were heavy, and, soon, they closed. Jed's mind drifted through his thoughts until it all faded into the embrace of welcomed rest.

\*\*\*

Abe trudged up the stairs with a heavy heart and in .desperate need to sleep. His discussion with Ezekiel had left him feeling drained and irritated. His thoughts lingered on the fight he knew was coming. He was going to die. He knew it deep in his inner being to be so. *I ain't ready for that.*

He climbed the stairs slowly, taking time to gather up his strength. Abe had no intention to die because of his deal with the dead Mr. McKay. But, if he didn't, he would be breaking his oath to bring back Marietta and to protect the boy. Among his kind, to break an oath was sentencing oneself to eternal damnation. *Damn rules. Can't ever get away from 'em.*

He reached the end of the hallway and quietly turned the handle and slipped into the room. He saw John had already claimed the bed and was out cold, snoring as usual. Jed was asleep in the window seat, silent and still. He was glad that Jed's night terrors had ceased long ago.

The only furniture left to sleep on was the long couch lounger. It was upholstered in red velvet with intricate wood carvings on the arms and feet. Abe ran his hand over it. *Jys would love somethin' like this.*

He sighed and put his hand back to his side, inwardly scolding himself. He hadn't felt this way in a very long time. Not since his mentor and friend had found him all those years ago. He felt the weight of fear.

Abe frowned to himself as he shirked his duster coat onto an adjacent chair and laid down on the lounger, stretching his weary legs. *Damn it all, I'm not supposed to be afraid of anything! I'm El Diablo, for Christ's sake.* He frowned and adjusted his hat to shade his eyes from the sun. *But I can't help but feel it...Eberheart...he's stronger than me. I won't be able to be with ya, Jys, like I promised.* He felt the heaviness bear down on his chest like lead. Fear always turned into regret. *I'm sorry.* He closed his eyes as he let dreamless sleep overtake him. When they woke, they would ride hard to Bodie. He just hoped Jystana would be there waiting for him, like she had said she would.

***

"Ow! What the hell, El Diablo?"

John's voice woke Jed from his deep sleep. He tilted his hat up as he yawned and stood from his perch. He saw Abe adjusting his duster and John rubbing his face with an irritated frown.

"I told ya to get up," Abe growled as he headed to the door. Jed gathered his coat and effects. It was time to ride again.

"Well, yeah, but did ya have to slap me?" John grumbled as he got up and put his gear back on as well. Abe paused at the door and looked back at John under his hat with a sinister glare. John quickly put his hands up in defense as he began walking to the door as well, "Alright, alright, I get it."

Jed kept a smile to himself as he adjusted his belt and pistols before the three of them left the room. Abe led the way down the flights of stairs to the main lobby. Abe passed the desk without so much as a glance to the man behind the desk. Jed passed, tipping his hat to him. He nodded back, nervously watching the three of them leave.

The food from the dining room smelled heavenly, but Abe seemed to be in a hurry. *Just as well. I can eat the cured meat we have for now.* John followed the two of them out to the porch and to the horses. They had been fed, it seemed, as any evidence of hay and grain were long gone. Jed walked over to his stallion and rubbed his forelock.

"Who fed our horses, El Diablo?" John asked, patting his horse's neck.

"Hell if I know," Abe replied, sounding disgruntled.

"They seemed hungry," Jed turned and looked to the voice. He was surprised to see the priest there, already on his dapple gray horse. It was odd to see a priest on top of a horse like that, but, then again, this priest was not a normal priest. The pale gold aura was still around him, like the faint glow of the sun. Jed watched him, still distrustful of him.

The priest smiled at the three of them. "Forgive me if that was the wrong feed for them."

Abe turned Dusk around to face him, clearly irritated with the man. "We have a deal, Ezekiel."

Jed looked back at Abe, then, at the priest. *Ezekiel? Like the prophet?*

"Yes, Absalom, I am fully aware. I will meet you at Bodie. I think it will be best if we are not seen riding together." Abe grunted taking out a cigarette and lighting it. The snow was still a light dust on the dry ground. Their breaths puffed clouds of pure white.

Abe nodded at Ezekiel's suggestion. Jed mounted up on his horse, and John followed suit. Abe turned Dusk towards the southern part of town, he was ready to go. Jed was only too happy to get going again. Their rest was needed, but Jed was anxious to keep going as fast as they could to Bodie. He knew they were very close to getting his sister back.

"And, child," Ezekiel's voice was commanding, but not harsh. Jed looked at the priest. He knew he was talking to him. His pale, amber eyes were almost eerie as he stared deep into Jed's being.

"Yessir?" Jed answered politely.

"Be cautious of your emotions." He urged his horse to walk forward, reining to a stop next to him. His eyes never left Jed. He shifted nervously in his seat, as he couldn't take his eyes off of the priest. "If you cannot control them, they are very dangerous." His words were calm and soft, almost a warning. Jed nodded, not entirely understanding what he had meant.

"I will do my best, sir."

He smiled and gently patted Jed's shoulder before turning his horse to the north, "See that you do." Without another word, he clucked and heeled his horse into a lope. Jed watched the strange priest ride off. *What the hell did he mean?*

"C'mon, Jed, we ain't got all day," he heard Abe's voice call out to him.

Jed put aside the man's warning for now. He would have to figure out what he meant later. For now, he had more important things at hand. Jed reined his horse to face John and Abe, who had started to ride off without him. He heeled his horse a little harder, making him go into a lope to catch up.

Jed rode next to John as the three of them urged their horses into a gallop. The cold bite of winter was harsh in their lungs and stung their faces as they turned south. For hours, they rode through the hills; mostly in silence. Bodie was in California, way away from where they were now. Jed was determined to get there swiftly.

***

Rolling hills gave way to rocky terrain, dry prairie, and steep mountain ranges that cut into the land. The snows they had been trying to outrun were gone. The temperatures were slowly returning to a tolerable temperature.

Days turned into weeks, and each day, Jed became more and more impatient to get to Bodie. On top of that, Jed was growing less and less patient with John. He was constantly talking, spinning tales of his own experiences and triumphs over his lifetime. Jed was amazed that Abe hadn't shot him yet. *Maybe he doesn't hear him.*

They had ridden through the night again, which had become more and more common as of late. It was taking its toll on the three men. Jed had concluded that John's talking was his way of concentrating. Jed, however, could feel the strain of the constant talking weighing on him. He could feel his patience wearing thin.

This worried him.

He rubbed his face and sighed, trying to calm himself down. He blamed it on his tiredness as they rode. John had talked about everything from women to guns. John had, ultimately, returned to women, once again.

"How about you, Jed? What do you like in a woman?" John called to Jed.

It was rare when John wanted to hear someone else talk. Jed almost didn't hear his name in John's voice. He glanced back and shrugged, "Dunno…"

"Oh, come on now, you gotta know what you like!" John urged his horse to ride up next to Jed.

Jed sighed and looked down at his gloves, "Brown hair, I guess."

John clasped Jed's shoulder as if in a brotherly gesture. "I had assumed as much," John chuckled and took his hand back, switching the reins from one hand to the other. "For me, I love 'em when they're red-headed or brilliant brunette."

"Wonder if this Marietta is pretty," John mused. Jed felt a prick of worry over his sister. He realized that he could hardly remember what she looked like.

A flare of anger welled inside Jed. He glared at John, "That's none of your damn business."

John looked at Jed, taken aback at the aggressive response. "What is she, yours, or somethin'?"

"No…" Jed set his jaw, returning his focus to riding. He was done talking. *I'll be damned if he gets his hands on her.*

"Then, what's your problem?" John scoffed, adjusting himself in his seat.

Abe glanced back; Jed knew he was hearing everything they were saying.

"I would appreciate it if you shut your damn mouth about her, John." Jed warned him in a dangerous tone. He was losing his patience. He could feel his anger burn deep in his gut.

"Oh, so you do like her, then? Well, if you like her, she must be pretty."

Jed snapped his head back to John, shooting him a furious glare. His anger was rising still. He couldn't keep his hands from shaking, and his vision becoming clouded.

"Guess we'll have to see who she likes best! I have yet to see a lady not throw herself at me—"

Jed couldn't take it anymore. A shout of pure raw anger ripped through his throat as he leaped out of his saddle, grabbing John's collar. The two men tumbled down to the soggy ground below them. John's horse whinnied and bolted in a panic. Jed's stallion nickered and trotted off to the side. Jed pinned John to the ground with his forearm and landed a couple punches on John's mouth and nose. He could feel the flesh and bone with each impact.

John shouted back at him, blocking one of Jed's punches with a free hand, and quickly pushing Jed off him. The two of them scrambled to their feet and squared off. Jed couldn't help but feel his rage course through him, like an uncontrollable river in spring. His vision was focused as he rushed John. The two of them landed blows to each other. John's punches felt like bats, and started to take their toll on Jed.

Jed watched John's next move and avoided a swing that would have split his lip. He took the opening to knee John in the abdomen and bash his head. John staggered, dazed by the blow. Jed growled and grabbed him by the collar, hitting him once, then twice. John collapsed to the ground again, but Jed wasn't done with him yet.

All the anger that he had kept pent-up inside was spilling out. His father's death, his sister's kidnapping, his odd friend sacrificing everything to help him, and the continuing string of leads they had to follow—it was all just too much for him to hold in anymore.

John raised his hands in surrender, breathless. Jed ignored his plea. Snarling, he kicked John hard in the side.

"Jed," the sound of Abe's voice echoed in his ears. He ignored it, kicking John over and over, the scent of blood now apparent. John's blood.

*This bastard deserves it! No one can take her away from me! Never again!*

"Jedidiah!" Abe's voice was stronger now. John was curled up in a ball, trying to defend himself from more blows.

"DAMN IT, BOY, I SAID *STOP*!" Abe shouted, his hands roughly pulling him away from John, snapping him out of his blind rage.

He was breathing hard, and his knuckles ached. He looked at Abe, who was frowning at him. He went over to John and bent to one knee.

Jed looked at what he had done with wide eyes. John was a bloody mess, moaning and writhing on the ground. Jed swallowed hard and looked down at his hands. *Why....? Why couldn't I stop...?*

Abe gently rolled John over to his back. He coughed and spat blood out to the side. His lip was in bad shape, and his nose was crooked as he coughed out, "Crazy...son of a bitch...ow!" Abe set the bone back in John's nose with a sick crack.

Jed backed up a few paces before running off. He needed to be alone for a while. *Something is wrong with me...I...I shouldn't be around people.*

He heard Abe's voice call after him, but he chose to ignore it. He couldn't face him, not now. His rage left him only with a heart heavy with guilt and despair.

***

Abe growled and let Jed run. He knew he needed some time. *Why is Ezekiel always fuckin' right about everything?* He returned his attention to John, who was still squirming in pain. He had never seen Jed react like that. He knew it was the blood in his veins. *I gave him too much...*

"Damn it, El Diablo, that fuckin' hurts!" John cried out as Abe shoved a piece of bandage up in his nostrils. The smell of John's blood was familiar. He had made a deal with John long ago.

"Shut your mouth, John. It's always getting' you in trouble." Abe growled and stood up. He went to Dusk, who hadn't moved the entire time. Abe opened his saddlebag and took out a small, wooden box that had seen better days, along with his water canteen.

*Damn you, John, now I gotta waste this on ya,* he thought, turning his back to John, who had made himself sit up and was holding his ribs. "One pinch, and lots of water," Abe instructed gruffly.

John opened the box and smelled the contents. He wrinkled his nose and coughed, "What the hell is it?"

"Just do as I say, John." Abe dug around in his coat for a cigarette. He knew that Umika was a foul-smelling and far worse-tasting herb that his kind used for bleeding and broken bones, but it was better than nothing. He had used the herb several times before, and it had always been hard to find. The only way to get it was through the black market—and not a human black market, either.

John did as he was told and took a pinch of it, making a disgusted face as he choked down the water. He took several gulps until he could stand the after taste of the Umika. "The hell was

Jed's problem, anyways?!" John grimaced. Abe knew it was putting his bones back to place and sealing his wounds.

Abe was silent for a moment before lighting up his cigarette, "Marietta is his sister, John."

John was silent, his irritated expression completely gone. Despite his conman nature, Abe knew that John was naturally good-hearted. Too kind for his own good. The cigarette smoke was calming on Abe's nerves as he watched John's expression fade into regret. He knew he felt guilty for what he had said.

"Why didn't you say anythin'?" John asked carefully as he shakily stood to his feet. He shouted in pain as the final rib popped into place. He doubled over and grunted as the pain subsided to a dull ache.

"Didn't think you to be an idiot, John..." Abe answered. "Should have been obvious in his eyes." Abe walked over to John and took the tiny box and his canteen back from him. "You're not as good as you used to be, John"

John sighed and looked at the various blood spots on his shirt, "Yeah, I know. Maybe I should—"

Abe cut him off with a hand motion. The last thing he needed was Jed's anger to resurface. Without a word, Abe turned and walked off to where Jed had gone. *I'll do it. Someone has to...might as well be me.*

\*\*\*

Jed had stopped hundreds of yards away, where it was just him and the wilderness. He was distraught over what he had done. He didn't understand what had come over him. He was kneeling, his head bowed and his hands clasped tightly together.

*God, I don't know what's wrong with me. I couldn't stop it... this... rage in me.* Jed could feel tears coming. He bit his lip to hold them back. He was a man, damn it. He shouldn't cry. "What have I become...?" he quietly asked himself. He knew his pa would not be pleased at all by his actions. He was a shame to his family. A shame to himself. He almost killed a man, just for talk.

"He can't hear ya, Jed."

Jed cringed at Abe's voice. He hadn't heard him come up behind him. With a sigh, Jed stood back to his feet. He couldn't bear to look at Abe. Not after what he had done. "Did I kill him?" The question was heavy in his mouth. After all the men he had killed, not one had been an innocent man. They had been men who worked for Eberheart or demons. Not innocent in the slightest meaning of the word.

Abe was silent. The silence was almost worse than an answer. Jed finally turned to face his friend.

"Am I a demon now, too?"

Abe took a drag, blowing the smoke out in a stream. He looked to the ground, "No, Jed, you ain't a demon." He dropped his finished cigarette and ground it in the damp earth with his heel, before he walked over to Jed. "And John will be just fine." Abe looked at Jed under his hat with strangely comforting eyes. "You stomped his sorry ass…he needed to be put in his place." Abe couldn't help but grin.

Jed didn't return the grin as he diverted his gaze to the ground. His guilt was still heavy in his chest. "But, you are stronger than him, Jed…" Abe clasped his shoulder in a comforting way as he spoke, "It's my fault, Jed…my blood…I gave you too much."

Jed looked up at him, confused, "What do you mean?"

Abe sighed, taking his hand off his shoulder, "When El Cabrio nearly killed ya, I was gonna lose ya…" He looked down at the ground, as if in shame, "I couldn't let that happen." Jed let the words sink in. Abe had rarely opened up this much to him.

"So, I did what I had to, to keep you alive…" Abe's eyes lifted to meet Jed's again. He could see the regret and guilt written all over the hunter's face. Jed had never seen that before. "I knew you had anger in you…an unquenchable anger. I figured I could control you, teach you how to suppress it…"

Jed looked at Abe, surprised at his admission. *Is he apologizing...?*

"I guess I was wrong..." Abe couldn't look at Jed.

"Abe I...I don't understand what's happenin' to me...I nearly killed John." Jed looked at his hands again, which had nearly healed from beating John. Abe looked up finally, pain in his eyes.

"My blood is in you, Jed. Each time a blood pact is made, a certain attribute is more prominent in the recipient than all others. Yours happens to be anger." He walked over to Jed and looked him right in the eye. "You have to control it yourself. I can't do it. Only you can."

Jed looked back at his friend. He was afraid still of what he could have done. He didn't want that to happen again. Not ever.

Jed nodded. *I hope I can. That priest knew what I was capable of, somehow...*

"He's fine," Abe answered Jed, before he could even ask. Jed had never meant to kill an innocent. Even though John from far from innocent, he was not evil, nor was he working for Eberheart.

Jed nodded again, a heavy burden lifted off his shoulders. *I have to control this...thing inside me. Whatever it is—anger is what Abe called it—I call it monster. My own inner demon.* After a moment of silence, they both walked back to where it all started. John was on his feet, chasing his skittish horse down, cursing to himself as the horse danced away from him. Jed looked on, relieved.

He hadn't killed an innocent man.

# Chapter 38

Jystana had come to Bodie before the summer season hit California. She loved the heat, and the money was flowing like a strong river through a basin. She wasn't here for money—at least that wasn't the *entire* reason. It had been months since she had seen her dearest love, Absalom. She was used to going months without seeing him. It was just how it was. He was a hunter, and she a soiled dove, gathering information for him while he was away.

This time was different.

She sat at the bar, her dress a beautiful Parisian blue with lace across the breast and on the layers of cloth. The silk always felt heavenly on her skin, and it looked so much better off. She smiled at the bartender, who had been eyeing her all evening. With a wink, she blew him a kiss. The bartender turned a brilliant scarlet as he slid over a shot of her favorite whiskey. "Thank you kindly," she said with a smile.

She took the drink in her hand and turned to face the filled saloon parlor. It was rambunctious, as it always was in the night time. She worked here, not very often, but sometimes. The most the men could afford was a touch. Looking was free, and many men were.

Jystana took a sip of her whiskey, listening intently for any more clues. She had already called for Abe about a month ago—a unique ability among devil pairs. She could feel and sense him always, no matter the distance; and he, her. She had extremely urgent findings he would need: she had found out who the main contact in this town was.

Casually, she glanced up the stairs to a door that was half-hidden from view. Silas, the main devil in control of this vast mining town, was elusive in his business dealings. He punished those who got in his way or displeased him. When his office door was closed, everyone knew not to bother him. A boy of no more than eighteen had been taken up a couple hours ago. Jystana could only imagine what he was doing behind his closed door.

With a sigh, she looked back to the parlor again. *Thank God I can't hear anythin' over tonight's crowd.* Her thoughts were soon interrupted by a large man who smelled like he had never heard of a bathtub in his life. He was human, and she was not in the mood to entertain any gentlemen callers tonight. She could feel that Absalom was very close. She didn't want to wait to see him again.

"How much are ya, darlin'?" He asked drunkenly slurring. Jystana made an innocent face, with a hint of deviousness. *That always seems to attract the men.*

"I'm too much for you tonight, sweetheart. I know someone else you might like, though," Jystana leaned around him and whistled to another girl, who was busy gaggling with other doves. Her mussed hair was intertwined with ribbons, and her clothes were half undone. "Marie! I need you over here, darlin'!"

The drunken miner looked from her to Jystana and belched. Jystana waved away the foul odor of his breath. She was irritated with him already. The girl wove her way through the crowd and slyly smiled up at the miner.

"What do ya want now, Jys?" She asked playfully. Jystana liked this girl. If she was interested in making deals, she would have made her an offer by now.

"This nice gentleman is lonely. Can you take care of that for me? I have an appointment later tonight I can't miss." Jystana was amused by the miner's confused stupor as Marie wrapped an arm around his and steered him away from the bar.

"Of course, Jys, but you owe me one," she winked as she walked off. The miner was already more interested in Marie and had completely forgotten the white-haired beauty. *La Dame Blanc*, as they had taken to calling her recently. She smiled at the name. *No matter where I go, that name always seems to catch up to me.*

She set her glass on the counter, scanning the crowd. It was the same bunch as it always was, night in and night out, but she kept her ear out for any sign of Eberheart's doings. She was cautious at the beginning of the season—she didn't want to be seen if his men were frequently visiting the town. Jystana couldn't risk her life, let alone her lover's.

She felt a tingle crawl up the back of her neck. Her surroundings seemed to slow down to a crawl as her senses became more acute. She could feel Absalom so very close now. She stood from her seat and watched the door with impatience. She missed him so much—more so than ever before.

***

The three men had stopped in front of the packed saloon, leaving their horses tied towards the end of the lineup of other horses. Abe didn't even hesitate as he led the way to the porch. Jed and John were quiet, and had come to terms with each other over the last week. They were more alike than they had originally thought.

John looked at Jed and adjusted his vest and belt. Jed nodded and followed John, a signal to be ready for a fight if need be. Abe was determined to find someone in this saloon, and Jed felt sorry for whomever it was. The parlor was filled with the usual types as the three of them entered. Smoke hung over the mass of people like a shroud, shifting and moving with the movements of the people.

John had already set his sights on a group of whores in the corner, who were trying their best to lure him over for a 'sample'. John grinned as he stepped towards their direction. Jed firmly grabbed his shoulder and leaned in to John's ear, "You don't want them, John."

John frowned, disgruntled that Jed had interrupted his possible night of pleasures. "Why's that?" John bit back irritably.

Jed looked at the girls, then, back at John, "First of all, John, they got what you don't want." John's disgruntled face soon changed to one of concern as Jed continued, "And, second, I'm pretty sure we got a job to do first." Jed patted his shoulder and released it. His eyes searched the room as John cleared his throat and stood next to Jed.

Jed couldn't help but smile to himself as he searched for anything that might hint at a clue. Abe was not far ahead, weaving through the rabble of miners and local drunks. Jed could feel that they were very close to something—to what he wasn't sure, but his gut instinct gnawed at him in the back of his mind.

Abe stopped suddenly, his shoulders squaring. It was subtle, but Jed could see it. Jed nudged John and pointed for him to go around. Jed moved forward towards Abe. His hand rested on the grip of his gun as he approached Abe.

*He sensed somethin'...*

Before he could reach him, a familiar woman stood in between him and his friend. "Jystana...?!" Jed asked, relieved. Her eyes were just as stunning as the first time he had met her. Her hair was perfectly laid over her shoulders and down her front, and her dress was expertly tailored.

She smiled and rested a hand on her hip as she looked him up and down. "My, my, you have grown, Jed!" Jed relaxed and eased his hand off his gun.

"Jys, we ain't got time for playin' your damn game," Abe's voice sounded behind them, his body language relaxed now.

With a sigh, she turned to him, her eyebrow raised, "You never do. Where the hell have you been, Absalom?" She quietly scolded him. Jed suppressed laughter as Abe shifted uncomfortably in place, his frown plastered on his brow.

"Workin', woman...what else would I be doin'?"

"Of course you were. I called for you months ago!"

He sighed and rummaged in his duster jacket. "We ran into...problems."

Jed turned back to the crowd as the two of them bickered. He saw John was at the bar ordering a whiskey, and several men clamored around him for the same thing. Among the auras that flowed and fluctuated around the room, a different one stood out to him. It was darker than the others. His attention focused on a short man who appeared to be no older than eighteen.

*Somethin' ain't right about him.* Jed watched him as he approached the counter and hastily ordered a drink. His eyes darted around the room nervously, almost as if someone or some*thing* was trying to get him when he wasn't looking.

Jed felt drawn to him. *I need to talk with him.*

He left his friend and Jystana where they stood as he made his way to the man. Jed didn't approach him directly. He didn't want him to run. John had noticed the man, too, but he hadn't made eye contact. John was smarter than he led on when Jed first met him.

Jed reached the counter and slid a bottle over from the edge of the counter. He would pay for the drink later, if the bartender even noticed. He poured himself a shot of whiskey and glanced at the young man, who had finally turned his full attention to his drink.

*He's frightened of something...but what?*

The downtrodden young man's hair was tousled.. Jed felt pity for him as he spoke softly, "You live around here?"

The young man snapped his gaze to Jed, his eyes wide. He licked his lips nervously and played with his glass repeatedly, "Y-yeah...why?"

Jed shrugged and knocked back his drink, "Jus' wondering. I was passing through—seeing some relatives in the area ,and I jus' wanted to know what the town was like."

The young man seemed to slightly relax as he looked back to his glass and drained the whole thing. "Best y'all get out of here, while you still can…" He spoke so softly, Jed almost couldn't hear it.

Jed uneasily adjusted his weight in the seat, turning to the young man who was refilling his glass. "Why?"

The young man paused, before downing his glass again. "Silas…" Upon mention of the name, the young man downed his glass and left the bar hastily. Jed stood and tried to follow him, "Hey!" He called after him. The young man didn't stop as he left the saloon. *Damn it! What the hell is goin' on here?!*

"Jed…" He turned to face Abe, irritation growing in his chest. "Head upstairs. You'll find the man who runs this place," Jystana was close to Abe's arm, and she was desperately trying to get his attention.

"Abe, wait—"

She tried to get her words in, but Abe stopped her with a growl, "Damn it, woman, let me speak." He ordered back at Jed, "Get what we need, and get out…"

Jed nodded. He knew what to do. He turned on his heel and he walked towards the stairs. After what Abe wanted him to do, he aimed to find out who this Silas was—and he would end whatever it was that was tormenting that young man.

*He reminds me of myself so many moons ago. Maybe, if I can help just one person, it might make a difference.*

He ascended the stairs, taking care not to draw attention. So far, he hadn't attracted a single suspicious eye. At the top of the flight, a larger man stopped him with a firm hand on his chest. Jed looked up at him under his hat brim.

"No one beyond this point," he snarled menacingly.

Jed watched the deep, blood red aura writhe around the man as the two looked each other in the eye. *Demon...*

"I need to speak with the owner of this place," Jed insisted firmly.

The demon grunted and firmly moved Jed back, "No one sees Silas, unless he calls fer ya."

*Silas...the same one the boy was talking about?* Jed frowned. He didn't have time for this bullshit.

"Let him through, Ben," a man's voice called from the other side of the balcony that surrounded the upper parlor. The two of them looked over to a man who was dressed in leather pants, chaps, a neatly tucked shirt, and a dark brown vest. Jed couldn't help but notice the bandolier and loaded gun belt. Ben—as the demon was named—unhappily grunted and hesitantly stepped aside.

Jed moved around him and headed towards the devil who called himself Silas. Jed noted the deep black aura that writhed around this one—an aura that was similar to Abe's.

*Devils and demons really* are *different...Abe wasn't jokin'.*

Silas slyly grinned, indicating for Jed to follow. Jed glanced at the parlor before following the man into his office. Silas entered first and stopped at the door, letting Jed pass through. He closed the door, locking it behind him. Jed frowned and looked back at the door, then, Silas. "Is it necessary to lock it?"

Silas chuckled and moved around Jed, looking him up and down with an odd hunger to his eyes. Jed's inner self was screaming for him to run, but he couldn't miss this opportunity. Abe wouldn't have sent him up here if this devil didn't know anything.

"I don't like interruptions when conductin' business," Silas answered calmly as he stood in front of Jed. "Care for a drink?"

Jed cleared his throat and locked eyes with Silas. He was extremely difficult to read. "No, thank you. I'm not here for a social call."

Silas chuckled, "No, of course not." He walked to his desk and sat on the edge of it. Jed didn't move. He didn't want to get any closer than he had to. "First, before we talk about whatever it is that you want to talk about, I would like to introduce myself." He reached behind him and grabbed a dark bottle, its label scrawled with odd text he had never seen before.

*I wonder what language that is...*

"I'm known as Silas in this town...a purveyor of sorts. Only those that want to make me an offer for my...specialty items...come to me directly." Silas uncorked the bottle and pressed his finger against the opening, tipping the bottle over once to cover his finger with is contents. He set the bottle down and euphorically licked his finger. Jed could only assume that it was a drug of some sort.

"My name ain't important, Silas." Jed could feel something was off about this devil. Something he hadn't faced before. Silas laughed, recorking the bottle and jumping to his feet.

"I'm afraid you're wrong, boy..."

Jed could feel a tingling at the back of his neck. *I don't like this...*

Before Jed could react, Silas leaped across the room and grappled Jed to the floor. Jed shouted as he landed with a hard thud on the wood floor. He glared at Silas, who held him in a chokehold, immobilizing his arms to keep him from his guns. He coughed and struggled against the devil's grip. "You see...I need your name, so I know what to write in my book."

Jed bared his teeth angrily at Silas. He could feel his rage build inside him again, but, this time, he wanted to let it out. "You best get off me!" Jed managed to choke out.

Silas just grinned and leaned in too close for Jed's comfort. "Oh, I don't think so, my boy. You're mine to play with for a while."

As Silas' hungry eyes gazed at him, Jed thought, *Oh I don't fuckin' think so.*

※※※

Abe had finally dragged Jystana over to a corner table. He had complete faith that Jed could handle one saloon owner. Jystana sat across from him, as beautiful as ever. He loved that blue silk dress.

"Abe! You don't understand what I'm sayin'!" Her sultry maiden façade was long gone.

"You talk too much, Jys…" Abe grunted as he lit up his cigarette. "Jed can handle this Silas character. Just because your charms couldn't seduce the bastard doesn't mean Jed can't do what I ask."

Jystana frowned at him and leaned in close, "No, Abe you really don't understand! I *couldn't* seduce him—"

"Because you ain't tryin' hard enough," Abe cut in as he poured himself a shot of his favorite whiskey.

"He's a boy-lover, Abe!" Jystana hissed at him.

Abe choked on his drag and fumbled his hold on the cigarette.

"What?!" He snarled back.

"I was tryin' to tell ya!" Jystana desperately added.

A shriek of pain was heard from a room upstairs. Immediately, Abe stood up sharply, knocking his chair to the floor. The patrons of the establishment less fazed by the shriek than Abe knocking his chair over. *Oh, hell no!* Without a second thought, Abe was rushing through the crowd, taking the steps two or three at a time. He had to get to Jed before it got any worse.

The large demon that protected the stairs drew his pistol to stop Abe. He didn't stand a chance as Abe punched him in the face with such force it knocked him on his back. Jystana was close behind him as Abe headed straight to the only closed door. He snarled angrily as he slammed his foot into the door, breaking the lock mechanism and causing the door handle to wobble out of its place. Abe had his guns drawn, ready to take revenge, if need be.

What he saw was not what he expected.

Jed had a man tied up with the black leather strapping on the floor. Blood was everywhere as a wound on the man's cheek gushed. Jed was standing over him, also bloody, but not as harmed as Abe had expected. He sighed, relieved that the shrieking was not from Jed at all.

Jed grinned at Abe, "'Bout time, El Diablo." Jed wiped his knife blade on the man's pants as he stepped over him. Abe went to put his cigarette back to his mouth, but realized he must have left it downstairs. He rummaged again and got out a new one, lighting up as Jystana sighed with relief.

"Get on with it boy, we ain't got all night…"

\*\*\*

When Abe had busted through the door, Jed had been ready to kill whoever was coming. Jed had been surprised to see that it was Abe.

*He must have heard this pig squeal,* Jed thought. He had gotten leverage against the devil as Silas had tried to have his way. He managed to get out from under him and grabbed his knife that El Cabrio had cut him with so long ago. Jed had slashed at the man's cheek, which, shockingly, had brought the devil to his knees. He'd have to ask Abe why El Cabrio's knife, in particular, could cause so much agony.

He had stepped around Silas, who was writhing in pain on the floor. Abe had taken up a smoke, and Jystana wandered around the carnage; clearly satisfied with Silas's fate. It wasn't too long thereafter that John showed, stopping just short of the door.

Abe looked at John and walked over to him, "Mind the door, John."

Before John could protest, Abe closed the door and leaned against it. Finally able to get what he needed, Jed turned his attention back to Silas. He would get the information they sought. Jed crouched down to Silas's level, tipping the devil's chin up to look at him.

He had taken off his hat and coat, so he didn't bloody them. "Alright, you nasty son of a bitch, where's Eberheart?"

Silas looked at Jed, then, at Abe, as if pleading for help. Jed snarled and grabbed his chin to make him look at him again, "Don't look at him. He won't help ya."

Silas whimpered with pain as Jed grabbed his face. The cheek wound was similar to Jed's scar. He knew it hurt like hell.

"I don't know what you're talking about..." His words trembled. Jed was tired of hearing those words.

Jed angrily shouted and hit the devil in the face, coating Jed's knuckles in blood from the wound. Silas screamed again as he tried to curl away from the blow.

Abe spoke once the screaming subsided, "You'd best answer him." Jed could smell Abe's cigarette smoke over the blood.

He was losing his patience. "Where is Eberheart?" Jed flashed the teeth of the knife in front of Silas' eyes. They widened in fear as he looked at the knife, then, at Jed. "Tell me, or I'm gonna cut somethin' off!"

Silas whimpered again, this time, it was mixed with a blubbering sob. The pathetic devil sniveled and shut his eyes."Eberheart is holed up in the desert, not far from here." Jed couldn't believe it; this devil was actually telling him. After all this time, he had never thought he would be this close. "He's east of town, about twenty miles or so." Jed looked at Abe as the man babbled. He nodded.

Jed looked back at Silas. *Pathetic...*

Jed stood as the devil looked at him pleadingly. He didn't want to leave behind any loose ends. He drew his pistol and aimed it at his main heart—at the center of his chest, below the sternum.

He pulled the trigger.

# Chapter 39

Abe had left the saloon shortly after Jed had pulled the trigger. Silas's death had almost been satisfying. Abe drew in a deep breath of fresh air, savoring their small victory.

They finally had the exact location of Eberheart, a devil he would soon see again. Jed and John had gone to a different part of town to bunker in for the night. John had told Jed he had a "talent" for finding the best inn and gambling establishment anywhere on the frontier.

Abe didn't follow them. He wanted to be alone.

The streets were relatively quiet as he walked toward the opposite end. Jystana had given him exact directions to her place of residence, an invitation he would never disregard. He hadn't seen her for far too long.

He always admired her tactics and her unique talent when it came to bargaining for a place to occupy. As she had put it so many years ago, "You have your connections, darlin', and I have mine."

He stopped at a taller building as he rummaged for a cigarette. He knew she would hate it if he smoked in her living space, but, tonight, he didn't care much. The building, itself, wasn't very old; freshly built by the looks of it. Its wood siding wasn't warped or tarnished by the test of time, nor had it been desecrated by its inhabitants. *She always did have good taste.*

Abe lit the tip of his cigarette and walked to the staircase that hugged the building. They were sturdy and hardly creaked as Abe climbed. She had told him which floor and which door was hers. He yearned to see her again. He wanted to forget the impending battle that would come with the rise of the sun.

He climbed a couple flights of stairs until he reached her door. He could smell her scent, strong to his nostrils. The memory of smelling her for the first time was still overpowering to him. She had the sweetest aroma of cloves and sweet jasmine—a scent that he could never forget. Abe sighed, discarding his cigarette. She had told him to invite himself in before he left the saloon. She would join him shortly.

He turned the knob of the door and let himself in. The main room was darkened, save the moon that was beginning its ascent. The interior, as he expected, was nothing short of lavish. Jystana always had to have to best. *She deserves the best...* Abe walked around the small parlor area, running his hand lightly over a lounger. *I just wish I could give it all to her...*

Abe sighed as he took his hat off and looked down at it. He was weary; tired of running from everything and everyone. It was time to put an end to Eberheart and find a way to live in relative peace.

"Fancy meetin' you here, Absalom."

Abe perked his head towards the door. Jystana's voice was always an ear-catcher, even in a room full of people. Her voice was quiet, confident, and stunningly beautiful all at once.

She had a sultry smile on her lips as she walked around him and ran a hand over his arm. The mere touch of her made his whole body ignite with passion. *Damn it, it has been too long.* She knew how hypnotic she was, chuckling softly as she walked to a dressing screen. He recognized that screen from their youth.

"Well, Abe, it would seem you leave quite the path of death behind ya." Her voice called to him as she began to undress. He could see her voluptuous figure through the screen. He didn't even know why she still used it. He knew what she looked like. Abe waited with patience as he sat on the red, velvet lounger, playing with his hat in his hands.

"Comes with the job, Jys." A grin toyed at the corners of mouth.

"I know that, Absalom," She looked around the corner of her cream-colored screen. Her complexion was beautiful in the moon's light. "You're always so damn messy." She retreated back, her blue dress falling over the top to rest for the night. He loved that color on her.

Abe's grin faded as he waited for her. *This could be my last with her.* The thought pained him as he stood. Moments later, she walked around and up to him. Her playful smile was gone at his expression.

"Absalom...?" She stopped in front of him, tying her silken sash to hold the robe closed, her expression now heavy.

He looked down at her. Her robe was Chinese silk, with an intricate flower design scrawled on its ivory fabric. He half smiled at it as he ran his hands over her arms, feeling the material ruffle and smooth as he did, "I bought this for you. It just about cost me a fortune to get it."

She smiled, running a hand down his chest. He ached for her. "I remember it well. Nearly made that chink piss himself." They both chuckled at the long-ago memory.

Silence spanned between them as Abe felt her arms and curvaceous sides through the silk. She was always so perfect in every way, and he knew every square inch of her. Her hair was flowing over her right shoulder, catching the filtered moonlight through the aged lace curtains that hung over the window, and he could feel her stunning eyes on him. He loved her more than he could ever express. He couldn't look her in the eye. He didn't want to die.

"Absalom," she whispered softly, her hands touched his scruffy jaw with her soft, slender hands. "You don't have to fight him alone."

"I know," he quietly answered. "I just...I don't know if I can do it, Jys." His own words shocked him as he gently gathered her hands into the grasp of his rough ones. Abe finally looked at her. Her piercing, sky blue eyes were fixed on his cobalt ones. With an agitated sigh, he turned from her and went to the window, gazing at the street below. He could sense her worry.

Abe heard her bare feet tread softly over the wooden floor boards. Her arms wrapped around him, resting her hands over his chest in a loving embrace. Her face was resting on his back. "You can do this. Eberheart needs to be put in the grave."

Abe looked down to his chest, where her hands were resting. His hearts were pounding heavily, and he could feel the rising need for her in his entire being. He remained silent as she moved around him to block his view of the street. "You're El Diablo, damn it. You're the only one who can—and will—put an end to his bullshit."

"Jys, I don't want you to get hurt…or worse." His admission of fear shocked her as he pulled her into his arms, his hands wandered over her body. He couldn't help it.

"I won't." Her voice was a whisper, her lips close to his.

He couldn't take it anymore. He pressed his lips to hers in a fury as he rubbed his hands along her ribs, feeling her curves. He hastily loosened the tie to her robe. He ripped the tie off, tossing it to the side. The robe gave way, exposing her naked front. She returned the favor as she hastily stripped him of his coat, letting it fall to the floor.

Their passion escalated as they made their way to the velvet chaise lounge. He wasn't going to wait. He couldn't wait. He needed her now; and he knew she needed him. They were a pair, sealed for all eternity. If this was to be their last, he wanted to show her that he loved her, even with the face of death looming over his shoulder.

# Chapter 40

Jed had woken up at dawn from a night of relentless dreams. He hardly slept, and he turned down several whores who desperately wanted to 'help him sleep'. All he wanted was for the morning to come as quickly as possible. His sister was so close now.

The sun was barely cresting the mining town as he pulled on his boots, put on his belt and hat, and adjusted his vest. Jed was ready for this day. A day he had waited for so long to see. He left the room and walked to where he knew John had gone to. He rasped his knuckles against the door. Silence answered him. Jed quietly grabbed the knob and turned it, cringing slightly at its squeaky protest. John was laying askew in bed, bottles of all kinds scattered everywhere; and he was still fully clothed.

"John," Jed spoke with a raised voice, knowing it would be the only thing that could cut through his drunken slumber. "Get your ass up. We need to go."

John responded with a groggy groan, unmoving. Jed couldn't help but grin at his odd comrade. He walked into the room and over to John. He lightly smacked his foot off the edge of the bed it was hanging over. With a heavy thud and a groan, John finally lifted his head from the pillow.

"Damn it, Jed, it's too early for this shit."

Jed contained a laugh as he watched John slowly sit himself up, catching himself before he tipped completely over. "Come on, John, El Diablo is probably waitin' for us downstairs," Jed hurriedly encouraged. He stooped down to John and wrapped his arm over his shoulder.

"I don't need no damn help," John snapped. Jed ignored him and continued to help him. As soon as John was on his own feet, he stopped protesting, as a belch ripped through his throat. Jed crinkled his nose and tried to wave away the rank smell of alcohol.

"Christ Almighty, John."

John laughed as he pushed Jed away from him. Jed was more-than-happy to oblige. John wove his way across the cluttered floor and towards the door.

\*\*\*

The two men ate a quick meal while they waited for El Diablo to show. Jed was certain he would come. Somehow, he always knew where he was. The two of them were attending to their horses, preparing for the ride ahead of them. John had sobered up after a couple cups of mediocre coffee and some food.

The sun was fully exposed now, and the heat was already baking the packed soil under their feet as Jed tightened the last strap and mounted up. *We need to find Abe and get going.* From what Silas had said the night before, he knew it might take them half a day.

John also mounted his horse and turned him towards the main street, squinting from the sharp rays, despite his hat shading his eyes. "Know where El Diablo ran off to?"

Jed had an idea of who he was with—but not where. Jed opened his mouth to make a guess, but was cut off by an all-too-familiar voice. "John, sometimes, you're as blind as a coal miner."

Jed grinned as he turned his horse to look at his friend approaching from a side street. Abe reined Dusk to a halt nearby and rested his hands on the horn of the saddle. To Jed's surprise, he saw Jystana not far behind him. She sat tall and elegant on top of her dapple white mare, whose eyes were just as red as Dusk's were.

Jed wondered, *Another European horse?*

Jystana was wearing dark brown leather pants, a different look from her usual attire. The ivory undershirt was slightly undone at the top, exposing the tops of her breasts. Her belt was loaded with ammunition and two ivory pistols at her sides.

Jed was surprised that Abe was going to let her accompany them on this last ride. He thought, *I somehow get the feelin' that she didn't give him a choice.*

"Well, now, there's the stud!" Her sultry voice called over to Jed. His ears began to burn. She still managed to fluster him. Without uttering a word, he tipped his hat towards her in respect.

Abe took up the reins in his hands again, turning his horse to the edge of town to his right side. "Shit, y'all talk too much." Before any could rebut his words, he spurred Dusk into a lope, leaving the rest in his dust trail.

Jed soon heeled his stallion to follow, knowing that the other two were, no doubt, not far behind. Jed felt a knot forming in his gut. The time was finally at hand.

He could, at last, get his sister back and claim revenge for his father's brutal murder, as well as the destruction of the only home he ever knew. The sound of horses' thundering hooves invigorated Jed as they picked up the pace to a gallop.

*Hell is comin' for ya, Eberheart. And I'll be the one to deliver it.*

***

Marietta was sitting in what was a poor excuse of a 'room'. The walls were made of old slat wood. It was more of a shack than a real building. It had been added to a bigger shack next door, which she avoided as much as she possibly could. The bastard who had taken her kept holding her here; for some reason that she didn't quite understand. He was confusing, almost radical at times. He never hurt her, touched her, or hit her. Nothing like that at all. Regardless, she had not let her guard down around him.

His underlings had tried their luck on more than one occasion. One of his men would get restless and want some sort of comfort. Since she was the only woman within miles, she was the most desired among the ranks. Every time someone tried, they were mercilessly slaughtered without hesitation.

She sighed, trying to focus on educating herself with the half-ruined books Eberhart Marks had allowed her. Most of the words were faded, some of the pages were missing, and others were so water-damaged it was difficult to grasp the concept of what she was reading. The delicate table was rickety, and the chair was small, barely able to hold her weight.

Marietta frowned, tucking stray hairs of auburn behind her ears. *It's so hot here*, she thought, glancing toward the open windowpane and listening to the busy hustle of the day. Eberhart's men were always in a rush; always doing something. Today was different, somehow.

She closed the damaged book and stood carefully; she didn't want to break her only chair. Lifting the tattered blue hem of her dress, she went to the door and pulled on the fraying rope that held the latch together. The door creaked as she swung it open, clacking shut when she stepped into the open air. Men were shouting and rushing every which way. Something was definitely different.

"Marietta, darlin', you should be inside."

Marietta's blood curdled in disgust as she frowned at Eberhart. It took every inch of her inner strength to not try and kill this man by herself. She had tried, but all he did was laugh as he demonstrated his preternatural healing ability. He frightened her, but she would rather let her hatred persist to the surface.

*I don't want to be inside*, she projected her thought loudly and bitterly in her head. She knew he could hear her. Over this course of time, Marietta had to learn very quickly not to let him hear her thoughts. She learned how to still think without letting him hear her by whispering in her mind.

Eberhart shrugged in an uncaring manner, "Suit yourself." He beat the brown hat he usually wore against his pant leg before setting it onto his head. He was dressed for something important, she could tell.

It made her uneasy. *What is he planning to do?* He wore his hip-length, dark brown coat, with two large bandoliers loaded with ammunition. A knife hung at this left leg, accompanied with two heavy-looking pistols and a large gun belt that held up his dark brown pants.

*He's ready for a fight, but...with whom?* She quietly asked herself. She watched him as he walked towards the center of the ramshackle settlement to intercept a rider coming from the westernmost part. He was coming in at a full gallop, only sliding to a stop in a flurry of dust and snorting horse. His eyes were wide with fear.

"Boss, they're headin' this way!"

Eberhart grinned, his sharp teeth flashing in the bright sunlight. "Good, let them come."

The man nervously nodded and rode off towards the lean-to stables that were erected a few months ago; Eberhart looked around at his men and spoke with a booming voice, "Alright, boys, you know what to do. Time to burn this loose end."

\*\*\*

Jed, Abe, Jystana, and John all rode their horses hard toward the east. Abe led the way, seeming to know exactly where to go. The sun was rising high towards the noon hour. It would be difficult to catch the Marks gang by surprise with little coverage from the land around them. Jed's desire to avenge his father and get his sister back burned deep in his soul as they rode for what seemed like hours.

Jed began to wonder if they would reach Eberhart's encampment before sundown at this rate. Without warning, Abe reined quickly to a stop. Jed and the others did the same.

Glancing around at the barren landscape, John said, "El Diablo, I'm startin' to think that bastard back in Bodie gave us shit directions…"

Jystana looked at John as Abe dismounted, a smirk toying at her plump lips, "John, you're truly, beautifully useless."

Jed held his laughter in as he watched Abe stoop to the ground and trace his fingers over what appeared to be hoof prints.

John frowned at her, "I could say the same to you, ma'am, but—"

"They passed this way," Abe growled as he stood up.

"How close?" Jed asked, eager to fight for his family.

"Closer than I damn like." Without another word, he threw the reins over the horn of his saddle and turned Dusk around. With a firm smack across his rump, Dusk bolted forward, running off in the distance. Jed didn't hesitate to follow. He was ready for this.

"John, you're goin' left. Take out as many as you can." Abe looked long and hard at John as he dismounted and retrieved a long barrel rifle from the back of his saddle. Jystana had dismounted and had relieved her pistols from their holsters, making sure each one was loaded and ready-to-kill. Jed had pulled his pistols as well as he waited for Abe's directions.

Abe turned his attention to Jed, satisfied that John was doing as he had been told. "Jed, you're gonna be helpin' him." His tone was low, but didn't lose its authoritative strength.

Jed frowned, wanting to be down in the fray with him, not stuck being his spotter. "But Abe…! I can fight. You know I can!" Jed spoke in an exasperated tone, hoping he could persuade his friend to let him fight alongside him.

Abe cut him off as he clapped a hand on his shoulder, his cobalt eyes piercing through Jed's soul. "Jed, you gotta get yer sister out of there. I can only distract Marks for so long. In and out."

Jed let the words soak in. They sounded heavy. *Why is he talkin' like this? Like he's about to die...*

"Abe—"

"Understand, boy?" Abe growled, clearly done talking. Jed stared straight into the hunter's eyes; his friend's eyes. Chills ran down his spine as he realized the truth: Abe was afraid of facing Eberhart. Even though there had only been a small inkling in his eyes, Jed saw it.

He swallowed, now worried about the fight ahead of them. He knew he had to focus all his strength in doing what Abe wanted him to do.

Jed nodded.

Abe grunted satisfactorily. He turned his gaze to Jystana as she began walking towards them. The sound of John's rifle hammering back sounded foreboding. Jed hoped many of Eberhart's men would fall by his skill.

"John. Jed. Head towards the ridge," Abe nodded towards the ridge not far from them. Jed nodded, waiting for John to reach him. Together, they began walking towards the rising ridge.

Jed looked back behind him as they went, watching Abe and Jystana talk amongst themselves. "You any good with that gun, John?"

"I haven't missed yet, Jed." John couldn't keep a grin from forming on his lips as he confidently held the rifle, as though it were just as much a part of him as his own arms.

Jed smiled. The nervousness in his gut was growing but he couldn't let that hold him back now.

# Chapter 41

Jed and John crawled into position on the ridge overlooking the small ravine that carved into the plains. Jed would never have guessed that it was there at all, if Abe hadn't spotted the horses tracks that led to it.

Several shacks and sheds dotted the inner lining of the ravine, but what disturbed him most was the absence of any life. *They're here. I can feel it.* Jed grew impatient. He adjusted his weight on his stomach as quietly as he could.

John was further down the ridge, his eyes focused down the narrow barrel and through sight that was attached to the rifle. Far to his left, Jystana was also laying on her stomach, her eyes scanning the scene below, like a bird of prey.

Abe was yet to be seen.

Jed understood what Abe was trying to do. He wanted to make a big enough distraction to draw out the bastard who had stolen his sister and changed his life in such a brutal way. His hands tightly gripped the handles of his pistols. The tension was so thick he could hardly breathe.

He looked towards the entrance of the ravine; he could barely see around the jagged edge of the ridge he rested on as he watched his friend walk down the windy beaten trail. *Damn it, Abe, I should be down there with you.* Jed adjusted his pistols and prepared to start covering. He knew they were there, somewhere.

His inner mind was screaming for him to help his tutor and comrade. Abe might die, just to help Jed. His inner conscious was torn. He wanted to help him, but, in doing so, he would be disobeying him. If he didn't, however…

*Shit…*

Jed slid back out of view before standing to his feet, crouching to avoid detection. *You ain't gonna do this alone, damn it! You trained me! I can help you!*

\*\*\*

Abe could feel the heat soaking through his black leather duster, baking his core with a welcomed heat. He could smell the tension in the air around him, and the smell of Eberhart's demons that were close by. He knew this was a setup.

The previous night, Jystana had told him he didn't have to do this alone. He knew he didn't need to martyr himself, but he also knew himself. Abe knew that he was a stubborn old bastard. The thought of anyone he cared about getting caught up into Eberhart's wrath pained him. In his mind, he had to do this alone.

He heard someone in a shack move as he past the first row. He didn't break his attention. He would be able to hear them coming.

*Where are you, you sack of shit?* Abe thought maliciously. He felt his own inner devil struggle against the mortal form. It wanted to taste blood, and in a bad way. *Soon.*

For a decade, Absalom had been running from Eberhart. And, for a decade, Eberhart had made sure that his life was made miserable and that he was constantly hunted. He was notorious in the frontier, even before he had joined with the Marks gang all those years ago. After his adopted father and mentor had perished abruptly, Abe had nowhere else to turn.

It was a mistake he would not soon forget and forever regret.

"I see you finally caught up with me, Absalom."

Abe snapped his head to the right, his pistols raised, ready for a fight. With bared teeth, he cautiously approached. He cocked the hammers back on his pistols. He hoped he could catch Eberhart off-guard.

"How long has it been, now? A couple years?" Eberhart's voice echoed off the walls of the ravine. It was difficult to pinpoint where he was, precisely. Abe growled under his breath as he felt the heat rise from deep within. His inner self was screeching to be let out. He forced it to remain contained. The rage was building to a steady peak. He wouldn't be able to hold it for much longer.

"Get your fuckin' ass out here, Eberhart!" Abe snarled as he came to the center of the encampment.

Abe stopped. He could sense that he was close. *He has grown stronger. Damn my luck.*

His laugh boomed over the encampment, filling every empty and hollow space with the sound of his amusement. Abe kept a sharp eye out, determined not to be the first one to fall.

Eberhart stepped out from an alley ahead of him, his hands free of any weapons. It felt like a cold stone dropped in Abe's gut as he watched the devil approach. He knew what that meant.

*I have to drop him, before he can reach me.* Abe gripped his pistols harder as he followed Eberhart's movements with them. He just needed a good shot, and Eberhart would be dead. Simple as that.

"I can tell you are just bursting with delight at this lil' reunion of ours, Absalom." Eberhart's smile flashed in the sun, stopping several yards away from Abe. Abe gritted his teeth. He couldn' get a clear shot of his heart. "Where is that sweet lil' whore of yours, Abe? I miss those legs of hers."

Anger flashed in his eyes as he snarled, "I don't have time for this bullshit."

"Oh, I think you *do*, Absalom." His chuckle chilled Abe to the bone. As Eberhart began to circle, Abe kept his eyes trained on him. "Or you wouldn't have come all this way…"

"Where is the girl?" Abe growled. His temper was beginning to flare.

"So, that is what all this is about?" Eberhart paused. "If you mean my daughter…" The words slammed into him like a train. *Daughter?! Oh, fuck, Jed, I didn't know…* "Then it ain't your damn business."

*\*\*\**

Jed stopped in his tracks at Eberhart's shattering words. *His daughter?! What the hell is goin' on?!* He had followed his friend through the rows of shacks, making sure to avoid the windows and open doors, in case one of the demons decided to try a quick kill. He had been listening to Eberhart and Abe talk to each other up to this point.

Anguish filled his heart as he crouched in his spot, not believing what he had just heard. "No…it can't be true," Jed murmured to himself. It angered him that Eberhart would dare imply his mother was anything but a good woman and loving mother. He could feel his rage build quickly inside him as forced himself to continue forward. His pistols were ready.

*I'm gonna tear you to pieces, you bastard.* Jed let the anger flow through him as he got closer to the center, where his friend and Eberhart were. He would drop him where he stood.

"My daughter stays with me, Absalom." Eberhart's cool voice pissed Jed off even more as he peeked around a corner to get an idea of his position. Eberhart was on the far-left side of the center. Abe was in front of Jed, his guns trained on his adversary.

"She ain't yours to possess, Eberhart," Abe growled irritably.

"Isn't she?" Eberhart scoffed and started to pace to the other direction. "She has my blood in her veins," Eberhart's tone darkened, grating on Jed's nerves as he began to slowly sneak forward. He would get this bastard. "She's a perfect species, Absalom, a Nephilim in its truest form."

Jed took the opportunity of Eberhart's distraction and stood to his full stature. He raised his pistol with his teeth and then bared them in fury. How dare he talk about his sister like that? "She ain't your child!" Jed shouted, catching both men off guard. Jed could see Abe's countenance turn into rage and anxiety all at once. Jed knew that Abe didn't want him down here with him.

Jed didn't care. He wanted revenge.

Eberhart's guffaw filled his ears as Jed cocked the hammer back on his gun, "Well! Looks like the pup made it after all! Well done, Absalom, well done." Eberhart turned his malicious grin to Jed, his eyes as red as hell, itself. "A pity my daughter has to watch him suffer…"

Jed couldn't hold it in any longer. His anger reached its boiling point, and he let loose. He squeezed the trigger, unfazed by the force of the shots as he let bullets fly towards Eberhart.

Abe fired as well, deftly moving to a different position. Eberhart avoided Jed's shots as he disappeared in a cloud of swirling, inky tendrils. Jed snarled under his breath as he quickly turned around, trying to anticipate where Eberhart might be next.

A heartbeat passed before he heard a roar behind him. He tried to turn to face Eberhart, but was too late. He felt the connective impact of Eberhart's fist at his back. The sheer strength of his blow sent Jed flying forward and tumbling to the ground, finally skidding into a shack. Jed saw stars for a moment as he got to his feet with a slight stagger. *Damn it!*

Jed watched as Abe and Eberhart locked into a close battle. Abe dodged and evaded many of what would have been severe blows, had they made contact. As he fired, each shot missed its mark. Jed started to run to help his friend. Now, he understood why Abe was hesitant to come here. Eberhart was just toying with Abe; he was much stronger than he.

*Shit, he won't be able to hold him much longer! I got to get to him!* Jed's anger flowed through him as he pumped his legs faster. He had an urgency to reach his friend. Jed felt a tingling sensation, like needles pricking the back of his neck. An unearthly shriek ripped through one of the shacks as he ran past, followed by a crash. It was answered by several similar calls. Windows began shattering, and doors began splintering from someone trying to break free.

He saw his friend take a blow to the jaw, knocking him off his balance for a moment before barely dodging another blow. Jed's vision was filled with movements of demons finally bursting through their shacks. Most of them were so pale that you could see their veins; their eyes were black and soulless. They had fanged teeth dripping with globs of saliva. Their bodies seemed to resemble human men.

They began to pour into the crooked streets. Jed could feel the tingle in the back of his mind shrieking at him to flee of the imminent flood of demons that were coming for him. He ignored it.

Jed didn't have time to deal with this. Without a second thought, Jed was able to control his anger, as he concentrated on their vital point—the main heart, just below the sternum. A shot was fired, and the demon screeching as it failed in its jump, tumbling to the ground and clawing at the hole that had been drilled right into its heart. Black blood coated its front, and its clawed hands screeched in its writhing agony. Jed didn't have a chance to revel in his small victory.

So many more were fast approaching. Jed glanced at Abe, who seemed to be gaining the upper hand, and, then, back at the approaching demons that were Eberhart's 'men'. Jed pulled the hammers back on his pistols, taking careful aim.

*I'll make sure you're all sent straight back to hell!*

\*\*\*

Abe heard the shrieks of the lesser demons come from the shacks. He knew it was a trap; a good reason why he didn't want Jed involved this time. *Damn kid is gonna get himself killed!* Abe ducked and rebutted with a swift upward jab of his elbow. He felt

Eberhart crumple slightly as he made contact with his lower abdomen.

The two devils were locked in close hand-to-hand combat. Eberhart had managed to disarm both of Abe's pistols, flinging them to the sides of their scuffle. Their blows became increasingly crafty as they fought. Abe could tell that Eberhart was toying with him, but he needed to try. He had to kill this bastard. For deceiving him all those years ago, for forcing him to commit all breeds of heinous acts he wouldn't normally take on; even for Jedidiah, and his sister, Marietta.

He had a score to settle with this bastard. Or he would die trying.

Eberhart grinned as they fought faster and faster, their blows growing in ferocity. Abe could feel his inner devil scream to be let out, to let him tear Eberhart to pieces. Abe missed landing a blow to Eberhart's jaw. He cursed himself, knowing that it left him open. Eberhart took his opening. Abe grunted and cried out as Eberhart viciously knocked Abe down to the dirt. Abe felt his breath get knocked out of his chest. He had to move. He heard Eberhart roar in anger as he quickly rolled out of the way of Eberhart's foot crashing down on top of him.

He nimbly regained his footing, breathing hard. He could feel the burn of several bruises and the sting of cuts that he knew were bleeding.

"You're gettin' weak, Absalom. What's the matter?" Eberhart taunted him, stalking towards him.

Abe would not allow Eberhart to kill him in this form. He regretted what Jed might see, but, at this moment, it didn't matter. Abe hoped Jed would forgive him; he needed to give everything for this final stand. He relaxed the internal seal that had been placed on his form so many years ago. The fire of his inner devil raced through his body, shaping his skin, his bone, and his muscle into a form that was oh-so-different from his human form. With a savage roar, Abe let his body transform into a tall, midnight black devil. As the last layer of smooth scales rippled across him, a long tail that extended from his spine. He felt his large wingspan spread aggressively as he crouched low, ready to spring at his enemy.

Abe felt his true nature take over as he heavily breathed through flared nostrils, his reptilian snout pulled into a ferocious snarl. His horns curled around his acutely pointed ears, resembling a ram. He could feel every muscle quivering with rage, shaking with anticipation, and tensing to tear into his enemy's flesh.

"I'm gonna fuckin' kill you, Eberhart!" His voice boomed over the calamitous sounds around him. He heard shots from afar, recognizing that John and Jystana were already doing what they could to help Jed. Abe couldn't focus on him now. He was ready for blood. Eberhart's blood. Eberhart's laugh pierced his acute hearing, "You see, Absalom?! It's not bad to give in to your nature!"

Eberhart laughed as he watched him loosen the seal he had on his own inner devil. In mere seconds, Eberhart's human shell transformed into a large beast, with four horns—two on the top, and two protruding from the sides of his jaw and curving towards the front of his face. His limbs were thick, riveted with muscle and veins.

He was much taller than Abe, a greater devil, yet he had no wings of any sort. Abe knew he had an advantage over him. *Always went for the brute force, Eberhart.*

As Eberhart's dark, greenish scales finished covering his body, Abe saw the devil standing before him; bigger, stronger, and more powerful than he had ever imagined he could be. His vicious, yellow eyes narrowed as he struggled to focus on Abe.

*Too much power, you dumb shit...* Abe hissed and crouched low; he was prepared. Eberhart snarled at Abe, as he, too, prepared for deadly combat.

"I'm going to enjoy this, Absalom..." The devil's hiss was menacing—it sounded like a thousand snakes all at once.

Abe let his grin show, white on black, his sharp teeth glinting in the light, "Likewise…" Their voices were much deeper, their natural sound.

In those few seconds, their true natures ached for a fight. They yearned for bloodshed. They yearned for dominance.

\*\*\*

Jed's muscles burned as he fought his way through the demons that constantly tried to block his path. He had seen Abe morph into some sort of creature It had frightened him at first, but he realized that the creature was still Abe and would still need his help.

He ran past bodies of demons, finally breaking through to the center, where Abe and Eberhart were battling. Blood was beginning to streak on the dirt. Roars of savagery were resonating against the ruined shacks and the ravine. Cracks of thunder overshadowed all as the two delivered bone-shattering blows. They tumbled and clawed at each other.

Abe roared with pain as Eberhart pinned him on his back with a clawed foot, almost like a bird of prey. His talons dug deep into Abe's flesh as he began tearing at his wingbase.

Jed's anger burned stronger inside as he watched his friend's black blood pour over his scaled skin to the ground below.

"No!!" Jed shouted as he reloaded his pistol with speed and accuracy. He took aim at the giant devil, Eberhart, and fired a few rounds into his chest. The giant howled and reeled back.

Jed reloaded again and watched the devil change his attention from Abe to Jed. His eyes burned fire red as he charged toward him. Jed glared at him as he aimed again, hoping he would get a shot to his main heart.

Jed heard a mighty roar—a battle cry of rage—as he watched Abe leap from his spot onto Eberhart's back. His black wings flared, with one barely able to hold itself up from the damage it had withstood. Abe's clawed, black hands began to tear furiously at Eberhart's shoulders, back—anything he could reach.

Jed watched in shock for a split second before he quickly began firing at Eberhart again. He wanted this devil dead. Eberhart screamed in a fit of rage, and, before Jed could fire a kill shot, Eberhart violently twisted his body. His large hands managed to grab Abe's upper half, flinging him to the ground. Abe howled as his wounds contacted the dirt.

"Abe!!" Jed shouted in horror as Eberhart pinned him to the ground, his talons raised. Jed fumbled as he tried to reload. *NO, God damn it!*

Eberhart's talons viciously descended. He meant to kill him. Abe shrieked in agony as he tried to fight Eberhart off him. His flesh was easy for Eberhart to tear through, and his insides became a slaughterhouse.

Jed's vision began to cloud over red as he let his rage take hold. He cocked the hammer back and took aim. Jed had finally found the shot he had been looking for.

The single shot cut through the air and ripped into the main heart of Eberhart. The devil stopped for a moment, as if in shock. He roared and began to charge him, leaving a squirming Abe to die of his grievous wounds.

Jed didn't wait. He loaded the last three bullets as fast as his fingers would allow. He fired again, and again, and again. Each hit pierced Eberhart's main heart. Each time, the devil slowed more and more, until, finally, he couldn't move. His lips were curled in a snarl, his red eyes beginning to dim.

With a boom, the devil fell first to his knees, then, to his arms. They shook to hold his mass up, blood flowing freely from his gunshot wounds and slashes that Abe had delivered. Silence descended upon the bloody scene as Eberhart completely surrendered to the ground, snarling. His breathing was sharp and erratic, until he shuddered his last.

It was over. His need to avenge his father was finally sated. A deep fear gripped his gut as he rushed toward his friend. Dark blood soaked the ground as the devil twitched and convulsed. *Abe...! Oh, my God... no!*

# Chapter 42

Jed was unsure if he could stomach the thick smell of blood, but he had to. His friend was dying, and he didn't know if he could save him. The sight nearly made him retch as he watched the large devil in front of him. His friend—Abe, El Diablo—was lying in a pile of his own blood and strewn insides.

He heard footsteps rush up from behind him.

"Absalom?!" Jystana's voice was high-strung, tight with anxiety. Jed closed his eyes as he felt her approach. "Absalom!" He knew she had seen him. She brushed past Jed and collapsed to his knees next to him. Her pants became coated in his blood as her hands hovered over his wounds and his chest, as though unsure if she should touch him or not.

"Christ Almighty..." John breathed. Jed had barely noticed him stop next to him. His face was paler than he had ever seen it. He retched, letting his stomach spill its contents off to the side. He couldn't handle it. Jed went to Jystana's side and gently touched her shoulder.

"Jystana I...I don't—"

"In the name of the Trinity..." Jed saw a frazzled Ezekiel to his right. Anger sparked anew in his chest as he confronted this strange priest.

"What are you doin' here?!"

"I'm here to help...I am afraid I came too late."

"No shit! Abe is dying!!" Jed almost lost his temper again, until Ezekiel calmly walked to him, touching his shoulder. An odd coolness flooded him, like a cold, hard rain putting out a wildfire. He looked at the old man as he kept moving past him.

"Jystana, please," Ezekiel was crouched next to her, and trying to get her off Abe. He was losing too much blood.

"Get away from him, you fallen son of a bitch!" Her eyes flashed a dangerous vibrant blue. Jed's eyes saw the fury of an icy blue tendril flare up around her body; her aura he realized, as her inner she-devil flared inside her. Ezekiel touched her shoulder, and her bristled opposition was quickly crumpled into silence, her flared aura somewhat subdued as she backed away from Ezekiel and Abe. She covered her mouth with her delicate hand, her eyes brimming with red tears. *Is that...blood...?* Jed had to tear his eyes from her as John came back, wiping the back of hand against his mouth.

Jed turned his attention back to the fading Absalom. *God damn it, Abe...* He made himself hold back burning tears that threatened to weaken his resolve. He was going to lose his friend.

"Jedidiah, I need you to do something for me," Ezekiel had grabbed Jed's shoulders firmly and made him look at him. Jed looked into the Fallen's amber eyes, listening.

"I am going to take him to a doctor." Jed swallowed hard and glanced at his friend, who was steadily fading.

*No amount of doctors can help this*, Jed thought, but he nodded. He had to trust him, or at least let him try. "In the meantime," Ezekiel said, "I need you to help these people." As he lifted Absalom's broken body into his arms, a heart-rending yowl ripped through Abe's throat as he contorted, his muscles spasming before he grew silent again. "I need you to lead these people."

Jed felt lost. Again. He didn't even know how Ezekiel was going to get him to a doctor in time. If it wasn't already too late. "I don't even know where you're takin' him," Jed said, exasperated.

Ezekiel nodded to a distraught Jystana, who was trying not to raise her hackles again. "She will know the way..."

"But how?"

Ezekiel didn't say another word as he lifted his head to the sky, his eyes closed. Jed could see his faded gold aura start to burn brighter and brighter, until fully extended wings protruded from his back, the light illuminating the area around them. Jed had to block his eyes from the intensity.

A strong rush of wind came from the illuminated Ezekiel, followed by the whoosh of powerful wings pushing upward. Several wing motions were heard before they faded into the distance, the light following them.

Jed lowered his arm and opened his eyes, only to see the remnants of the battle around them. Abe's blood and indistinguishable carnage was all that was left. He glanced to the sky, turning to face John and Jystana.

"Jystana, get the horses…There's one more thing I have to do."

She choked back a worried sob and disappeared in shadow, acknowledging him with a nod. John took a couple startled steps backward, "The hell is goin' on?!"

Jed frowned and looked at John, "John we ain't got time for this. I need to find my sister."

He vowed that Abe's sacrifice would not be in vain.

***

Jed and John searched the shacks hurriedly, hoping to find her. Now that the battle was over, Jed was frantic to find her. He felt horrible for not trying to find her first, but he also knew that she had more of a chance being hurt if he had.

Shack after shack, they searched and searched. John adjusted his rifle over his shoulder and worriedly licked his lips. "Jed, I'm gonna check up there, see if he stashed her in those upper cervices." John pointed above and began running towards it; Jed never even noticed the ladder leading up to what he could assume was a lookout. He continued straight, searching the last of the shacks. Jed was beginning to wonder if she was here. After searching the last shack, he felt the weight of failure burden his shoulders.

*Where are you, Marietta? I won't give up 'til I get you back.*

*Tap. Tap. Tap.* A faint sound broke the silence. A normal man wouldn't have been able to hear it, but Jed could. Jed frowned, knowing that it wasn't a natural sound. He walked cautiously to it, keeping his senses alert. The sound grew louder, as if it were stone on stone, like someone trying to send a message.

Turning the bend in the ravine, he saw a makeshift entrance to a cave, like pathway that lead into the underground.

"Marietta?!" Jed loudly called out. The tapping stopped for a moment, before erratically starting its pattern again. Jed's heart began to lift. *Please, Lord, let it be her!* Jed desperately thought as he jogged over to it. The entrance drew closer and closer to him. He saw movement beyond the rough metal gate.

"Marietta!" Jed saw her. He couldn't mistake that auburn hair anywhere in the world. His heart leaped into his throat, raw emotion letting loose through his body. He sprinted the rest of the distance, sliding to a stop at the gate. Its lock was heated shut. She wasn't going to be able to get out on her own.

Shattered rocks the size of his head were smashed all around her. It looked like she had tried to break out. She was wearing a different dress; one he didn't recognize. It was light yellow with white trim around the sleeves, neck, and hem of the dress. It was covered in dirt and stains. Her face was tear-stained, carving through the dirt on her cheeks. Her hands were wrapped around the bars.

Jed got as close as he could. Her hands reached for his shoulders, trying to hug him, even from a distance. He looked into her frightened blue eyes. A tsunami of relief washed over him. She was safe and unharmed. After all this time, he had had so many worrisome nightmares of what he might find whenever he did find her—if he ever did find her. All of it was put to rest as he let a smile—a real smile— spread on his lips and opened his arms to her. It felt so foreign to him, after all these long months, but he didn't care. Tears stung his eyes as he reached through and touched her face in brotherly compassion. Her shoulders racked with silent sobs as she gripped his shirt and vest, trying to get closer.

Jed gently rested their foreheads together, "It's okay, I got ya. He's dead now." He felt her nod through her silent hysteria. He couldn't believe he had found her. He gently broke the reunion as he stood back. "I need ya to step back, Marietta. I don't want ya to get hurt."

She nodded and backed away from the gate. Jed looked at the lock, hoping he could do this. He knew that rage was still inside of him. It was quelled for now, but he needed its strength again. He drew a deep breath before gripping the rough metal bars. He knew he could spread them far enough.

He planted his feet wide, to get the leverage he needed. With a heave, Jed pulled outward on the bars. At first, they didn't move. Jed breathed hard, doubling his efforts to set his sister free. The metal began to groan in protest as he shouted in anger—he wanted to get her free. He had to. His eyes were lit with the flame of determination as he gave all the strength he had. Finally, with a loud squeal of bending metal, the bars were wide enough for her to pass through.

He stepped back to let her through. Her eyes were wide with shock. Jed felt the tips of his ears burn red as she sidled her way through carefully. He cleared his throat sheepishly as he held his hand out to her. Her hand gripped his, accepting his help as she left that ramshackle prison. Once she was on solid ground, Jed couldn't help but pull her into a strong embrace. She was really here, in front of him, unharmed. All his anger, all his hatred and despair, disappeared as he held her tightly. Sobs of joy and relief ripped through him as he let it all fade away. Her body trembled as she gripped the back of his shirt. He would never let anything happen to her ever again. He kissed her forehead and rocked her as she sobbed with him. Jed looked up, speaking in a cracked voice through his blubbering, "Thank you...I hope you can rest now, Pa..."

They wept and held each other for what seemed like hours, until both had settled their emotions. They smiled at each other. Marietta's lips trembled from the overwhelming emotion.

"I, uh, have some things to tell ya later on," Jed spoke quietly to her, not knowing how he could tell her everything he had gone through to get her back.

"You found her?!"

Jed heard John's voice call out to him from behind. He must have heard Jed's shouts. Jed nodded, "Yeah...John, this is my sister, Marietta."

Marietta looked at John closely as John extended his hand for her to shake. A grin plastered his weary features as she cautiously took his hand. "Nice ta meet ya, Marietta. I'm John, John Carson."

She nodded, trying to hide the smile on her cracked lips.

Jed heard horses in the distance, coming through encampment. Jed moved Marietta behind him, just in case it was someone other than Jystana. John turned around as well. The three of them watched as Jystana rounded the bend and reined her horse to a sliding stop, the other three horses following suit in a torrent of dust.

No words were spoken as Jed and John hurried to their horses. Jystana had Dusk tied off to the back of her saddle. Jed loosed his and mounted, helping his sister up behind him. He adjusted in his saddle quickly, glancing back at her as Marietta wrapped her arms around his waist, "Hold on tight, okay?" She nodded, tightening her grip.

Jystana turned the way she had come and kicked her mare into a gallop. She was not wasting any time. Without hesitation, Jed and John raced after her.

# Chapter 43

They rode hard for several days, heading north. They were quiet for most of the ride, all of them worried about Abe's condition. Jed hoped that he was still alive and that Ezekiel had found a doctor, like he had said he would. Jystana had told Jed that they were heading in the direction of a small settlement, only known as Arium to a very select few. It was a very foreign name, it didn't seem like it would be a real place. "It's a sanctuary, a neutral zone, for beings like us," was all she would say on the matter.

The riders and their horses were all exhausted. They all wanted to get to where they were going as fast as possible. Jystana was not letting them take any sort of break from the grueling pace she set. They wove through the hills, always heading north. Jed made sure that Marietta was t stable in the saddle. He knew she, most likely, hadn't ridden much since her abduction.

It was early morning, the air was crisp, and the horses were barely mobile. Jed kept urging his stallion forward. The animal was heavily lathered and its breathing was heavy, and its stride was jerky with muscle stiffness. Jed looked to his left and saw that John was barely awake. He was bobbing with his horse, leaning this way and that, catching himself before completely falling asleep and tumbling off. Marietta was fast asleep, sore from all the riding. Her dirt-stained face was patchy from her earlier tears.

Jystana was ahead of them, her white hair pulled up with a tie, keeping it out of her vision. Her white mare never broke its stride and it never seemed to tire. Jed's heart weighed heavy every time he saw Dusk, who had been tied to the rear of her saddle. It didn't look right at all.

He could only imagine how it was for Jystana. Jed felt for her. He felt sadness, fear, and an intense feeling of dread—all for her and what might have become of his friend. They wove around a dip in the hill, revealing a tiny, sleepy town down below. *Arium...*

Jystana clucked, urging her mare to speed up, as if it weren't going fast enough already. Jed could feel the urgency in her body language. Jed hurried after her, John doing the same. The four of them galloped into town and finally stopped in front of a two-story building on the edge of town. Jed's horse came to an abrupt stop, chewing the bit and hanging its head low to the ground. Jed gently withdrew Marietta's arms off his midriff and dismounted before helping her down.

John dismounted and rubbed his horse's forelock. It, too, was exhausted from the long ride. Jystana dismounted before her horse even stopped. Dusk stopped next to the mare with a nicker, pawing the ground with impatience. Jed watched her rush into the building. Jed felt cool dread rising in his stomach. He wasn't sure what they were going to find.

Jed followed her, looking up at the crooked sign over the threshold. In faded red letters, it read: Medicine. Jed glanced at Marietta, who looked ragged. He gently took her hand and squeezed it, "I'll get ya somethin' to eat soon and somewhere to rest." She nodded as she looked up at the sign, mouthing the word to herself.

Jed gently pushed the half-open door inward, letting them through. He heard movement upstairs and a frantic voice. *Jystana must have found him. Lord, please let him live.*

John stopped next to him, observing the odd front room. "Well, I certainly wouldn't wanna live here..." John looked toward the wall lined with racks filled with various apothecary medicine bottles. Jed looked at John and spoke sincerely, "John, I need you to watch Marietta for me, okay? I'm goin' upstairs."

Jed looked at Marietta, who seemed to be irritated that she was to be watched by someone she didn't know. "Look, Marietta, I don't know what it's like up there. Please, stay here, with John. He's a good man, he'll protect ya."

John nodded, straightening his crinkled vest, as if he were meeting the lady of a lifetime. She reluctantly let go of Jed's hand and walked over to John, who motioned for her to sit down on a small, padded bench against the wall. Jed swallowed hard, preparing himself for what he might see. He closed the space between him and the landing of the staircase. The wood railing was rough in his hand as he jogged up the steps. His legs burned from the new motion; he had been in the saddle for too long.

The steps creaked and groaned under his weight until, finally, he reached the top. The hallway was short, with only two or three doors, one of which was open with light peering through.

He heard the voices more clearly, "I'm sorry, ma'am. There's only so much I coulda done for him."

"That's not good, enough damn it!" Jystana's voice was cracked. She had been crying.

"Jystana, please…you're exhausted…the doctor is doing all that he can."

Jed recognized that voice—Ezekiel was there. He frowned with concern as he reached the door and looked inside. Ezekiel was gently holding Jystana's shoulders from behind her, attempting to keep her calm. Jystana was crying; red streaks of blood ran down her cheekbones, dripping on the floor in heavy droplets. *Devils cry blood?* He stepped all the way in, staying out of the way as an old man with wiry gray hair moved around a large table.

He saw his friend. He was paler now, almost gray-black in color now. He hadn't transformed back into his usual, recognizable form. Jed felt the weight of guilt on his heart as he removed his hat in respect. *Damn it, Abe, I'm sorry…I shoulda done better.*

His presence was noted as the old man looked up at him through large glasses that were much too big for his face. His scowl seemed to be a permanent fixture on his brow. He kept working, barely acknowledging Jed, "What do you want boy? We're closed today."

Jed opened his mouth to speak, but Ezekiel beat him to it, "This is Mr. McKay. He is a close friend and colleague of Absalom."

The old man grunted, moving around to Abe's newly patched mid-torso. The bandages were already soaked again. "Fine! No more after him. This devil needs his rest. Hell willin', he'll survive this."

Ezekiel nodded, taking that as a cue to leave the doctor and Abe alone. With gentle coaxing, he managed to escort a distraught Jystana out of the room and back towards the staircase. Jed placed his hat back on, starting to leave.

The old man called out, "Just wait now, boy, I need ya." Jed stopped in his tracks, puzzled.

"I thought he needed his rest."

"He does! But first I need your help changin' this bandage. It's all dirtied again," the old man grumbled as he pushed his rolled sleeves back up his arms. Jed stepped forward and stood next to the old man. His eyes looked over Abe, feeling the seed of despair begin to take root.

"He ain't gonna make it, is he?" Jed asked quietly, turning his viridian eyes to the old man.

The doctor paused as he cleaned his hands in a bowl of water that was on a stand. "He might, if he has a strong will…" The man sighed as he moved to Abe's side, peeling away the first layer and tossing it to the side. Jed could see the red stains where previous bandages had been. "I haven't seen this sort of wound in over a century…"

Jed looked at the old man, confused, "A century, sir?"

The doctor kept taking the old bandages off as he looked at Jed, "You deaf, son? I said a century! And, before you ask, no, I ain't human neither."

Jed raised his eyebrows in surprise, but, now that he looked at the old man, he could just make out the faded golden aura around his features. *He hid himself well. I didn't realize that he was an—*

"*Was*—keyword, boy. Make yourself useful, and grab me them scissors." Jed was taken aback as the old man pointed to a tray that held all sorts instruments Jed didn't recognize. Jed reached over and grabbed a tool that he assumed was what the man asked for as he frowned at the man, "I didn't say a damn word, sir."

"You don't have to. Us angels can see into the hearts and minds of men," he explained, cutting away the last layer of bandage to reveal several jagged stitch lines. The black thread was barely able to hold the flesh together. Each shallow breath from Abe stretched the tension of the stitches, threatening to loose and expose his near-fatal wounds anew. A strange herb was padded in between the stitching that Jed couldn't identify. His curiosity was quickly replaced by nausea from the sight and the smell.

"Don't even think about it, boy," the angel grumbled, motioning for Jed to grab the bandages on the table behind him. Jed swallowed the feeling. He had to do this for Abe. He grabbed the fresh linen and handed it to the doctor. He soaked it in a different bowl of water and rung it out until it was just damp. He tenderly started to clean the stitches.

Hours seemed to drag by as he helped the old angel clean the fresh blood and reapply the bandaging. When he was done, he washed his hands and adjusted his glasses. "That should do for now. We'll see how he does in the next few days. His body will either fight this nasty wound and live…or he will die a slow death." The old man gently patted Jed's shoulder and walked to the door, all frustration gone, replaced with genuine empathy. Jed watched the old angel leave.

It was just Jed and Abe now. Jed walked around Abe and grabbed a chair. He pulled it close and sat in it quietly. He didn't want to leave him. *I don't want him to die alone.* Jed wiped his face with a tired hand, taking off his hat and running his fingers through his messy hair.

It was over. All of it. It was finally over. The feeling of completion flooded his weary body with relief and satisfaction. He did it. He finally did it. He had done everything he could do to kill Eberhart and get his sister back. Jed was thankful that she appeared to be unharmed. He leaned back in his chair, sighing as he let go of his burden.

Abe was going to be alright. He had to be.

Jed leaned forward, resting his elbows on his knees, his hands clasped together. "...Abe..." he spoke quietly, "I dunno if you can hear me, but..." He swallowed hard, taking a breath as sorrow ripped through his heart again. He didn't want to lose another friend. A mentor. A father. The angel's words laid heavy on his heart as he made himself keep talking out loud, "I-I...I want to thank you...for everything you have done...even if I didn't deserve it..." Jed felt a hot tear roll down his grizzled cheek, his throat choking up, "Don't leave me here, Abe. Please don't leave me, too..." Jed's plea faded into a quiet whisper as he hung his head, softly crying.

*** 

Those few days had been a nerve-wracking waiting game as the doctor attended to him every hour on the hour. Jed hoped and prayed with all his might that his friend would live through this, that he had heard his plea.

Soon, a week had gone by, and Abe was slowly seeming to get stronger. The first indication was the color of his skin beginning to return, the dull black returning to a shiny midnight shade Jed had seen before. He took turns with Jystana and Ezekiel to watch over him, and the doctor was constantly checking on him.

Each time the bandages were changed, the stitches looked more and more solid and firm. Jed was hopeful in feeling that Abe might just pull through this.

He sat now at a bedside, in the same room. Abe had changed back into his human self in the middle of night. The sound of cracking bone and stretching tissue had startled Jed awake as he watched his friend change from a black devil to the human form he recognized most.

Abe was still asleep. His breathing was steadier and deeper. His face, though, remained pale and gaunt. Dark circles outlined his eyes, and his stubble was longer. Three layers of blankets were covering his body. Jed had asked if it was really necessary to have three blankets. The doctor had insisted that it would help Abe's natural body temperature remain constant and help him heal.

He assumed he was right. And it made sense. A devil from hell would like more heat than a human would. Jed was resting his eyes, his hat pulled low to block out the midday sun. Jystana and Marietta were wandering the town. It was good for the two of them. Jystana needed a distraction, and Marietta was beginning to feel a stirring that she had never felt before. Most importantly, though, it kept the women from nagging Jed about how badly dressed his sister was.

"...Where the hell am I...?" The cracked deep voice sounded.

Jed pulled his hat back and sat up straight. Relief pulsed through him as he saw Abe moving his head and lifting a hand to rub his face. Jed pulled his chair closer, a grin spreading on his lips.

"Abe! Thank God you're alright!" Abe winced at his voice. *His ears must be sensitive.*

"Shit, boy...you're too damn loud." He groaned, opening an eye to look at him. His cobalt blue eye stared at Jed. He blinked, then, they both opened. "You look like shit..."

Jed couldn't help but laugh. Emotion threatened to overwhelm him again; he was so thankful that Abe was alright. "Should look at yourself, Abe. You don't look any prettier."

He grunted before closing his eyes again. Jed was eager to talk with him, to thank him for everything and for almost giving his life to fulfill his promise. There was so much Jed owed to him that he knew he could never repay in his lifetime.

"Jed…" Abe cleared his throat and looked at him again, "Marietta…is she…?"

"She's fine, she's with Jystana," Jed spoke quietly. The grin on his face was starting to hurt. He didn't care. He was happy to see his friend was on the mend.

"Ah, hell…best you get her away from that woman…"

Jed chuckled and reached over to the nightstand, where water was sitting in the tin cup. "Well, Abe, I don't think that's possible. Jystana has her mind set to get her new clothes."

"With my money…damn it all," Abe grumbled and winced as he started to prop himself up on his elbows. Jed tried to help him, only to be batted away. Abe grunted and groaned until he finally sat up. The blankets that were layered on top of him fell almost completely away. He frowned down at himself and looked around the room. "Where the hell are my clothes?"

Jed looked to the corner of the room nearest the door, then, back at his friend. "I'll get 'em when the doc says you're ready." Jed knew what he was like. He wanted to leave, and quickly. Abe never liked to linger in one place for too long.

"To hell with him," he grumbled.

"I'm afraid that ain't gonna happen, Absalom." Jed looked at the old doctor as he strode through the door. Jed got up from his seat to make room for the angel as he took his spot. As the angel started to check on his vitals and his stitches, Abe crinkled his nose at the doctor. "You're lucky to be alive…Ezekiel did well to bring ya to me."

Abe bared his teeth at him. Jed got the feeling that Abe and Ezekiel had a history that was much older than he. The doctor ignored his silent protest as he looked at the bandages. It was spotty, but not nearly as soaked as when Jed first saw him. "Well, looks like a few more days and your stitches can come out. It seems your body took well to the Mana Herb." *So that is what was in those stitches...*

"I ain't got a few more days," Abe grumbled, continuing to try to get up on his own.

The doctor frowned and firmly tried to keep Abe seated, "Now wait a damn minute! You ain't done healin' yet! You might be just barely able walk, but certainly not able to ride just yet! Sit down!"

"Abe, please just listen to the doctor," Jed cautiously pleaded with his friend. He tried to restrain himself from laughing aloud; it was quite comical to watch his friend try and get his way in his condition. He was definitely feeling better.

Jed felt his hair stand on end as he heard the familiar clack of boots coming up the stairs. He knew Jystana was coming. *Oh, hell, here we go...* The sound grew louder and louder until she appeared in the doorway. Her eyes were alight with a fury that could only be meant for Abe. She had gotten a new dress; a deep violet silk one with ivory lacing and ties to hold the bodice of the dress in place. As usual, her bosom was slightly exposed. "What the hell do ya think you're doin'?" Her voice cut through the argument like a butcher's knife.

Both the doctor and Abe paused in their squabble. Abe growled at the old angel when he tried to make him lay back down, "What does it look like, Jys?"

Jed hid his grin behind a hand over his mouth. The last thing he wanted was to draw Jystana's wrath upon himself. With a fluid motion, she stalked from the doorway to the bedside, pushing the doctor away. No one wanted to intervene in this one. "You ain't done yet, and you know it!" She firmly made Abe lay back down, making a point to cover him back up. His scowl said it all; he was not amused.

"I ain't a fuckin' child, damn it."

She looked at him hard; an icy stab that Jed could feel from where he stood. "Then, stop actin' like one and do what you're told. I will not lose you to your damn stubbornness."

He was quiet for a moment, his eyes closing and slowly reopening. *His body must be exhausted.* "Damn it, Jys, you know I don't like this."

Her expression softened, and a smile replaced her scowl. "I know...but you're almost done." She leaned forward and lightly planted a kiss on his cracked lips. Jed had never seen a tender moment between the two-- not ven when they were first introduced. It made him happy to see that Abe had someone who cared about him. At the kiss, Abe slipped back into sleep.

Jystana stood up straight, satisfied that he was resting again, and turned to the doctor, "I apologize for his behavior...he's unruly most of the time." She glanced back at the form of her sleeping lover, and, then, back at the doctor. He adjusted his glasses on the bridge of his nose and ran a hand through his gray, wiry hair. "It's nothin', ma'am. I'm just glad he hasn't tried to bite me yet."

Jystana chuckled and moved around him back to the door, "Don't worry, honey, he doesn't bite...at least not on people he doesn't show an interest in."

Jed chuckled at her wicked smirk before moving from his safe corner toward the door. He knew she wanted to take her turn to watch over him. The doctor grunted and finished cleaning his hands before leaving, muttering to himself, "Damn devils..."

Jed followed the doctor, adjusting the hat on his head. He paused for a moment and looked at Jystana, "Jystana, thank you..."

She looked at him puzzled, the smirk gone, "Whatever for?"

"Helpin' my sister get adjusted again…It means a lot to her, and to me."

She smiled and leaned up, lightly placing a kiss on his lower cheek. Jed felt his ears burn at the gesture.

"Of course, Jed. It's my way of sayin' thank you for helping Absalom. I would have lost him, for sure, if you hadn't killed Eberhart."

Jed smiled and nodded, "You're welcome, ma'am. I was just doin' what I knew needed to be done."

They nodded at each other, and Jed tipped his hat and walked out the door, to the lobby below. He wanted to find Marietta, who was, most likely, exploring the settlement. Or, perhaps, he could grab a drink with John and Ezekiel. *Why not both?* Jed smiled to himself as he strode out the door to the main part of the town.

\*\*\*

Jed and the others were talking amongst themselves. Jed knew it was coming.

"OUCH! Fuck!"

John stifled a snort as Abe's cry was heard from the floor above them. Ezekiel paused from his reading of the Holy Word to glance at the ceiling above them. "It would seem he is much better…"

Jed chuckled at the remark and leaned his back against the wall. He was sitting with his sister, who was also feeling much better. She was wearing a powder blue dress that oddly resembled Jystana's style and taste. *She really has turned into a beautiful woman. I'm so thankful I was able to get her back.*

"Enough! Damn it!"

"Hold still! You'll only make it hurt more!" The doctor shouted back at him. Silence filled the room as Jystana sighed and shook her head.

"Still stubborn..." She spoke casually. Her blue eyes set their focus on Marietta, "Just remember, Mari, men are stubborn, regardless of who they are."

John looked at her and spoke, "Not always, ma'am, sometimes, we just like to do things our way."

"You mean the most ignorant, stubborn way?" Jystana grinned. Marietta giggled silently next to Jed. No sound was heard, but he could hear her voice in his head. He was still taken by surprise every time she spoke or laughed or shouted in her mind. He never thought he would hear her voice. Ezekiel had told him that he was able to convince her to at least unlock some of her abilities, given that she was a Nephilim.

That word, *Nephilim*, still rang fresh in his mind as he pulled Ezekiel to the side one evening. He had been reading his bible, which was normal for him. He asked if he could explain what that term *Nephilim* meant. Ezekiel's face had become concerned as he looked over toward where Marietta was sleeping on a makeshift cot. When he was sure that she was sound asleep, he spoke in a low tone.

A Nephilim, he said, was a rare being. A gift, some had called it. Neither pure human, nor pure supernatural. A being that could see and hear all things, and one that could, potentially, destroy both the realm of God and that of Lucifer. "

"She's one of millions who have been born that's survived for so long," Ezekiel whispered carefully. "She will be hunted if she is discovered. Marietta would not be looked at as an individual, but as an abomination and threat to our worlds." Ezekiel gently rested a hand on Jed's shoulder. "As long as she remains as she is now, Marietta will continue on as a normal, human woman." He squeezed his shoulder and headed up the stairs to relieve Jytana.

Jed would never forget the angel's words.

"Son of a bitch!!"

Jed glanced up the stairs at the sudden outburst, "It's all done, you big pussy. You're good enough to ride now." Jed sighed relief to hear that; and so were the others. Abe had narrowly escaped death, twice now, since Jed had known him.

He heard the footsteps of the doctor coming down. Jed stood, eager to hear what the doctor had to say. He descended the steps one at a time, wiping his hands with a towel. He stopped at the landing, looking irritated.

"He's all done…make sure he doesn't do any sort of grueling labor or feats of strength or he could rupture his insides," he spoke in Jystana's direction. She stood and nodded as she smoothed out the front of her dress.

Jed heard Abe coming. The familiar brush of leather and clinking of the heavy gear he always wore made his presence ominous to most, but, to Jed, it was a relief to hear. The doctor moved down to the parlor, behind his desk. He rummaged for something on the wall behind him.

Abe showed and stopped in his tracks, rummaging for a cigarette. Jed's relief was beyond anything he had felt before. His friend—more like a father to him—had survived, and he looked well. It was as if it had never happened. Abe found his cigarette box and pulled one out, lighting up.

The doctor frowned as he set a couple of labeled bottles out on the counter. "I would rather you not smoke in here."

Abe grunted and took in a drag as he walked over to the counter, "I don't give a damn."

The doctor wrinkled his nose and shook his head, "Take your damn medicine twice a day. Should keep the pain levels down."

Abe stood and grabbed the bottles, observing them in his hands. Jed watched in silence as Abe tucked the bottles into his jacket and nodded a curt thank you. Abe took another drag and looked at the room. He frowned, "What are y'all starin' at…?"

Jystana couldn't help but laugh and loop her arm through his, "Let's go, Abe…"

He grunted and walked out of the doctor's shop into the bright morning sun.

They all followed. Jed knew a goodbye was near. John and Jed had groomed the horses and made sure they were all fit for riding. His stallion was sniffing the ground around him, John's gelding was half asleep, and the 'European' horses were watching people as they walked by. Ezekiel was talking with John and Marietta, and Jystana and Abe were walking to their horses.

Jed walked to his horse and untied it, mounting up. He had a long way to go, he was sure. He wanted to go back to the ranch where it had all started. He wanted to rebuild and to continue what his father had begun there.

Abe mounted Dusk with a weary grunt. The exertion must have hurt his wounds. Jed turned his stallion to face Abe, who was grimacing and adjusting himself in the seat of the saddle. Jystana had mounted her white mare and stayed close to him.

"Abe...?"

Abe gently heeled Dusk forward, reining him to a stop beside him, "What is it, Jed?"

Jed smiled. "Thank you...for everything."

Abe nodded, adjusting his hat better over his eyes, "Didn't have a choice, boy."

"You did. You could have let me die on my own, but you didn't. I have my sister back, my father is avenged..." Jed paused, not wanting his emotions to show through. He looked him in the eye, "You're like a father to me Abe. I'll never forget you or what you did to help me."

Abe's grizzled features finally broke through the disgruntlement, a grin spreading on his lips, "You turned out alright, Jed. You're still a shitty shot, though."

Jed laughed, and, to his surprise, he heard Abe quietly laugh with him. The laughter died some as Abe spoke again, "Good luck, Jedidiah McKay, you're a good man. Keep it that way."

Jed nodded. "I'll do my best, Abe. You've taught me a lot over the past months."

Abe nodded, proddingDusk forward. Jystana smiled as she passed by, blowing a kiss to him. He shook his head as he watched the two ride past him, only pausing for Abe to talk with John.

"Your debt is paid, John… don't fuck it up. I don't wanna hear that you went and got into trouble again."

John nervously smiled at Abe's threat. He reached out to pat Dusk's neck, only to have Dusk nearly bite him. He quickly retracted his hand as he responded, "Don't worry. I'm not doin' anymore 'business' as far as I'm concerned."

Abe nodded his curt approval. "Oh…and you better take care of her." Abe nodded to Marietta. "If Jed don't gut you first, you can guarantee I will."

John looked at him, bewildered, as Abe winked at him and chuckled. Jed couldn't help but chuckle at John's reaction as Abe heeled Dusk in the sides, spurring him into a lope. Jed prodded his horse forward, stopping next to his sister, John, and Ezekiel, who was smiling, watching the two of them ride off before returning to the doctor's home.

Jed watched with a heavy heart as his friend rode off towards the wild frontier. He was going to miss him. After all the time that he had spent preparing for anything, he was never prepared for saying goodbye to his friend.

He felt a hand gently rest on his knee. He looked down and saw his sister, smiling at him with encouragement. Jed heard her voice, *Don't worry, Jed, I'm sure you'll see him again.*

Jed smiled sadly as he returned his gaze back to the fading figures. "We'll see, Marietta. He's a roamer." He helped her up and seated her behind him. John had mounted his horse and walked him to the two of them. Jed looked at John, "You got anywhere to go, John?"

John grinned as he adjusted the reins in his hands, "Not anywhere in particular, no."

"Good. I could use your help as a ranch hand, if you're interested," Jed grinned back. He had grown fond of John. Even though they were the same age, John was like the little brother he never had.

"I'd be glad to help," John answered with a smile.

Jed nodded. With a few clucks and prodding at the sides of his stallion, he started out at a lope. He was ready to return home. It felt good to be heading home, to where he belonged. Ezekiel watched them all depart with a soft smile, knowing that the worst had come to an end.

*Be careful in your travels, Mr. McKay. May God protect and watch over you.* He touched his fingers to his forehead, to his heart, then his left to right shoulder as the three figures faded into the distance.

# Epilogue

It was fall now. The grass was brown and scarce, and the sage brush that carpeted the ground for miles still bore their teal-green leaves. The air was starting to cool again. The mornings smelled different, and the few trees that still had leaves had turned deep shades of crimson and burnt orange.

The morning was crisp, and Jed took the opportunity to roam the several hundred acres of land that was his father's. It had been a couple years now since he had said goodbye to Abe. He often wondered what he was doing, who he was hunting, and where he was going. Jed struggled every day with the urge to roam the way that Abe did. Abe had warned him that he would never be the same—not after the deal with a devil.

Jed forced the thoughts back into the recesses of his mind. He had duties to perform. He urged his stallion into a trot, guiding him carefully through the rugged terrain. Jed watched the horizon as the sun crested the familiar red rock mesas in the distance. He loved this land, and he knew every inch of it. The cattle were healthy this year, and the herd was growing quite steadily.

John had done well here at the property. He was an honest worker, and a good ranch hand. Jed had appreciated his presence on the property. He was a sharp shooter, and made damned sure that nothing would get the cattle at night. They still had a mounted wolf's pelt above the newly built mantle in the ranch house.

Jed stopped atop a jagged rock outcropping, the edge of the property. All the memories of the past couple years almost seemed hollow. He was happy that Marietta had married John. He treated her like gold. Jed was surprised when John had approached him to ask for her hand. Jed was the head of the household; it was only proper for John to ask him. Jed had granted his permission. He smiled at the memory.

It was time to head back for a spot of breakfast and to mend the fences again. The air was much cooler than it had been the previous day, and Jed welcomed it. It didn't take long to approach the house. He paused. The weight of his thoughts was almost too much to bear. He knew it was only a matter of time before he had to move on. He needed the open country again. He craved it.

He sighed, scratching his scruffy chin, and continuing to the house. Jed could smell the fresh cooking from the barnyard. Marietta had become a fabulous cook; much better than Jed had ever tasted. He dismounted and affectionately patted his horse's neck.

He walked up the steps and quietly went inside, turning towards the parlor and stopping to admire all that was in there. They had been able to fully furnish the house, thanks to John's silver-tongued bartering skills. Jed often joked that John could sell snake oil to a rock and make a fortune out of it.

"You're up early, Jed!" John's jovial voice called out. Jed was so deep in his memories he didn't hear John come from upstairs.

Jed looked over his shoulder at him. John had grown to be a fine man, tall with dark brown hair, and dancing sapphire blue eyes. His grin was contagious and always made the room light up. Jed turned to face his brother-in-law, "I'm always up at this hour. You know that, John."

He chuckled and stood next to him, admiring the wolf's pelt. Both men were silent for a moment. Jed could tell that John wanted to talk, but he wanted to let him take that first step.

"Jed...Marietta and I have been talkin'..." He scratched the back of his head. He always did that when he was nervous. Jed looked at him, patiently waiting. "We're, uh... we're both worried about ya..."

Jed looked at the floor. He knew they were worried. He just wasn't sure if he could tell them what he yearned to do. Jed nodded and looked back at John. "You're gone more often than not, and we just want ta know if you're alright...that's all."

Jed smiled and clasped John's shoulder, "John, in all honesty, I've been needin' to talk to you both about something."

*Talk about what?* Jed looked to the doorway; his sister's voice was always clear in his mind. He smiled sadly at her as she wiped her hands on a linen. She was pregnant now with her first child and was starting to get big.

"Sit down. I'll explain." John looked to Marietta, a little unnerved by what Jed might have to say. He knew Marietta would take it hard, but he would never leave her, unless she had someone to protect her. John filled that spot for him. John helped Marietta sit down on the couch closest to the window. He could feel both of their gazes on him. He dreaded talking to them about this, but he knew it had to be done.

"You all know that I had to make a deal with El Diablo, to do what I needed to do a couple years ago..." They both nodded. Marietta held John's hand tightly. Jed sighed. The tension was growing, and he couldn't stop it. "Before I agreed to it, he told me that I wouldn't be the same after it. And he was right...I ain't the same no more." He turned his eyes to the window as he continued, "I have a need to roam, to hunt down those that stray too far out of line." He glanced at the floor, his hands resting on his hips, "I can't do this no more..." He looked John and Marietta in the eyes.

John was worried; it was written all over his face. And Marietta, she was heartbroken. Her eyes said it all. As much as it pained him, he had to say it.

"I have to leave."

Marietta stood, tears dribbling down her cheeks as she came to hug his neck. He tightly wrapped his arms around her, feeling a pain that cut deep. On one hand, he didn't want to leave her here. But, as much as he loved this land and his family, he couldn't stand being here any longer. *Perhaps this is why Abe couldn't stay in one place for too long...I understand now.*

She sniffled as her shoulders shook. Jed gently pried her from him and looked at her in the eyes, "Marietta, look…I ain't goin' away forever. I'll come back from time to time." He gently smiled at her.

She nodded as she touched her swollen belly, *You better! This child needs to know his Uncle Jed.* Jed couldn't help but grin.

"Oh, I'm sure they'll hear all about me."

John stood, clearly shaken by Jed's desire to leave, "Jed…You need to be careful out there…" Marietta moved out of John's way as they embraced in a brotherly fashion. He was going to miss his brother-in-law.

"I'm always careful, John. You know that."

John scoffed with a sad smile, "Bullshit, Jed, and you know it."

Jed chuckled as he adjusted his hat and gave his sister one last embrace. It was time for him to leave. He had packed his saddle and all the necessities he would need. He left the parlor, letting his sister go. He would miss them dearly, but his soul craved the open plains again. He needed to hunt.

He went to his stallion and mounted up, taking the dark leather reins into his hands again. John went to his side and patted the horse's neck. "You come back now. I don't wanna hear that you got up shit creek without a rower."

Jed smiled and reached down to pat John's shoulder, "Same to you…I don't wanna get news that my brother-in-law got himself into trouble."

John smiled sadly and backed away. He held Marietta close to him as Jed tipped his hat to John with respect. John nodded a silent, final farewell in return. With a few clucks and a prod into his stallion's sides, Jed headed towards the north. He didn't believe in goodbyes anymore; he knew he would see them again.

The sound of his horse's breath filled his ears, and he felt the controlled power under him surge with elegance and eagerness. He didn't know what he would find, but he would not stop until he found it. His instincts were leading him; he knew that Abe had given him this ability. *I understand now, Abe*, he thought as he urged his horse into a gallop. *This need to roam is part of our nature...and, in this world of dust and blood, it's a rare gift given to few.*

## *Acknowledgements*

I want to thank Michael with Beyond Publishing for taking a chance on a first-time author and a new-ish genre. I also want to thank my first writing college professor, Chris Nordquist, for teaching me how to write freely with my "creative hat" and to go back and prune with my "editor's hat"; it has helped me even when I thought I couldn't write anymore, and it has saved me a lot of pain through the process. I want to take the time and thank Marcin as well, the illustrator of the cover to this book. You're amazing! And lastly, I want to thank all my friends and family for helping me through this, for all the long nights of watching classic Clint Eastwood blaze across the screen, The Magnificent 7 fighting for a good cause, and Django: Unchained beating all the odds. What a wonderful journey this has been, and many more to come.

*Author*

**M. E. Krueger** was born and raised in Oregon. She has always been fascinated with history. Particularly the early American history, which has been a continuous journey for more of an understanding. Stemming from a college writing project, her first work has developed from a short story into a rich and fulfilled novel.

When M. E. Krueger is not researching or writing, she loves to enjoy time with family and close friends.

www.ingramcontent.com/pod-product-compliance
Lightning Source LLC
LaVergne TN
LVHW091529060526
838200LV00036B/538